CW01067249

To Katie & George
Lovely Saintly x

The KAIROS

and the Amazing Mystery of Zionica

Michelle Isabella Cashin

Bethelonia
www.bethelonia.com

All rights reserved; no part of this publication may be reproduced or transmitted or stored in a retrieval system by any means, electronic, mechanical, photocopying or otherwise without the prior permission in writing from the publisher and the author. The moral right of the author has been asserted.

The Kairos and the Amazing Mystery of Zionica, this edition, published in 2015 by Bethelonia, United Kingdom. Copyright © 2015 Michelle I Cashin. ISBN 978-0-9546460-2-8

Printed and bound in Great Britain.
Cover illustration from original artwork by Christine Bennett.
Cover compiled by The Agency Creative, Altrincham.
Typeset by Bethelonia.
Selected Bible quotes taken from the King James Bible.
Selected Bible quotes taken from the New King James Bible.
Copyright © 1979,1980,1982 by Thomas Nelson, Inc. Used by permission. All rights reserved.

Quotation from Sydney Carter's 'Lord of the Dance,'
reproduced by kind permission of Stainer & Bell Ltd, London, England.

Sample text verses of Cecil Frances Alexander's (1818-95) hymn, There is a green hill far away.

A CIP catalogue record of this book is available from the British Library.

But it is written:
"Eye has not seen, nor ear heard,
Nor have entered into the heart of man
The things which God has prepared for
those who love him."
1 Corinthians 2: 9

Note from the author:

I believe that Heaven is beyond the scope of man's imagination, therefore, I am confident that my humble portrayal of Heaven, for the purpose of this story, would pale into insignificance compared to the real Heaven that all true Saints will enjoy for all eternity.

I thank God for my wonderful husband, John.
I could not have written this book without his love,
support, help, dedication, faith and financial assistance!
Thank you so much!

Michelle Isabella Cashin

Chapters

CHAPTER ONE

A Miracle after a Storm

Wings could be heard gently fluttering, high above in the cavernous hall. Tall, golden archways flanked either side. Each archway had a different coloured light shining within it, which corresponded to the colour of a sparkling precious jewel at its pinnacle – jasper, sapphire, emerald, topaz, amethyst and every precious jewel that there ever was. Everywhere sparkled with light and colour, like a prismatic effect from thousands of crystals, as if in the centre of a glorious rainbow.

Anna glided along with apparent urgency. Droplets of light fell like tiny golden snowflakes on her wavy blonde hair and flowing white gown, then seemed to evaporate, blending into the aura of golden light that framed her. She came to an archway lit with turquoise-blue and, without stopping, she turned and glided straight through it, emerging into a small chamber which was also bathed in the soft, turquoise-blue light.

A man, dressed in white and enveloped in the same aura of golden light, stood in front of a large screen, watching what appeared to be images of a school rugby match. The Vista was not so much a specifically defined screen, but rather a 3D virtual viewing area, about two metres square.

'Nathan…' Anna breathed, a little hesitantly. Despite the hint of an anxious frown, Anna's face radiated beauty – the kind of beauty that can only be a reflection of a soul filled with love.

The man turned and a smile beamed from his handsome face.

'Oh...' Anna looked into the Vista. 'Is that your son again, Nathan? Good-looking young boy. How old is he now?'

'Yes, that's my Joel – he's twelve years old,' Nathan replied. 'He's just been made Captain of his school's junior rugby team.'

'He really is following in your footsteps, then,' she smiled. 'It's nearly time, isn't it?'

'Yes, I think it will be this Easter holiday. I'm so looking forward to him joining the Kairos. Excuse me one moment,

Anna. I think Joel is about to score a try.' Nathan turned back to the Vista and they both watched together.

When Joel was promoted to Captain of the School's Junior Rugby Team, he was overjoyed, along with his friends, being one of the most popular boys in the school. However, not everyone was overjoyed. In fact, one boy in particular was furious – Phinehas Belch! Phinehas was a rather large boy and considered that the promotion to the position of Captain should have been his. He was though, the *only* person in the whole school of that opinion. Joel, on the other hand, was the boy with the best record of scoring, and it was all about winning, after all! That, sadly, did not stop Phinehas from making a nuisance of himself and he had made it quite clear to Joel exactly how he felt about the matter; making several attempts to thwart Joel with silly activities, such as letting down the tyres of his bike and writing unpleasant graffiti (*I stink!* for instance) on Joel's exercise books when he wasn't looking...

Consequently, as the home game got underway on the school field, Joel was a little uneasy about his first Rugby match in the role of Captain, expecting that there would be trouble from Phinehas. He was right to be concerned as Phinehas seized every opportunity to "accidentally" bump into Joel. However, Joel was much fitter and more nimble and managed to swerve most of Phinehas's sabotage attempts.

As the game continued, a pair of large ravens appeared and perched on a low branch of a tree near the pitch. Joel had possession of the ball and was running well with it, able to dodge every attacker but, determined to stop him, Phinehas rushed at Joel, heading straight towards him. It looked as if he was going to crash right into him, like a battering ram! Suddenly, one of the ravens took off from its perch like a black javelin and it looked as if he was heading for Joel's back and as the raven was coming from behind, Joel couldn't see it. Then, as the raven reached Joel, it flew over him, squawking in Phinehas's face. This so took Phinehas by surprise that he fell flat on his face in the mud! This left the way clear for Joel to continue and score the try!

'Go, Joel! Yes!' Nathan punched the air as he watched, through the Vista.

Meanwhile, Phinehas had a "mud supper" and the raven flew back to the branch, where its partner was waiting, shaking her head disapprovingly.

'Tut-tut, Magee!' Nathan chuckled.

'That cheeky Magee! He really pushes his guardianship to the limits, doesn't he?' Anna remarked with a smile.

'So, Anna,' he turned to the young woman, 'what brings you here in such a hurry?' he asked, although he really knew the answer.

Then, she became serious. 'It's Jean, Nathan. She and the three little ones have just arrived through the Fugue in the nursery,' she explained, a little anxiously.

Nathan's face dropped, as he nodded. Anna put a supportive hand on his arm, causing droplets of glittery light to coruscate around them.

'I'm sorry, Nathan,' she added softly.

'I know, Anna,' Nathan sighed. 'Jean will get over it, of course she will. It's such a sad loss for the Kairos, though. There's so much more she could have done.'

'Well, your Joel will be a very welcome recruit, Nathan, and now, with Jean's untimely exit from the Kairos, we're going to need a replacement for her, too!'

'Don't worry, Anna,' Nathan reassured her, with a glint in his eye. 'I already have someone in mind for that second vacancy.'

'Oh?' Anna looked surprised. 'Anyone I know?'

'As it happens, Anna, it's someone you know very well…'

'Not – my Peter?' Anna's eyes filled as she looked up at him.

'I believe your Peter will be just perfect for the Kairos, Anna.'

'Oh, Nathan!' Anna beamed. 'That's wonderful news!' A small tear dropped onto her cheek, glistening like a sparkling diamond.

Nathan gently wiped the sparkling tear with a golden finger. 'You know, Anna, He wipes away every tear, except perhaps tears of joy. Now, run along to the Garden of Lilies. Check on

Jean; tell her I'll be along soon and not to worry, everything is going to be fine,' Nathan reassured her. 'I just want to watch my son for a little while longer.'

'Right, I'll see you later – and thank you, Nathan,' Anna beamed, as she glided back through the archway. Even if there *had* been gravity, she would still have been floating on air.

†

It was early April and school had just broken up for Easter. Joel was in his bedroom, cramming last-minute stuff into his case.

'Come on, Joel!' Mum yelled from downstairs. 'We need to get on the road now, to avoid the traffic!'

'Coming!' Joel shouted back, carefully wrapping a large lantern inside a jumper and pushing it into an already bulging suitcase. Finally, he managed to zip the case shut, and he dragged it out of his room, then *it* dragged him down the stairs.

'Are you sure you couldn't get anything else in that case, Joel?' Mum chortled, as Joel's case landed at the bottom of the stairs with a resounding thump.

'I wish I could fit my TV in,' Joel remarked, with a cheeky grin.

'It's only for two weeks, love, I'm sure you can manage without television for that long!' Mum remarked, apologetically. 'I'm sorry to dump you on Grandad every holiday, Joel; you know I don't have a choice, don't you?'

'I know, Mum, and I don't mind,' Joel shrugged. 'I like staying with Grandad and there's Peter, from the farm nearby. He's fun.'

'Oh, the crippled boy? Grandad told me you're kind to him and stick up for him when he's teased about those callipers.'

'Oh yes. I like Peter. He's a very interesting person and he's one of the best friends anyone could have,' Joel frowned. 'He's not crippled, Mum, he's just got a limp from having polio when he was young. Those callipers make it look worse than it is – it's just that they clatter when he walks. Most kids are nice to him.

It's Tamara's brother, Presten, who bullies him and calls him "Tin Legs."'

'See, you're doing it now – defending him,' Mum smiled.

Joel grimaced – he really did like Peter – he wasn't just nice to him out of pity.

'I promise we'll have a good holiday together in the Summer, Joel,' Mum said affectionately. 'Come on.' She struggled to drag his case out to the car. 'You know, I always miss your father,' she said, straining with the effort of lifting the heavily packed case. 'At times like this, I realise how much I took for granted when he was alive.'

It had been the same routine every holiday, since Joel's dad tragically died four years ago. Joel was eight then; he remembered very little about the accident. Nathan Asher, Joel's dad, had been a brilliant barrister for the prosecution, working closely with top detectives from the Drug Squad. He was constantly approached by head-hunters, who tried to poach him for private law firms as a defence barrister, but he said there were enough barristers earning shed-loads of money defending people, some of whom were blatantly guilty. He said he couldn't put his hand on his heart and defend someone he knew to be dangerous, who should be locked up for the safety of others. Whatever the pay, no amount of money could compensate for the sleepless nights, knowing violent criminals had escaped justice to continue their nefarious crimes against young and vulnerable people. Dad's mission had been to ensure that these criminals were put where they belonged – behind bars.

Joel's dad had been working on an important case which required him to work late at night, and he would often arrive home well after Joel had gone to bed. Prior to that case, Dad was very often home early enough to read with him at bedtime. Joel had treasured those times.

Then came the devastating news that Nathan had fallen asleep at the wheel of his car, crashing through a barrier into a river. The car was fitted with all the latest technology – electric windows and sunroof, anti-theft devices; everything designed for ease, comfort and to protect the vehicle. You almost had to be a computer boffin to get into it, and Hercules to get out – when it was at the bottom of a river. He couldn't even open a window to escape and swim to the surface.

Mum blamed the accident on his working too hard and too late at the office; she said he was so committed to his job, it killed him. The funeral was just a blur to Joel; he went through it like a robot, hardly able to take it all in.

Soon afterwards, Mum got a job in the city and then *she* started working late. Joel took the bus home from school, then Naomi looked after him until Mum got home. Naomi was a young and pretty Native American, studying English. She let Joel eat anything he wanted and had lots of time to go to the park, the cinema and do fun stuff. Joel thought she was cool.

When Mum had her annual four-week holiday, she and Joel spent it together. Joel spent the rest of the school holidays with Grandad, so that Mum could keep on working when Naomi went to stay with her family. Grandad's smallholding was – well, Mum called it "the country," but Joel called it a *complete wilderness!* It was a stark contrast to their hi-tech, busy life in the city.

Grandad was the original country bumpkin; he kept a few sheep and hens and grew a few vegetables. He didn't own a TV. Then, there was his noisy, rickety old jeep – thank goodness Joel's school friends at home couldn't see him there!

Grandad's place had been in Joel's family for three generations. It was Grandad's childhood home and also Mum's. There was a special secret part of his land; a hilly field where a shallow stream trickled down into a small pond. A few planks and logs provided a makeshift bridge. Several trees gave secluded shelter, but there was one huge, old special tree near the edge of the pond. This was where Joel had a really cool den. Blocks of wood nailed onto its trunk made a ladder up to the den. A rope-swing allowed for a faster descent to the ground. On the far side of the pond, a sandy bank led up to a small, grassy plateau, also fringed with trees. It was "child-heaven" – the perfect place to while away the school holidays, feast on good things to eat, and share secrets. It was Grandad's den first; when he was a young boy he named it 'Zionica,' because Zion is another name for Heaven. Then it was Mum's (she had been a real tomboy) and now it was Joel's – and the *secret* of Zionica was about to become his, also.

Joel had made some good friends near Grandad's. His best friend was Peter, the boy with the callipers. He was the adopted son of Mr and Mrs Jordan – local farmers who couldn't have children of their own. They found him when he was only two years old, abandoned in an orphanage in Hungary. They fell in love with him and fought complicated red tape to adopt him and bring him home to England. That was ten years ago.

When he wasn't at school, Peter helped his father on the farm. He knew a lot about the land, animals and nature. He had a feel for things – it was a gift. He could even read cloud formations and predict the weather as well as any radio forecaster.

The two boys were quite different. Joel was the image of his father. Captain of his school's junior rugby team, he was a good size for his age. He was fit and strong with dark, wavy hair and eyes a warm amber colour; gregarious, quick-witted, with a somewhat dry sense of humour.

Peter was slightly built although quite tall, despite his crooked legs. With his blonde hair, big blue eyes – and long eyelashes most girls would die for – he had an almost angelic look about him. He was very popular with the girls, who paid him lots of attention at school, which he often found quite embarrassing. He looked forward to the holidays when Joel came to stay with his grandad.

To Peter, Joel was a link with the outside world; a glimpse that there was civilization beyond this rural haven of tranquillity. They had spent many hours in Zionica, swapping stories about their very different lives, but just how special Zionica was, Joel and Peter were very soon to find out. This holiday would be different – just about as different as it could possibly be. In fact, after this holiday, their whole lives would be very different. They were about to discover the fantastic secret of Zionica, and then they would have to keep the secret. For the next four years, Joel and Peter would both have to lead a *double life!*

Peter was constantly tormented by Presten, whose family lived in a large house near where Joel's grandad lived and whose father was the headmaster of the local high school. He was in Peter's year at school and seized every opportunity to bully him. Though roughly the same height as Joel, Presten was not fit or athletic at all – in fact he was rather lazy and chubby. His favourite sport seemed to be causing some sort of havoc, or making someone's life a misery – usually Peter's. He had a mean, threatening manner. His brown hair was cropped very close to his head, which enhanced his bully/thug-like image. Added to this, he almost lived in a patterned grey tracksuit that made him resemble a prison convict.

In the school holidays, life was easier for Peter because Joel's presence was enough to keep Presten at bay; Presten wouldn't dare try anything with Joel in the vicinity! Presten's enmity though had been further compounded recently, due to an incident in the previous school holidays. Presten had been bullying two young boys who were playing in the snow, and he had trashed a snowman they were building. Joel, intervening, held Presten's arm behind his back and let the two young boys pelt him with snowballs – in front of his posse of delinquent friends – who all found the incident immensely amusing. Although it hadn't physically hurt him, the hurt was to his pride and Presten had sworn revenge for this humiliating experience.

†

Grandad stood in his bedroom, staring at the small wooden box on his dressing table. He picked up the box and a vague, misty memory flashed through his head. He was a young boy, about twelve years of age. The pond in Zionica had frozen over; there was snow everywhere. The sun was shining but there must have been moisture in the air, as a huge, vivid rainbow dusted the snow with a hint of glowing colour, like a reflection of Heaven.

He couldn't resist skating on the ice, although he knew he shouldn't. Then, suddenly it cracked beneath him – he had been too close to the edge where the ice must have been thinner. The freezing water caused him to catch his breath as he slipped helplessly beneath the surface, unable to break through the solid sheet of ice. He felt himself drifting into blackness. Then, a bright stick was suddenly thrust in front of him and light exploded all around it, melting the ice as if it was a burning-hot poker. He grasped frantically for the stick and felt himself being hauled out of the water and dragged onto the snowy bank. He felt warm breath blowing on his face. Looking up, he saw two incredible, flared pink nostrils. The pure white horse lifted its head – and a sparkling horn glowed between its ears! Then it galloped onto the plateau and vanished up into a powerful, blinding flash of light. He slowly opened his fingers and there, in his hand, was a small piece of pointed crystal, glowing brightly. Then, right before his very eyes, it faded into a dull piece of horn…

Suddenly, the sound of tyres on the yard outside brought him back to the present. Grandad carefully replaced the box on the dressing table and looked out of the window. It was his daughter, Elizabeth, arriving with his grandson, Joel. Dusk was descending and the rustling trees and dark clouds threatened a mighty storm. He hurried down to help them in before the heavens opened.

†

'Goodbye, civilization and real life – hello, wilderness and eccentricity!' Joel exclaimed, as he jumped out of the car in Grandad's yard. Much as he poked fun at Grandad's simple country lifestyle, Joel still felt that little spark of excitement; he loved staying with Grandad really. He ran swiftly to the porch, not only in his eagerness to see Grandad, but also to get out of the fierce, chilly wind that was whipping up a frenzy.

Grandad came straight out to help Mum with Joel's case.

'Hi, Grandad,' Joel grinned, running past him into the house, just as a massive flash of lightning lit up the sky, followed by a loud peal of thunder.

'Hello, Joel.' Grandad returned the grin.

Inside, there was a welcome roaring fire, blazing in the grate. Grandad's cottage was an "Aladdin's Cave" of knick-knacks; every corner and shelf packed with all manner of paraphernalia he'd collected over the years; every item with its own tale to tell.

In a corner, in a very large dog basket, lay a very large dog. Grandad's ancient black Labrador, Rodney, at one time would have come bounding noisily outside to investigate the arrival of visitors. Now that he was happily retired, guarding was to Rodney, a dim and distant memory, as he snoozed on regardless.

Grandma had passed away five years ago. She was diagnosed with cancer, but unfortunately too late to be treated. Grandad missed her lots and he kept the house going in much the same way as when she was alive. He was well able to look after himself though; he was fit, looked younger than his sixty-five years and wasn't a bad cook. Elizabeth, Joel's mum, was their only child. He was proud of the way she had brought Joel up on her own these past four years. He enjoyed his role as Grandad and looked forward to Joel coming to stay during the school holidays. He put his large black kettle on the old-fashioned fire-grate, while Mum flopped down in a rocking chair and sighed with exhaustion.

'A nice cup of tea will perk you up, love, after that long drive,' Grandad said, cheerily, as he settled on a little wooden stool by the fireplace.

'Thanks, Dad,' Mum yawned.

'I'm going up to my room, Grandad,' Joel announced, dragging his suitcase up the uneven, twisty stairs.

'Don't forget to duck, Joel!' Grandad shouted after him.

Grandad's tiny cottage had been built a few hundred years ago, when the average adult height was considerably shorter than it is now. So, despite Joel's tender age, the tops of the doorways were actually level with his forehead. He ducked into his room and heaved his case onto a trunk at the bottom of the bed. Opening his case, he took out the battery-powered lantern. He unwrapped it and, carefully placing it on the bedside table next to a picture of him and his parents, he switched it on. The yellow light flooded the room and a slightly wistful look came upon his face, as he gazed at the photograph and remembered his dad.

The lantern was the last thing Dad had given him before his fatal accident. He had said, *"Make use of the light, Joel, while there is still time; then you will become a light bearer*." Although Joel didn't fully understand this statement, it had always stuck in his mind.

Joel crossed the uneven floor to the tiny window, which Grandad had left open to air the room. He knelt down to gaze outside as the sun disappeared beyond the horizon – he had to kneel because the sill only came up to his knees.

The whole place was at the unrelenting mercy of an angry, howling wind. Joel watched the last fingers of light wave goodbye, as the night fell like a final curtain on the day. He could just make out the silhouetted shapes of the barn and other outbuildings, with the swirling trees and the wild, rustic landscape. It was going to be a very dark night indeed; thick cloud limited the chance of moon or starlight. He couldn't wait for morning, when he could go down to Zionica with Peter and open up the den for the holidays.

The open window was rattling a little in the wind. Joel shivered and leaned out to grab its handle to pull it shut. Suddenly, a fierce gust snatched it from his fingers. He gasped in fright as he lost his balance and began to fall headlong out of the window, towards the gravely yard below. Then, before he knew what was happening, he felt a force on his shoulders which stopped him and actually started to push him up and back through the window! The next thing he knew, he was sitting on his bedroom floor – and the window was mysteriously closed!

Straining his eyes, he could just make out the shape of a bird – a raven, perched on the window-ledge outside. As Joel stared, the bird cocked its head to one side and then, to his immense surprise, it appeared to raise an eyebrow. Then, it spread its wings and flew off into the night. Joel shook his head and blinked, a little dazed. He rushed quickly back to the window, but there was nothing – or no one – there. Joel thought it must have been his imagination or something – maybe the fading light playing tricks on his eyes. Probably a strong gust of wind had blown him back inside and slammed the window shut…

'Joel!' Grandad called up the stairs. 'Come and have some supper, lad, and tell me all your news. I want to hear about this promotion in the rugby team.'

†

At first light, Joel was woken by Cedric, the cockerel. He sprang out of bed, put on his trainers and ran downstairs, almost tripping over Rodney at the bottom. Joel loved to go out to the coop first thing and collect fresh eggs for breakfast. Cedric had a harem of seven hens and considered it his role in life to protect them, a duty to which he was fiercely loyal. So, venturing unarmed into the coop was not advisable, especially when Cedric was hungry. However, he was easily bought – a bucketful of grain usually did the trick.

The hens provided free-range eggs which Grandad sold, along with other organic produce, to the locals. His smallholding provided most of his own food and covered his modest living expenses. His one luxury was a good stock of brandy and Benedictine which, mixed together, was Grandad's favourite tipple and also, he was convinced, the best cure for any cold or flu. The odd bottle of old malt whisky occasionally found its way into Grandad's store cupboard, too. However, this usually lasted for a very long time as just a few sips were guaranteed to send him straight to sleep.

Picking up a small basket, Joel unlatched the back door and almost stepped onto a present left by Martha, Grandad's old tabby cat. She was sitting proudly over the lifeless field mouse, waiting to be congratulated on her prize, hopeful that the gesture would be returned in the shape of a bowl of fresh milk.

'Martha! You murderer!' Joel shouted at the cat, before running off up the yard.

The gale force wind of the previous night had been replaced by a steady breeze and, though chilly, it promised a sunny day. Grandad was already out on the yard, feeding his small menagerie of sheep and goats.

'Morning, Joel!' Grandad called. 'The hens are waiting for their breakfast!'

'OK Grandad!' Joel picked up the bucket of grain which Grandad had left by the coop, and let himself in.

Cedric immediately attacked the bucket, pecking at it furiously and trying to jump onto it. Joel quickly flung a handful of grain on the ground. The mercenary Cedric abandoned the bucket (and temporarily his role of defender of the coop) swooping greedily onto the grain. The sound of the bucket and Cedric's squawks were all that were needed to lure the hens away from their beds and they came over to join him, squawking their little heads off. This left the way clear for Joel to collect the newly-laid eggs, still warm as he put them into the basket.

†

'These eggs are just how I like them, Grandad,' Joel enthused, as he sat at the breakfast table with Grandad and Mum. He stabbed another toast soldier into a boiled egg and the yellow yolk oozed gungily up over the toast. Joel stuffed the whole soggy mess into his mouth. 'Perfect!'

'You shouldn't talk with food in your mouth, Joel,' Mum said, delicately pushing scrambled egg onto her fork.

'Oh leave him be, Liz. The lad is on holiday; he's just enjoying his food,' Grandad winked at Joel.

'Don't you go spoiling him again over the next two weeks, Dad,' Mum insisted. 'He'll be expecting the same star treatment when he comes home!'

'Well, if I can't spoil my only grandson occasionally, it's a poor do. What do you say, Joel?' Grandad grinned.

'That's fine by me, you can spoil me any time you like,' Joel replied, returning the grin as he got up from the table. 'Can I phone Peter now, Grandad?'

'Of course you can, lad.'

When Joel came racing back into the kitchen after phoning Peter, Mum was ready to return to the hustle and bustle of city life.

'Thanks, Dad,' Mum said hugging Grandad.

'Not at all, don't you worry; we'll be fine. We'll look after each other, won't we, Joel?'

'Yeah, that's cool, Grandad,' Joel nodded.

'You just take care of you,' Grandad smiled affectionately.

'Well, I'll see you two in a couple of weeks, then.' Mum gave Joel a kiss on the forehead.

'Bye, Mum.' Joel turned to Grandad. 'I'm just going to meet Peter, Grandad. He's on his way over.'

Joel ran behind Mum's car, down the yard to the gate, waving her off. The car disappeared round the bend. He waved to Grandad, then set off down the narrow country lane to meet Peter. He was striding happily along, expecting to bump into Peter, but he didn't expect what he found. Suddenly he stopped, on hearing a muffled sort of moaning sound which seemed to be coming from the ditch. He crept slowly over the grass. There was something moving. He began to edge cautiously towards it.

'Peter!' Joel jumped into the ditch and pulled his friend's head up. There was about three inches of water in the bottom of the ditch. Peter was all wet and covered in mud; he tried to open his eyes to look at Joel. His face was bruised, one of his eyes was swollen and his top lip was bleeding. Joel hauled him up onto the grass and wiped some of the mud from his face with his sleeve.

'Peter – what happened?'

'Presten,' Peter coughed. 'He ambushed me in the lane – he's demented – he's torn my coat! My mum will be furious.' Peter looked down at his torn jacket.

'Never mind the jacket! Are you all right? Can you get up?'

'Yeah, I don't think anything is broken; I'm just a bit sore.'

Joel supported him as he struggled, in his metal callipers, to stand up. 'Come on, let's get you home and clean you up.'

'No! I can't let my mum see me looking like this! You know how she'll fuss. Can we go to your Grandad's?'

'Of course we can,' Joel nodded.

'Thanks, Joel.'

Joel put Peter's arm over his shoulder and they set off back in the direction of Grandad's place. Before they had gone far, they heard the sound of hooves cantering up behind them along the grass verge. It was Tamara, riding on her small brown and white pony, Cherokee.

'It's Miss bla - de - bla on her pony,' Joel said, joking fondly. He liked Tamara really. Her family were well-to-do and her dad was headmaster of the local high school.

'Oh no! That's all we need – Presten's sister!' Peter whined. 'Joel, don't tell her it was Presten – she'll go straight to her dad. I know she means well but it'll just make Presten worse.'

Tamara came to an abrupt halt and leapt off the pony.

'Joel! You're back!' she cried with excitement.

At ten, she was a couple of years younger than Joel and Peter. Nevertheless, she had a smart head on her shoulders and the three of them were very good friends. She adored the two boys and had, for some time, had a secret crush on Joel – although she'd have died of embarrassment if he ever found out. Suddenly, Tamara gasped, as she saw Peter's face.

'Oh, no! What happened to you, Peter?'

'I slipped off the hay stack,' Peter muttered unconvincingly.

'Yeah, right…' Tamara raised a suspicious eyebrow. 'It's not a coincidence that I've just passed my evil brother in the lane!'

'I – I know what you're thinking, Tamara, but don't,' Peter pleaded. 'Telling your dad will just make things worse. Anyway, Presten will find out that Joel is here now for the holidays and I'll get two weeks of peace.'

'Oh, you really think so, Peter – after last holiday? Presten has sworn revenge, you know,' Tamara sighed. 'Come on, get on Cherokee – you look as if you can hardly walk.'

They both helped Peter to mount Cherokee.

Being Presten's younger sister, Tamara was well aware of his reputation as a bully and she found her elder brother a constant embarrassment. As Peter was pretty much defenceless, he appeared to be Presten's main target. Tamara did what she could though, to help Peter.

Tamara was a confirmed tomboy – one of those girls who are "one of the boys." She'd always preferred boy-type activities and would more likely be found climbing trees than playing with dolls. However, she couldn't have looked more like a girl: long, silky, golden hair; cheeky, sparkly blue eyes; pale, English rose complexion; perfect rosebud lips. She was full of life and fun, though sometimes her impetuous nature caused her to speak first and think later! But no one could have been kinder or more generous. In fact, it was hard to believe that Tamara and Presten were even related – let alone had the same parents! Even their father sometimes joked that when Presten was born, they must have brought the wrong baby home from the hospital and Tamara kept begging them to take him back! Mr Goodchild (yes, a fitting surname for Tamara – but Presten?) was constantly having to apologise for his son's latest stupid prank.

†

Peter sat on a chair in Grandad's kitchen, and winced as Grandad gently applied some cotton wool and antiseptic to his wounds, while Joel did his best to clean up Peter's muddy coat.

'It's just ripped a little under the arm, Peter,' Joel observed.

'Yes, Presten was swinging me round by my sleeve – until he suddenly let go and I went flying into the ditch,' Peter muttered.

'Boy, I'd like to have a go at Presten with my cricket bat!' Joel shook his head in fury.

'It wouldn't do any good, Joel. He'd just take it out on me again,' Peter muttered, despondently.

'I'm afraid Peter is right, Joel,' Grandad agreed. 'You will never stop violence with violence; it just makes bullies like Presten worse. You mustn't retaliate. Anyway, you're only here for two weeks. Peter has to deal with Presten on a daily basis.

'Can't the police do anything?' Joel asked in frustration.

'Huh – the police? They're as much use as a wheel on a walking stick in such matters,' Grandad murmured. 'They'd say it's a case of domestic fighting between two juveniles. It's a sad and ironic situation, but the police are handcuffed by the law! Basically, Presten would have to murder Peter before the police could act! Besides, Presten's father is well-respected in the community; a member of the Church Council and Head of the High School. No one would want to risk upsetting him, despite his unruly son.'

'Unruly? Demonic, if you ask me!' Joel frowned.

'Yeah, he knows there's nothing we can do,' Peter added, weakly. 'We should just try to keep out of his way.'

The door opened and Tamara entered.

'Cherokee is quite happy in your barn, Mr Jacob; thanks for the hay.' She smiled.

'You're welcome, Tamara love,' Grandad replied.

'How are you, Peter? Eoow…' She crinkled up her nose as she inspected Peter's swollen face. 'Oh, how could I possibly be related to Presten?'

'There you go, Peter.' Grandad stood back. 'I'm afraid you'll have a black eye and a big fat lip tomorrow, though.'

'Look on the bright side, Peter,' Joel teased. 'It'll keep the girls off you for a while.'

'You're joking aren't you?' Peter squirmed. 'This'll make them ten times worse – they'll mother me to death! It's just as well it's the school holidays.'

'Hey, I bet there's loads of frogspawn in the pond,' Tamara remarked, changing the subject. 'Let's go up to Zionica and see. Can we have some jam-jars and some string, Mr Jacob?'

Collecting frogspawn and watching them hatch into tadpoles was one of those country activities that seemed a world apart from Joel's life in the city. There wasn't actually much to do as life seemed so much slower when he visited Grandad.

A soft breeze carried the sound of their laughter, together with the dull clatter of Peter's callipers, as the three friends made their way over the field to Zionica. Patches of blue sky allowed the sun to shine intermittently through the trees, causing the gently rippling pond to glisten.

They dangled their jam-jars into the water and scooped up masses of frog-spawn. A coloured twist-tie round the string of each jar clearly identified its owner: red for Joel's, white for Peter's and blue for Tamara's. This way they could monitor the hatching progress, to see who hatched the biggest and best tadpoles.

'I wish you'd let me tell my dad what Presten has done to Peter,' Tamara said to Joel, as they retrieved the full jars from the water.

'Well, you can't,' Joel replied, firmly. 'That'll just make things worse for Peter.'

'You're not mad at me, are you, Joel?'

'No, sorry, Tamara – I'm mad at myself,' Joel muttered with a sigh. 'I should be able to protect Peter, but it seems I can't even do that.'

'It's not your fault, Joel,' Tamara insisted. 'How can you protect him when most of the time you're not even here!'

Peter carried his jar to the tree and began to climb up the nails and wood blocks to the den, an art he'd mastered quite well despite his callipers.

'Hey, chill, guys. Forget it – Presten is not worth getting upset about,' Peter insisted, as he reached the den and began tying his jar to a branch. 'Honestly, I don't think we'll get any trouble from him now you're here, Joel.'

'I don't know, Peter,' Tamara mused, following him up to the den. 'Presten is mad as anything about, you know, the snowballing incident last holiday. He's determined to get his revenge.'

'Yeah, that was the funniest thing ever – I'm so glad I was there to see it,' Peter chuckled. 'Anyway, he got his revenge this morning, didn't he? Witness my face!' Peter pointed the first finger of each hand at either side of his face.

'No, Tamara is right, Peter,' Joel replied. 'That's just playtime
for Presten. I suspect he's got some evil retribution planned for me, too.'

After they'd secured their jam-jars to a branch in the den, they restocked supplies. An important event at the start of each holiday was replenishing the various storage boxes and tins with essential items such as sweets, pop, biscuits, books, etc.

They stayed in the den all day, catching up on each other's news since the last holiday, only going back to the house to get some sandwiches and cake for lunch – which they took back to the den to eat.

By late afternoon, the chill wind seemed to get brisker. A green woodpecker laughingly called, and Peter looked up at the thickening cloud. 'I think we'd better head on back – there's going to be a corker of a storm,' he observed. 'If you don't get Cherokee home soon, Tamara, you'll have to leave her overnight. Within an hour, it'll be too dangerous to ride back.'

'Hey, do you want to sleep over tonight, Peter?' Joel asked.

'Yeah, cool – and my mum won't get to see my bruises!' Peter replied, enthusiastically.

'Great!' Tamara sulked. 'Oh, why did I have to be born a girl? Boys have all the fun. I have to go home and put up with Presten, while you two have a midnight feast!'

'Yeah, it stinks, doesn't it?' Joel sympathised. 'If it was up to us you could stay too, but you know the rules.'

'Yeah, I know, it's in case we do bla - de - bla…' Tamara complained irritably.

The boys both looked at her, then exchanged amused glances.

'You know, this bla - de - bla sex thing.' Tamara raised her eyes in a rather bored gesture. 'I don't know what all the fuss is about. It's not fair.'

'Well, there must be something to it, Tamara, or they wouldn't go on about it the way they do,' Joel teased, winking at Peter. 'Grown-ups seem to think it's pretty important.'

'Yeah, but we all know it's how you get babies,' Tamara went on flatly. 'I mean, come on,' she mocked. 'I bet neither of you know how to do it anyway – and I certainly don't!' she added hastily.

'I know how animals do it, I've seen them,' Peter volunteered, in a matter of fact way.

'Eoow, you mean you've watched them?' Tamara screwed up her nose in disgust.

'I live on a farm, Tamara – my dad breeds cows! Sometimes I have to help my dad.'

'So, what do they do then – the cows?' Tamara asked, casually twisting a lock of hair round her finger and trying to look as if she wasn't really interested.

'Well,' Peter answered, you take the male bull into a big shed where the female cow is waiting…'

'And?' Tamara urged, leaning forward.

Peter leaned forward to whisper in her ear. 'The cow goes… MOO!'

'Oh – grow up!' Tamara huffed hotly. 'Anyway, people are very different from animals.'

'Hey, come on, if Peter says there's going to be a storm, then there's going to be a storm – let's get going.' Joel leapt from the den onto the rope and swung to the ground.

'Oh, bla - de - bla…' Tamara muttered, then, catching hold of the swinging rope she pushed it to Peter. 'Here, Peter.'

†

By the time they reached Grandad's cottage, the weather had worsened considerably. Tamara was still in a bit of a sulk as they entered the kitchen from outside. Joel poured out three tumblers of milk and put the biscuit tin on the kitchen table and the three friends sat round it, munching.

'Oh, look, Peter, Grandad has mended your jacket,' Joel mumbled through a mouthful of biscuit.

Peter took the jacket from Joel and inspected it.

'Hey, that's great!' Peter beamed. 'He's cleaned it up too.

Mum will never know!'

'The old man has his uses, doesn't he?' Joel remarked, dryly.

'I still think it's not fair,' Tamara whined, miserably.

'Look, Tamara,' Joel replied, a little impatiently now. 'We know you don't think it's fair, neither do we, but do you have to keep saying it?'

'Actually Joel,' Peter announced, gazing out of the window. 'I think Tamara might just have to stay. The storm is almost upon us; it wouldn't be safe to let her ride home.'

'Oh, brilliant!' Tamara exclaimed excitedly. 'We can have a midnight feast while we watch the lightning flashing in the sky!' She jumped, startled, as a loud clap of thunder peeled.

'Well, OK, let's see what Grandad says. Maybe he could phone your parents, Tamara, and tell them you'll be sleeping in the spare room.'

'I didn't think you had a spare room, Joel...' Peter asked, puzzled.

'We don't really. This is Grandad's cottage, remember – built for pygmies – you can't swing a cat in it. There's Grandad's bedroom and mine. My room *is* the spare room!'

'Oh, yippee!' Tamara cried in amazement.

'Maybe Grandad will sleep on the couch, like he does when Mum stays, and let Tamara have his room,' Joel added.

'Aah, but that won't be as much fun!' Tamara argued. 'What about our midnight feast – and ghost stories?'

Just then Grandad walked in from outside.

'I've bedded Cherokee down for the night, Tamara,' he said. 'It's not safe to ride home; there's a storm building up and it's going to be a corker. What do you say, Peter?'

'It's going to be a corker all right, Mr Jacob,' Peter replied. 'We heard a green woodpecker calling earlier. Oh, and thanks for mending my jacket,' he added gratefully.

'Well, we couldn't send you back to your mum with it the way it was, could we?' Grandad smiled. 'A green woodpecker, eh! I think we'll batten down the hatches for the evening. You two had better stay over; there may be trees down in the lane – it's safer to stay indoors. I'm sure Joel can find you something to wear for bed.'

They all tried hard to keep straight faces as Grandad went on.

'Peter, you'd better ring your parents and let them know you're staying. Tamara, you'd better let me speak to your parents first. I think it will be better coming from me, don't you?'

'Oh absolutely, Mr Jacob, thank you.' Tamara now found it impossible to keep the wide grin off her face, as Grandad headed for the phone in the hall.

'Wow, you'd think your grandad had been listening to us talking, wouldn't you?' Tamara whispered under her breath.

They weren't wrong – an almighty storm attacked them from all quarters. Lightning lit up the sky with blinding flashes, as the rain lashed, the wind thrashed, and thunder crashed all around. The roofs of the barn and outbuildings flapped and clattered as if some terrifying beast was trying to get out. They heard the sound of the lambs bleating and Cherokee whinnying, from the barn.

Grandad snuggled in his rocking chair by the open fire, a glass of his favourite tipple in his hand. Rodney whimpered and padded morosely around the lounge, finally finding solace at Grandad's feet. Even Martha, who normally spent the night outside, was happy to forego a night's hunting and instead, curl up in Rodney's bed for the night.

Meanwhile, the three friends, who were not in the least bit tired, had organised their sleeping arrangements. They'd tossed a coin: Peter got the camp bed and Tamara got the airbed, which they set up in Joel's room with mounds of pillows, blankets and quilts. Peter was quite comfortable in a pair of Joel's pyjamas. However, they all fell about laughing at Tamara, who, completely swamped by another pair, elected instead to wear one of Grandad's T-shirts, which also swamped her like a tent but at least there were no trousers to try and keep up.

Grandad wasn't supposed to know about the feast they smuggled upstairs, but he'd enjoyed enough midnight feasts himself to guess the probability. He smiled to himself, pretending not to notice their padded nightclothes stuffed full of booty, when they said goodnight and slipped upstairs.

They settled down comfortably with a feast of peanuts, cake, chocolate and crisps. Joel switched off the light; it was much more exciting with just his lantern and the flashing lightning, which lit up the whole room when it struck. He closed the curtains. 'I've never seen such a furious storm! I wonder if God is really angry about something...' he mused, with a frown.

'Oh, leave the curtains, Joel!' Tamara cried, ignoring his remark. 'We'll be able to see the lightning flashing in the sky and it'll be more exciting!'

'I think we'd better shut them, Tamara.' Joel murmured, with a shiver, as he remembered his scary experience of the previous evening.

'You're not scared of a bit of thunder and lightning, are you, Joel?' Tamara teased.

'Of course not!' Joel retorted quickly.

'I think we should leave them shut,' Peter said, coming to Joel's defence. 'The lightning is so bright, we'll still see its effect through the curtains.'

'Yeah,' Joel teased. 'They'll stop it coming right into the room and striking us! Unless frazzled hair and popping-out eyes is the look you're going for, Tamara?'

'Eoow...' Tamara pulled a face. 'Joel, sometimes you can be so bla - de - bla…'

They stayed awake till after midnight, talking, feasting and playing games, as the storm raged on. Grandad boosted supplies, bringing up hot cocoa and (more) chocolate cake. They hastily hid all the sweet wrappers under the bedclothes when he entered the room. Then he sat and told them all a mysterious story, while the lightning continued to illuminate the room with brilliant blue flashes. It was kind of scary and exciting, but cosy, all at the same time, because they were safely tucked up inside.

Finally, they drifted off to sleep. Grandad switched off Joel's lantern, before tiptoeing off to bed himself.

†

The early-morning call from Cedric was right on time. He seemed to be demanding, 'Get up and feed me!'

Tamara climbed out of her air-bed. Yawning and still half asleep, she ambled over to the window. 'It's so eerily quiet after last night's storm,' she mumbled, pulling back the curtains and rubbing her eyes. 'Apart from Cedric's squawking, it's still as a post.'

'I feel like I've had about three minutes sleep,' Joel moaned, turning over. 'Anyway it's "still as a mill-pond" and "deaf as a post," Tamara.' He covered his head with a pillow.

Peter, immune to early-morning farm noises, slumbered on.

'Oh, cockerels!' Tamara cried suddenly, as she looked out of the window.

'I know, Cedric can be really annoying,' Joel said. 'Here, open the window and throw this boot at him.' He reached for a boot and flung it over to Tamara.

'I don't mean Cedric, Joel.' Tamara beckoned. 'Come and look at this!'

'Don't tell me, the barn has disintegrated in the storm,' Joel murmured, sleepily climbing out of bed and joining her at the window.

'Wow…' he whistled. 'Hey, Peter! Wake up!' Joel rushed over to Peter's camp bed and shook him. 'Peter, come on! What do you make of this? Come and look!'

'What is it? Is there a fire?' Peter sat up and reached for his callipers.

'Leave those – there isn't time; come on!' Joel urged, helping him up and supporting him across the room.

'Alleluia!' Peter exclaimed, staring out of the window. 'Looks like God is as sorry this morning as he was angry last night! I've never seen anything like it!'

'Neither have I!' Tamara gasped in amazement.

For, what they were looking at was the hugest, brightest, most colourful rainbow they had ever seen. It was so big it seemed to fill the whole sky, stretching right down to the land.

'Look where it ends – it seems to vanish into the ground right at…' Joel gasped and looked earnestly at the others.

'ZIONICA!' they all shouted in unison.

'Isn't there supposed to be a pot of gold at the end of a rainbow?' Tamara asked.

'What are we waiting for?' Joel shouted. 'Let's get a closer Look!'

The boys hastily threw on their clothes, while Tamara ran into the bathroom to do the same. All three jumped and slid down the stairs, then ran out of the door. Tamara and Joel were half-carrying, half-dragging Peter, callipers clanging.

When they reached the brow of the small hill at the edge of Zionica, they stopped to stare at the rainbow's almost iridescent hue. It was still very early and the sun was only just up, but the rainbow filled everywhere with warmth and light. It was so real and so close, they felt bathed in its warm and brilliant glow.

'It's awesome!' Tamara murmured.

'Awesome!' Joel and Peter echoed.

'A rainbow is a sign from God, isn't it?' Tamara stated, curiously.

'He must have something very important to say,' Peter replied. 'I wonder what it is?'

'Yes. This could almost be Heaven itself…' Joel pondered.

Then, without warning, the rainbow dissolved, right before their eyes.

'Oh, come back…' Tamara begged, in disappointment. 'How can it just vanish?'

The warm glow had been so wonderful, they hadn't wanted it to end. Then, as they slowly walked down the hill towards their tree, Peter stopped suddenly.

'What's that?' He cocked his head to listen.

Then they all heard it: a sort of soft, laboured breathing and grunting.

'Where's it coming from?' Joel cried, puzzled, as he continued down the dip. Then kneeling down, he shouted. 'Over here!'

The others rushed over to Joel.

'It's an injured animal. A hare or something; it's too big to be a rabbit; it's alive – only just.'

Peter and Tamara knelt down beside Joel and looked at the animal. It was white as snow and they could see its sides slowly moving up and down with weak breaths.

'Since when have you seen a hare with ears that small, Joel?' Peter asked, lifting the animal's head. 'This isn't a hare – it's a foal!'

'A foal? But how has a foal got here?' Tamara asked in astonishment. 'Where's his mother?'

'Dunno,' Peter answered, mystified.

'What? Did he just drop out of the sky, or something?' Tamara demanded curiously, expecting the boys to come up with some credible explanation.

'Well, it looks like that, doesn't it?' Joel mused.

'The most likely explanation is that his stable must have been damaged in the storm last night and he escaped,' Peter surmised. 'His owner will probably come looking for him when he discovers he's missing. We'd better take him to your grandad's barn; he'll perish out here. Can you manage to carry him, Joel?'

'Yeah, no sweat.' Joel picked up the tiny creature. The foal was a little smaller than Rodney and Joel guessed, rightly, not nearly as heavy. Too weak to struggle, the foal allowed himself to be carried.

When they got to the barn, Joel laid him down in some fresh straw.

'Isn't he beautiful?' Tamara whispered. 'He's positively *titchy-cuticus*, just like a miniature Cherokee. What shall we do with him now?'

'We'd better check him over, to see if he's injured,' Peter replied, authoritatively.

Peter was used to caring for animals, particularly when they were injured or sick. At home he often tended to the sick bay animals, while his dad concentrated on the productive ones. He began to gently feel the foal all over, checking his legs, back and stomach.

'I can't see anything wrong with him; I think he's just plain exhausted,' Peter concluded, as he moved the little animal's head, checking its eyes and ears. Then, suddenly, as he moved his hand between its ears, Peter froze like a statue.

It appeared to Joel and Tamara as if a bolt of lightning had struck Peter! An almost blinding light seemed to shoot from the foal straight into him, surrounding him with a glowing aura. This alarming apparition lasted only about two seconds. Then, the bright light disappeared and he snapped out of suspended animation. He shook his head, as though dazed. Joel and Tamara stared at him, with their mouths wide open.

'Tell me I didn't see that, Tamara,' Joel murmured, weakly.

'You – didn't – see – that – Joel and neither did I…' Tamara stammered.

'Then, what exactly *did* we see?' asked Joel, with an air of disbelief.

'I, er – what exactly?' Tamara pulled a confused face.

Peter stood up. He looked at them, a little apprehensively.

'Something just happened, didn't it?'

'Er, something…' Joel shrugged, visibly shaken, but trying to play it down so not to alarm the others before he could speak to Grandad about it. 'I think it must have been the sun coming up at a strange angle through the window. It seemed to shine right on you – made you look a bit weird.'

Peter started to walk towards them, but tripped.

'Ouch!' He sat down on the floor and started to adjust his callipers. 'These callipers are pinching.' He looked up at his two friends, who were staring at him very strangely indeed.

'What's the matter with you two? You look like you've just seen a ghost.' Peter sounded worried.

'Peter…' Tamara murmured incredulously. 'Your face…'

'What? What about my face? Oh right, my black eye; it looks ten times worse this morning,' Peter remarked with a forced laugh. 'It doesn't feel that bad though – in fact, it doesn't hurt at all...'

'W – what black eye, P – Peter? Your face looks f – fine to

me,' Tamara stammered.

'You're right, Peter,' Joel said, seriously. 'It did look worse when you got up this morning, but now your bruises have gone – your face is back to normal!'

'It can't be!' Peter exclaimed. 'It was like my mum's blueberry pie half an hour ago!'

'Well, it's peaches and cream now,' Joel mused.

Peter stared at Joel in disbelief.

'You're serious, aren't you?'

'I can't explain it, Peter. Come on.' Joel leaned down and helped Peter up. 'Let's go in for breakfast – see what Grandad says about the foal.'

They cooked a breakfast feast in the kitchen, while Grandad was still out feeding his flock and attempting to repair the storm damage. They couldn't understand the mystery of Peter's missing bruises, although Peter certainly didn't miss them. By the time Grandad came back inside, they were sitting at the table tucking into bacon, eggs, sausages, beans and toast. The kitchen almost looked as if it had been hit by a nuclear blast; however, the food was delicious.

Grandad pulled up a chair and joined them. They all marvelled at the rainbow, the children exclaiming that they'd never seen one quite like it.

'Have you ever seen a rainbow like that before, Mr Jacob?' Tamara inquired.

'I have,' Grandad surprised them. 'We do see some spectacular rainbows here, but I only ever remember seeing one other that brilliant,' he replied, thoughtfully.

'When was that, Mr Jacob?' Tamara urged.

They all looked at Grandad with eager anticipation.

'Many years ago – in fact I must have been about your age, Joel. But there was something most extraordinary about that rainbow.'

'What was that, Mr Jacob?' asked Tamara, intrigued.

'Well, we'd had an incredible storm the night before,' Grandad began enthusiastically, 'just like last night, only it was different...'

'Please go on,' Tamara pressed.

'Well, it was a snow storm. It was winter and the following morning, there was snow everywhere. There were just a few clouds in the sky and this huge, brilliant rainbow. It was in the same place as the one this morning and, just like you, I raced over to Zionica to look at it. It was so big and bright; the light from it made the snow rainbow-coloured. It was the most incredible sight. The pond had frozen over and – well...' Grandad shrugged, as though he had been going to say something else, but suddenly changed his mind.

'Wow!' Peter whistled.

'What happened, Grandad?' Joel urged.

'Nothing... that's it,' Grandad replied, somewhat abruptly.

Tamara nudged Joel. 'Go on,' she whispered to Joel. 'Tell your grandad about the foal we found, Joel.'

Grandad sat up with interest.

'Yeah, Grandad, do you know anyone local whose mare has recently had a white foal?'

'Pure white, Mr Jacob,' Tamara added eagerly.

Grandad looked at Joel with some concern.

'No, no one. What's this about finding a foal – white, you say?'

'Yes, Mr Jacob,' Tamara beamed, excitedly. 'It's beautiful, like snow.'

'It must have got out in the storm last night,' Joel explained. 'Only we found it, half-dead, down in Zionica when we went to look at the rainbow.'

'I'm sure it's just exhausted, Mr Jacob.' Peter added 'I couldn't find anything wrong with...'

'But, Mr Jacob, look at Peter's face!' Tamara interrupted.

Grandad looked up at Peter and gasped with astonishment.

'Oh, my hat!' The last time I saw that face, it was nearly the colour of a rainbow!' Grandad leaned forward to scrutinise Peter's face. 'How radically curious...' he mused. 'You'd better tell me exactly what happened.'

They explained the earlier incident in the barn when, after they had found the little foal, the light had seemed to have a climacteric effect on Peter. Grandad listened quietly, then sat back in his chair pondering. They wondered if he believed them, or if he thought they were making it all up, though Peter's face spoke for itself. The suspense ended with Grandad standing up.

'Is it still in the barn?' he asked, a little anxiously.

'Yes, it's in the stall next to Cherokee,' Joel answered.

'Well, we can't leave it there; it might be in danger. Go and fetch it into the house – and bring some fresh straw.'

The children all stared at Grandad, then at each other, utterly confused.

'What on earth do you mean, Grandad?' Joel asked. 'How can our barn be dangerous? This is just absurd!'

'Yes, Mr Jacob. If the little foal's life is in danger, shouldn't we call out a vet?' Tamara asked, concerned.

'Oh, no, there's no need for that, Tamara,' Grandad answered. 'No, you just go and fetch it here and let me look at it.'

'Oh dear, what about my Cherokee? If the barn is dangerous, shouldn't we get her out, too?' Tamara sounded quite alarmed.

'No, Cherokee is perfectly alright, Tamara. Just go and get the little foal you found. Now go on children, make haste!' Grandad insisted.

'All right, Grandad, if you say so,' Joel muttered with a shrug. 'Come on, let's go.'

All three children set off for the barn as instructed, though rather bewildered.

†

The three friends hurried across the yard to the barn.

'Has your grandad gone completely batty, Joel?' Tamara asked, earnestly. 'Since when has a barn been dangerous to horses? Why are Cherokee and the other animals in there if it's dangerous and why does the danger only apply to the foal?'

'I just don't know, Tamara…' Joel shook his head, 'But I'm

sure that Grandad knows something.' Then suddenly, he caught Tamara by the arm and stopped her. She followed his bewildered gaze to Peter – and her jaw dropped. He was striding out towards the barn as they'd never seen him before; callipers clanging as usual – but not a limp in sight!

CHAPTER TWO

Victory in the Lane

Ever since he could remember, Peter had always had a limp. He needed to wear callipers to support his crooked legs and feet, which were ravaged by polio and general malnutrition when he was a baby. But now, crazy as it seemed, Peter was walking with two perfectly normal, straight and strong legs. It was a miracle – pure and simple!

Inside the barn, Cherokee was leaning over the side of her stall, her nostrils blowing softly over the foal, as though comforting him. Peter and Joel carefully lifted the little foal and carried him out of the barn. Cherokee whinnied, almost as if she was calling after them not to take the baby away.

They took him into the kitchen. Tamara brought some straw and Grandad made a little bed in the alcove under the stairs, then they laid the little foal in it.

'Well now, aren't we a beauty?' Grandad declared, smiling at the little animal.

The foal seemed to be recovering already and raised his head, blinking his big eyes at Grandad, as if he was answering him, acknowledging the compliment.

'Ooh, it's almost like Christmas!' Tamara swooned, clearly taken with the little foal.

The boys looked at her, then at each other, rolling their eyes.

'You know, it's like when they laid baby Jesus in a little bed of straw…' Tamara explained.

'I suppose, but then foals usually sleep in a bed of straw, Tamara,' Joel pointed out. 'Baby Jesus was an actual person.'

'Well, it reminds me of the nativity, anyway,' Tamara insisted.

'Here, Peter, I keep this bottle for the sickly lambs. I've warmed some milk; you know what to do.' Grandad handed a small baby feeding bottle to Peter.

'OK, Mr Jacob.' Peter knelt down and held the bottle for the foal to drink.

'Can we give him a name, Mr Jacob?' Tamara begged. 'I mean, we've got to call him something till his owner comes for him.'

'Yes, Tamara love. What do you suggest?'

'Well, he arrived in a storm; how about we call him Storm?'

'Fits him perfectly, love.'

Tamara knelt down next to Peter and cradled Storm's head, while Peter gave him the milk.

'Hello, Storm, my name is Tamara, and this is Peter, Joel and Mr Jacob – and we're going to look after you. Oh, I wish we could keep him, he's so cute.'

'That's impossible, I'm afraid,' said Grandad. 'Make the most of him, Tamara because he won't be with us for long. He will have to go back, you know.'

Peter gave the bottle to Tamara and struggled to stand up in his callipers.

'Peter, you might as well take those callipers off, lad,' Grandad said. 'You won't be needing them anymore; they're more of a hindrance now.' With that, Grandad headed for the door to the hall, calling back, 'You'd better get ready, it's Sunday. We'll have to leave for church in half an hour.'

They all looked down at Peter's legs, then up at each other, perplexed at Grandad's mysterious comment.

†

Grandad always attended church on Sundays, but it was only recently that the local church had grown in popularity. The front-row pews were now full every Sunday morning. This was largely owing to the sudden spiritual awakening of almost the entire female teenage population of the parish, who were always early (first there get the best seats). This spate of Christian fervour amongst these blushing young girls was undoubtedly connected with G.R. JAM. That was the girls' code for Gorgeous Reverend John. The young, enigmatic (and single) Reverend John Aaron

Matthews was installed as the incumbent vicar of St Mary's, when the old vicar retired the previous year. John Matthews brought a refreshingly modern approach to worship. His services were not old-fashioned or steeped in stuffy religious ceremonial pomp, but they celebrated the love of God as shown by Jesus. The children also loved him; he played the guitar and sang as he preached. In fact, if he hadn't been a vicar, Matthews could have been a successful singer and musician. He was popular with older ladies too. Unlike most vicars with their shiny heads fringed by the "Friar's ring of grey," Matthews had a good head of hair!

†

Peter felt very self-conscious as he walked into the church minus his callipers. He felt as if every eye was staring at him, like hot pinpricks in his back.

'Stay close behind me, Peter,' Grandad instructed protectively. 'Joel, you stay at the back, behind Peter and Tamara.'

The three friends followed Grandad up the aisle of the church. Joel thought the fact that Grandad took it all so calmly was evidence that he knew more than he was telling, and Joel was determined to find out exactly what that was.

A slight murmur stirred through the congregation as Peter walked straight and silently up the aisle, without the familiar clanging of callipers, and there were audible gasps as he passed each row of pews. However, Peter's parents were thankfully right at the front of the church. Although they turned round like everyone else, they didn't have a good view of Peter because he was shielded behind Grandad. The last thing Peter wanted was some sort of scene in front of everyone – where he would have to explain the absence of his callipers.

Tamara's parents were not far from the back of the church and Presten was with them, seated next to the aisle. As Grandad passed them, he suddenly stopped, immediately turned his head and looked down at Presten, who had furtively stuck his foot out, ready to trip Peter, as he followed after Grandad.

'You should be careful, Presten,' Grandad frowned reproachfully. 'Your foot may get hurt – should anyone happen to trip over it.'

Presten's smirking face dissolved into an irritated scowl as he slowly pulled in his foot.

Grandad and Mr and Mrs Goodchild exchanged greetings with a smile and a nod. Then, Grandad continued to lead his young troupe on up the aisle.

Tamara glared at Presten disapprovingly then smiled sweetly at her parents, who beamed and waved back. She was their pride and joy and generally made up for all the headaches Presten caused. Presten shrank back in his seat, a look of loathing on his face, as Joel walked past and threw him a piercing stare.

Reaching an empty pew, they filed in to take their seats. Grandad immediately leaned forward to pray while the three children leaned forward to whisper among themselves.

'Joel, it's like your grandad seems to know about things before they happen – it's weird,' Tamara whispered.

'You mean, Presten's foot? I could have guessed myself that Presten would try something sneaky and unimaginative like that,' Joel replied. 'He's so predictable.'

'He's so embarrassing...' she snapped under her breath.

'Anyway, I'm convinced that Grandad knows more than he's letting on,' Joel continued in a hurried whisper. 'There's something mysterious going on and I'm going to get to the bottom of it!' He sighed and lightly thumped the hymn-book shelf in front of him; this vibrated down the whole shelf along the pew, which caused Grandad to glare at him reprovingly.

'Sorry,' Joel mouthed, to Grandad. Then, he turned back to his two friends. 'See if you two can get your parents to let you stay over again tonight and we'll drag it out of him.'

They both nodded eagerly.

Matthews welcomed everyone into the house of God and announced the opening hymn. The music began to play and everyone stood up to sing.

There is a green hill far away
without a city wall,
where the dear Lord was crucified,
Who died to save us all.
We may not know, we cannot tell
what pains He had to bear;
but we believe it was for us
He hung and suffered there

When they came out of the church, Joel asked Grandad if Peter and Tamara could stay over again. Grandad said it was fine by him, as long as it was OK with their parents. Tamara's parents were surprisingly accommodating, much to her glee and Presten's annoyance as he snarled behind their backs. Their main concern was that it might be inconveniencing Joel's grandad, but Joel explained that Grandad spent too much time on his own and loved having them to stay.

The awkward ones were Peter's parents. When they saw him without his callipers, they were very shocked; they couldn't believe that he was suddenly healed! Reluctantly though, they gave their consent, but Peter had to promise to go with his mum to see the doctor first thing Monday morning.

Tamara went home with her parents to pick up some clothes and her toothbrush. Joel accompanied Peter and his parents back to their farm to collect Peter's overnight stuff.

Peter ran up the stairs to quickly pack a bag, while Joel waited in the farmhouse kitchen with a glass of fresh farm milk and a little piece of heaven on earth – a huge chunk of Mrs Jordan's famous chocolate cake. Peter's mum was a fantastic cook and she was always in the kitchen, baking.

As Joel drank the milk and scoffed the cake, Mr and Mrs Jordan marvelled that never before in his whole life had Peter run up the stairs. They tried to prise some information out of Joel about what had happened.

'It could be one of those unexplained phenomena you read about, Mrs Jordan,' Joel answered a little cagily, then he took a large bite of cake so he didn't have to speak. He breathed a sigh of relief as Peter came to the rescue, carrying his small holdall.

'Here, Joel, take this for your grandad.' Mrs Jordan presented Joel with an enormous chocolate cake, which almost completely covered the dinner plate it was sitting on.

'Thanks, Mrs Jordan; your chocolate cake is the best!' Joel grinned.

Joel and Peter set off down the lane to Grandad's place, Joel carefully carrying the chocolate cake. Suddenly, who should spring out from behind a large tree but Presten and two members of his delinquent posse: Will and Jud. Of course, Presten wouldn't have risked a confrontation on his own while Joel was around – he was too chicken!

Presten stood in the middle of the lane, barring Joel and Peter's way. Will and Jud stood behind him, goading him on. Presten carried a heavy baseball bat and slapped the palm of his hand with it intimidatingly.

'Where are your stilts, "Tin Legs?"' Presten sneered at Peter.

'Do one, Presten!' Joel threatened. 'Let us past.'

'I obviously didn't do a good-enough job on you yesterday, Jordan. I thought you'd be looking like a pickled cabbage by now. We're gonna have to do something about that, aren't we lads?' He tipped his head to Will and Jud who guffawed, nodding their heads stupidly.

'Yeah, that's right, we'll have t' do a better job this time, Pres',' Jud sneered.

'What's that you've got, Asher?' Presten looked at the cake Joel was carrying.

Of all the things Joel needed in his mitts right now, a massive sticky chocolate cake was not one of them.

'None of your business, Presten. Get out of our way!' Joel shouted with a confidence he wished he was feeling. Presten on his own was a pushover, but three of them – and one armed with a baseball bat – greatly reduced the odds of victory.

'Give that to me and I'll let you go,' Presten lied.

Will and Jud smirked as Presten raised his baseball bat and

scowled threateningly.

'Yeah, Asher, give us that cake!' Jud demanded.

'No chance, Jud. But I'd happily give you a knuckle butty if you like!' Joel mocked.

'Get them, Pres'!' Will snarled.

'Shouldn't you be on a lead, Will?' Joel sniped back.

Presten started towards Joel and Peter.

'Your mate ain't gonna be able to help you now, Jordan,' he sneered, swinging his bat threateningly. 'You're outnumbered!'

'Presten, you're a clown! Who do you think you are – Mighty Mouse?' Joel put the cake down on the lane and rolled up his sleeves. 'Clear off and take Coco and Buttons with you.'

'Yeah, sling your hook, Porky!' Peter surprised himself with his new-found fearlessness. Dropping his bag, he quickly rolled up his sleeves.

'Getting brave all of a sudden, aren't you, Jordan?' Presten sniggered. 'Want another thrashing, do you?'

'You heard, Presten!' Joel threatened. 'Back off!'

Presten took a quick backward glance, checking Will and Jud were right behind him. Reassured that they were, he was filled with a sudden surge of conceited confidence.

'Or what, Asher?' Presten challenged, defiantly.

Joel suddenly saw red and, imagining himself on the rugby pitch playing for the Cup of the Year, he lurched forward. 'OR THIS!' he shouted. Diving head-first like a charging bull, Joel's head landed smack in the middle of Presten's stomach. This knocked Presten backwards with such a force that he might have been catapulted right over the hedge, had Will and Jud not been there to break his fall. This in turn, sent Will and Jud flying like skittles and all three of them lay winded and groaning on the muddy grass verge.

Peter and Joel slapped their right hands together in the air.

'Way to go!' they cried in unison.

'Get the cake, Peter!' Joel yelled, grabbing Peter's bag.

Peter picked up the cake and the pair of them scarpered, laughing their heads off, before Presten and his two minions had a chance to recover.

'I'll get you, Asher!' Presten groaned, defiantly.
Joel couldn't resist shouting back.

'Well, we've still got the cake. So, who's the loser now?'

†

By the time they arrived back at Grandad's, Tamara was already there. Her parents had dropped her off in their posh car and Grandad had given them a basket of fresh eggs. Tamara had spent the time bottle-feeding Storm, until he dropped off to sleep just like a baby. He seemed quite at home in Grandad's kitchen, (although some health inspectors might have had something to say about it). Grandad had now made a baby stable under the stairs with some wood, and Storm looked cosy and settled.

Rodney was skulking about, jealous of this cute new guest that was demanding everyone's attention. He'd collected all his belongings: Grandad's old slipper, a half-eaten dog chew and a squeaky toy that had lost its squeak – and tried to lie on them all at once, guarding them. Occasionally, he ventured up to sniff Storm.

It was lunchtime, so the three friends made a load of sandwiches and packed them with some of Mrs Jordan's chocolate cake. Then they set off for Zionica, to spend the afternoon there.

When they climbed up to the den, they were thrilled to find that masses of tadpoles had hatched out in the jam jars. They decided by a vote that Peter had the largest tadpole, but Joel had the most tadpoles. However, Tamara claimed to have the cutest tadpole, a point the boys couldn't (or decided not to) contest.

By this time, they were ravenously hungry and tucked into the nosh with relish. Tamara almost cried with laughter as they told her about their victory over Presten and his two clownish cronies, in the lane outside Peter's farm.

'Yeah, they went flying like skittles,' Peter chuckled. 'It's the funniest thing I've seen since – well – since the snowballing.'

All three of them roared with laughter.

'I'd love to have seen that!' Tamara giggled, helplessly.

'Anyway, on a more serious note,' Joel continued earnestly, 'I'm convinced there's something Grandad is not telling us – he knows something.'

'Yes, he was so matter-of-fact when we told him about the light affecting Peter in the barn,' Tamara added curiously. 'And the way he told him he wouldn't need the callipers anymore. How did he know?'

'And why did he think the foal would be in danger – in the barn?' Peter remarked, baffled.

'That's what I just don't understand,' Joel added. 'I mean, if it's dangerous for the foal, why are the other animals in there? What's in the barn that's only dangerous to foals?'

'Or is it this particular foal…?' Peter mused.

'Yes!' Joel cried, excitedly. 'Maybe there's something unusual about *this* foal!'

'And I hate to sound weird but…' Tamara shrugged, '…what about the light thing? We both saw it, Joel. Was it really the sun through the window?'

'Hmm, I don't know, but the fact remains,' Joel stated firmly, 'something *did* heal Peter.'

'Yes,' Tamara agreed. 'How can bruises just simply disappear and – sorry Peter – crooked legs get straight? What exactly did happen? Guys – we have witnessed an actual miracle!'

'I know, awesome isn't it. I haven't got any answers, but I'm convinced Grandad has,' Joel frowned, thoughtfully.

'So, how are we going to get him to spill?' Tamara asked, eagerly.

'Well, that's one of the reasons I thought you two should stay over again. It's Sunday. If we can't get Grandad talking on a Sunday evening, we never will,' Joel remarked, knowingly.

They both looked quizzically at Joel.

'Grandad is a great one for traditions,' Joel explained. 'On Sundays, Grandma always cooked a big roast dinner, followed by a sticky pudding or a juicy pie. She always started with a small glass of sherry while she made the gravy, then a glass of wine with the meal. She usually followed this with a cherry brandy by the fire after the dishes were done. The only thing Grandad has changed is the drink after dinner – he has a brandy and Benedictine mixed together! Do you get my drift, now?' Joel spread his hands.

'Sure do, by the time he has his brandy and Benedictine…' Peter began.

'He'll be singing like a parrot!' Tamara interrupted impetuously.

'Exactly,' Joel grinned smugly. 'But it's a canary, Tamara – singing like a canary.'

'Oh, bla - de - bla!' Tamara shrugged.

'But we'll have to be careful how we do it,' Joel warned. 'If he thinks he's being tricked he'll just clam-up and send us to bed. Grandad loves talking once he gets going. We'll get him started on something safe, then engineer the subject round to the mystery of the foal.' Joel gave a heavy sigh. 'We've *got* to get him to talk; I can't stand not knowing!'

CHAPTER THREE

Thieves in the Night

After the Sunday roast, which they had in the early evening, the three friends insisted that Grandad went into the lounge while they cleared up the dishes. When there were just a few left to put away, Peter and Tamara joined Grandad in the lounge while Joel finished off in the kitchen.

Grandad was standing by the fireplace with his brandy cocktail in one hand and was gazing affectionately at a small, framed photograph he held in the other.

'Is that your wife, Mr Jacob?' Tamara asked hesitantly, looking at the woman in the photograph.

'Yes, Tamara love – that's Mrs Jacob,' he replied fondly.

'You must miss her,' Tamara said, softly.

'More than I can say,' he smiled. 'It's a terrible thing, you know, cancer. She was a good woman, a good wife and mother, always thinking of others before herself.'

Just then, Joel joined them from the kitchen.

'Don't you wonder sometimes, Mr Jacob,' Tamara continued, 'why God lets these things happen? I mean, why does He let a nice lady like Mrs Jacob get cancer?'

Grandad replaced the picture on the mantelpiece, and sat down in his rocking chair with a sigh.

'Come, sit down,' he beckoned the children.

They made themselves comfortable on the rug by the fire, then looked expectantly at Grandad, waiting for him to speak.

'This is a mistake that people tend to make, children; it's easy to blame God for things, like cancer,' he explained. 'But, the reality is that God provides the great minds of eminent doctors and scientists, to fight against this evil disease, giving them the skills to develop the technology and drugs necessary. It is the devil who has corrupted, what God created perfect. No, Tamara, love, everything that God created was good, but there is an enemy of our souls who is the devil and the evil of cancer is the devil's efforts to corrupt what God made good. Many people think the devil is a myth – not real – something conjured up in the imaginations of story tellers: a monstrous red, two horned evil creature with burning coals for eyes and a pointed tail. That visual image may very well be a myth, although part of it is true – the devil really is an evil creature. The devil is an evil spirit, invisible to the human eye. This allows him to prowl around unseen, which makes him dangerous and deadly. Some say his greatest achievement is convincing people that he *doesn't* exist. Children, the devil is as real as you and me!'

The three friends stared up at Grandad, transfixed.

'You know, kids, the devil used to be an angel in Heaven, a very beautiful angel, apparently, his name used to be Lucifer,' Grandad continued. 'He became extremely greedy and selfish and rebelled against God. He was jealous of God; he wanted all the power and the glory for himself. That old serpent, the devil, enticed other angels to follow him and about a third of the angels in Heaven were fooled by him and believed his lies. They joined him in his rebellion and a war broke out in Heaven. God is all-powerful, all-seeing and all-knowing. He was wise to the devil's nefarious plotting and threw him out of Heaven in disgrace, along with all his followers – fallen angels, the lot of them! From that moment onward God renamed him Satan and the devil, now Satan, has been burning with rage and consumed with hate, because he knows his own fate, his final destination – the fiery pit of hell which God made especially for the him and the fallen angels. Ever since then, the devil has waged a war against God's people, with the aim of taking as many souls as possible with him into darkness, and the ultimate destruction of hell. Children, the devil is evil itself and the Bible says he is a liar and the father of lies.' Grandad paused to sip his drink.

By now the children were so mesmerised by Grandad's story that they'd clean forgotten about the secrets they believed he was hiding from them.

'How shocking!' Tamara exclaimed. 'Please carry on, Mr Jacob.'

'Well, after they were thrown out of Heaven,' Grandad continued, 'these fallen angels became ugly demons and bad spirits. It's the devil and his evil followers that are behind all the evil and corruption in the world. Everything you see around you, Tamara love, is the physical, natural world. There is also a spiritual realm, only you and I cannot see it. Nevertheless, it is very real. Sometimes though, some people can "see" with "spiritual" eyes, and bad spirits or demons have been known to trick these people by pretending to be someone who has died.'

'Can they really do that, Mr Jacob?' Tamara asked.

'Yes and tragically children, these people who have the ability to see spirits often think they are seeing and hearing from people who have died…'

'You mean ghosts?' Tamara asked, with a shudder.

'Yes, but Tamara, although there are many popular "ghost stories," these are just myths. What these people see are not dead people at all, but what are called in the Bible "familiar spirits." These are bad spirits without a body – demons – and they can take on the form of a person! You see, demons also have knowledge; they know, for example, that you have a particular picture on the mantelpiece of your late Aunty Betty, wearing a purple dress. But unfortunately, people who call themselves "mediums" or "spiritualists" are very much deceived. They claim to be "in touch" with other people's dead loved ones, when in fact, it's not Aunty Betty they're talking to at all – it's a demon, familiar spirit masquerading as Aunty Betty. However, because they appear to know things that only Aunty Betty and you would have known *and* are able to appear to look like her, they can cause great deception. That, children, is the devil's greatest weapon – deception – causing people to believe a lie!'

'Oh! So grieving relatives think they are getting messages from their loved ones, when in fact they're hearing from these evil imposter demons!' Joel cried, horrified.

'Lamentably, that's it in a nutshell!' Grandad nodded. 'This is just one of the devil's very cruel deceptions. But, in reality, there is no communication with the dead. If people think they've seen or heard from the ghost of a dead person, they're wrong. The Bible says that it is appointed once for man to die and then judgement.'

'Mr Jacob?' Peter began.

'Yes, Peter?'

'Some people claim to have seen a vision of Jesus. How do they know that it's Jesus and not one of these, er – familiar spirits?'

'Good question, Peter. I'm glad you're paying attention. The Bible says that the devil himself can masquerade as an angel of light. You must remember that whenever Jesus has appeared to someone, He always identifies himself as Jesus, the Son of God, who died on the cross and is *obviously* risen – otherwise He wouldn't be able to appear, would He? Demons pretend to be someone they're not, or sometimes they are seen as the monstrous beings they really are. Anyway, you would always know if Jesus Himself appeared to you because His presence always brings warmth, light and an overwhelming feeling of love. If you can't feel the love, peace and comfort, then it's not Him. Remember, the Bible says, "God is love."' Grandad leaned back and smiled at the mesmerised faces before him. 'Unfortunately,' he continued, 'the devil brought sin into the world by taking advantage of the cunning serpent and deceiving Eve, and subsequently Adam, into deliberately doing something that they shouldn't – that is, to take and eat the fruit that God had specifically forbidden them to eat. It was this first act of rebellion that brought sin into the world. The result was what is commonly known as "the fall" – they "fell" from grace. God's heart was broken, because the penalty of sin is death and the crowning glory of God's creation – "man" – began to die, along with the whole world God had created.'

'Is that why *everyone* eventually has to die, Mr Jacob?' Tamara asked.

'Yes, death is the inevitable result of sin, Tamara, but God never intended for men to die. He created our souls to live forever and neither did God make Hell for men. He made Hell for the rebellious fallen angels, but now it is the tragic final destination of sinful man. You see, kids, because sin had spread to man from the devil, the end that God had decreed for the devil and his followers then became the destiny of all men, condemning all of us to hell – and that's not what God wanted at all! God loves us all! But because God is holy, righteous and just, He cannot go back on His word. Sin is what separates us from God and because of it, we are not worthy to be in His presence. Even Mother Theresa and all her fine charity, could not have come close to the perfect holiness of God. The Bible says, "There are none righteous, no, not one." We all sin because sin is in our DNA; from Adam's seed, generation to generation, we're all born with it.'

'How terrible!' Tamara gasped. 'You mean that, we've all got to go to hell when we die because the devil made Eve eat that fruit?' she asked, indignantly. 'But I don't want to go to hell, Mr Jacob. I didn't eat that fruit, so why should I suffer because of what Eve did?'

'But what about Jesus?' Peter asked. 'Wasn't that why He was crucified – to save us from our sins so that we could go to Heaven?'

'Oh, you've stolen my good news end to the story, Peter,' Grandad grinned.

'Oh, so there *is* some good news then,' Joel muttered, weakly.

'Yes, Jesus Christ and what He did at the cross is the "*silver bullet*" – the "*stake in the heart*" of sin!' Grandad announced with a grin. 'The blessed Son of God, conceived by the Holy Spirit and not of sinful man. In Jesus there was not the slightest trace of sin, praise God! Jesus was the perfect Lamb of God.'

'Grandad, I know that Jesus was crucified on a cross and rose again from the dead, but I don't really understand how that applies to us, now,' Joel pondered.

'Well, you see, Joel, the devil thought he'd won a victory over God by stealing the souls of men. That evil creature knew that if he introduced sin into the world, God, being holy and just, would have no choice but to send all sinners to hell. They would then be separated from Him forever because He cannot have sin in His presence. That of course would have applied to the entire human race, but, for the grace of God! The plan of salvation offered to all men a free pardon, an opportunity to be saved by the sacrifice of God's Son, Jesus! What this means, Joel, is that you don't have to go to hell and neither does anyone else. God Himself provided the solution to man's greatest dilemma.

'I think I understand what you're saying, Grandad,' Joel nodded. 'Jesus took our punishment, didn't He? God treated Him on the cross, as though *He* had committed all of our sins.'

'Correct, Joel, you have well understood what is called the "Divine Exchange." Through the cross of Jesus Christ and His blood, shed thereon, Jesus took the "fall" for all of our sins which enabled God to freely offer us a clean slate, without compromising His just and holy nature.'

'Is that why Jesus is called the "Lamb of God" – because he was sacrificed?' Tamara asked.

'Yes, love,' Grandad answered. 'Jesus was the only one who could have done this though, because we have all sinned and deserve the punishment. Jesus was innocent and He didn't deserve to die but volunteered to take our place. He was in Heaven with God the Father before being born down here. Jesus was not descended from Adam because Mary, His mother, conceived Jesus in her womb by the Holy Spirit of God, hence the "virgin birth." Mary's husband, Joseph, was the "legal" father of Jesus, but not his biological father. Therefore, Jesus did not inherit the sinful DNA nature, but instead, He had the righteous DNA nature of God, His true Father, which made Him sinless.'

'Jesus didn't stay dead though, Mr Jacob, did He,' Peter stated. 'He is alive in Heaven now.'

'Praise God! And this is key, Peter, to the salvation of men,' Grandad replied. 'Because God is holy, just and fair, He could not allow His innocent Son, Jesus, to stay dead – that would not be fair and just! Hence, the resurrection – God the Father raised Jesus from the dead and He is alive forevermore. The penalty for sin has been paid for by Jesus' innocent blood, shed on the cross, and all who believe this receive everlasting life – a free gift of grace from God!'

'Thank God, a "get-out clause," as Dad used to say,' Joel sighed with relief.

'A great mercy!' Grandad agreed. 'However, the lamentable fact is, children, that unfortunately, many poor souls still go to Hell,' he said, shaking his head.

'Oh?' Tamara frowned. 'Why, Mr Jacob? Are some people too bad to be saved?'

'No, Tamara love. It doesn't matter what a person has done, there is forgiveness available through what Jesus did at the cross. His blood is powerful enough to cleanse the vilest and most evil men – whosoever trusts in Jesus will be saved – as long as they make that commitment before they die, of course.'

'So, what's the problem, Grandad?' Joel asked. 'Why are some people not saved?'

'In a word, Joel – unbelief!' Grandad replied. 'You see, to get the free pardon, you've got to *believe* that God did this. Many people don't believe it, and they find out, to their cost when they die, just what they have rejected! God sent His only Son, so that *all* who *believe* in Him shall not perish but have everlasting life. No one comes to the Father unless they accept Jesus Christ as their Saviour; faith in the cross is essential to be saved.'

'So, some people *choose* to go to hell because they reject Jesus?' Joel cried, in astonishment.

'Alas, Joel, that is a lamentable fact,' Grandad nodded. 'Rejecting God's grace, offered through the sacrifice of His Son, Jesus, is a guaranteed one-way ticket to Hell.'

'But that's tragic, Mr Jacob, when all they have to do is believe!' Tamara exclaimed.

'Yes, it is,' he agreed. 'But God decreed that everyone should have free will to choose. Some people think they can earn their own way to Heaven by doing good deeds, but that is an impossibility. All too many people discover, when it's too late, that rejecting the Lord Jesus Christ was *the **most insane** decision* of their entire lives!'

'Wow...' Tamara exclaimed, rather stunned. 'Mr Jacob, what exactly are our souls?'

'Well, Tamara,' Grandad replied. 'Your soul is your mind, your will and your emotions. In other words, it is everything that is you – Tamara the person, your memories your thoughts, likes and dislikes. When someone dies it is only their body that dies, their soul doesn't die. No, ten thousand years from now, your soul – that is you – will be alive somewhere. Glorious Heaven if you trust Jesus or the horror of Hell if you don't.'

'Ooh,' Tamara murmured, pondering the seriousness of this statement.

'Remember though, children,' Grandad warned. 'The devil is still in the world and he is *trouble*! He is determined to drag as many souls to hell as he can. His strategy – to do everything possible to prevent people from discovering the truth and he actually uses people in the world to accomplish his evil plans.'

'How, Mr Jacob?' Tamara asked.

'Again, by deception, just like in the garden of Eden – causing people to believe a lie. He whispers bad things and lies into their ears. They think it's their own thoughts, but it's not. This is how he gets some people to do bad things,' Grandad explained. 'He will do anything to discredit Jesus and the cross – that is his main focus. If he can keep people from believing what Jesus has done for them at the cross, he has destroyed their souls and they will perish.'

'Sounds like Presten could be one of them,' Joel remarked, tersely.

'Well, there's time for Presten yet, Joel; he's young, he may grow out of this…' Grandad began, but was interrupted by Tamara.

'Beastliness!' Tamara cried.

'I was going to say "phase,"' Grandad continued with an amused smile. 'Presten could eventually see the light and turn into a very nice young man – who knows?'

'Oh yeah, and I might turn into a singing peacock!' Joel muttered scathingly.

'Well anyway, for now Presten is someone to be wary of, as you very well know,' Grandad warned. 'Curious though, if you jumble up the letters in "Presten" what you might end up with…' Joel picked up a pen and paper from a nearby table, and the three of them started to work out what Grandad meant.

'Serpent!' Peter cried, first to solve the anagram. 'The devil disguised himself as a serpent when he tempted Eve in the Garden of Eden, didn't he, Mr Jacob?'

'That's right, Peter,' Grandad nodded.

'Well, that explains a lot,' sighed Joel.

'Oh, you mustn't read anything into that, Joel – we're only talking about a twelve-year-old boy,' Grandad chuckled. He savoured another sip of his drink and this pause reminded Joel about the pressing subject of Peter's healing.

'So, Grandad, what do you think about the young foal that we found? Where do you think he's from?'

'Storm is not an ordinary foal,' Grandad replied, mysteriously, his eyes narrowing slightly.

'Oh?' Joel asked, curiously.

The three children sat up and exchanged puzzled glances.

'Yes, I'm quite certain that what we have in our kitchen is…'

The three friends leaned forward in anticipation.

'…is a young unicorn,' Grandad announced simply.

'A unicorn!' the three sang in unison.

'But – I thought that unicorns were…' Tamara started.

'Just another mythical creature, that doesn't really exist?' Grandad finished Tamara's sentence. 'Well, technically speaking, that's what they are – now. No one that we know about has ever actually seen one.'

'But, Grandad, I don't understand. How can they be mythical, non-existent creatures if we've got one in our kitchen?' Joel insisted.

Grandad gave a deep sigh.

'Well now, where shall I start?' Grandad rubbed his chin pensively. 'Unicorns were allegedly not always just mythical creatures. Rumour has it that they roamed the earth a few thousand years ago, just like other animals. But they were sadly mistreated by some unscrupulous individuals, who hunted and killed them for their horns.'

'Oh, how beastly!' Tamara cried. 'Why, Mr Jacob?'

'It was widely believed that the horns of unicorns had healing properties; therefore they became very valuable and people would pay a fortune to get hold of one. However, for all practical purposes, the horn had to be removed from the animal and ground up to make a potion. Consequently, like the elephants and rhinos of today, unicorns paid the price with their lives because of evil, greedy poachers,' Grandad sighed. 'And this depleted their numbers, making them rare and consequently...'

'Even more valuable!' Joel surmised.

'Precisely,' Grandad nodded. 'And so the vicious circle went on. That is, until the great flood in Noah's day.'

The children frowned as Grandad continued in a low voice.

'I would appear that when God sent the animals to Noah to be put into the ark and thereby saved from the flood, evidently the unicorns were left out. God simply didn't send any to Noah. Then God himself shut the door of the ark at the appointed time, with not a single unicorn on board.'

'But why didn't He want them saved as well?' Tamara cried.

'Isn't it blindingly obvious?' Joel answered, sadly. 'He was probably very upset about all the cruelty and killing. I mean, that's why He flooded the earth in the first place, isn't it, because He was upset about all the evil in the world.'

'Well, you've got a point there, Joel,' Grandad agreed.

'So, that means that the unicorn must have become extinct with the great flood,' Joel began. 'But…

'You don't understand where the one in the kitchen came from,' Grandad interrupted. 'Hmm, I must admit that is rather puzzling, to say the least!'

'Oh, please go on, Mr Jacob,' Tamara pleaded. 'How do you *know* that Storm is a unicorn and not just a baby pony?' I thought unicorns had a long horn on their foreheads?'

Grandad put down his glass and stood up.

'Come with me,' he beckoned, mysteriously, as he headed for the kitchen.

Bursting with curiosity, the three friends followed him. Once in the kitchen, Grandad knelt down next to Storm in the straw bed under the stairs. Then, he carefully lifted the foal's wispy forelock from its forehead. The three friends all gasped as they looked on. For there, protruding from the tiny animal's forehead, was the burgeon of a very small horn, barely a centimetre long.

'Of course, it will get much bigger as he grows,' Grandad explained. 'The horns of very young unicorns are short, to protect their mother as they are born and to protect them from injury during play. By the time Storm is fully grown though, this horn could be anything from thirty to fifty centimetres long!'

'Wow!' Peter cried in amazement. 'This is incredible!'

'A real unicorn – how amazing is that!' Tamara purred.

The children then began to bombard Grandad with a multitude of questions.

'Are you saying then, Mr Jacob, that it was Storm's horn that healed me?' Peter asked.

'I thought the horn had to be ground up to make a potion?' Tamara asked, somewhat confused.

'How did he get here, Grandad?' Joel asked. 'Where did he come from – if unicorns were wiped out of existence?'

'And why is he in the kitchen? What's so dangerous about the barn?' Tamara asked. 'Do you think someone will try to kill him – for his horn?'

'Is that why we can't leave him in the barn, Mr Jacob?' Peter asked. 'Should we be concerned about the other animals, too?'

'And how do you know all this unicorn stuff, Grandad?' Joel pressed.

'All right! All right!' Grandad chortled. 'You must understand, children, that there is no magical healing power whatsoever in the actual horn itself. I suppose there may be some health promoting properties in the horn that could be beneficial if eaten. However, in Peter's case, the radical and total healing wa done supernaturally from above; only God has those powers and

He is the one who chooses the method He will use to heal someone. He gives Christian believers the authority to use the name of Jesus, but it's not the believer that does the healing – it is still Jesus. The unicorn's horn was merely the mechanism used in this case.'

'Like Jesus healed a blind man by making mud out of clay and spit and rubbing into his eyes, Mr Jacob,' Peter added. 'It wasn't the clay – it was Who was doing it, that healed him.'

'Yes, Peter, that's right, you've got it,' Grandad replied.

'But, Grandad, where *did* this unicorn come from and how come he was used to heal Peter?' Joel cried, confused.

'Yes, do tell us, Mr Jacob?' Tamara pleaded.

'I don't know, children, but I have a theory. First though, get into your pyjamas while I make some cocoa. Then, I'll try to explain.'

'Oh!' they wailed in frustration, then immediately raced up the stairs. Three kids had never got ready for bed faster.

'Are you sure your grandad isn't bonkers, Joel?' Tamara whispered.

Joel laughed. 'Of course he's bonkers! You know full well my grandad is a dyed-in-the-wool eccentric! Nevertheless, he's no fool and I trust that what he says is true. Ask Peter – he actually reads the Bible, don't you, Peter?'

'Yeah, it's pretty much as your grandad tells it,' Peter affirmed.

In no time at all they were back downstairs on the rug, as Grandad came in with a tray of steaming cocoa. He shook his head and chuckled in amusement at their eager faces.

'So,' Grandad smiled, as he settled comfortably in his chair, 'you want to hear about unicorns, eh?'

'Please, Grandad, tell us what you know,' Joel urged.

'OK,' Grandad continued. 'There's lots of evidence that unicorns existed, most notably in the Bible itself. Unicorns have, of old, been regarded as biblical creatures, mainly because of references to them in the King James Bible, where they are used as a symbol of strength and it is believed by some that they are a symbolic of God's salvation through Jesus. Similarly, a horn is used *symbolically* to describe strength and power. There's no power in an actual horn itself, it is *only* symbolic. For example, in the New Testament, Luke chapter one and verse 69 says that He, God, has raised up a horn of salvation for us. This is obviously a reference to Jesus, His Son, and the symbol of the horn appears to represent strength and purity. The Bible uses a great deal of symbolism.'

'Yes, Mr Jacob. Jesus is also called the "Lion of Judah," isn't he?' Peter pointed out.

'That's correct, Peter,' Grandad replied. 'But clearly, He's not a lion...'

'And He's the "Lamb of God,"' Tamara added.

'Yes love, He is. However, for some unknown reason, the unicorn was written out of the modern Bible.' Grandad picked up his Bible from the table by his chair. It looked quite old and well used. 'This is a very old Bible, kids. It belonged to my mother, your great grandma, Joel,' Grandad reminisced. 'It is what is known as the King James Version, which was translated from the original Hebrew, Greek and Aramaic, into English, in 1611. Because of this, it is written in an old-fashioned style and contains some words which seem unfamiliar to us nowadays.' He opened it up. 'Deuteronomy, chapter 33 and verse 17. Here, Tamara, read the first sentence of this verse.'

Tamara read aloud from the Bible. '"*His glory is like the firstling of his bullock, and his horns are like the horns of unicorns*."'

'The symbolism here appears to be strength and purity,' Grandad explained. 'Now,' he reached into a small drawer in the table and pulled out a Bible that looked in much better shape. 'Look at the same verse in a more modern translation – the New King James Version of the Bible.' Grandad handed the Bible to Tamara and again she read aloud.

'"*His glory is like a firstborn bull, And his horns like the horns of the wild ox*..." Oh, my word, Mr Jacob! You're right – they've changed the unicorn to a wild ox! But who would change it, and why?'

'Yes, unicorns must have been mentioned for a reason, Grandad? Isn't the Bible the inspired word of God?' Peter asked.

'That's right, Peter, and the Scriptures were written thousands of years ago. Now, who indeed changed what was originally written by those Holy Spirit inspired people? Under whose authority – and why? Now that's just one example but there are others.' Grandad sipped his cocoa pensively, he loved a real mystery like this.

'But that's so sad, Mr Jacob. Unicorns are such beautiful creatures,' Tamara sighed.

'Quite,' Grandad agreed. 'The name "unicorn" is also significant. Derived from Latin, "uni" means "one" and "cornu" means "horn," thereby distinguishing a single horn, as in the verse we've just read. Unicorns have one long and straight horn, which grows and points upwards, while the devil, who is evil, is generally depicted as having two short curved horns which point downwards. All very curious, don't you think?'

They all nodded in agreement.

'There are other Christian symbols: a fish for instance and of course the cross, and the bread and wine that symbolise the body and blood of Jesus. As you know, Jesus told many parables which were full of symbolism.' Grandad smiled, then continued. 'One of the reasons for the unicorn being a Christian symbol must be its image of goodness and purity. This is probably because of its references in the Bible – but, how did it get to be written in there in the first place? Some people think that since the unicorn became extinct on the earth, it may be alive in Heaven as a heavenly being.'

'Like Jesus is alive in Heaven now, Mr Jacob?' Tamara asked.

'Yes. We know that the Lord Jesus Christ is alive and sitting at the right hand of God the Father. Whether or not there are any unicorns in Heaven is not actually known,' Grandad smiled. 'I guess we'll have to wait till we get there to find out, love. But, that unicorn in the kitchen came from somewhere. I believe that there are all kinds of wonderful things up there that none of us have ever seen. In fact, the Bible tells us that this is the case: "*Eye has not seen, nor ear heard, nor have entered into the heart of man the things that God has prepared for those who love Him.*"'

'Mm, so, Grandad,' Joel asked. 'How did a heavenly being…?'

'…manifest itself here?' Grandad shrugged. 'I don't know, but I have an idea that it might be something to do with that unusual rainbow. I think that maybe, somehow, the rainbow was some sort of "gateway" which allowed Storm to come here.'

The three children gasped in amazement.

'Wow!' Joel exclaimed. 'This is even more bizarre than I imagined! So, what you're implying, Grandad, is that the rainbow is a gateway between Heaven and Earth and that somehow, Storm has found his way through it?'

'Well, crazy as it sounds, Joel, yes. You see, we know for a fact that there is a supernatural dimension outside of time and space. Jesus ascended on a cloud after his resurrection. Also, Elisha was taken up in a chariot of fire. They both went to what we call Heaven. What I don't know though, is how or why Storm arrived here!'

'Mr Jacob?' Tamara asked, thoughtfully.

'Yes Tamara, love?'

'Do you think Storm fell by accident – or – was he – sent?'

'What an insightful question from someone so young, Tamara!' Grandad exclaimed in astonishment. 'That I don't know, love, but I suspect that while he is here, he could be in grave danger,' Grandad warned.

'Why, Mr Jacob, what's in the barn that could harm him?' Peter asked.

'Well, maybe I'm being over-cautious,' Grandad replied. 'But while he's here, he's mortal, which means that he could be harmed…'

'Oh,' Tamara gasped. 'You mean that someone might want to kill him?'

'Remember what the devil did through Herod two thousand

years ago, in a desperate attempt to destroy the infant Christ. He had all the baby boys of two years and under ruthlessly slaughtered. The devil was behind that, children. Imagine if the devil knew that this living symbol of purity and goodness, a symbol of Christ Himself, had come here. What might the devil do, just for revenge? The devil is evil and seething with rage. That's why we cannot leave Storm in the barn. A stable fooled the devil once before, when he expected God's Son to be born among royalty and worldly riches, but God in His wisdom delivered His Son in a lowly and poor position.' Grandad leaned forward as he continued earnestly. 'If the devil got his hands on this little symbol of purity and goodness, it could have unspeakable consequences.'

Joel, Peter and Tamara turned suddenly pale and gulped, while Grandad continued with urgency.

'Storm must be protected at all costs and returned from whence he came, as soon as possible. Now, the devil is crafty; he may even know that something has slipped through. You can bet he'll be searching everywhere, even as we speak, to find our little Storm – and remember, he has those evil demons and spirits all around at his beck and call. They'll be on the lookout, too.'

'How come you know all this, Mr Jacob?' Tamara asked.

'I've studied and done a lot of research, love. I've always been fascinated by unicorns, ever since…' Grandad suddenly stopped. '…I'm talking too much now. Perhaps I shouldn't have had that last brandy and Benedictine.'

'Please go on, Grandad – ever since what?' Joel urged.

The three of them looked up, anxious for Grandad to continue. Then suddenly, Rodney seemed to remember that he was actually a dog and not a couch potato; he started growling, then, with a fierce bark he leapt out of his basket and sped into the kitchen. There followed an almighty crashing sound, then Rodney could be heard yelping. They all ran quickly into the kitchen. The back door was swinging on its hinges and the baby stable that Grandad had made under the stairs had been demolished! Rodney lay panting by the broken pieces of wood – but there was no sign of

Storm! Peter knelt down in the straw, then looked up at the others.

'Storm has gone!' he wailed, morosely.

'No! no!' Tamara cried desperately, bursting into tears. She turned to Joel. 'Joel, we've got to find him; we've got to get him back!'

Grandad peered outside and inspected the back door for damage, while Peter checked Rodney over. After carefully examining the dog (who was lapping up the sympathy and attention) Peter stood up.

'Good old Rodney, he's obviously tried to protect Storm. I think he's OK – just had a bit of a fright. But look at this!'

Peter held up a small piece of cloth. 'Rodney had this in his teeth!'

Joel took the cloth from Peter and inspected it.

'What is it?' Tamara moved in for a closer look.

'It appears we have some forensic evidence,' Joel mused. 'Looks like the culprit didn't get away scot-free. I think it's a piece of someone's pants. There are tiny spots of blood on it…'

'Eoow,' Tamara winced.

'…probably caused by Rodney's teeth sinking into the villain's backside.' Joel bent down and patted Rodney. 'Well done, Rodders.'

Tamara suddenly leapt forward and snatched the cloth from Joel.

'Presten!' she screamed. 'This is off Presten's jogging pants!'

Joel and Peter looked stunned.

'Tamara is right!' Joel confirmed, scornfully. 'Who else would wear anything that un-cool? How dare he sneak in here!'

'And what does he want with our Storm? Where could he have taken him?' Tamara raised an eyebrow in fury as her distress turned to anger. 'That beastly brother of mine!' With that, Tamara fled from the house and ran down the yard to the gate.

'Joel! Stop her!' Grandad yelled.

They all ran outside into the dark night, chasing after Tamara.

It had been raining and the ground was still wet.

'Tamara! Wait!' Joel shouted after her.

But she was determined to catch her wicked brother. She reached the gate and ran straight out into the lane without thinking. Joel was closest; he saw her for a split second in the headlights of the passing car. Then, there was a terrible screeching of tyres as the driver desperately tried to stop on the wet road. Then, a dull thud…

Joel felt as if his heart had stopped. He reached Tamara and threw himself down. She was lying face down on the road; the headlights of the car were shining on her. He turned her over but she was unconscious, the bloodstained cloth still in her hand.

'Tamara… no…' Joel gasped faintly.

Peter and Grandad reached them and looked on in horror, as the driver jumped out of his car and rushed over to look at Tamara where she lay, motionless.

'I – I couldn't stop in time!' the distraught motorist cried. 'She ran out so fast …'

CHAPTER FOUR

Storm's Passion

Little sobs as Mrs Goodchild wept into her handkerchief, punctuated by the annoyingly loud tick-tock of a wall clock and Grandad occasionally blowing his nose, were the only sounds that could be heard in the waiting room of St David's Hospital. Tamara's distraught father and mother held hands. Joel and Peter sat in silence, every tick of the clock a painful reminder that all they could do was wait. They were hardly able to believe that such a dreadful thing could have happened to Tamara. They felt responsible – that they should have taken better care of her. They were all too upset to speak.

Presten stood next to his parents. He still had on the same old jogging pants that he must have been wearing when he sneaked into Grandad's kitchen – evidenced by a dog-bite-sized hole on the backside – it must have been too painful for him to sit down.

Eventually a doctor entered the room and everyone jumped up expectantly, as he approached Mr and Mrs Goodchild.

'I'm afraid your daughter is still unconscious,' the doctor began in a low voice. 'There's been some internal bleeding and we've had to put her on a life-support machine…'

'Oh...' Mrs Goodchild gasped.

'Just till we know what we're dealing with, Mrs Goodchild,' the doctor added reassuringly. 'We will be running some more tests in the morning but for now, she's comfortable. You may see her for a few moments.'

Joel and Peter began to follow, but the doctor stopped them.

'I'm sorry, but only the parents for now, please.' He proceeded to lead Tamara's parents away.

Joel and Peter sat down again, looking defeated.

'Well, lads, I'll go and call a taxi to take us home; there's nothing we can do here now,' Grandad muttered woefully. Then he walked off to find a phone.

Joel looked ferociously at Presten, who trembled in fear like a frightened rabbit.

'You – you can't touch me here…' Presten squeaked, looking as if he was about to wet himself. 'Not in the hospital – I'll shout for the doctor and you'll be in big trouble, Asher.'

'We don't give a stuff about you, Presten! Where's our foal?' Joel spat. He hoped that Presten hadn't overheard their conversation with Grandad earlier, about Storm being a unicorn.

'It's quite safe – Will and Jud are taking care of it – and it'll be safe as long as I am,' Presten threatened, smugly.

'Safe? With Will and Jud? They couldn't take care of a coldsore!' Joel scowled. 'If anything happens to that foal, Presten, I'll come after you and thrash your fat, scaredy butt.'

'My dad might have something to say about that, Asher,' Presten smirked, pompously. He had a habit of abusing his father's good standing in the local community.

Joel stepped closer to Presten and glared at him angrily.

'Your dad is too concerned about your sister to bother about you, you little wimp. By the way, does he know it's your fault she's where she is?'

Fear suddenly gripped Presten's face at the thought of his dad finding out what he'd done, and he looked as if he was about to be sick.

'Hmm, I thought not,' Joel snarled with contempt.

'Don't you dare! Don't you dare say anything, or I'll…'

'Or you'll what, Presten – wet your pants?'

'…I'll beat "Tin Legs" to pulp when you've gone, Asher.'

Joel moved close up to Presten's face.

'"Tin Legs?" Can you see any... tin legs around here, Peter?' Joel asked, giving Peter a sidelong glance.

Peter, moving up to Joel's side, looked Presten straight in the eye. 'Nope, Joel, don't believe I do,' he confirmed, with a grin and a new boldness that he never knew before his miraculous healing.

'Presten, do you see any tin legs around here?' Joel snapped.

Presten looked feverishly from Peter to Joel, then shook his head.

'Good! Now, you just make sure you bring that foal back

tonight. Oh, and don't *you* dare hurt a hair on his head,' Joel added.

'Taxi will be here in a few minutes, lads,' Grandad announced as he entered the room. 'We'll wait outside, shall we, boys?'

Peter and Joel followed Grandad outside. As he was leaving, Joel threw Presten a warning glance, causing Presten to give an involuntary, cowardly whimper.

†

Later that evening, Grandad lit a candle and said some prayers for Tamara. Joel and Peter sat in Joel's bedroom, miserably mulling over how they could have avoided the accident. If only Joel had kept hold of Tamara and not let her run off. If only he could have run faster and stopped her. If only Peter hadn't shown her the material from Presten's pants. If only Presten wasn't such a jerk…

Suddenly, they heard a knock at the front door, immediately followed by Rodney's ferocious bark. Recent events seemed to have revived Rodney's instincts and given him a new lease of life.

Joel and Peter rushed downstairs, hoping it was good news about Tamara. Grandad was already standing in the open doorway, with Rodney hiding behind him and peering round Grandad's legs.

'Mr Goodchild…' Grandad was surprised to see Tamara's father on the doorstep. '…is Tamara…?'

'There's no change yet, I'm afraid, Mr Jacob. We've come to apologise,' Mr Goodchild announced, soberly.

'Apologise? But…'

'William and George came round to our house with their parents,' Mr Goodchild explained. 'It seems the boys got scared after Tamara was hurt.'

Joel and Peter exchanged glances, then they walked up behind Grandad, as Mr Goodchild continued.

'They've come clean about their little prank; sneaking into

your kitchen with Presten.' He stepped aside. 'I believe Presten has something that belongs to you, Mr Jacob.'

Presten had been hiding behind his father. Joel and Peter gasped as they saw the little foal in Presten's arms. Presten looked down, sheepishly.

Rodney, recognising Presten, growled, curling up his lip. Whimpering with fear, Presten stepped backwards attempting to hide behind his father again.

Joel took Storm from Presten and immediately handed him to Peter to be checked over.

'Well?' Mr Goodchild snapped sternly at Presten. 'Haven't you got something to say to Mr Jacob, Presten?'

'I'm – I'm s – sorry, M – Mr Jacob,' Presten stammered nervously. 'We d – didn't mean to s – steal your foal. Will and Jud a – and me, we were j – just spying on Joel and Peter – it was just a game, when we s – saw the foal, we – we thought…'

'Go on, Presten,' Mr Goodchild urged, crossly.

'We thought it would be f – fun t – to borrow it. We were going to bring it back. Your dog tried to stop us an... and before we knew it, all the wood came crashing down…' Presten looked down miserably '…I hope your dog is all right.'

'Obviously, I will pay for any damage or vet's bills, Mr Jacob,' Mr Goodchild added.

'That's not necessary, Mr Goodchild. It's very brave of Presten to come and own up like this,' Grandad reassured them. 'Rodney seems OK and I'm sure the foal is alright too. We must pray for your sister, Presten – her full recovery – that's all that matters now.'

Presten studied his feet intently.

'I'll send Presten over in the morning to collect Tamara's pony,' Mr Goodchild offered.

Presten looked at his father with sudden alarm and swallowed hard.

'Oh no – I – I don't want to go near that animal, Dad. It doesn't like me – it tries to bite me!'

Joel and Peter exchanged glances. If the situation hadn't been so serious, they would have cracked up at that entertaining, cowardly outburst from Presten.

'The pony is all right here, Mr Goodchild. She can stay as long as you want – till Tamara is well enough to come and collect Cherokee herself.

'That's very generous, Mr Jacob, and much appreciated.' Mr Goodchild answered. Then he turned to Presten. 'Go and get in the car now, Presten – and be thankful that Mr Jacob hasn't reported this theft to the police!'

Without looking up, Presten shuffled off to the car.

'Thank you,' Mr Goodchild gulped emotionally, gripping Grandad's hand.

Grandad nodded sorrowfully.

†

Next morning, Joel and Peter collected the eggs in silence while Grandad fed the animals and let Cherokee into the paddock for some exercise. Then Peter made up a bottle of warm milk to feed Storm. Grandad had already repaired the baby stable, under the stairs in the kitchen and Rodney lay on guard in front of it. The affable hound appeared to have become quite attached to Storm – either that or he was hoping some milk might get spilt and *need* licking up!

Shortly after breakfast, Peter's mum arrived to take him for the dreaded (and as far as Peter was concerned, pointless) visit to the doctor's surgery. As Peter expected, the doctor didn't have an explanation for this apparent "miracle recovery." He used the stock reply doctors tend to use when they don't have an answer: "It's just one of those things." But there was no doubt about it, Peter's legs and feet were now completely normal, just as if he'd never had polio at all.

The next couple of days were almost intolerable. Joel and Peter couldn't think about anything but Tamara, lying there unconscious in the hospital. The results of the tests had not been very encouraging and she was still on a life-support machine. A general gloom had descended over everyone; they were all desperately worried about her.

To make things worse, Storm was deteriorating. He was now so weak that he could hardly lift his little head to drink from the bottle. A few feeble gulps were all that he could manage at a time. Grandad was feeding him every fifteen minutes or so and they took it in turns to massage his little body and legs to keep him warm. The poor creature just lay there, looking pitiful, hardly opening his eyes.

In between feeding Storm and looking after the other animals, Grandad spent much of his time on his knees, praying for Tamara and another miracle. Also, he secretly enjoyed temporarily taking over Tamara's role of pampering the pony, and was much amused to discover the little tricks Tamara had taught her.

By Wednesday, at least they were allowed to see Tamara. She was still in a coma and the doctors were unable to give them any encouraging words about her possible recovery. She was in a private room, and family and friends were allowed to visit her any time within reason. So, instead of spending the day up in Zionica in the den, Joel and Peter packed a rucksack with loads of food, CDs and books – and spent the time with Tamara. They played her music, read to her and brought her up to date with Storm's condition, hoping all of this would somehow wake her up.

Tamara's mum and dad popped in regularly, but Presten was warned to stay away. They thought that if she sensed he was there, it might distress her. He was in terrible disgrace, being held responsible for Tamara having run out onto the road.

Tamara's hospital room was full of flowers, cuddly toys and all manner of presents and cards from everybody in the village, and from her school. She'd have been thrilled if she'd seen it all; it was as if three Christmases had all come at once.

By Thursday, there was still no sign of Tamara waking up. The doctors were shaking their heads – which was not a good sign at all. Doom had settled like a dark cloud and hope was fading. As yet another nurse checked Tamara's vital signs and left the room, also shaking her head.

Closing the door, Joel whispered to Peter.

'Peter, we should bring Storm here. If he healed you, then maybe he could heal Tamara, too.'

'Yes, Joel, that crossed my mind, too. It's worth a try, but how do you think we could get him past the doctors and nurses? How would we explain bringing a small pony into the hospital? Besides that, Storm is very weak! Then, don't forget your grandad – I don't think he would agree to it.'

'I know you're right,' Joel nodded. 'I'm sure that he wouldn't, but he won't know. Look, it's not going to be easy, but there must be a way.'

'Maybe we could try, tomorrow,' Peter suggested. 'It's Good Friday and there'll just be a skeleton staff here.'

'Hey, good thinking, Peter. Grandad will be going to church in the morning. It's this witness-procession thing – he does it every year on Good Friday. You know, when a man dresses up like Jesus and drags a big cross around the village. They call it "Acting out the Passion," then they have a service in church. He'll be out most of the morning. We can sneak out with Storm and bring him back before Grandad returns.' Joel leaned over Tamara and took hold of her limp hand. 'Don't worry, Tamara, we'll have you back with us before you know it.'

During the holidays, Joel sometimes spent the odd night at Peter's farm. Now though, Joel didn't want to leave Grandad on his own because he was so upset about Tamara and felt responsible for what had happened, as she was staying in his house when she had the accident. Also, Storm's condition was critical and he needed round-the-clock care. So, the boys decided that it would be a good idea if Peter moved in to Grandad's for a few days, to help look after Storm. As Peter was quite experienced at looking after sick animals, his parents agreed.

The following morning, Good Friday, Joel and Peter were up early, battling Cedric for the eggs. They didn't want to lose any time. They planned to set off for St David's Hospital with Storm wrapped in a blanket as soon as Grandad had left for church.

Joel busied himself making their breakfast, while Peter made up the baby bottle with some warm milk, then knelt down under the stairs to feed Storm.

Suddenly, Peter shouted. 'Joel! Here – quick!'

Joel rushed over to the stair alcove, where Peter was anxiously inspecting Storm. There were spots of blood in the straw. 'Peter, what's wrong? Are you hurt?'

'No – it's not my blood, Joel. It's Storm, he's bleeding... Look, there's blood on the straw!'

'That weasel, Presten!' Joel spat. 'What's he done?' Joel jumped up immediately and ran to the back door to shout Grandad.

'Grandad! Come, quickly!' Joel yelled.

Grandad dropped the bucket he was holding and ran into the kitchen.

'What's happened?' he puffed anxiously.

'It's Storm, Grandad – he's injured!'

Grandad rushed over to Storm and after inspecting him, he stood up scratching his head and looked rather confused.

'What's wrong with him, Grandad? Is he badly hurt?' Joel cried anxiously.

'No, he's all right. Sit down, lads.' Grandad pulled up a chair at the kitchen table and he too sat down.

'This is more serious than I thought, boys,' Grandad began, gravely. 'I just can't believe it – it's too incredible!'

'What, Grandad – what is it?'

'Amazing as this might sound, Storm appears to have what you would call, "stigmata."'

'*Stigmata*? Isn't that something to do with the wounds on Jesus' hands and feet?' Peter asked, mystified.

'Yes, Peter, that's correct,' Grandad nodded.

'Huh?' Joel frowned.

'Oh it's happened before, Joel, but as far as I know, only to people. This is the first time I've ever heard of this happening to an animal. The first recorded example was, I believe, in the thirteenth century and involved Saint Francis of Assisi, who later became the Patron Saint of animals. It's when someone experiences an extreme spiritual encounter with Jesus – their hands and feet have been known to bleed inexplicably – identifying with the suffering of Jesus, as He was nailed to the cross,' Grandad explained. 'Bizarre as it seems, it looks like our little Storm is acting out the "Passion of Jesus." It's Good Friday – the anniversary of the crucifixion. What concerns me, boys, is if Storm acts out the Passion to its conclusion!'

'You mean that he might die!?' Joel cried.

'The longer he stays here, the more he is in mortal danger. We've somehow got to get him back where he came from. If he dies…' Grandad looked very grave '…it could have unspeakable consequences.'

Joel and Peter gulped as they stared at Grandad in horror.

'But, Mr Jacob, we don't know where Storm is from – not really!' Peter cried in exasperation.

'Or how to get him back...' Joel added.

'I think I might know a way,' Grandad continued. 'But we need another storm, or at least a little rain.' He gazed pensively out of the window. 'I suspect, boys, that the only way we'll get him back is the same way he arrived...'

Joel and Peter exchanged confused glances, as Grandad continued earnestly.

'All this week you've seen me on my knees praying, for Tamara, mostly. But, you see, boys, I've also been praying for another storm because, what usually follows a storm?'

'A rainbow,' they both replied in unison.

'Yes, well, if a rainbow can bring him here, then presumably it can take him home again, too,' suggested Grandad.

'Yes, but Grandad, we can't exactly stuff him back up a rainbow!' Joel cried, sceptically. 'How do you plan on getting him back?'

'Well, yes that is a rather imponderable situation, I have to agree. However, we've already had one miracle recently; we just need to pray for two more. One thing is for sure though...' Grandad grinned.

'What's that, Grandad?' Joel asked.

'There ain't nothing too hard for God!' he proclaimed, confidently.

The two boys stared at Grandad. With all of this upset about Tamara, they'd almost forgotten about the fantastic circumstances surrounding Storm's arrival, and Grandad's insistence that he be sent back as soon as possible.

'Trouble is,' Grandad went on, 'I think the energy that came out of him, and into Peter, left Storm very weak and vulnerable. I fear that if he stays with us much longer, he may be unable to return home at all! He could turn irreversibly mortal, in which case he will die, with tragic consequences!'

'You mean, it's my fault he's dying?' Peter wailed, morosely, 'because healing me drained his power?' He was clearly distressed as he wiped a tear from his cheek with the back of his hand.

'Oh no, Peter. He would have gradually become weaker anyway. He's so young and tiny and, due to where he is from, his horn had a small amount of supernatural healing power, which has now worn off, because he is in the world – not Heaven.'

'Does this mean that he hasn't got enough power to heal Tamara?' Joel asked hesitantly.

'I'm afraid so, Joel. I don't think he could heal a pimple at the moment,' Grandad shrugged.

'Oh, if only he hadn't healed me!' Peter cried. 'I'd gladly have my callipers back, if only he had enough power to heal Tamara.'

'Peter, it must have been in God's plan that you were healed, there is a reason for it. That tells me that God has a big plan for your life. Hey, you two weren't seriously thinking of taking Storm into the hospital, were you?' Grandad looked at them in surprise.

They both looked down sorrowfully. Grandad shook his head and sighed deeply.

'Had you not thought about how you would get him past the

doctors and nurses? They wouldn't allow you to take an animal into the hospital! I'm not convinced it would be the right thing to do, anyway.' Joel and Peter looked at each other, mortified. They had been banking on smuggling Storm into the hospital to heal Tamara. Now, their one hope of saving her was gone. Peter suddenly jumped up, tears welling in his eyes.

'It's my fault! Tamara might die and it's my fault! It should be me in that hospital! Why can't it be me?' he cried, beside himself with sorrow.

'Of course it's not your fault, Peter!' Grandad tried to explain. 'Tamara had an accident. That's what it was – an accident.'

'I'll never forgive myself if she dies!' Peter cried, distraught. With that he fled outside.

Joel stood up too.

'I'd better go after him, Grandad,' he said, sadly. 'I think I know where he'll be.'

Grandad nodded, too upset to speak.

CHAPTER FIVE

Fire and Brimstone

Leaning into the wind, which was growing stronger by the minute, Joel shivered a little and pulled his coat round him as he walked over the field to Zionica. The sky was becoming darker and the temperature had dropped considerably. He climbed up the tree to the den and, sure enough, Peter was sitting there, staring glumly at his feet. Joel sat down next to him.

'You OK, Peter?' he muttered.

'Yeah, I guess,' Peter replied awkwardly, without looking up. Then, after a pause he continued. 'I've let all the tadpoles go. The wind was blowing the jars about.'

Joel nodded.

'Grandad is right, you know, Peter,' he said quietly. 'You can't blame yourself – any more than I could blame myself for not running fast enough to catch her. She'd tell you off big-style if she could see you now. What do you think she'd say?'

'Probably, "Pickled tadpoles, Peter! Pull yourself together, you're so bla - de – bla,"' he mimicked.

'Hey, you've got that right, pal. I reckon that's just about what she would say!' Joel chuckled.

'What are we gonna do, Joel? We can't just sit here.'

'There's nothing we can do, Peter. We've no choice but to leave it to the doctors. Well, actually, there is something we can do,' Joel mused thoughtfully.

Peter looked up with a glimmer of hope.

'We could save Storm,' Joel continued. 'That's what she would want us to do. She would want us to get him home so that he wouldn't die.'

'You're right, Joel.' Peter suddenly cheered up. 'In fact, if she was here now, she'd be driving us batty talking of nothing else but saving Storm – and you know what?'

'What?'

'If your grandad's theory about a storm is right, we won't

have long to wait because his prayers have been answered. Do you see that rabbit wandering about over there?'

Joel looked at the rabbit.

'It's the wrong time of day for rabbits to be out and about,' Peter explained. 'It means there's a mighty storm brewing. Joel, the heavens are about to open!'

'Well, come on! What are we waiting for?' Joel grabbed the rope swing and, out of habit, held it out for Peter.

'No, after you. I can leap as well as anyone now,' said Peter.

They exchanged grins, then Joel slid down the rope and Peter followed swiftly after him. They both set off at a brisk pace, feeling so much better now they had a plan.

The heavens opened all right, and the rain pelted down. By the time the boys arrived back at Grandad's kitchen, they were completely drenched. Grandad seemed to have perked up, too.

'Well, we've got our storm now, lads,' he remarked cheerily.

'We know, Grandad – we're soaked!' Joel replied. 'Just tell us what you want us to do.'

'First of all, get out of those wet things then I'll tell you.'

Ten minutes later the boys were back in the kitchen, warm and dry again, with mugs of soup in their hands.

'Right,' Grandad began. 'Whatever you do today, lads, you must be back before nightfall. One of us has got to be with Storm all through the night until first light. We'll feed him every half-hour, just a few sips at a time. We need to monitor his breathing, noting any change – however slight. Keep up some gentle massage to keep him warm and help his circulation; he's very weak,' Grandad paused and smiled at the boys. 'If we can just keep him alive until morning, at dawn we can take him to Zionica. I believe God will provide the rainbow we need and Storm will be alright. It's going to be testing, boys – so, we're in for a long night.'

'OK, Grandad. We'll just to go to the hospital for an hour or two, and then we'll come straight back,' Joel promised.

'All right, Joel, but eat something first before you go.' Grandad replied.

They all turned to look at Storm, so frail and forlorn, breathing weakly in his little bed under the stairs. Grandad had put tiny bandages on Storms heels, over the stigmata wounds.

Joel and Peter picked at a light lunch but they weren't really hungry. Joel's mum telephoned. Grandad said not to worry her with all that was going on; he didn't want her driving over in a panic, and anyway she was very busy with her work. Joel found it a strain just chatting cheerily to her, when he really wanted to blurt everything out. However, he managed to exercise some self- control and kept the conversation light.

When the boys arrived at St David's Hospital, Tamara looked exactly the same, as if she was just sleeping. All the technology: tubes, pipes and drips, were connected and working as before. They told her of their plan for Storm at first light. They talked as though she could really hear them, hoping that maybe deep down in her subconscious mind, she could. Peter found a frog puppet, with a crown on its head, amongst all the gifts sent by well-wishers. He talked in a funny voice pretending to be the frog.

'Hello, you look just like a sleeping princess. I wonder if a kiss from a prince will wake you up?' Peter put the puppet to Tamara's cheek. 'I guess it's not the same from a puppet,' he mumbled despondently.

Mr and Mrs Goodchild entered the room.

'You boys are such good friends to our Tamara,' Mrs Goodchild said softly. 'I'm sure she would appreciate all this – if she only knew,' she added glumly, with a sigh.

'I've heard of people in comas coming round when they hear familiar sounds,' Joel replied encouragingly. 'Maybe that'll work with Tamara.'

'Bless you, Joel. I hope you're right, dear,' she smiled weakly. Then, they were interrupted as the doctor entered the room.

'Hello, Mr and Mrs Goodchild,' the doctor greeted them, politely.

'Hello doctor,' they both replied.

'Would you step inside my consulting room for a moment? I need to speak with you.'

'Of course, doctor,' Mr Goodchild replied, a little hesitantly. The Goodchilds exchanged an anxious frown and then followed the doctor.

'I wonder what that's all about,' whispered Peter, curiously.

'They won't tell us anything, Peter – we're not family…' Joel replied, glancing out of the window. 'Come on, we'd better get back. What's the weather outlook?'

'Oh, don't worry, Joel, it's going to bucket down all night and there'll be a fair wind, too,' Peter answered, without even looking out of the window.

†

That evening, Grandad lit the fire in the kitchen and the three of them stayed in the kitchen, playing various board games, taking it in turns to tend Storm, while yet another storm raged outside.

As dusk descended, Grandad lit a paschal candle and then took a glass bottle, filled with water and poured some into a small dish. Then he unlatched the back door, stepped outside and, with a brand new paint brush, painted a large cross on the outside of the door with the water.

'What are you doing, Grandad?' Joel asked, puzzled. 'Surely you're not going to start decorating now?'

'I got this from the vicar this morning; it's holy water – it's been blessed in the name of Jesus,' Grandad explained. He stepped back inside and locked and bolted the door. Then, he began to paint a line of the holy water round all the walls of the room. He then refilled the dish and took it over to Storm, along with some gauze, and proceeded to unravel the bandages from around Storm's heels.

Joel and Peter leaned over to watch Grandad as he gently dabbed the holy water on the tiny wounds on the undersides of Storm's heels. At this point, the boys began to wonder if Grandad was losing his marbles!

'Mr Jacob, you're really taking this seriously, aren't you?' Peter marvelled. He'd helped his dad many times with the cattle on the farm, but he'd never seen anything like this before!

'Yeah, come on Grandad, isn't this a bit over-the-top?' Joel added, with a deep sigh, rolling his eyes at Peter.

'You don't realise what we are dealing with here, boys,' Grandad explained earnestly. 'We're not fighting flesh and blood, but spiritual wickedness – the unseen enemy of our souls, who would love to destroy this pure symbol of all that is good.'

The boys' bemused expressions transformed into sheer amazement when, as the water seeped over the stigmata wounds, the tiny holes instantly shrank!

'Wow! That's amazing! Did you see that, Joel?' Peter cried incredulously.

'Yeah, the holes are healing up!' Joel could hardly believe it either.

'Peter – Joel – the responsibility has been inadvertently thrust upon us to return this creature to where he belongs. If he remains here, he will become mortal and die. We cannot let that happen, it would be unthinkable. He is a heavenly creature; he shouldn't be here at all!'

'Yes, Grandad, I'm sorry,' said Joel apologetically.

'We'll do whatever you say, Mr Jacob,' Peter agreed.

'Good lads,' Grandad smiled. 'The devil may very well be out looking for Storm tonight; he may even know where Storm is right now. But the devil works in darkness; he won't see past the holy water cross on the door, neither will he be able to enter through it. We're safe – as long as we don't let him in.'

'Well, we wouldn't be that stupid, Grandad!' Joel laughed, nervously.

'Don't underestimate the devil, Joel; he's a trickster. Don't expect him to come knocking on the door to introduce himself; he's a master of deception and disguise. We could unwittingly let him in if we let down our guard. It's best to be vigilant and whatever happens, that door *must* stay locked and bolted until sunrise.'

'Mr Jacob? What is spiritual wickedness?' Peter asked, 'And how can we protect ourselves from it?'

'Good questions, Peter. Well,' Grandad continued, 'spiritual wickedness, in essence, is evil schemes concocted by the devil and his demons. However, there are three things the devil is scared of: the name of Jesus Christ, the cross of Jesus Christ and the blood of Jesus Christ shed thereupon; it's all summed up in the Word of God – the Bible – if only people would actually read it instead of mocking what they don't understand.'

'So, how can a locked and bolted door keep the devil out?' Joel asked.

'It's not the door, Joel. On its own, the door is just a piece of wood, that wouldn't keep the devil out and neither would water painted on it. Remember, I said the water was blessed in the name of Jesus – it's the *name* the water was blessed in, lad, by faith. There is power in the name of Jesus; I mean, real power, but where the power to protect us comes from is *faith* in that name and faith in what Jesus did at the cross being sufficient for every need and every victory. This is what will turn that door into a spiritual "brick wall." The devil won't be able to come through it because Jesus defeated all evil at the cross, boys, and that is at the heart of our deliverance from every evil – but it won't do you any good if you don't believe it. Without faith in that grace – Jesus Christ and Him crucified to pay for our sins, every human being is doomed – without exception!'

The two boys stared at Grandad in amazement; they were struggling to take it all in.

'The day before the children of Israel were set free and came out of Egypt,' Grandad continued to explain, 'God instructed them, through Moses, to kill a lamb and paint its blood on their doorposts and above the doors. God's people were held in slavery and Pharaoh had refused to let them go. So God sent the angel of death to kill the firstborn of every house in Egypt. However, when the angel of death saw the blood, he would pass over those houses and only kill the first born of the families who did not have the blood on their houses as instructed. The blood was to point forward to the coming redeemer, Jesus, the Lamb of God, who would give his life on the cross. Now of course, Jesus has been and made that sacrifice of Himself – and risen again! Painting the water blessed in His name is confessing by faith that we believe His sacrifice is sufficient – we don't need to kill another lamb because the blood of Jesus shed at the cross was a once-for-all sacrifice. Now, we have the covering of the blood of Jesus – that is an all-powerful spiritual weapon against which the devil cannot stand. All our weapons against evil are spiritual and are all linked in some way with Jesus Christ and His victory at the cross, without our faith in this victory, we are all powerless.'

'Wow, Grandad, that is powerful indeed!' Joel murmured.

During the last few days, they'd been bombarded with so much fantastic information and witnessed such strange events, that their minds were reeling dizzily, like Ferris wheels. With all this excitement, neither the boys or Grandad wanted to go to bed at all; they simply weren't tired. The old rule of safety in numbers definitely applied in this situation so they decided to stay together, in the kitchen, the whole night. Throughout the night, in between playing Scrabble and other board games, they took it in turns to repeat the bathing of Storm's heels every so often, till the holes were miniscule.

After some time, Peter looked up from the game they were playing and nodded towards Storm. 'You know, he definitely looks brighter. What do you think, Mr Jacob?'

Grandad glanced at Storm. 'Peter, you're right; his eyes look wider and brighter and his breathing seems easier. What time is it?'

'Quarter-past eleven,' Peter replied, with a yawn.

'We must stay vigilant,' Grandad added. 'There's time for mischief yet.' He had hardly finished speaking when a sudden chill swept over them, making them shiver, and the paschal candle flickered.

'Brr, that was a chilly draught,' Joel remarked, with a shudder.

Grandad got up from the table and poked the fire, putting more coal on it.

'What's that noise?' Peter asked, looking around nervously.

They all listened and heard scratching coming from the back door, then they heard a meow.

'Oh, it's only Martha,' Joel laughed, pushing back his chair.

'Sit down, Joel!' Grandad ordered, firmly.

'What? Surely we can let Martha in, out of the rain?'

'We don't know that it *is* Martha. I said, sit down, Joel. If it is Martha, she can find a sheltered spot in the barn for tonight.'

'OK.' Joel shrugged a little reluctantly, and sat back down. They continued their game. The scratching stopped and the meowing faded, then disappeared.

'Great! The last station – I'll buy it!' Joel cried with a smug grin. 'Now I own all the stations. You'd better watch out if you land on my property, you'll pay a massive fine now.' Joel had just started to count out his fake money to pay the banker when an eerie chill seemed to brush over them again, and once more, they all shuddered uneasily and exchanged nervous glances. No sooner had this happened than they were startled by an unexpected knock at the door.

'Who could that be?' Joel asked.

'Either of you two expecting anyone?' Grandad checked, with an air of suspicion.

The two boys shook their heads and shrugged.

'Then we just ignore it. Your throw, Peter,' Grandad instructed and calmly took Joel's money, giving him the deed card for the station.

The knocking came again, then there was the sound of a familiar voice shouting.

'Hey, open the door! Let me in!'

This made them all jump. They were suddenly ice-cold and could feel little prickles creeping up the backs of their necks. The candle flickered again, and this time it went out!

'It's Mum!' Joel gasped in astonishment. 'Grandad, Mum is here! She must have been driving all night!' Joel jumped up to answer the door.

Grandad leapt from his chair and grabbed Joel by the arm.

'Ignore it, Joel!' he ordered, to Joel's surprise.

'Now you're going too far, Grandad! That's Mum out there and I'm going to let her in!' Joel struggled to break free.

'No!' Grandad commanded, firmly.

'Hey, come on guys! It's cold and wet out here – open up!' the voice pleaded again.

'Grandad – please!' Joel begged. 'That's Mum's voice! We've got to let her in!'

'Didn't you speak to Mum at lunch time?' Grandad asked.

'Yes, but…' Joel started.

'Didn't we tell her everything was alright?'

'Yes…'

'Joel – I can't explain what that is out there, but I know it's not your mum. She would not drive all this way without telling us she was coming,' Grandad insisted firmly. 'If you don't believe me, pick up the phone now and ring her.'

Joel's eyes filled slightly; he was beginning to get scared, thinking that Grandad may have really lost the plot this time.

'Don't be silly, Grandad! Mum's outside – please, open the door…'

'I said, pick up the phone and call her, NOW!' Grandad demanded.

Taken aback at Grandad's sudden forthright command, Joel reluctantly went to the hall, picked up the phone, and dialled Mum's number.

'Grandad,' he pleaded in exasperation. 'I really don't know why I'm doing this. What is the point in ringing Mum at home, when she's out there on the doorstep, getting drenched? It's one thing banishing Martha to the barn but…' Joel suddenly froze mid-sentence and the blood seemed to drain from his face, as he stared at Grandad and gasped.

'Hello…' Mum's sleepy voice could be heard from the phone.

'Mum – is that you?' Joel murmured in disbelief.

'Joel? Of course it's me – who else would be answering our phone? It's almost midnight; is there a problem? Is Grandad alright?'

Momentarily speechless, Joel stared at Grandad and Peter, who were sitting at the kitchen table, looking somewhat bemused.

'Joel…' Mum pressed. 'What is it? Say something…'

'N – no – I mean yes…' Joel stammered.

'What do you mean, Joel? *Is* Grandad alright or isn't he?' Mum sounded very concerned.

'I'm sorry Mum – Grandad is fine,' Joel found his voice and tried to pull himself together. 'There's nothing wrong at all, Mum. I just wanted to – er, to – to say goodnight – and I love you, Mum. I'm sorry I woke you.'

'Oh, how sweet. Thank you darling – I love you too. I'm sorry I can't be with you this Easter weekend, love. This project has me tied up but I'll see you next weekend. Goodnight, love.'

'Goodnight, Mum.' Joel slowly replaced the receiver. An icy feeling came over him, chilling him to his very soul and he somehow wobbled, on his jelly-like legs, back into the kitchen.

Peter looked up in astonishment. 'Joel, you've gone all white – like you've seen a ghost or something.'

'If that was Mum on the phone – then wh –who…?' Joel stammered.

Peter's look of astonishment dissolved into an alarmed frown.

'Whoever, whatever, is gone,' Grandad replied, calmly lighting the candle again. 'It was probably just the wind.'

'Yeah, right,' said Joel, sceptically. 'Since when has the wind been able to impersonate people's voices?'

'Let's continue our game, shall we?' Grandad urged hastily. 'Come and sit down, Joel, it's your go again.'

Joel moved, a little shakily, to the table and sat down, but his heart wasn't in the game.

'I'm sorry, Grandad, I can't get into this right now. Can we have a break?'

'OK, I guess it's about time to do Storm again. You get the bottle of milk, Joel, and I'll do his feet.'

Grandad and Joel stood up. Then, suddenly, there was a tremendous bang on the back door – as though a cannon ball had been shot at it with full force. The three of them almost jumped out of their skins and Rodney fled upstairs, yelping in fear.

'What on earth was that?' Peter cried.

'Well, I don't think it was the wind!' Joel remarked, with a shrug.

'Oh, why didn't I send you two to Peter's tonight and deal with this myself?' Grandad reproached himself.

'We wouldn't have gone – you know that,' Joel answered.

Then, suddenly – BANG! There it went again. Then, whatever it was, it started hammering on the door – hammering and banging. The door rattled and vibrated noisily like a pneumatic drill, as though it would fall off its hinges at any moment.

'Grandad! We're under attack! What are we going to do?' Joel cried, fearfully.

'Don't panic, it can't get in unless we let it in,' Grandad replied.

'It!' Peter shrieked. 'What do you mean – it? What is it?'

'It appears, Peter, to be a fiery serpent – as if straight from the pit of Hell. Just remember though, it's no match for the power of the One in Whom we trust.' Grandad answered, reassuringly.

The banging suddenly stopped and there was another eerie silence, like the calm before a storm, when you know something is about to erupt – but *this* was something else! Something creepy seemed to be tangible in the air. They waited silently with trepidation. Then, sure enough, BANG! This time it was on the wall, then again, BANG further along the wall, followed by a series of bangs, as if bouncing along the walls like a heavy ball.

'I think it may be looking for a weak spot, to try to break through...' Grandad muttered, looking rather confused.

Then, came a further cold silence. The three of them exchanged nervous glances, as though they knew it hadn't gone away, but was a lurking, evil, menacing threat, regrouping to return with its next attack. Then suddenly: WHOOSH! The wind seemed to gust right down the chimney, making the fire flare in the grate, extinguishing the candle and, despite the roaring fire, a chill once more brushed over the three of them, making the hairs stand up on the backs of their necks. Then, just as quickly, the fire died down.

'Grandad – what's happening?' Joel shrieked.

Peter and Joel looked anxiously at Grandad.

Grandad struck a match and, with a shaky hand, re-lit the candle.

'Try to stay calm, Joel,' he urged. 'It can't harm us. We're protected, remember what I told you about the holy water being blessed in that all-powerful name of Jesus. God gives us the victory through Jesus – the Lord has won this battle already – at the cross when He said, "It is finished." The waterline I painted on the walls has created a barrier that is not visible to our eyes, but the enemy knows it is there and he will not dare to cross it. This does confirm to me however, that we have stumbled upon something important – important enough to be the cause of this ferocious attack from the enemy. This means, boys, that, it is even more crucial than I had previously thought that we protect this little creature and return him, alive, as soon as possible.' Grandad sighed, then continued. 'Let's get on with bathing Storm again, shall we? Peter, sit down – and try to calm down. Everything is going to be alright.'

Peter hesitantly returned to his seat, while Joel and Grandad crouched down to tend Storm. Peter was white as a sheet and a little shivery. He stared into the fire and as he watched the glowing embers, the flames began to rise and dance hypnotically before him. His tired eyes danced with the flames and his mind drifted into a daze. He felt light-headed as the flames seemed to grow and dance more and more wildly, seeming to entice him. The wind again blew fiercely down the chimney, making the fire flare and roar, like an angry wild beast trying to break out of its cage. The cards and fake money were flung into the air and scattered around the room, then the candle went out yet again. Joel leapt up.

'Grandad, you've got to do something!' he cried in fear.

The flames of the fire were growing unnaturally long. They seemed to be reaching out into the room, like hideous snakes, hissing – their forked tongues darting further and further, spitting burning-hot coals. Then, to Joel's surprise, Peter stood up and, as if in slow motion, he started walking towards the fire in a trance-like state.

'Peter!' Grandad shouted.

Peter didn't appear to hear; he seemed to be irresistibly drawn towards the fire. The snake-like flames seemed to take on the appearance of a huge red dragon with several heads, gnashing its fierce jaws as flames roared out of its mouths. It appeared to engulf half the room and the monstrous apparition looked as if it was about to consume them!

'It's pulling Peter into the fire!' Joel shrieked, horrified.

'PETER! Come away from the fire! Turn away, Peter!' Joel tried to approach Peter but it seemed the flames were actually trying to separate them, as though they had a mind of their own.

'Quick!' Grandad cried. He pulled Joel back to the stair alcove. 'Hold my hand and grab the stair rail with your other hand, we'll make a barrier in front of Storm. Jesus has already won this battle at the cross! When he proclaimed, "It is finished" he disarmed and put to shame the devil and all his demons!'

Joel did as instructed and they held fast, amid the fiery furnace raging around them. Peter was perilously close to the fireplace.

'PETER! - PETER!' Joel implored him again.

'Peter! Don't look at the fire! Turn around!' Grandad yelled.

'Why's he not hearing us, Grandad?' Joel cried desperately.

Grandad closed his eyes and prayed aloud.

'Lord Jesus, Lamb of God, have mercy on us. Holy Spirit, help us!' Suddenly, Grandad opened his eyes and in a flash, the revelation came to him. 'CHIMNEY! How could I forget? Joel, I put the holy water all around the room, but not across the fire! The chimney is the weak spot. It's a break in the spiritual barrier!'

Joel glanced over at the sink, where the bottle of holy water was sitting on the draining board – out of reach. Then, without warning, he let go of Grandad's hand and leapt across the room to the sink. He snatched the bottle and with grim determination he turned to face the dragon.

'WHAT PART OF, **"IT IS FINISHED"** DON'T YOU UNDERSTAND!' he bellowed at the top of his voice. Then, he aimed the bottle at the fireplace and with all his might hurled it into the centre of the fire. The bottle exploded like a Molotov cocktail, smashing to smithereens in the fire grate and the holy water splashed up the chimney and all around the fireplace. Immediately, there followed a horrid piercing screech – like that of an injured wild animal. It sounded so hideously evil, it chilled them to the depths of their souls!

Instantly, the flames and the coals were sucked back into the fireplace, as if drawn by a powerful vacuum. Then, in a matter of seconds, the fire died down to a natural glow and everything miraculously returned to normal and was, by contrast, incredibly calm and still. Peter collapsed in a heap on the hearth rug, while Joel and Grandad rushed over and knelt beside him. Joel lifted Peter's shoulders and tried to rouse his unconscious friend.

'Peter, are you alright?' Joel cried.

Peter opened his eyes and gazed up at Joel and Grandad, a little whoozy.

'It was the weirdest thing!' he explained. 'I was being drawn towards the fire. I knew it would mean utter doom, but I – I couldn't stop myself. Thank you, Joel. You saved my life! How is Storm?'

'Storm!' Grandad cried, anxiously.

They all turned towards the alcove under the stairs. Grandad rushed over to Storm and knelt down to check him.

'The holes have completely disappeared!' Grandad chuckled, in amazement.

Joel and Peter joined Grandad. Storm looked up with big, bright-blue eyes and blinked.

'Well, hello, little fella,' Grandad beamed.

Then, for the first time, Storm began to stir.

'Look! He's trying to stand up! Peter, he's going to be OK! Grandad, he's going to be alright!' Joel cried, beaming.

With one final heave, the little unicorn struggled up onto his feet. To their utter amazement, he had grown to about twice the size he was before. His white coat seemed to have become iridescent and shiny. Then, to their astonishment, Storm's horn suddenly sprouted to about ten centimetres long and began to sparkle like crystal shimmering in sunlight.

The candle suddenly flickered, then burst into a brightly burning flame. They all wiped their brows and sighed, relieved that the nightmare was over and that Storm had made a miraculous recovery. Then they heard Cedric crow and suddenly realised it was Saturday morning.

'Phew, I never thought I would be so glad to hear Cedric crow so early in the morning!' Joel sighed, with relief. 'This has been the longest night of my life!'

Grandad went over to the window, opened the curtains and peered outside. The first fingers of light were stretching up from the east, fanning out over the horizon. The rain had stopped and the wind had dropped to a gentle breeze. Joel and Peter joined Grandad at the window. Exhausted and thankful, they all watched the miracle birth of a brand new day.

'Thank God for a new dawn,' said Grandad, with a sigh of relief. He put a reassuring arm around the boys, as they gazed through the window together. 'A new dawn and renewed hope, hey lads?'

The two boys looked up at Grandad and smiled in agreement.

'I'm very proud of you, Joel; it took some guts to face that thing. You did good, lad,' Grandad said with a smile.

Then, they heard a weak little bark and looked round. Rodney was crouching halfway down the stairs, peering apprehensively at them, no doubt wondering if it was safe to come down into the kitchen.

'Some guard dog you are, Rodney!' Joel mocked, with a chuckle.

'Yes, you can come down now – now the action has finished!' Grandad chortled.

They all laughed as Rodney ran downstairs, wagging his tail.

CHAPTER SIX

Two Dispatched Heavenwards

Ludicrous as it seemed, compared with the previous night's adventures, sending a baby unicorn back to Heaven didn't seem all that bizarre. So the two boys went along with Grandad's instructions, without any notion of anything being odd at all. They wrapped up against the chilly weather, while Grandad wrapped a woollen blanket around Storm.

'We mustn't lose any time, boys,' Grandad urged. 'Judging by last night's attack, much evidently depends on getting this little creature back to where he belongs. The window of opportunity will be short. One of us should carry Storm; he's obviously feeling better and we don't want him romping off for a play. I suspect that's how he ended up here in the first place – by scampering into places he shouldn't.

'I'll carry him, Grandad,' Joel volunteered, picking up the baby unicorn all snuggled in the blanket.

Although he'd grown to nearly twice his original size, Storm was still light enough for a fit and strong twelve-year-old rugby captain to carry.

'I wish Tamara could see him,' said Peter, wistfully.

'Don't worry, Peter, we'll tell her exactly how cute he looked, won't we, Grandad?' Joel remarked with a smile.

'We can show her!' Grandad grinned, pointing a camera at the two boys with Storm, and taking a snapshot.

†

As the three of them reached the brow of the hill on the fringe of Zionica, the sun was shedding its new light over all the land. They stopped for a moment, then gasped as they watched the most fantastic rainbow materialise before their very eyes. It spanned the whole sky in a huge arc, with Zionica at its centre. Just as before, the light was so bright and powerful that it shone all the way down to earth and encompassed them in the dome of its warm glow. It was the most wonderful experience! Then, to their sheer astonishment, another amazing thing happened! They could hardly believe their eyes as they watched a beautiful full-grown unicorn appear at the centre of the plateau! With power he gracefully reared up and then stood bathed in the light, head and tail held majestically high. Although he was pure white, the rainbow seemed to reflect off him, shimmering like a prism. The soft breeze ruffled through his mane against his steely neck.

Grandad caught his breath; he was clearly overwhelmed. Then, pulling himself together, he urged in a low whisper, 'Go on, boys – he's waiting for Storm.'

The two boys stepped onto the plateau together, Joel carrying the baby unicorn. Peter helped Joel to place Storm within a few feet of the magnificent creature. They removed the blanket and stood back a little. The large unicorn walked forward and bowed his head down to Storm. As their two muzzles met, a piercingly bright light shot upwards, and, instantly the pair seemed to vanish up into it. The rainbow continued to glow for a few seconds, then it too vanished.

Grandad walked down to the plateau as Joel turned excitedly to face him.

'You saw that, didn't you? It wasn't a dream! You saw it too!' Joel cried with elation.

'It was the most awesome sight ever!' Peter shrilled.

Dazed, Grandad turned and silently headed back to his cottage, too overcome to speak.

†

Over breakfast, the boys talked excitedly about the amazing experience that they had just witnessed at Zionica.

'No one must hear of this, boys,' Grandad warned. 'We should keep it a secret; you must both promise me.'

'Of course,' they both nodded.

'If this leaks out, we'll have all manner of reporters and TV crews – to say nothing of opportunist crooks – looking to exploit the situation. Zionica would be spoilt forever. You do understand, don't you, boys?' Grandad implored.

'We certainly do, Grandad. We want a media circus as much as we want toothache!' Joel quipped, dryly.

'Yeah, for sure Mr Jacob, no one will hear of it from my lips. The press would make a meal out of my *miracle healing* too!'' Peter agreed emphatically. 'Except – perhaps – could we – I mean would it be all right to…?'

'I think Peter means Tamara, Grandad. You know we've been talking to her while she's been in this coma. We've told her everything about Storm, so far. Can we tell her he's home safely now?'

'I can't see a problem with that, lads – as long as you make sure nobody else is listening,' Grandad answered, with a smile.

'Hey, you know, the big unicorn that came for Storm? His horn was all jagged at the end – I was really surprised. I had imagined that unicorn horns would be smooth, round and pointed – like you see in pictures of them,' said Joel, curiously.

'It must have been the early morning light, Joel,' Grandad muttered, mysteriously eager to change the subject.

'No, Grandad, it wasn't the light! I was so close, I could almost touch him. It looked like a piece of the end had broken off…'

'Maybe he broke it in a fierce battle for the herd,' Peter dramatised.

'Oh my hat!' Grandad suddenly stood up. 'I've not fed the animals yet. Why don't you two give me a hand before you go off to the hospital?'

'Sure, Mr Jacob.' Peter jumped up. 'Come on, Joel. I can't wait to tell Tamara about this morning. Surely something this exciting must wake her up!'

They rushed round the yard feeding Grandad's animals, which were all impatient and irritable at being kept waiting for their breakfast. There were a few protesting bleats and some pushing and shoving, as the animals dived greedily into the troughs.

Joel's foot was trampled on by a particularly impatient and heavy sheep. Also, Cedric made it known that he was quite cross and Joel and Peter both learned that it was not a good idea to let Cedric get cross. By the time the boys got to Cherokee in the barn, Grandad had already fed her. Then they moaned, as Grandad suggested they should muck out her stall.

'I wonder if we should ride her,' Peter suggested. 'You know, so she's not too wild and frisky when Tamara is better. We don't want Tamara to be thrown and end up back in hospital, do we?'

'Have you gone completely bonkers, Peter?' Joel looked at him as if he was crazy. 'You never learned to ride because of your callipers and there's not a chance of me getting on it! There's more chance of me entering a beauty contest! And there's less than zero chance of that!'

'How bad can she be? She's only a small pony…' Peter shrugged.

Joel glared at Peter – nothing would get *him* on the pony!

'So – we'll let her into the paddock again then…' Peter conceded.

'Correction, Peter. YOU can let her into the paddock. I think I'll start mucking out her stable.'

Peter led the pony outside, then he returned to help Joel.

'The things we do for mates,' Joel huffed, as he piled manure onto a wheelbarrow.

'I'm sure if the tables were turned, Tamara would put herself out for us,' Peter replied.

'Oh yes, what a picture – Tamara painstakingly rubbing linseed oil on my cricket bat, or cleaning mud off my rugby boots,' Joel laughed. He picked up the wheelbarrow and wheeled it outside to the muck-heap. Peter followed, grinning.

'You know, Joel,' Peter pulled a face as his boots sank and squelched into the water-logged mixture of mud and manure. 'I think we should have made Presten do this.'

'Maybe Peter, but personally I'd rather muck out fifty stables than have that goon around,' Joel retorted.

'Yeah, I guess you're right,' Peter shrugged. 'At least we're doing something for Tamara. I still feel terribly guilty that because of me, Storm's healing power depleted.'

'Well, you know what Grandad said about that, Peter. He said Storm wouldn't have had enough power by now, anyway. We've got to have faith. She'll come round – you'll see.'

'Do you really think so, Joel?' Peter bit his lip anxiously.

'Yeah, I do, especially with all the prayers Grandad is saying. I bet, in a few days, the three of us will be stuffing ourselves with Easter eggs in the den at Zionica.'

'I hope so, Joel.'

'Hey, come on, cheer up. Let's go and get cleaned up; we can't visit Tamara reeking of manure, can we? Then again, the smell might be enough to wake her up!' Joel chuckled.

†

About half an hour later, the two boys were both spick and span and saying goodbye to Grandad. They walked the short distance down the lane to the bus stop.

When Joel and Peter arrived at St David's Hospital and entered Tamara's room, Mr and Mrs Goodchild were sitting at her bedside, looking more distraught than ever. Mrs Goodchild was sobbing again, while Mr Goodchild held her hand.

'What is it?' What's wrong?' Joel asked, anxiously.

Mrs Goodchild jumped up and fled from the room in tears. Mr Goodchild glanced sorrowfully at the two boys, then hurriedly followed his wife. Peter and Joel rushed up to Tamara.

'She's still breathing,' Peter murmured, as he scrutinised the equipment. 'Everything is still connected and seems to be working OK. So, what can have happened?'

'I wish I knew, Peter,' Joel sighed with frustration. 'It's not fair! Friends care about people, too. Why won't they tell us what's going on?'

No sooner had Joel said this, than the doctor entered the room.

'Hello. Peter and Joel, isn't it?'

'Yes, doctor,' Joel replied, a little surprised. 'Why are Mr and

Mrs Goodchild so upset? What's wrong, doctor?'

'I'm afraid it's not good news, boys,' the doctor began quietly. 'All our tests are complete now and we cannot ascertain that there is sufficient brain activity to indicate that Tamara will recover.'

'What do you mean – "sufficient brain activity"?' Joel demanded hesitantly. 'Surely if there's any brain function at all, then she's still alive, isn't she, doctor?'

'Yes, doctor. She's still breathing! her heart is still beating…' Peter pleaded, '… she's just asleep, isn't she?'

'Yes, she is still alive and she's breathing because this equipment is breathing for her,' the doctor explained, solemnly. 'Her vital functions would not be sustained without the equipment. Soon, her internal organs will start to shut down, and before long they will cease to function completely. I'm afraid there's nothing more we can do. In this sort of situation, it's kinder to switch off the machine and let nature take its course. We've got to let her go, boys.'

'Let her go?' Peter cried desperately. 'No! We can't let her die! She's only ten! It's her eleventh birthday soon! Please, doctor – there *must* be something you can do…'

As Peter pleaded with the doctor, Joel was too shocked to even speak. He just stared blankly at the doctor.

'Believe me, boys,' the doctor continued. 'We've done everything humanly possible; there's no other option open to us. Mr and Mrs Goodchild asked me to tell you this, because they're too upset.'

The doctor's words seemed to waft over Joel; he became suddenly dizzy and wasn't really taking it in. In fact he didn't even feel as if he was still in the room, but felt strangely detached as if he was somehow outside, looking in – like in a dream.

'There's going to be a short service of blessing here tomorrow,' the doctor continued. 'As it will be Easter Sunday and there's a church service in the morning, Reverend Matthews will be coming in the afternoon. The blessing will take place at half past two, then the machine will be switched off.'

'Switched off!' Peter exclaimed in disbelief. 'But that's too sudden! We need more time, doctor!'

'I'm really sorry, boys.' The doctor sounded genuinely upset. 'I have a nine year old daughter myself – this is such a terrible tragedy. If you believe in God, may I suggest you pray for a miracle – nothing short of a miracle will save her now.' With that, the doctor turned and left the room.

'Switch the machine off?' Peter repeated. 'Joel, we can't let them do it – we just can't!' He turned back to Tamara. 'Tamara, we've saved Storm!' Tears welled up in Peter's eyes as he spoke, willing her to wake up and listen. 'You should have seen it, Tamara. We took Storm to Zionica at dawn this morning and a wonderful rainbow appeared – like the one we saw the other day when Storm arrived, remember? Storm stood up on all four feet, fully recovered. Then, the most magnificent adult unicorn came; he was huge and the colours of the rainbow sparkled all around him, as if from a crystal. He bent his head down to nuzzle Storm and, as the two muzzles touched, a blinding light shot upwards to Heaven and they both disappeared, up into the light. It was the most fantastic sight ever! I wish you could have seen it!'

'What a beautiful story, Peter,' came a voice.

The two boys, taken aback, turned quickly towards the doorway to find Mrs Goodchild standing there, sniffing into her handkerchief.

Peter gasped as he remembered his promise to Grandad to make sure no one heard him talking about Storm.

'You know, I'm sure that's how Tamara would imagine Heaven to be,' Mrs Goodchild added, distantly. 'Thank you so much. You will both come to the blessing tomorrow, won't you – and bring Mr Jacob?'

'Yes, Mrs Goodchild, we'll be here,' Peter sniffed and wiped his cheek with the back of his hand.

Usually, Joel was the spokesperson and Peter the quiet one. This time though, Joel was lost for words. He stared at Tamara, unable to believe what he'd just been told. He felt as though he'd got chewing gum stuffed inside his head.

'Joel? Are you alright, Joel?' Mrs Goodchild asked.

Joel slowly raised his eyes to look at Mrs Goodchild. He had no idea how much of the story she'd heard, and right then he didn't care.

'How could God let this happen, Mrs Goodchild? After all our prayers! Grandad has almost worn his knees out!' Joel cried weakly.

Suddenly Mr Goodchild swept into the room, his face twisted with rage. The hurt and frustration was proving too much to bear and he was angry.

'You can't blame God for this!' His voice almost squeaked as he choked on his anger and grief. 'This terrible tragedy that has taken our beautiful daughter from us prematurely was not the result of Divine action, or inaction!' He gave a little sardonic laugh. 'It's all too easy, isn't it? Oh, here we go – another disaster. Well, we can't blame ourselves, can we, so let's blame God for everything again…' Then his distraught expression dissolved into one of contempt as he continued coldly. 'There's no escaping the fact that this is the result of a naughty boy's prank. Killed – by her own brother! God gave us all free will; Presten chose to break into your grandad's house and steal that foal. Had Presten not done this, Tamara would have been safe inside and would not have run out onto the road after him. The culpability clearly lies with Presten – our own son…'

Joel gasped; he was still speechless and now even more so. Much as he disliked Presten, he now almost felt sorry for him. Mr Goodchild spoke with such a chilling lack of compassion for his own son, as if forgiveness and redemption were beyond him. Joel thought of his own father and felt for a moment how terrible it would have been for him turn against him like that. Presten may be paying for this for the rest of his life; the resulting bitterness could turn him irreversibly evil. Without his parent's love and support, Presten could be a lost cause. Joel shuddered at the thought.

Then, Joel blinked hard. What was the matter with him? He suddenly became aware that he was standing there, in the hospital,with thoughts racing through his head about Presten's future – even feeling sorry for him, when he'd just heard that Tamara was going to die and it was Presten's fault! He felt confused and just wanted to get out of the hospital; he couldn't deal with it any more.

'I'm sorry, Mr Goodchild,' Joel's voice was shaky. 'I'm truly sorry, for you all.' He glanced at Peter. 'Come on, Peter, I think we should go. Goodbye, Mrs Goodchild.'

'We'll see you tomorrow, Joel,' Mrs Goodchild answered, wiping a tear from her eyes.

†

The two boys sat in silence on the bus home. Three times now in his twelve short years, Joel had been forced to deal with the loss of someone close. First Grandma, then Dad, now Tamara. He sat wondering to himself, who would be next? It made him feel vulnerable and brought home to him in a very real sense, how fragile life really was. Nothing is guaranteed – except that, one day we all have to die. Most people probably go through life not thinking about it, but having seen death strike in his own family at people who had so much to live for, Joel even found himself wondering how long *he* would be around! Peter was the first to break the silence.

'We should have kept Storm for a bit longer.'

'Hey?' Joel snapped out of his private thoughts.

'He was getting better – stronger. If we'd kept him for a few more days, he might have been strong enough to heal Tamara.'

'Sssh,' Joel whispered. 'Keep your voice down, Peter. You're wrong, you know what Grandad said: the longer he stayed, the more danger he was in. Don't you remember? He said Storm would have become mortal and died, with unspeakable consequences. I don't know about you, but personally I wouldn't want to have to go through a repeat of last night, either!'

Peter looked aghast. 'Me neither,' he replied quickly, with a shudder.

'Storm wouldn't have been able to heal Tamara, anyway. What healed you was his supernatural heavenly power, which depleted. Had he become mortal, his horn would have had to be ground up to make some sort of potion and Tamara would have had to *swallow* it, and for that she would have to be *awake.* Anyway, even if it worked, she would never forgive you for killing him for his horn.'

'I know, you're right, Joel,' Peter replied mournfully. 'I'm just finding it very hard to accept. She looked so peaceful lying there, as though she was just sleeping. I can't believe that we'll never see her again after tomorrow...' he turned away, choking back tears.

'You're not the only one, Peter; we're all upset by it.' Joel sympathised. 'It's Grandad I'm worried about though. He'll blame himself for this,' Joel surmised.

The bus pulled up at the stop before theirs, just outside the village church. Joel stood up.

'Come on, Peter, we're getting off here.'

Peter stood up and followed him dejectedly off the bus.

'Why are we getting off here, Joel? Ours is the next stop.'

'Because, Peter, I have a question for the vicar.'

Joel strode up to the huge, heavy, wooden door of the old country church. The door creaked spookily as he pushed it open. They were conscious of their footsteps, which echoed loudly as they entered and crossed the stone flagged floor. Then, slowly and silently, they made their way up the carpeted aisle of the church. Matthews must have heard them come in, as he came straight out of the vestry to greet them.

'Hello Joel, hello Peter.' Matthews said cheerily. 'How nice to see you. What can I do for you, boys?'

'I've got a question, Vicar,' Joel said quickly. 'I want to know why Tamara has to die. Why hasn't God answered our prayers – especially as Grandad's knees must be worn to the bone by now? Why did God let this happen, Reverend Matthews? What has Tamara done to deserve this?'

'Phew, cut straight to the quick, don't you, Joel?' Matthews remarked, with a heavy sigh. 'Now then, you'd better come and sit down, boys. This may take a while.'

The three of them sat in the choir pews in the chancel at the top of the Church, and Matthews paused momentarily to collect his thoughts.

'It's a terribly sad thing – to lose someone close, especially someone so young and vibrant like our lovely Tamara,' Matthews began. 'I'll try and give you some words of comfort.'

'We don't want words of comfort, Reverend,' Joel remarked, somewhat tersely. 'We want answers!'

'Yes, I can see how upset you are, Joel – and quite understandably. You three are very close, aren't you?'

The boys nodded.

'Well, you can be sure that somewhere in all of this business with Tamara, God has a plan for good. You may find that hard to swallow now, but eventually something good will come out of this.'

'But, Reverend Matthews, I can't for the life of me see what possible good could come out of Tamara dying at the age of ten! Why isn't God answering our prayers?' Joel demanded, in frustration.

'Well, Joel, let me ask you this,' Matthews continued. 'When you ask your parents for something, how often is the answer a clear and immediate yes?'

'Hardly ever,' Joel muttered.

'That's right. Don't they usually say: "perhaps" or "I'll think about it," or then again, sometimes the answer is a clear "no,"' Matthews went on. 'But you're in no doubt that they love you, right?'

'Right,' Joel and Peter nodded together.

'Well, it's like that with God. He does answer our prayers but very often it's not the answer we expected or wanted, and sometimes the answer is "no,"' Matthews explained. 'Because, God has a better way – His Kairos is perfect.'

'Are you saying then, Reverend, that because the life-support machine is to be switched off tomorrow, God is saying no to us?' Joel asked. 'And what does Kairos mean, anyway?'

'No, I'm not saying that, Joel but we do need to be prepared for that, if it is God's answer. "Kairos" is a Greek word meaning "an opportune moment in time." God always knows the right time for everything. But in any case – she's not dead yet, is she?'

'You mean, there's still a chance for God to send us a miracle and that Tamara might wake up?' Peter asked, with a glimmer of hope.

'I don't want to lead you to think that a miracle "will" happen because you may be very bitter if it doesn't. But my own view is that where there's life, there's always hope. We must have faith and keep on praying. If we want God to listen to us, we must keep on speaking to Him and not give up. Do you understand, boys?'

'I think so, Reverend. You mean the more we ask God, the more likely He is to say yes?' Joel asked, hesitantly.

'Well, how many times has your persistent asking changed your parents "maybe" into a "yes?" Bear in mind though, boys when we speak to God, we must ask in the way that He has ordained, that is, in the name of His Son, Jesus.'

'Well, we have prayed in the name of Jesus, Reverend. So, why then has God not answered our prayers?' Joel persisted.

'Well Joel, if you've done that and still not got an answer, then the most likely cause is…' Matthews answered solemnly.

'Go on, Reverend,' Peter urged. 'Have we done something bad and are we being punished?'

'Oh, no, Peter, not at all; we have a very merciful God! The Reverend answered with a smile. Remember, forgiveness plays an important part in receiving answers to our prayers. So, you should forgive others who have hurt you. I mean really forgive in your hearts. Some people harbour grudges for years, but the only person that really affects is themselves. Un-forgiveness can block blessings God has for you. This is the crux of the Christian message. God forgives all of us on the basis of what Jesus did for us at the cross, but only if we also forgive others. Anyone who refuses to forgive another could never enter Heaven. You know, boys, you often find that when you take that courageous step to forgive someone who's hurt you, the last obstacle to your prayer being answered is removed.' Matthews looked at the two boys earnestly. 'Is – is there someone that you have not forgiven, that you are possibly holding some sort of grudge against?'

Joel and Peter both looked down uneasily.

'I see,' Matthews smiled, knowingly. 'Boys, for your prayers to have the best chance of being answered, you must forgive this person – even if you don't think he or she deserves it, or even wants it. Believe me, boys, God's judgement is infinitely more powerful than anything man can do.'

'But Presten is a…!' Joel blurted out.

'Remember where you are, Joel,' Matthews interrupted with a frown. 'This is God's house.'

'Sorry, Reverend,' Joel murmured humbly.

'Good. Now you need to ask yourselves this question. Which is the stronger feeling? Your love and concern for Tamara or your – shall we say, disapproval of this other person?'

Joel and Peter knew he was right, and put like that there was no contest; they were desperate for a miracle.

'You know, boys,' Matthews went on, 'Jesus said that when two or more pray in his name, He will be there with them. I've been meaning to talk to you two and I think now is an appropriate time. You see, until you ask Jesus to come into your heart and forgive you of your sins – which He took the punishment for at the cross – you're still burdened by your own sins. You need to personally accept the grace of what God has done for you, through His Son. God has a plan for your lives, boys. Would you two like to ask Jesus into your heart – to be *your* Lord and Saviour?'

The two boys nodded.

'Yes, Reverend Matthews,' Peter replied with conviction. 'I don't want there to be any doubt about it; I want to end up in Heaven. I don't want that vile creature, the devil, dragging me to hell!' he continued, remembering the traumatic ordeal of the previous evening, in Mr Jacob's kitchen, when the flames of the fire appeared to engulf him.

'Me too, Reverend Matthews,' Joel agreed seriously.

'Whatever it takes – whatever I have to do, I'm on the good side. If God has a plan for me, then that's what I want for my life.'

'And that's what you shall have, both of you. God takes commitment like that very seriously. Shall we pray?'

The boys nodded and bowed their heads

'Then, repeat these words after me, boys,' Said Matthews, as he led them in a simple prayer.

(Why don't you say this prayer with them. If you really mean what you say, then you too can know your eternal destiny is secure in the loving arms of God, Heavenly Father.)

'Heavenly Father,
Thank you for sending your Son, Jesus,
to die on the cross for my sins.
I'm sorry for all the things I've done wrong;
please forgive me. I forgive anyone who has
done wrong to me. Jesus, come into my heart
and into my life, be my Lord and Saviour and
fill me with your Holy Spirit. Amen.'

'Amen,' Joel and Peter repeated together.

'There'll be rejoicing in Heaven right now, because now your names are written in the Lamb's Book of Life. You are now "born again," into new life.' Matthews proclaimed. 'You now saved. The enemy, the devil, can never take you to Hell; you're in the care and protection of Jesus – the mighty Saviour. Not only that, but Jesus is a mighty warrior and He is gathering a mighty army of soldiers in the light, in His war against evil. I believe, boys, that you two will also be mighty warriors, in the Lord's End-Time-Army. "Thanks be to God who has delivered you from the powers of darkness and conveyed you into the Kingdom of the Son of His love."' Matthews accompanied the boys to the door of the church. 'I'm proud of you two boys. Be assured that your prayer has been despatched Heavenwards. Remember, everything is in God's timing, which is never too early and never late, but always perfect, as God Himself is perfect.'

'Time is the one thing we don't have, Reverend Matthews. They're planning to switch the machine off tomorrow, as you know,' Joel pointed out.

'Yes, things do look bleak at the moment, Joel, but just remember that with God all things are possible. You're both coming to the blessing, aren't you?'

'We'll be there Reverend,' Joel nodded, '...hoping for a miracle.'

'Quite. Give my regards to your grandad, Joel. He must be feeling dreadful. We mustn't let him blame himself.'

CHAPTER SEVEN

A Holy Reunion

One of the hardest things Joel would ever have to do was to tell Grandad the grim news about Tamara. He wanted to put off this unpleasant task for as long as possible so, instead of going straight back to Grandad's cottage, he and Peter slipped past the gate and made their way up to Zionica. This would give them a chance to discuss everything on their own, which they both felt the need to do.

When they climbed up to the den, everywhere was quiet, still and relatively warm, in contrast to all the inclement weather they'd been having lately. There was plenty of food in the rucksack they'd taken to the hospital, but all they could manage was to pick at some biscuits and crisps.

'I'm sorry about Tamara's mum hearing me telling Tamara about, you know, Storm and everything,' Peter muttered ruefully, as he bit into a ginger nut, 'especially after I promised your Grandad that no one would hear it from me. I wonder how much she heard?'

'Oh, I shouldn't worry about that, Peter. I'm sure Mrs Goodchild thought you were making it all up for Tamara. I mean, she would, wouldn't she, in the circumstances? Nobody else heard and even if they did, it would have sounded much too far-fetched for anyone to believe you were describing something that had actually happened!' Joel tipped the last crumbs out of a bag of crisps into his mouth, blew the empty bag up like a balloon and popped it loudly with a clap of his hands.

'Mr Goodchild gave you a bit of a roasting, didn't he? Were you scared?' Peter asked.

'No, not really. He wasn't angry at me; he was just upset. Anyway, he was right. People do blame God for things that go wrong.'

Peter nodded.

'Strangely, I found myself feeling sorry for Presten,' Joel added.

'Huh?' Peter pulled a mystified face.

'Oh, I know, Presten is a pain in the butt and we'd all like to see him fall into a vat of pig muck – but the way his dad spoke about him…' Joel shook his head, sadly. 'I don't see my dad now, Peter – he's been dead for four years, but I always feel he's with me – watching over me – cheering me on. I can't imagine anything worse than being despised by your own father. I'd rather die than lose the love and respect of my dad.'

Peter shuffled a little uncomfortably. Mr and Mrs Jordan were the best parents he could wish for and he loved them dearly, but he was adopted and he didn't want to talk about it.

'What do you think about the Reverend's explanation of hope for Tamara?' Peter asked, quickly changing the subject. 'I mean, he said, with God all things are possible.'

'Well, there are two possibilities, aren't there, Peter?' Joel replied, thoughtfully. 'Either Matthews is a lunatic and it's all a load of codswallop, in which case millions of people have been hoodwinked for centuries, or, Matthews is right and, if that's the case, it's the most staggeringly important thing I've ever heard in my whole life! Matthews said we need to have faith. He said there was time yet, and remember – he's the one conducting the blessing service tomorrow!' Joel continued earnestly. 'Peter, Matthews doesn't strike me as a lunatic. So, if he still thinks there's a chance…'

Peter stared at Joel, the light suddenly dawning in his eyes, as Joel continued...

'I've *got* to believe that Matthews is right because, if he isn't what's the alternative? If Matthews is wrong and it's all a load of codswallop, then all hope has gone, there's nothing to hang onto and Tamara will die. But, Peter, if Matthews is right we've still got a chance – we've got hope! So, I'm with Matthews! I believe it like I believe my own name is Joel. How about you?'

'I guess, if you put it like that, Joel,' Peter agreed. 'Did you forgive Presten in that prayer?'

'I did,' Joel grimaced. 'It was really hard, but once I realised that Tamara's life is more important than any silly feud, it seemed the right thing to do.'

'Yeah, that's pretty much how I saw it too,' Peter agreed. 'The things you do for mates!'

'Imagine if she could see us now, deciding to forgive Presten. She'd be laughing her socks off,' Joel replied, humorously.

'Yeah, especially at you on the muck heap this morning,' Peter chuckled. 'Joel…' he became suddenly serious again, 'do you think we should go and tell your grandad about the blessing now? He has a right to know.'

'Yeah,' Joel nodded, breathing a loud sigh. 'I've been putting it off, but you're right. OK, let's go.'

With heavy hearts, the two boys crept into Grandad's cottage. He was sitting in his rocking chair by the fire in the lounge. The boys detected a hint of a sniffle – he was either starting with a cold or he was upset and they guessed it was the latter. Although it was only just after five o'clock in the afternoon, he already had a brandy and Benedictine in his hand.

'It's OK, lads,' Grandad muttered, faintly. 'You've been spared the grim job of telling me; I already know. Mr Goodchild telephoned and invited me to the blessing tomorrow.'

The boys nodded, both quite relieved that they did not have to tell him themselves.

'I've succumbed to my weakness, lads,' Grandad murmured tilting his glass.

'I suppose it's OK to have a drink now and then, Grandad,' Joel replied sympathetically.

'No, it's not.' Grandad unexpectedly placed his whisky glass down on the table. 'I think I'll turn to the comfort of the Holy Spirit, instead. Pass me my Bible, will you, Joel.' He sniffed as he took the Bible from Joel and opened it on his knee. 'Why don't you two go up and get ready for tea?'

†

Joel tossed and turned and hardly slept at all. It was the night before Easter and it dragged on interminably. He just wanted the night to be over so that he could get back to the hospital. He hoped that by morning, surely everything would be all right – after the prayer that the Reverend called a "Heavenly despatch."

On Easter morning, they were all up before dawn – even before Cedric! Grandad held a dawn vigil on the plateau in Zionica. This was normal Easter Sunday routine for Grandad: celebrating the resurrection of Jesus Christ, on the third day after His crucifixion, which is what Easter is all about.

After that, Joel and Peter fed all the animals while Grandad cooked breakfast. However, none of them could eat much at all.

Easter Sunday meant a special service in church, but Grandad didn't take much persuading to take the boys to the hospital first. They all piled into Grandad's old jeep and set off. It was sunny for a change. Joel thought this was a good sign and this seemed to cheer them up.

On arriving at St David's Hospital, Joel and Peter rushed in, each with a large Easter egg for Tamara but their faces dropped as they entered her room. Everything was just the same; Mrs Goodchild, aided by a nurse, was brushing Tamara's silky blond hair. There was a frilly dress, which even Joel knew that Tamara would have hated, hanging by the bed. Tamara was a "tomboy" not a "frilly-girl" he thought.

'Has she woken up yet?' Peter asked, hopefully.

Mrs Goodchild shook her head slowly as she replied. 'I'm afraid not, love; there's no change at all.'

'But how can that be?' Joel cried in disbelief. 'I was certain God would have answered our prayers by now! I mean that's what God does, isn't it – miracles?'

'We've all been praying for a miracle, Joel,' Mrs Goodchild answered sadly. 'But I guess it's not to be.'

Grandad entered the room and his hopeful expression also dissolved immediately.

'I'm so sorry, Mrs Goodchild,' Grandad murmured, weakly.

Mrs Goodchild nodded and smiled bravely.

'Come on, boys,' Grandad urged, 'there's nothing we can do here. Let's go to church.'

With heavy hearts, Joel and Peter put down their chocolate eggs amongst all the other presents and followed Grandad outside.

'Did you see that dress hanging up?' Peter whispered on their way down the corridor.

'It would be hard to miss it, Peter,' Joel replied quietly. 'I don't profess to be a great follower of fashion, but I think it's a good job that Tamara doesn't know about it. I think she'd positively explode with horror at the thought of wearing it. I'm astonished that Tamara's mother doesn't know her own daughter well enough to understand that.'

'She does know,' boys,' Grandad answered them. 'I'm sorry, I couldn't help overhearing you. Mrs Goodchild knows only too well that her daughter is a tomboy, but probably sees this as her only chance to see her little girl dressed up like a prom queen. I don't think Tamara would object to this brief indulgence of her mother – in the circumstances, do you?'

The boys nodded that they understood.

At the church there was a Holy Communion service. Joel and Peter went up to the altar with Grandad, to receive the bread and the wine: the emblems of the Lord's body and blood.

'The Body of Christ; feed on Him and remember that He died for you,' Reverend Matthews repeated, as he offered the bread to them individually.

'The blood of Christ; shed for the sins of the world.' Matthews repeated, as he offered the cup of wine to everyone.

After the church service, it was still over two hours till the blessing service at the hospital so Grandad and the boys made their way home. They made a pretence of eating – pushing food around their plates, but couldn't really eat much at all.

'May I be excused, Grandad? I'm not hungry,' Joel murmured with a sigh.

'And me, Mr Jacob?' echoed Peter.

Grandad nodded and pushed his own plate away, too. 'It's nearly one o'clock. Don't go far, boys. We should leave for the hospital by two, so we arrive in good time.'

Joel and Peter wandered outside and made their way gloomily up to Zionica. Instead of climbing up the tree to the den, they made their way to the plateau, where only the day before they had said goodbye to Storm; it all seemed such a faraway dream now. They sat on the grass and although the sun was shining through patchy clouds, a faint sprinkle of rain began to fall.

'Great!' Joel muttered. 'Now we come out without our coats and get rained on.'

'It's only a shower, Joel. It'll soon pass. Hey, maybe there'll be another rainbow and Storm will return!' Peter remarked, groping for some glimmer of hope. 'Do you think he would come back if we asked him?'

'I don't know, Peter,' Joel replied. 'He may have got into trouble for coming in the first place; who knows what goes on up there. He may even be grounded – in a heavenly kind of way.' Joel rubbed his chilly arms and stood up. 'Let's ask him!'

'What?' Peter stared at Joel as if his friend had gone crazy.

'Let's shout him – ask him to come back. What have we got to lose?' Joel asked, with a shrug.

'Joel, you're mental!' Peter cried in bemused astonishment.

'This is the last ditch, Peter. I'll try anything!'

They were getting quite wet; the rain was running down their hair and faces. Joel looked upwards and began to shout.

'Come back, Storm! Please – please – come back!'

Peter stood up and joined in.

'We're both mental!' he grinned. Looking upwards, Peter also began to yell. 'Come back! Please, Storm, come back!'

The boys exchanged grins as they both continued to shout at the tops of their voices. The rain was soaking the pair of them. Then – all of a sudden, colour exploded from the sky and a bolt of light shot down to the plateau. Before they knew what was happening, everything suddenly went black and they felt as if they were being pulled through a long tunnel. Then they saw a very bright light and they were heading straight towards it. There was nothing they could do, but neither did they want to. The light was so warm and bright, inviting and wonderful; they just had to reach it! As they got nearer, they could just make out the vague, misty outlines of people in the light at the top of the tunnel. Then, they both passed out.

'Joel…' a soft voice spoke.

Joel opened his eyes and looked up. Everywhere was very bright, warm and glowing. Flashes of colour like crystals in sunlight gently swept and swirled around, while sparkling lights twinkled like stars in a moonlit sky. He could hear the most beautiful music and soft angelic singing from the sweetest voices, like nothing on earth. He was looking into a face which could only have belonged to an angel. Joel just knew that, because her smile could have melted an iceberg! His eyes seemed drawn to hers. She was surrounded by a glowing aura of light, which moved with her as she moved. The light glittered all around her like gold dust.

'You're with us now, are you, Joel?' she laughed. 'My name is Charis.'

Joel couldn't take his eyes off her; he was momentarily speechless! Then, he heard Peter.

'What's happened? Where are we?' Peter whispered, totally awestruck.

As Joel turned around, it seemed as if everything was in slow motion. He saw Peter next to him and noticed that he also had a beautiful angel smiling over him.

'Everything is all right, Peter,' his angel murmured softly. 'My name is Aletheia and I'm here to take care of you.'

Charis took hold of Joel's hand and he felt as if he was floating on air as she helped him up. He looked down, still holding the angel's hand and realised that he *was* floating on air. His head was a little above the angel's. He looked at Peter and saw that he too had floated up. Joel returned his gaze to Charis and frowned. She laughed again and gently tugged him back down to her level.

'There's no gravity here, Joel; you'll get used to it,' she said softly, with a smile.

'Used to it? Is this Heaven? Are we dead?' Joel asked,

anxiously.

'I'll take over here, Charis,' came a man's voice. The man stood with his back to Joel and Peter, while talking to the angels.

'Oh, is there a problem, Nathan?' Charis asked.

'It's family business – and they're both Kairos.'

'Oh, my wings!' Charis exclaimed. 'The second in only twenty-three years – and two at once! We'll be catching up with the Morisco Zone at this rate.'

'That'll take some doing, Charis; they've held the record for five hundred years,' Aletheia replied, with a smile.

'Well, we'll leave you to it then, Nathan. Blessed is He,' Charis said cheerily.

'Blessed is He,' Aletheia murmured sweetly.

'Blessed is He,' Nathan replied.

Dressed all in white, Nathan was surrounded by the same aura of light as the angels. He bowed his head as Charis and Aletheia floated away. Then, he turned to Joel and Peter and flashed a massive grin.

'Well, now then,' Nathan began. 'What have you two got yourselves into?'

Joel's eyes almost popped out of his head as he stared in disbelief.

'DAD!' Joel shrieked in utter shock.

For, the man standing in front of him was none other than Nathan Asher, deceased – Joel's dad!

CHAPTER EIGHT

Angelic Hosts

Vague memories of his dad's funeral flashed through Joel's head as he gaped, open-mouthed, at his dad. He thought he must be dreaming! How could this be? Dad had died four years ago and yet, there he was – large as life! A sudden feeling of panic came over Joel – was he dead, too?

Nathan Asher smiled reassuringly at the boys. A soft, golden glow ebbed all around him; he was so real.

'Hello, son,' he beamed, spreading out his arms.

Joel sank softly into his dad's arms, melting into the fabulous glow. He felt as if he was totally immersed in pure love and an overwhelming sense of peace suddenly engulfed him; it was like nothing he'd ever experienced before! He felt so safe, he could have stayed there forever. Nathan held out an arm to Peter.

'Peter, come,' he invited him warmly.

Peter floated over to Nathan and Joel, and he too became immersed in the wonderful glow. After a while, Nathan stood back to look at the boys.

'It's wonderful to see the two of you,' he said with a huge smile.

'This is incredible…' Joel choked. 'I – I thought you were dead!'

'Only my earthly body died, Joel. I – that is, my soul and my spirit – did not die.'

'But that – that means you're – you're in Heaven?' Joel stammered in amazement.

Nathan nodded.

'And we're here too! That means – me and Peter must be dead!'

'No.' Nathan shook his head. 'Don't worry, I'll explain everything,' he reassured them. 'So much has happened to you two recently, your heads must be in a bit of a spin.'

'A big ferris wheel, more like!' Joel exclaimed.

'You've both been worried about your friend, Tamara.' Nathan remarked solemnly.

They both nodded.

Joel felt a lump rising in his throat; he felt so responsible. He should have been able to catch up with her and stop her from running out onto the road. After all, he was supposed to be the big, school rugby star! If only he'd run faster, Tamara wouldn't be in the hospital at all.

'It's all my fault!' he blurted out, mournfully.

'No, Joel,' Nathan assured him. 'You cannot be held responsible for circumstances beyond your control. I pronounce you not guilty. You must accept that, or those negative feelings will hold you back and that's just what the enemy wants. The battlefield is in the mind. Thoughts of guilt are a weapon the enemy uses – but *your* weapons are mighty in God, for overcoming those thoughts. With practice, you can learn to use the weapons God has given you; we'll talk more about that later. Now though, God has heard your prayers and this morning at the altar rail, He heard you again. You both said exactly the same thing as you received the Eucharist sacrament. What was it you said when you received the communion bread, Joel?'

'T – t – take me instead…' Joel replied, hesitantly.

Peter threw Joel a shocked look.

'What did you say, Peter?' Nathan asked.

'Er, I said that too…' he murmured weakly.

'That was the point when the next stage of God's plan for you two boys was set in motion. He had already decided *how* He was going to answer your prayers, well before you even said them,' Nathan grinned.

'So, Tamara has woken up then, and she's going to be all right because we've died in her place. Is that why we're here – in Heaven?' Joel asked.

'Well, not exactly…' Nathan began.

'But I don't understand, Mr Asher…' Peter interrupted. 'Surely, she must have recovered – if we're here in her place?'

Nathan smiled patiently. 'You haven't died in Tamara's

place; in fact, you haven't died at all.'

'Phew! You're sure? You mean, we're not dead?' Joel gasped in relief.

'But, how can we be in Heaven if we haven't died?' Peter asked with a puzzled frown.

'Well, you haven't arrived in the usual way – that's for sure,' Nathan explained. 'You've found the Kairos gateway. The unicorns discovered that a rainbow can be used as a bridge between the earthly and celestial realms. As you can see, looking around here, this whole place consists of light and colour. God made light and you know that colour is just different degrees of light. That's why a rainbow is a sign from God, He makes them; it's like a reflection from Heaven. The unicorns are not supposed to use them, but sometimes they slip down out of curiosity – and to play. Grandad's place is ideal for them; it's very private and of course the Kairos gateway is there. Unfortunately though, when you went rushing out to see the rainbow last week, the other unicorns scarpered and the baby unicorn was left behind.' Nathan smiled in amusement at the boys' bewildered expressions. 'Thank you for all you did to protect the baby and return him.'

'It was a pleasure,' Peter grinned. 'Mr Asher, does anyone else use this Kairos gateway?'

'Not this one at the moment. But don't worry, there's no danger of people falling into it by accident. Only a child of good, pure and true heart can pass through it, and then only on God's invitation.'

'God's invitation?' Peter echoed, incredulously.

'Yes, you didn't fall into it by accident, boys; you were summoned,' Nathan declared mysteriously.

'We were summoned?' Joel cried in astonishment.

'Yes, chosen, if you like. In fact, *you've* been destined for the Kairos since before you were born – both of you.'

'*Hey*?' Joel whistled, wide-eyed, hardly able to believe what was he was hearing.

'Even before *I* was born,' Nathan continued. 'You see, God has a plan and every one of us has a role to play,' he smiled.

'Wait a minute,' Peter interrupted. 'When we asked about the Kairos gateway, you said "not this one." Do you mean that there are other similar gateways, Mr Asher?'

'That's right, Peter, there are other special places like your Zionica. In fact there's at least one in almost every country, but they're not in constant use. As you heard Charis say, this one has not been used by the Kairos for twenty-three earth years. Some of these gateways have been unused for centuries. Only children of a very special kind can enter this way; everyone else has to come through the normal route – the way I did four years ago – and Grandma before that. So, when such a child is found, it's an occasion for much rejoicing; there's so much we can do.'

'What do you mean, Dad?' Joel asked eagerly. 'What kind of things? What have we been chosen for?'

'Well Joel, we can see so much from up here, but those of us who've come here in the normal way are not allowed to communicate with people in the world. Interfering with human free-will is also forbidden – everyone has to make their own choice. However, there are things we can do with special children, who are able to visit us in the way you two have,' Nathan continued earnestly. 'You see, boys, you can go back! We can tell, or even show you things that will enable you to be of great service in the war against evil, back in the world.'

'Wow!' Peter whistled.

'But, what, can *we* do, Dad?' Joel asked curiously.

'Yes, Mr Asher,' Peter added. 'I thought Jesus had already won that war. Isn't that the whole point of the cross?'

'Yes, Peter, that's true,' Nathan nodded.

'But, I don't understand, Dad. What can we do if Jesus has already done it all?' Joel shrugged in confusion.

'Well, Jesus has done the part that was impossible for any ordinary man to do. He's provided the door – the way back to God and into Heaven. However, there's still a war going on, boys,' Nathan explained. 'Many people in the world have been deceived by the unseen enemy. People are dying every day without knowing this powerful truth that can save them, and Hell is full of people who need not have gone there – they've had a "get-out-of-Hell-free card" but they've failed to use it. You see, boys, it's not just the knowledge that Jesus died on the cross; most people know that. The question is: why? They do not know that on the cross, Jesus took the punishment for *everyone's* sins, to reconcile us to God, that we may be saved. The enemy's strategy is to prevent people from finding out the truth. So, even though the victory was settled at the cross, the battle between good and evil still rages on – it's a spiritual battle, you see, boys.'

'A spiritual battle! But what's that got to do with us, Dad?'

'Well, it's like this, Joel. Jesus is holding out His hand – the lifeline to drowning mankind – having done all He can to save everyone. It's very difficult though, boys, to try to save people who do not know they are drowning! Jesus dealt with the problem – sin – once and for all at the cross, by taking the punishment for everyone's wrong-doing, so that God our Father, having punished His own Son for our sins, could receive all who believe this. That's the key: faith – faith to believe this saving truth of what Jesus did at the cross to save all of humanity. Salvation can only be received by the grace of God, through faith, and can never be earned by any amount of good deeds. The trouble is, most people actually believe that they will go to Heaven when they die, because they are, in their own eyes, "a good person." That is a lie and believing that lie is guaranteed to send them to Hell! There are none righteous, no, not one because all have fallen short of our Holy God and His perfect glory. The price for salvation was paid at the cross by the only One qualified to pay it, that is Jesus – the sinless Son of God – and there is no other way or other name under Heaven by which man can be saved.'

The boys gulped as they struggled to comprehend the seriousness of Nathan's explanation.

'The devil and his demons on the other side: the powers of darkness and evil, are constantly trying to discredit Jesus and the cross; whispering lies, saying the gospel is not true and doing all they can to prevent people from hearing and knowing the truth so that many people perish when they die and find, to their abject horror, that they are in the pit – that terrible place called Hell – and there is no way out, ever! God made Hell for the devil and for the fallen angels who also rebelled; it was not made for man.'

Joel and Peter gasped at the chilling thought of all those unsuspecting people, many of whom expected to go to Heaven, suddenly finding themselves in that place of eternal torment.

'Neither side, though, can be seen with the physical eye,' Nathan continued. 'There is a war going on in heavenly places, and the human mind is a battlefield where the enemy tries to take control by gaining footholds through thought and turning those footholds into strongholds in the minds of the people.'

'But why does God allow the enemy to continue with all that, Dad?' Joel asked, in exasperation.

'Because of His grace and mercy, son,' Nathan answered. 'Crazy as that might sound to you now. You see, more people are coming to the saving knowledge of the cross every day and, for the sake of those who will believe, God allows precious time, because in God's eyes the price has already been paid and all sin has been punished. Soon though, and very soon, the door of salvation through grace will close. Just as God closed the door with Noah and the first ark, the door of this final "ark" will close when the Lord Jesus Christ returns for His church.'

'So people need to make a decision before it's too late,' Joel surmised.

'Yes, Joel, the world has entered the end-times foretold in the Bible, and the time left to choose eternal life is short. Rejecters of Christ Jesus reject God's grace and those people pay for their own sins in eternal Hell, separated from God forever.

'But why would people choose Hell, Mr Asher?' cried Peter, gravely. 'That's insane, when a free pardon is available!'

'Yes, it is, Peter. Of course, the devil knows his "goose is cooked" and eternal torment is his end, but he is still a dangerous adversary,' Nathan continued. 'He is in the world, along with the evil fallen angels, and he is determined to deceive and use unsuspecting people in his mission to *kill, steal and destroy,* and ultimately, to take as many souls down to Hell as he can.'

'How does the devil use people, Mr Asher?' Peter asked.

'Well, as I said, this is a spiritual battle, Peter. He manipulates people by whispering evil thoughts into their minds and because he's invisible, they think these are their own thoughts. All the evil going on in the world stems from the enemy – the devil and his demons: the fallen angels who were cast out of Heaven with him in the "great rebellion." Wicked men do wicked things because they are manipulated in their minds like puppets, by the enemy. One of his favourite tricks is to whisper, into people's minds, accusations about other people. This is particularly nasty as it creates feelings of resentment and anger which can cause people to behave out of character. He can cause lots of trouble this way: breaking up friendships, marriages and even whole families. Family and political strife, even wars, can result from the enemy's evil whispering – it is called spiritual wickedness in high places.'

'So basically,' Joel exclaimed in outrage, 'the enemy and his demons can run riot in the world because they are all evil spirits that cannot be seen!'

'Like a wily fox in a coop full of helpless chickens, on a dark night,' Nathan nodded, with a wry smile.

'So, how can *we* help, Dad?' Joel asked, with a shrug. 'What's this Kairos all about, and what is it that we've been chosen to do?'

'The Kairos, boys, is a very special group of children, like yourselves. They are able to come and go here until they reach the age of sixteen. They are part of *God's* army of warriors, engaged in the battle against evil,' Nathan explained.

'That sounds like some sort of science-fiction story. What does it all mean, Dad?' Joel asked incredulously.

'Yeah!' Peter cried excitedly. 'It sounds fantastic! I want to get involved – to make a difference! Tell us more, Mr Asher.'

'Well, as I explained before, there is a very real battle going on with a very real enemy, and you two really can make a difference. How amazing is that – the opportunity to help bring oppressed people to the freedom and the life that Jesus died to give them!'

'I always felt as if there was some special destiny for me – that one day my life would be worthwhile...' Peter replied with wide-eyed wonder.

'Why are only children able to use this er, gateway, Dad?' Joel interrupted. 'You said we could come and go until we were sixteen. What happens then? Do we stay here for good?'

'And why are we special, Mr Asher?' Peter asked.

'Children have a special quality that, sadly, most adults lose,' Nathan continued. 'Jesus said that only if you become like little children, can you enter Heaven. This doesn't mean that everyone has to start behaving like children. We all know that children can be mischievous. But generally, children have a special capacity to love unconditionally and expect to be loved regardless of circumstances, influences, behaviour or anything else.'

The boys nodded that they understood.

'Also, of course,' Nathan smiled broadly, 'children are dependent on their parents, and that's how God wants all people to live – completely relying on and trusting in Him as their Heavenly Father, in the way a child trusts their earthly parents.'

'Ah, that used to confuse me – what Jesus said about becoming like little children to get into Heaven, but I understand it now, I think.' Peter returned the smile.

'Excellent! You'll both learn a lot more about the Kairos in due time; I have much to show you and much to explain,' Nathan replied.

'But Dad, what's happening about Tamara?' Joel pleaded. 'You said that God had decided how to answer our prayers. Please – just tell us that she's woken from the coma and that she's alright.'

'Well, it depends on you, Joel. She hasn't woken up yet. You're the one who is to wake her.'

'Me!' Joel cried in astonishment.

'I said that He had made His decision long ago about how to

answer your prayers. You see, boys, His next plan for you was set in motion by your choice at the altar rail, this morning. You both chose to put another before yourselves and God's word says that, "*Greater love has no man than to lay down his life for a friend.*" That selfless choice has confirmed your place in the Kairos, boys, because it was an act of love – the first and most powerful weapon against the enemy. It wasn't nails that held Jesus to the cross, it was love.'

'Will we see Jesus? Is He here?' Joel asked in awe.

'He is always here...' Nathan answered.

'But Mr Asher, shouldn't Jesus be with Tamara now – making her well so that she can wake up?' Peter asked.

'He *is* with Tamara, Peter, just as He is with any lonely, sick or frightened child, anywhere in the world. He doesn't have to be just in one place at a time. God can be everywhere at once! He is omnipresent and omniscient. He is God in three Persons: God the Father, God the Son and God the Holy Spirit – the three members of the Holy Trinity, complete and inseparable.'

Joel and Peter frowned, trying to understand it all.

'I'll let you into a secret,' Nathan smiled. 'No one up here fully understands either; we're not meant to. To put it bluntly, we're none of us clever enough – despite the fact that we have immeasurably more intelligence here than when we were mortal in the world.'

'Really? How come, Dad?' Joel asked, thoughtfully.

'Humans on earth only use a very small percentage of their brains. I don't know why, but most of man's brain capacity is dormant in the world. However, that physiological restriction is removed up here. So, even the most intelligent human, such as Einstein for instance, could never be as clever in the world as anyone up here.'

'Wow!' Peter exclaimed. 'Mr Asher, are we allowed to see Jesus?'

'Not yet, Peter. You would be too overwhelmed by His glory. You will not be allowed to see much of the true beauty up here because I'm very limited as to how much I can show you.

If I were to let you see the extent of what it's like here, you would not want to go back,' Nathan smiled, 'and we can't have that just yet because you still have much to do. He has prepared work for you.'

'Work? You mean, He's going to give us a mission?' Joel asked excitedly.

'Yes, I guess you could call it that, Joel,' Nathan answered.

'Wow! How phenomenal! But Dad, how am I going to wake Tamara?'

'We'll get to that, son. First though, there is someone here who you *are* allowed to see.' Nathan answered. He turned aside and a young woman appeared before him. She was very pretty, with blonde hair and blue eyes – and looked remarkably like Peter! She was surrounded by the soft golden aura, like that of Nathan and the angels.

'Peter, this is Anna, your natural mother,' Nathan introduced them. 'Anna, this is your son, Peter.'

Peter gasped in astonishment, hardly able to believe it.

'Peter, my son...' Anna beamed a beautiful smile and held out her golden arms.

Peter moved forward, a little awkwardly at first, but as he nestled softly into the arms of his natural mother for the first time since he was a baby, it felt so natural that his nervousness melted away.

'Contrary to what Mr and Mrs Jordan were told, and subsequently told you,' Nathan continued, 'your mother did not abandon you at the orphanage, Peter. She did everything she could to keep you and feed you, often going hungry herself. She was only sixteen and unmarried when she gave birth to you. Your biological father had taken her by force and abused her. She was forbidden to see him again and ordered by her family to give you up. She refused to let you go and as a result was ostracised by her entire family. She became an outcast, forced to live on the streets with down-and-outs, drug addicts, beggars and villains. She did very menial jobs for a pittance but through lack of proper food and care she became ill and when you were eighteen months old, she died. You were put into the orphanage by the authorities where you were found six months later by the Jordans, your adoptive parents. It was, of course, God who led them to the orphanage in Hungary. He used a Kairos child just like you to help them, and smoothed over the obstacles and red-tape so they could adopt you and get you out of the country.'

'Praise God!' Peter smiled, happily.

'Quite. Now, before we discuss the mission God has for you,' Nathan continued. 'Is there anything you want to ask me?'

'I'm worried about Tamara, Dad. We haven't got a lot of time. The doctors are switching off her life-support machine this afternoon. We need to leave for the hospital at two o'clock,' Joel explained with some urgency.

'I'm so proud you're my son, Joel,' Nathan smiled affectionately. 'Here you are in Heaven, with the opportunity to ask the ultimate questions, but you are still concerned about the plight of your sick friend. There's no need to worry. God invented time for earth. Time as you know it doesn't exist up here; this is eternity. You could be here for a hundred years and it would seem like no time at all. A thousand years is like a day here. When you go back, you'll find hardly any time has passed.' The boys stared at Nathan, overwhelmed and bewildered – to put it mildly.

'Awesome!' Peter gulped.

'Now, about Tamara,' Nathan continued. 'Your prayers will be granted and He has designed a way for you to wake her.' Suddenly, another woman, also surrounded in an aura of light, appeared in front of them with a beaming smile. Joel recognised her immediately, despite her appearing much younger than he remembered her.

'Grandma!' he cried with joy.

'Hello boys,' Grandma beamed. 'I'm here to give you a message for Grandad – it's regarding young Tamara. I want you to tell him: What wasn't right for a sixty-year-old woman *is* right for a ten-year-old girl and that he has to give to you the secret he keeps, and the mystery will be no more. Finally Joel, I must stress to you that it can only be used once and for the purpose for which it has been granted. Then, it must be returned to its rightful owner, who's been waiting fifty-three years for it.'

'But what is it – and who is the rightful owner?' Joel asked in complete bewilderment, as he stared at Grandma.

'You'll know, Joel. God bless you both, and Grandad.' With that, Grandma vanished.

'I'm sorry Joel,' Nathan explained. 'As I said before, it's not normally permitted for anyone here to communicate with the world. Grandma was granted a special dispensation to appear to you in this vision, only in answer to your prayers on this one occasion – you already know how much time Grandad spends on his knees!' he chuckled.

Joel nodded. He knew very well that Grandad always seemed to be praying – never more than since Tamara's accident.

'It's a very special honour and blessing for you and for Grandma, as it is extremely rare for this to be granted. Very occasionally, God allows someone to return to their physical bodies just after they've died, and they come back to life again. Some have dramatic experiences to tell people when they wake up. In the world, these are known as "near-death experiences." Obviously, Anna and I are allowed to see you because we are acting guardians here. God has His reasons for what He allows – just remember, He means everything for good.'

'But what's Grandad got to do with all of this, Dad?' Joel asked, uncertainly.

'Grandad was once standing where you are now, Joel,' Nathan said simply.

'Bingo!' Joel cried. 'I knew there was something! No wonder he knows all about unicorns! But why didn't he tell us?'

'Oh, he doesn't remember any of it. Come – follow me.' Nathan beckoned the boys.

They floated after him, proceeding along the large, cavernous hall, looking around in amazement. Anna followed behind. There were no real boundaries; even as they looked up, everything seemed to go on forever. Twinkling crystals cast prismatic effects everywhere the boys looked. There were many golden archways on either side of the hall, but they couldn't see through them because each archway had a different coloured misty light shining within it. A sparkling precious jewel shone from the pinnacle of every archway, corresponding to the colour within.

Nathan led them to a golden archway with a pearl at its pinnacle. There was written on the pearl: Welcome Room 159. They followed Nathan through the archway and he beckoned them to sit on pearl and gold chairs. The cushions did not indent at all as the two boys settled like feathers on them. Joel thought it really did feel heavenly, as he and Peter sat with his dad and Anna. He was beaming with so much happiness that he felt he could burst. Nathan smiled at the boys as he watched them bouncing lightly on the chairs and laughing at their strange weightlessness.

'This must be what it's like walking on the moon!' Joel exclaimed joyfully.

'Not quite, Joel; the moon has a smidgeon of gravity,' Nathan chuckled in amusement.

'Tell us about Grandad and the unicorns, Dad,' Joel pleaded.

'Well, Grandad was only about your age when he came here, Joel. He named the special place in the field where you have your tree den, "Zionica" after coming here but he doesn't remember that now, all he remembers is the name. He knows about unicorns because he's studied the subject – but he cannot remember that he has been here, or the real reason why he has a fascination for them in the first place.'

'Why doesn't he remember, Dad?' Joel persisted.

'Yeah, how could you forget something like this?' Peter added in amazement.

'Well, boys, as I said earlier, only children of a good, pure and true heart can come here the way you two have – through one of the Kairos gateways and Grandad came in the same way but once he reached sixteen, everything about this place was erased from his memory. The same thing will happen to both of you on the eve of your sixteenth birthdays. Yesterday Grandad was allowed to see the vision of Storm's heavenly return as a gift, knowing he would keep it secret.'

'I see,' Joel muttered, uncertainly.

'But didn't Charis say we were the second in twenty-three years, Mr Asher?'

'Yes, Dad, that would make Grandad forty-two when he came here!'

'No,' Nathan shook his head. 'That would make your mother eleven when *she* came here.'

'Mum too?'

'Uh huh. You see, Joel, Zionica's special gateway is a third-generation secret in our family,' Nathan explained.

Joel looked momentarily stunned. He wondered what on earth – or in Heaven – would be revealed next!

'So, I guess Mum doesn't remember anything about this either?'

'Correct. Neither can she remember why she wanted to call you *Joel*, but she made herself a note on the eve of her sixteenth birthday to call her first-born son Joel. Oh, she knew she wouldn't remember why she'd written it, but it was a comfort to her to write it before her memory of the Kairos was erased.'

'Is that allowed – to make a note before you forget all this?' Joel asked, in surprise.

'You will each be allowed to make yourself a brief note before your sixteenth birthday. Be warned though, it must not give anything away about the Kairos and your visits here. Just something simple; most kids find it helps, as obviously they don't want to leave the Kairos. That's why your memory of this is erased – to minimise the upset and to enable you to get on with your grown-up lives. Incidentally, you do get these memories back when you come here permanently.'

Joel and Peter nodded, incredulously.

'Anyway, why *did* Mum want to call me Joel?'

'Well, when you get back, have a look in Grandad's Bible. Turn to the book of Joel and see what the last line of the last chapter says. That should give you a clue.' Anna, who had sat quietly by while Nathan did most of the talking, added, 'You must remember not to tell anyone about any of this. To do so would not only be a betrayal of trust, but it would result in your immediate expulsion from the Kairos and instant memory erasure.'

'Also, Joel,' Nathan added, 'Peter will reach sixteen a short while before you. Once Peter reaches sixteen, you will not be able to discuss any of this with him, either. Do you both understand this? It's extremely important that you do.'

They nodded, although their minds were in a bit of a whirl.

'Did Grandad write himself a note, Dad?' Joel asked.

'Yes, he was allowed to keep a special memento too, but it's only on loan for a special purpose which is about to be fulfilled, I believe,' Nathan smiled knowingly.

'Oh, can you tell us what that is, Dad?'

'No, it's not my place; that's up to Grandad. You will find out when you deliver Grandma's message to him. This will also confirm that life on earth is not just a pot-luck game of chance. God really does have a plan – and He has a special plan for your lives.'

'I see...' Joel marvelled, wondering what all this meant.

'Tell us about the angels, Mr Asher,' Peter asked. 'Are they all that beautiful – like Charis and Aletheia?'

'Yes Peter, they're all just as beautiful, but they don't all look like Charis and Aletheia,' Nathan explained. 'There are many angels, Peter, and they all have different jobs. Charis and Aletheia look the way they do because they're reception angels – that is, they receive new arrivals. Their role is to put people at ease as soon as they get here. As you can imagine, many new arrivals have suffered one trauma or another and some require several angels to care for them and settle them in. Some people were not prepared for their earthly lives to end but had them cut short abruptly and unexpectedly. Much sensitivity is required and the regular angels are well suited to this work.'

'Regular angels?' Peter asked.

'Oh yes, there are several orders of angels, Peter,' Nathan

went on. 'You will see some of them: seraphs, cherubim and maybe an archangel or two…'

'Cool!' Joel murmured quietly, as he struggled to take it all in.

'This is just mind-blowing, isn't it, Joel?' Peter marvelled.

'Yes, Peter it is,' Nathan continued with a smile. 'Some angels are blessed with a special blessing. These are the ones who have been chosen to serve the Lord in a special way. I don't know if you'll get to see any of these, but you never know...'

'How do you mean, Mr Asher – in what way are they special?' Peter asked, eager to know more.

'Well, Peter, angels are very often God's messengers,' Nathan answered. 'Imagine the privilege of being the angel who informed Mary that she was to conceive the baby Jesus – or the angel who announced His birth! Or, the ones that informed the ladies that the Lord Jesus had risen from the dead, when they saw that the stone had been rolled away from the Lord's tomb, three days after His death!'

'Wow, I see what you mean, Mr Asher,' Peter agreed. 'That would be a pretty awesome responsibility.

'Precisely,' Nathan grinned, 'and a tremendous honour.'

'What happens to ordinary people when they arrive here, Dad?' Joel asked.

'Each one is individual, Joel,' Nathan explained. 'You see, everyone who arrives here has a personal relationship with the Lord and they are all cared for, whatever their need. There are so many different circumstances. For instance, some are victims of war, terrorism or crime – or simply an unexpected accident. Their deaths may have been sudden and violent. On the other hand, some have been ill for a long time and were expecting to come here – some even looking forward to it – they leap for joy to be suddenly free of pain and, of course, some simply die of old age and are overjoyed to meet up with loved ones who are already here.'

'The whole experience of our very short lives on earth is supposed to teach us something. We all face opportunities, challenges and choices. It's our choices that matter and that shape our destiny and these choices are especially important after we come to know the Lord Jesus. Life on earth is temporary – a blink in eternity. The real life is up here – eternal, never-ending. You really want to make sure that you make the right choices. Eternity is a long time to spend in the wrong place. So, the first and most important choice to make, of course, is to accept what Jesus did for us all at the cross and to ask Him to be your Lord and Saviour. Then you know for sure that you'll be spending eternity in the right place – here.'

'Well, it's a good job we said that prayer with Reverend Matthews, then,' said Joel, with relief.

'And you've no idea how happy that made me, Joel, and how awesome was the rejoicing up here as you two were born again,' Nathan smiled happily.

'What else do the angels do, Mr Asher? Do they all have jobs?' Peter asked.

'Well, they all have roles, which are many and varied. Some go down to earth to work among people, making great sacrifices in His name. They tend to work among suffering and needy people. These angels usually look plain, very different from Charis and Aletheia, so that they blend in with ordinary people. You should think twice before you judge the shabby, unshaven old man hanging about the street corner outside a pub. He might be an angel, waiting for the hapless drunk who may fall out of the pub and need help. Of course, all of God's elect people have guardian angels who are assigned to help and protect them – and they are charged with this very serious mission.'

'Do people become angels when they die, Dad?' Joel asked.

'No, son, angels have always been angels and they always will be angels. They are different from us and although they may sometimes take on a human appearance, they're as different from us as we are from plants.'

The boys nodded, open-mouthed, as Nathan continued.

'God sends ambassadors into the world on various missions. The most famous of all was, of course, His own Son, Jesus, who had a life up here before He was sent on His Great Commission to the world. After his earthly ministry, He returned here to Heaven, having won the victory and defeated the devil. John the Baptist was another, along with various saints and prophets through the ages. God arranges divine appointments.'

'So, what's it like here in Heaven, Dad?' Joel asked. 'What do you do?'

'Well, as you can see, we're not dead. Obviously, we're very much alive. Like you I was born again when I was in the world and so, when I died, I came straight up here. There is no fear here. No fear of crime, illness, accidents, loss or death. It's true! God wipes away every tear. We have love, peace and happiness. We get to meet people who've gone before us and find out how perfect God's plan really is. We all have our particular jobs and because God's love is infinite, we live in perfect love. You see, on earth, man's capacity to love is different. Think of someone you really love – Mum, for instance.

That is the kind of love everyone up here has for everyone else. We're all part of the same big family. It's not something that can be described, only experienced.'

The mesmerised boys looked on in wonder, as they listened to Nathan.

'You two will have to wait a long time to find that out for yourselves,' Anna added with a smile. 'There are many earthly experiences awaiting you yet.'

'Quite,' Nathan agreed. Then he rose from his chair and beckoned the boys to follow him, before floating off up the hallway again.

Joel and Peter exchanged astonished glances, then rose from their chairs and followed after him with Anna close behind. They were starting to get used to the floating thing and now found that being weightless was rather fun. Peter nudged Joel lightly in the back and grinned as Joel soared several metres. When he came to a stop, Joel did a roll in mid-air and giggled as Peter spread out his arms and glided upwards like a bird in flight. They both laughed whimsically. Then Peter noticed an archway with a beautiful pale lilac light that seemed to impel him to go through it.

'What's through there, Mr Asher?' Peter asked curiously, as he floated towards it. Then, suddenly, he froze and looked up in astonishment. A huge figure, at least three metres tall, appeared in the entrance, blocking the way. Although this Mighty Man appeared initially intimidating with his arms folded, his face was not threatening at all but gentle, kind even, which seemed to contradict the formidable guard-like stance. Suddenly Nathan appeared like a flash between Peter and the guard, who then vanished inside the archway.

'No, no, no, not that one,' Nathan insisted, barring the way.

'Hey, how did you do that?' Peter cried in astonishment.

'Well, it's easy when you know how, Peter,' Nathan smiled with a shrug. 'Unfortunately there are some things you must not see yet,' he warned.

'Who, or what, was that?' Joel asked, bewildered.

'That was one of the gatekeepers. You must not attempt to enter any of these archways, either of you. You're restricted to this area till it's time for you to go back.'

'What is this area, Dad,' Joel asked inquisitively.

'This is reception – a kind of hospitality area,' Nathan replied.

'You mean like the arrival lounge at airports?' Joel asked.

'Yes,' Nathan replied simply. 'That's basically what it is. Come, I want to show you something. This is one archway you *can* go through, and you will use it frequently while you're in the Kairos.'

They followed Nathan through a turquoise-blue archway. As he glided through it, the area opened up before him as if a room was forming in his path. It reminded the boys of the story of Joshua, when God parted the Jordan river for the Children of Israel.

The same warm, glowing light ebbed all around; the prismatic effect gently swirling and sparkling. It was as if the whole fabric of Heaven was a mass of rainbows, intermingled with twinkling crystal stars.

'Wow, this place is awesome!' Peter whistled.

Joel and Peter looked around, wide-eyed. Nathan came to a halt and turned towards the two boys.

'You like it then?' he grinned.

'Like it? It's amazing!' Joel declared.

'We call this the Vista,' Nathan announced. 'We can see anything we want here, boys. We can play back the past or watch the present in real-time and see what's happening right now in the world. We can even glimpse the potential future, but it can only be potential, because the future hasn't happened yet and it is dependant on people making choices.'

'Wow, that's cool, Dad!' Joel enthused.

'It's brilliant!' Peter agreed. 'Can I see me in ten years from now, Mr Asher?'

'I'm not sure that's a good idea, Peter, and anyway it would only show the *potential* you in ten years' time. It's not good to see your own future. I can tell you though, Peter that you have the potential to become a great veterinary surgeon, if you study hard. Remember though, that anything revealed to you here will be erased from your memory on the eve of your sixteenth birthday,' Nathan warned.

'Can you show us Tamara, Dad?' Joel interrupted, still preoccupied with her welfare.

The boys turned and followed Nathan's gaze, not really knowing what they were supposed to be looking at, as everywhere looked just the same. But, as they watched, a vision of Tamara appeared, almost like a hologram. It was like watching a large screen, but there were no edges to it. Curiously, she wasn't lying in bed at the hospital as they had expected. The view was of Tamara stuck in some sort of vortex-like tunnel. She appeared to be having a bit of a struggle, as though she wasn't sure whether to continue up the tunnel or turn back. She kept looking back, not seeming to know what to do; her lips were mouthing words but no sound came out.

'What's happening to her, Mr Asher?' Peter cried, anxiously.

'It's the life-support machine,' Nathan informed them. 'She's neither one thing or the other at the moment. Technically, she should have died and come through the tunnel and have been here by now but, because the machine is keeping her alive, she cannot make the journey up the tunnel. She'll be in suspended animation until action is taken on earth which is beyond her control. Sadly, this is all too common with people in comas on life-support machines.'

'Poor Tamara,' Joel muttered weakly. 'Isn't there anything you can do, Dad?'

'Oh, don't worry, she doesn't know what's happening. The struggle you see taking place is in her subconscious – rather like in a dream. From up here, there's nothing we can do for people in this situation. People can sometimes be trapped like this for years. Their loved ones refuse to let them go, considering their own loss rather than letting the victim move on.'

'But Tamara won't be stuck like this for long, will she, Dad? Didn't you and Grandma say God had answered our prayers?' Joel asked anxiously.

'Yes, Joel. When you get back, you will be able to free her one way or the other,' Nathan replied.

The two boys stared at him, completely bewildered.

'You can either let the doctors switch off the machine and she will complete the journey up the tunnel, where you know she'll be in good hands,' Nathan explained. 'Or, you can give Grandad the message from Grandma and see what he comes up with. There you go, see – another choice.'

'Dad, you said earlier that God had a mission for us. Can you tell us what this is?' Joel asked, pensively.

'Yes, I'm coming to that, Joel. It's why I've brought you to the Vista,' Nathan answered.

'What – does He want us to convert Presten into a good, caring and sensible person?' Joel said, mockingly. 'There's more chance of Rodney becoming a star racing whippet!'

'It's much more serious than purging a young delinquent, Joel,' Nathan answered, gravely, 'and it's not without some considerable danger. You could choose to decline this great responsibility but, if you did refuse it, your memory of all this would be erased instantly and you would be returned to the world oblivious of having been here.'

'You mean, we'd forget about seeing you?' Joel uttered, horrified.

'That's about the size of it, yes,' Nathan nodded.

'There's no way either of us would turn this down, Dad, however dangerous it might be! Right, Peter?' Joel glanced at Peter for reassurance.

'That's right, Mr Asher. Whatever it is, we want to do it,' Peter replied, determinedly.

'As you wish.' Nathan took a deep breath. 'OK, Joel, I know you were only eight when I died, but do you remember anything about that time?'

'I remember you were working on a very big case. It kept you in the office late most nights. I missed you coming in to say goodnight and reading a bed-time story, like you used to. Mum missed you too… She blamed the accident on your working too hard. She said you must have been very tired and fallen asleep at the wheel.'

'I'm sorry I wasn't there for you, Joel. The case that I was working on was very serious. I was collaborating with the police at Scotland Yard and we were nearing a critical point. We were about to unmask a dangerous criminal and expose details of his evil operations. I had intended making it up to you and Mum. I was planning on taking you away on holiday... but Joel, I didn't fall asleep at the wheel…' Nathan paused and looked at Joel in earnest. '…I was murdered – in cold blood…'

Joel and Peter looked aghast. Joel felt as if he had been suddenly stabbed in the heart.

'Murdered?' Joel and Peter gasped in horrified unison.

CHAPTER NINE

A Great Co - Mission

Every drop of blood seemed to drain from Joel's face; his mouth suddenly became very dry and he went weak at the knees. This couldn't be true, he told himself; how could it be? Why would anyone want to murder his dad? Then, as the grim reality started to sink in, shock turned to rage and he felt the anger rise in his chest as if it would burst. Someone had intentionally killed his dad! He didn't want to believe it; there must be some mistake!

'No! You mean someone deliberately took you away from us?' Joel cried, angrily. 'But how come the police didn't know that?'

'They assumed, like everyone else, that I'd been working too hard and had fallen asleep while driving the car near the river. There was no evidence or apparent motive to suggest otherwise.'

'Who did it, Dad?'

'I know you're upset, Joel.' Nathan murmured gently, trying to comfort him.

'Upset? I'm furious! Who could possibly have wanted to kill you?'

Unable to contain his grief, Joel flopped down on a nearby chair, sinking his head into his hands, but because of his weightlessness he bounced straight up again several metres into the air. There he hovered, still in a sitting position, head buried in his hands.

Peter made as if to follow him up, but Anna tapped his arm.

'I should leave this to Nathan, Peter,' Anna whispered. 'Joel needs to deal with this shock and come to terms with it, in order to carry out his mission.'

'Can you see any clearer up there, son?' Nathan called, then floated up and put an arm around him. 'It's not a sin to be angry, Joel; it's how you deal with your anger that is important. I know it's hard for you, bringing back all that pain and I'm sorry to be the one to do it. But, son, I need you to get past your own grief now, because what's at stake is too important. You see, my murder was just the tip of the iceberg. Your mission is to expose the evil plethora of crime behind it. You must be strong, son, then we can do something about it. It was suggested that someone else should tell you and work with you on this because I'm so personally involved. But, I felt it would be better to tell you myself and this will give us a chance to work together, you know, dad and son, as we might have done in the world had this not happened,' Nathan paused. 'I'm sorry I cracked a joke about seeing clearer up there; it just looked so funny the way you catapulted upwards.'

Joel looked up through tearful eyes.

'It felt funny, too,' he murmured with a weak smile.

'That's better. Let's put a brave face on; we can do this, son,' Nathan declared.

Joel nodded.

The pair floated down to the others. Peter looked at Joel sympathetically. Joel was his best friend and he hated seeing the hurt he was going through.

'All right, mate?' Peter asked, awkwardly.

'Yeah, sure, I'm cool,' Joel replied, with a strained smile.

'That's the spirit,' Nathan said, smiling. 'I can tell you, Joel, that you have the potential to become a great lawyer and barrister. You can make a difference, son; lives can be saved by putting vicious villains behind bars.'

Joel looked at his dad wistfully and swallowed weakly. He felt humbled by the wonderful, idealistic magnanimity of his dad and he decided, there and then, that he wanted to be just like him.

'Alternatively, you would make a half-decent rugby player!' Nathan grinned.

'That's some choice, Dad,' Joel returned the grin.

'Are we in business then, boys?' Nathan asked, seriously.

'You bet we are, Dad!' Joel replied firmly.

'Ready and willing, Mr Asher,' Peter grinned.

Nathan turned to the Vista and images began to appear.

'I've had to scratch around for views that would not be too

upsetting for you guys but would still give you an insight into the gravity of the situation,' Nathan explained.

First they saw kids – teenagers mostly, some younger maybe as young as ten or eleven. These youngsters were evidently sleeping rough on the streets and hanging around street corners, begging. There were obvious signs of alcohol and drug abuse: a shocking vision of poverty, neglect and shameful exploitation.

'These kids are sitting ducks, lads,' Nathan choked. 'Vulnerable, hurting, unloved – the results of a broken and lost world, were corruption and exploitation are the norm.'

The Vista views continued with shots of unsavoury characters prowling around, seeing whom they could devour with their drugs and perverted desires. Joel and Peter looked on, almost too shocked to speak.

The view changed to a dirty room, with two toddlers in a cot. The children were alone, dirty, hungry and visibly distressed. An empty baby bottle lay in the cot. As the scene moved into the next room, the mother lay, stupefied with drugs, unconscious on the floor.

'Switch it off!' Joel cried. 'I can't look at any more, Dad!'

The screen went blank and disappeared.

'Shocking, isn't it?' Nathan agreed. '...and these are the mildest views I could find – so as not to distress you too much...'

'This is pretty hard to stomach, Mr Asher,' Peter said mournfully. 'I certainly wouldn't like to see anything worse. I can't believe that kids live like that.'

'Who's responsible for all this, Dad?' Joel choked.

'This man,' Nathan nodded towards the Vista again.

A large, black car pulled up outside some houses and the Vista took them inside the car. Joel and Peter were overwhelmed with the virtual reality of the situation. It was like they really were actually inside the car, although they knew that they couldn't be; they were just onlookers – invisible to the people they were watching.

A stocky, middle-aged, dark-haired man dressed in a black suit was sitting in the back of this chauffeur-driven saloon.

The man was shouting something down a mobile phone and smoking a big, fat cigar. He opened a black attaché case; it was full of huge wads of money.

'Blood-money, boys,' Nathan sighed. 'From organised crime; causing pain, suffering, misery and even death; exploiting the young and vulnerable. This is what I and others were fighting against, and it's the reason I was killed.'

'Who is this man, Dad?' Joel asked.

'The man I was about to put behind bars for a very long time, son. Joaquin Lilith – Mr Evil himself, an infectious ulcer permeating humanity – police code name: "The Black Mamba."'

'The Dendroaspis Polylepis,' Peter interjected.

'The Dendro... what?' Joel quizzed, bemused.

'The deadliest snake in Africa,' Peter explained. 'Its venom can kill in minutes and it can run faster than most people.'

'Correct, Peter,' Nathan confirmed. 'But this Black Mamba is getting fat sucking the life-blood out of his victims by getting them hooked on illegal drugs and leading them into crime to fund the habit. The police have no idea who he is. He runs one of the largest organised crime rackets in the country, but every time the police get close Lilith slinks away, evading capture and keeping his identity secret, as if he knows every move of the police.'

'How does he get away with it, Dad?' Joel sounded horrified.

'Watch the Vista and it will all become clear to you both,' Nathan replied in a low voice.

They all turned to look into the Vista. A chauffeur alighted from the black car and opened the back passenger door. Lilith stepped out and entered one of the houses through a door held open by a policeman. As the door was shut behind Lilith, the boys recognised where it was immediately – it was blindingly obvious by the number "10" on the door – it was none other than the residence of the Prime Minister!

Both boys gasped in horror.

'Is that where I think it is? Peter asked, stunned.

'Yes, I'm afraid it is, Peter. The Prime Minister of course is oblivious to the unsavoury double life of this criminal he is entertaining. You see, boys, the "Black Mamba," this a kingpin of crime, is a senior officer in the Metropolitan Police Force! The mastermind behind a network of criminals, spreading destruction and misery and at the same time, he is one of the very men entrusted with shaping the country's fight against the festering sore that he is himself perpetrating! Of course he's laughing at the police – he even knows his own police code name – being one of the "top-dogs" at New Scotland Yard he has access to top-secret files *and* the Gold Control Room! Basically, if the law were on to him, he'd be one of the first people to know about it and consequently, he's always able to stay ahead and slither out of sight.'

'So, he just might as well be invisible!' Joel cried in frustration.

'It certainly seems that way,' Nathan replied. 'With a network of villains and gangsters under his control, it's easy to see how he remains incognito.'

There was silence for a moment. Both Joel and Peter wanted to ask the question but it somehow couldn't come out.

'Is – is…' Joel hesitated, not wanting to say the words.

'Is he the one who…?' Peter couldn't say them either.

'Who murdered me?' Nathan said it for them. 'Indirectly, boys – that is, he gave the order. The grim act was carried out by someone you may recognise, Joel.'

As they continued to watch the Vista they saw a mousy-haired man sitting at a desk, typing on a laptop computer.

'Isn't that your old office, Dad?' Joel asked.

'Yes, son,' Nathan nodded.

The view pushed in to the man's face as he looked up. Joel suddenly gasped.

'Dan Sadler!' Joel exclaimed in disbelief.

'Uh huh,' Nathan affirmed, grimly.

'But he was one of your partners in the firm – and one of your best friends – he was at your funeral!'

'A dog will always return to its own vomit' Peter commented.

'A "faux ami," as it turned out, Joel,' Nathan sighed sadly.

'What's he got to do with this crime racket of Lilith's? I don't understand. Why would Dan Sadler want you dead?' Joel cried.

'To stop me – he's with Lilith; they're in cahoots together.' Nathan shrugged. 'Sadler, unfortunately can be bought; he was paid a very large sum to help keep Lilith's identity secret and to keep him out of court. I had been working on this case with Detective John Smith whom you may remember, Joel. He came to the house a few times.'

'He still does. He seems concerned about Mum, and she likes him.' Joel suddenly caught his breath. 'So does Sadler! Mum trusts him! She may be in danger, Dad…'

'No, she's not,' Nathan reassured him calmly. 'Mum is not a threat to Sadler; he won't hurt her, I'm sure of that.'

'Phew, you had me worried for a minute then… but how do you know he wouldn't hurt her?'

'She's no idea of his duplicitous life-style. Like you said, Mum trusts Sadler. She would only be at risk if she knew – or suspected something, but she doesn't,' Nathan answered.

'So, what are we going to do about all this, Dad?'

'Well, son, just before I was killed, Detective John Smith was collaborating with those we called the "squealers."

'Hey?' Peter interjected.

'Informers – crims who tell on each other,' Joel volunteered. 'Isn't that right, Dad?'

'Yes, Joel, in the criminal world they're called grasses and it's considered a heinous offence to "grass" their own.' Nathan nodded. 'They're generally criminals who are involved in crime themselves to a lesser extent. They give inside information to enable the police to catch the bigger fish, in return for leniency for themselves or a cash payout. You may have heard the saying: "Set a thief to catch a thief." Smith has access to a slush fund, privately referred to as "*the squeal deal,*" for this purpose.'

'The day before I was killed,' Nathan continued, 'Smith telephoned me at the office. He was really excited because he believed he was close to discovering the identity of the "Black Mamba"

I mean, this would have been a monumental feather in Smith's cap, so it's hardly surprising he was excited about it. This kind of Detective-work would put him in line for serious promotion. Smith had made a major breakthrough with a squealer who was quite high up in Lilith's camp. The squealer had provided Smith with critical and damning evidence: a case full of audio and video recordings and a computer disc with files, listing names, addresses, dealing venues, import routes, targets, money-laundering details and drug sources. In short, operational details sufficient to blast the rats right out of the sewers and cage the lot.'

'Sadler being the traitorous, king rat!' Joel spat.

'With Lilith, the chief swine!' Peter sneered.

'Caught with their "snouts" firmly in the trough!' Joel added, contemptuously.

'Touché,' Nathan grinned. 'It was to be the coup of all time, flushing out those vermin with one yank of the chain. Of course, at this point, neither Smith nor I knew of Lilith's or Sadler's involvement. In fact, Smith still doesn't know – although he has certain suspicions.' Nathan sighed and shook his head. 'Sadler had listened in to our telephone discussion. He heard Smith arranging to come to my office the following evening, with the case full of evidence. He heard Smith say that he had not, at that point, had a chance to look at this evidence and we planned to go over it together, to consolidate our case which would give Smith one) the green light to swoop on the whole brood of vipers while they were napping in their pits – and two) a huge promotion. It was then that Sadler hatched his evil plot to kill me and rob the evidence, before I discovered the truth.'

The view on the Vista changed to the past; it was Nathan sitting at his desk in his office. The boys watched in silence as Nathan narrated the fateful events.

'This is the night I was killed. Smith came in with a small briefcase that contained the evidence he had just secured. He told me, apologetically, that he had been called to a meeting and had to postpone our session until the following morning and, having said that, he just dropped the case off and left. That divergence saved Smith's life. Had he stayed with me, Sadler would have killed him too. It was late; everyone had left the office for the evening – except for Sadler and myself. I had started to make notes on my laptop when Sadler came into my office, on the pretence of a chat. He knew Smith had left the case containing the evidence and he knew both his and Lilith's names would be in the file.'

The boys watched the Vista intently. They saw Sadler walk behind Nathan, pretending to look out of the window as he talked.

'I had my back to him,' Nathan went on. 'He took a chloroform-soaked handkerchief from his pocket and held it over my face from behind. After a struggle, I passed out. Sadler put a virus on my laptop to destroy any evidence there, and he took the briefcase. Then, he dragged me to the lift and took me down to the basement car park. He drove my car to the bend by the river. He belted me up in the driver's seat, locked me in the car and pushed it into the river. The rest is history.'

Distraught, Joel buried his head in his hands. He shuddered as he realised he had just witnessed his dad's murder. Nathan put his arm around Joel to support him.

'You're the last person I wanted to see that, Joel,' Nathan murmured, emotionally. 'But we need you… I need you to be strong. With your help can we expose these culprits and end their reign of misery, death and destruction.'

'The two-faced rat!' Joel spat angrily, clenching his fists.

'It gets even more bizarre,' Nathan continued. 'Sadler was supposed to take the case straight round to Lilith, but he knew that, along with his name, the names of all the squealers – including the one who provided the evidence – would be on the file. Giving the case to Lilith would have spelt certain death for the squealers. Sadler kept the case himself. Oh, not out of any loyalty or compassion for the squealers, but as insurance for himself! He told Lilith that he had made copies of everything and that he'd made certain arrangements: if anything happened to him, these copies would turn up in places that would make Lilith's hair stand on end. So, Sadler now gets a big fat wodge of untraceable moolah from Lilith, as regular as clockwork; a nice retirement fund for Sadler.'

'The jammy git!' Joel hissed.

'Quite, son,' Nathan grimaced. 'Now though, Lilith is petrified that something might happen to Sadler. If someone else tried to do away with him, or if Sadler simply had an accident, it would spell disaster for Lilith. So, Lilith employs two heavies – vicious, murderous thugs, to watch Sadler round the clock, just to make sure no harm comes to him. They're his own personal bodyguards.'

The two boys stared at Nathan in stunned silence.

'In short, they almost have to chew Sadler's food for him lest he chokes.' Nathan sighed.

'Ha! I bet Sadler can hardly even go to the toilet without these two swamp-brains standing guard! ' Joel observed.

'Oh, and that's not all,' Nathan added. 'Get this, Og and Nog have other orders. Lilith is so furious that Sadler has double-crossed him, he's organised a nice little personal present for him; if anything happens to Lilith, these two thugs have orders to kill Sadler immediately. That's the double-edged sword, lads. Lilith and Sadler are now living on a knife-edge, both scared to the bones that something might happen to either one of them, which would spell curtains for the other. To top it all, boys, Sadler now has all the squealers running scared. Almost the entire criminal fraternity in England wants Sadler dead but, at the same time, they're all terrified of what might happen to them on his demise. They all know he's the insider that can shop them to the law and to Lilith – and it doesn't take Einstein to work out what their fate would be if Lilith knew who the squealers were. Now, Smith is frustrated because not one squealer will go near him – they've all turned into scaredy-cats! It's a right mess, boys – blackmail and double blackmail, bluff and counter-bluff. The end result is that Lilith is still free to continue his nefarious reign of crime unhindered, and the devil is laughing all the way to hell.'

'That's despicable!' Peter cried.

'OK, Dad, how can we help?' Joel asked, determinedly.

'This is an extremely dangerous mission, boys, as I warned you. We can offer you very little actual physical assistance when you're back in the world. We can tell you where something or someone is, and we can predict with reasonable accuracy what they might do. But, we cannot *make* anyone do something or stop them from doing something – it's the "free will" thing. In short, if you get into trouble down there, generally, we cannot intervene. By and large, you're on your own – but not entirely…' Nathan paused.

'Go on, Dad,' Joel urged.

'I can tell you though, that you can always trust the ravens.'

'Ravens?' the boys both repeated, curiously.

'What about the ravens, Mr Asher,' Peter asked enthusiastically.

'Well, Peter, ravens have a special affinity with humans. They're ambassadors for good: brave and sensitive – sometimes too sensitive,' Nathan smiled. 'They're Intelligent too. They'll go forth in reconnaissance; report important detail and warn you of danger; they'll even bring you food if you're hungry; they'll look after you and defend you with their lives. They're also a little cheeky and I must warn you, however, that they can be extremely irritating at times,' he added with a knowing look.

'Oh?' Joel looked at Nathan, eager to know more.

'You'll soon see what I mean,' Nathan replied, with a wry smile.

'Are we going to wake up in a minute and find that this has all been a confusing dream?' Joel asked, incredulously.

'No, Joel, it's all real. People don't usually have the same dream at the same time. When you get back to the world, you'll both find that you can remember every detail.

'Let's cut to the chase, Dad; what are we to do?' Joel asked with conviction.

'Good, glad to see you're still keen,' Nathan responded with a grin. 'Now, somehow, you've got to locate the briefcase that is currently in Sadler's possession and ensure that it – and all of its contents – get to Detective Smith, the original intended recipient. Smith, unfortunately, never got to scrutinise the file; he still doesn't know that Sadler is a duplicitous traitor. You have to get Smith to look at the file and discover Lilith and Sadler's names on the list, otherwise Smith may just give the wretched case straight back to Sadler!' Nathan sighed. 'Yes, I'm afraid that as Sadler has been appointed a barrister for the prosecution, this basically means the evidence would never get to court.'

'I thought you said that Sadler had made several copies of the evidence, Mr Asher?'

'Smart of you, Peter, you're paying attention aren't you,' Nathan grinned and clicked his tongue. 'I said that Sadler *told* Lilith he'd made several copies. But, I can guarantee, boys, that Sadler never bothered – it's just a sword of Damocles he's dangling over Lilith's head! As long as Lilith *thinks* Sadler has several copies, Sadler is safe. These two villains need to be locked up for a very long time. That is why it has got to be done right; we can't afford to make any mistakes. If that evidence is destroyed, our case – excuse the pun, goes out of the window and we can't let that happen; there's too much at stake. These people are perpetrating despicable evil. We don't want them getting away with a short sentence on flimsy, circumstantial evidence – or, worse still, getting off altogether!'

'What? Do you think there's a chance of that, Dad?' Joel asked, concerned.

'Not if we do our jobs right, Joel – not a chance,' Nathan assured him.

'Good,' Joel muttered with relief.

'You don't have to accept this mission, boys.' Nathan looked at Joel and Peter earnestly. 'It would not be held against you at all. In fact, neither of you even have to accept your post in the Kairos; it is entirely your own decision. It would be a shame to lose you though because, as you heard earlier, the last one was twenty-three years ago and it is impossible for anyone over the age of sixteen to be in the Kairos. We hope you will accept. If you two were to join the Kairos, there's so much we could achieve in the next four years.'

'How many children are there in the Kairos?' Joel asked.

'There are one hundred and fifty – no more and no less. As soon as a Kairos child reaches sixteen and has to leave, a new replacement child is already chosen – it just happens that way.'

'So, two kids have just reached sixteen, then?' Peter asked. Nathan hesitated as the boys looked at him expectantly.

'I'm afraid, only one… ' His voice faltered.

'Oh – does that mean that only one of us can join, Dad?' Joel asked, dismayed.

'No, Joel. You're both in,' Anna interjected, as she gently placed a golden hand of support on Nathan's arm. 'I'm afraid one has just been lost.'

'Lost? What do you mean?' Joel asked with concern.

'Thank you, Anna,' Nathan squeezed her hand. 'Fortunately, it doesn't happen often, but as I said earlier, Kairos missions can be very dangerous and it is imperative to keep to the rules,' he explained.

'What happened, Mr Asher?' Peter asked hesitantly.

'A young Kairos member, for honourable reasons but wrongly, tried to intervene in a mission and did not follow the rules. Sadly, she paid for this mistake with her life. She's in Heaven now, but before her time.'

'Oh,' Peter murmured, awkwardly. 'Well, what if we said "no" to the Kairos? You would only have a hundred and forty-eight?'

'That has never happened,' Nathan replied. 'The nature of the children chosen is such that none of them has ever turned down the opportunity to fight for good against evil. If that was a possibility, they would not have been chosen in the first place.'

'Dad, did Mum take on any missions?' Joel asked.

'Yes, son, I'm sure you'll get to hear about some of them –and Grandad's exploits, too.'

'I feel humbled that we've been chosen,' Peter murmured.

'Yes, it's an awesome thing, isn't it?' Nathan smiled. 'Joel,

Peter, we can give you the information you need and the opportunity, that could see Lilith and Sadler placed where they belong – behind bars for a very long time. Many lives would be saved and misery avoided,' Nathan continued, earnestly.

'We wouldn't dream of turning this opportunity down, Mr Asher,' Peter said, determinedly.

'That's right, Dad. Anyway, if the worst came to the worst, at least we know where we'd be coming,' Joel chuckled, a little nervously.

'I knew that's what your answer would be – both of you,' Nathan grinned proudly.

Suddenly, Peter felt a soft nudge in his back and he floated round. It was a beautiful unicorn, about 12 hands high. As the creature stood shimmering like fluorescent silver satin, it almost looked as if it was made of glass. Beautiful rainbow colours reflected all around it and its horn seemed to sprinkle glitter like gold dust. Aletheia, the angel, was sitting on the unicorn's back.

'Hello again,' Aletheia beamed. 'I thought you might like to see your friend. This is Farga – or as you named him, Storm.'

'Storm!' Peter cried in amazement. 'You've grown so much!' He fussed over the unicorn, who had grown from the size of Rodney to the size of Cherokee.

'Farga is going to take you back to the Fugue, when you're ready, in gratitude for all you did to rescue him,' Anna smiled.

'The Fugue?' Peter frowned.

'The Fugue is the tunnel you travelled through to get here,' she explained.

Another shimmering unicorn glided up majestically behind Storm. This one looked almost twice as high as Storm, and Charis was perched high on his back. It was the same unicorn that had come to the plateau in Zionica to bring Storm home. Joel recognised its jagged horn.

'Cheyiea is going to take you, Joel,' Charis smiled down at him.

Joel looked at Cheyiea with some reservation; he'd never ridden an animal before, neither had he ever felt the urge to try. To be truthful, Joel would have been nervous of mounting the much smaller Farga, never mind this enormous animal that towered over all of them – Farga included. Horses just weren't his thing and Grandad's occasional suggestion of purchasing a donkey made Joel cringe. He was glad that Grandad lived a long way away from his school and school friends, who would have found Grandad odd enough, even without a donkey!

'There's nothing to be afraid of, Joel. He's quite safe, you know.' Charis smiled reassuringly, sensing his nervousness.

In an attempt to delay the inevitable unicorn ride as long as possible, Joel turned to his dad, hurriedly changing the subject.

'So, where is this briefcase, Dad? How do you suggest we get it? Sadler is miles away, in the City.'

'We can talk about that when you come back, son. First though, don't you have a friend to save?'

'Tamara!' Joel cried, in sudden panic. 'How long have we been here, Dad?'

'As I told you, time doesn't exist here – this is eternity. You haven't been here any time at all. Now, you should go back and do what you have to do for your friend. Think carefully about the challenges you face – and the risks. Then, when you are absolutely positive about your decision, you must come back and we'll discuss the plan.'

'When shall we come back?' Joel asked.

'As soon as you're ready – the sooner the better. It would be good to get this mission accomplished before you go back to school. The Kairos do not operate during term-time. So you've got one week, but if you do not return here within three earth-days, your memory of all this will be automatically erased and you will live your lives as normal – oblivious to the Kairos.'

'You mean, I'd forget about seeing you and the fact that you were murdered?' Joel asked.

'Yes – everything. Now, off you go. Your rides are waiting.'

Aletheia helped Peter glide up onto Storm's back, where he perched lightly behind her, grinning like a Cheshire cat.

'Wow, this is amazing!' Peter marvelled.

'Joel...' Charis beckoned softly and held out a golden hand. Joel looked up at Charis with trepidation and gave her his hand. As she cupped it in hers, Cheyiea bowed down lowering his shoulder. Charis gave a slight tug and Joel floated up onto Cheyiea's back, behind her.

'I'll be seeing you real soon, Dad,' Joel called, trying to appear undaunted, although he was feeling rather apprehensive about the unicorn ride.

'Yes, I believe you will, son,' Nathan replied.

'Goodbye for now, Anna,' Peter muttered a little awkwardly, unsure of what to call her.

'Yes, Peter love, for now,' Anna beamed happily.

The unicorns began to float up. Joel had expected the ride to be bouncy, but it actually felt as if he was sitting on a bed of feathers. He seemed to be floating round on a very soft carousel, round and round and round...

CHAPTER TEN

Arrival of the Magi

'You'll catch your death of cold, if you're not careful, Joel!' Grandad threw Joel's coat over his shoulders. 'Joel... Joel!'

Joel slowly opened his eyes and did a double-take as he saw Grandad leaning over him.

'I thought you might need your coats,' Grandad mumbled briskly, as he wrapped Peter's coat around him also.

Joel looked around at Peter. The boys were both now sitting on the plateau in Zionica, in a state of stunned bewilderment.

'It's getting a little chilly; I think we're going to have showers all afternoon. Look at you – you're both half-soaked already. You'd better come back to the house and dry out. We don't want colds and chills on top of everything else!'

Joel and Peter clambered to their feet and put their coats on, as Grandad set off in the direction of home.

'Did you just…?' Peter whispered to Joel, but Joel cut him short before he could say anymore.

'Yes – ssh – we'll talk about it later,' Joel whispered back. Then he called after Grandad: 'What time is it, Grandad?'

'It's only just after one o'clock, Joel. There's plenty of time,' he called back.

'But it was nearly one o'clock when we left the house!' Peter whispered to Joel, blinking and rubbing his eyes as if trying to wake himself up. 'That means we've hardly been gone at all…'

Joel shrugged, giving Peter a warning glance and they both hurried after Grandad, back to the house.

'Grandad!' Joel called, running up behind him. 'Grandad, I've got a message for you.'

'A message? What kind of message? From whom?' he replied inquisitively.

'Well, it's probably nothing – it may not mean anything at all really. Grandad, what would you say if I said it's a message from Grandma?' Joel waited hesitantly, expecting Grandad to tell him not to be so silly, but he didn't; he just sighed.

'Did you hear me, Grandad? I said I had a message from Grandma…' Joel persisted.

Grandad stopped walking and turned to face Joel, who returned his gaze, anxiously.

'Joel,' he smiled sympathetically. 'I know this thing with Tamara has got you really upset – and it's made me think more about Grandma too, but don't get things out of perspective, son. You'll feel better after the blessing – then we can all move on.'

'Grandad, I mean it. Grandma said to tell you! She said, "What wasn't right for a sixty-year old woman *is* right for a ten-year-old girl!" She said you had what we needed to make Tamara better, and that you would understand.'

Grandad caught his breath and looked momentarily startled. Then, collecting his thoughts he continued, 'Joel, the doctors have said there is nothing they can do for Tamara now. Hard as this is you must be strong and let go, son,' he replied firmly.

'Please, Grandad you've got to listen to me,' Joel pleaded again. 'What is it that you've got? Whatever it is, Grandma said you must give it to me – it could save Tamara!'

'People do have vivid dreams that appear very real, Joel. Come on back to the house, we'll talk it over with some hot soup to warm you up,' Grandad answered with an encouraging smile.

†

After Joel and Peter had dried out and changed, they sat in the kitchen with mugs of hot soup. Grandad had been sitting waiting for them. On the table in front of him was a small, carved wooden box and next to it lay an old brass key.

'So, the riddle is finally going to be solved, although it still doesn't make much sense,' Grandad remarked mysteriously.

'What riddle, Grandad?'

'This box has been on my dressing table for a long time. You must have seen it there, Joel,' said Grandad.

'Yes, it's been there as long as I can remember. You always

keep it locked, don't you?' Joel replied. 'Not that I've been snooping…' he quickly added, as he remembered the times he had attempted to force the box open when he was younger.
Grandad nodded.

'That's because I've always known that it is important. The trouble is, I don't know why. The contents of the box are a complete mystery. There's a note that I've written to myself, but the strange thing is – I don't for the life of me remember writing it!'

'How weird! What does the note say, Grandad?' Joel asked with intrigue.

Grandad picked up the key. Joel could hardly contain his excitement; he'd been bursting to get that box open for as long as he could remember, and Grandad had always changed the subject whenever he mentioned it. Grandad unlocked the box and pushed it, still closed, over the table to Joel, who looked at it with eager anticipation. Joel carefully opened the lid, as if he expected something to fly out of it. He put in his hand and pulled out a small object, which was wrapped in note-paper. He unfolded the paper and a piece of what looked like dull, grey horn fell out of it, landing in the box. He flattened out the note. Peter leaned over, eager to see what it said.

'There's a heading, it says: *Genuine unicorn horn*.' Joel read.

'What does the rest of it say, Joel,' Peter urged.

'*Marcus*,' Joel began,
'*You won't remember writing this note,
but you're writing it to yourself because
it is important. You must keep this horn
safe and not let it out of your possession,
until a young messenger asks for it.
Then, you must give it up and you'll
know why. God bless*.'

Joel looked up excitedly.

'It's signed "Marcus Jacob!" You're right, Grandad; this is definitely your handwriting – and it's your signature!'

'Just a minute…' Peter cried, 'there's something else in the box, too.' Peter put his hand in the box and pulled out another piece of paper. 'There's something wrapped inside.' He carefully unfolded the paper and the object dropped into the box.

'It's a pin – a gold pin – like a tie pin or something,' Joel said. He picked up the pin and scrutinized it. 'Looks like it's in the shape of some letters – K...'

'No!' Peter interrupted excitedly, taking the pin off Joel. 'One letter and a number – K 87!'

'What does the note say, Peter?' Joel asked.

'It's Psalm eighty-seven...' Peter murmured slowly.

Suddenly, Joel and Peter understood the significance of the pin.

'Hey, that must be...' Peter exclaimed.

But a quick nudge in the ankle from Joel stopped him, just in time, from blurting out the mystery that they were to keep secret.

'Ouch – er – it must be a very valuable pin...' Peter winced, rubbing his ankle.

'Do you remember where you got these things, Grandad?' Joel asked quickly.

'Yes, well, the horn anyway, I think.' Grandad's brow furrowed in thought.

'You do?' Joel and Peter cried together in surprise. They were confused because they had both obviously expected Grandad to answer "no" to this question.

'Hmm, well er, it's all a bit of a blur, really,' Grandad began, rubbing his chin. 'I have vague and very strange recollections – flashbacks I suppose – of how it came into my possession. However, why it's so important, why I wrote the note and what it all means is a complete mystery – except for Grandma's message – that makes sense.'

'Well, how did you come by it, Grandad?' Joel asked with some confusion. 'Surely you didn't kill a unicorn for it?'

'Of course not!' Grandad retorted, with some indignation.

'Sorry, Grandad, that was a stupid question,' Joel muttered, apologetically.

'All right, son,' Grandad paused. 'Remember when we saw that big bright rainbow, the morning Storm arrived?'

The boys both nodded.

'Yeah – you couldn't forget that in a hurry!' Peter replied.

'I told you I'd seen one just like it before, when I was about your age, Joel, but that it had been on a beautiful morning, after a snow storm – most unusual.'

'Yes, Grandad, I remember you saying that,' Joel replied, with intrigue.

'Well, like you, I rushed down to Zionica to look at it. When I got there, I noticed with glee that the pond was completely frozen over and – like most twelve-year-old boys, I couldn't resist the temptation of solid ice. Well, it looked solid when I started sliding about on it. I remember I had such a wonderful time skating about. The sun was shining, there was pure white snow everywhere and Zionica looked like a Christmas card,' Grandad reminisced. 'Then, I must have got too close to the edge of the pond, where the ice was thinner and had begun to melt a little in the sun. Before I knew it, the ice cracked under me and I slipped into the freezing-cold water. It was so cold,' he shuddered as he remembered the feeling, 'that it took my breath away. Then, I found myself trapped under the thick solid ice and I couldn't find a way to break out.'

'How terrifying!' Peter gasped.

'Yes, it was, Peter,' Grandad went on. 'I tried to punch a hole in the ice, but it was like punching a brick wall in slow motion. I was getting very weak and my lungs felt like they were going to burst. Everything turned black – I thought I was going to die!'

'Thank God you didn't! How did you get out, Grandad?' Joel asked, mesmerised by the story.

'Well, the strangest thing happened. Just as I was about to sink into unconsciousness, something, rather like a sharp stick or branch, was suddenly thrust through the ice – right in front of me! There was an explosion of light, the ice all around the stick melted instantly and the water became warm – like a spa. I reached up and grabbed hold of the stick and immediately I felt myself being hauled out of the water! Then, I was dragged a little way from the pond and left, lying on my back on the snow. I felt warm breath blowing into my nose and mouth, and I coughed up some water. The warm breath somehow warmed my whole body and revived me. I opened my eyes and saw what had pulled me out of the water and saved me from certain death.'

'What was it, Grandad?' Joel asked, although he thought he already knew the answer.

'Well, I know this may sound like the crazy ranting of an old man, boys, but – without a shadow of a doubt – it was a unicorn!' Grandad announced, emphatically. 'An enormous powerful, white unicorn, glistening in the sunshine. He was standing over me, his head lowered, his soft muzzle brushing over my face. Then, he swung round swiftly and galloped down onto the plateau. As quickly as he arrived, he vanished. Like a shooting star, he soared up into Heaven in a flash of light.'

'Wow!' Peter exclaimed. 'You actually saw that?'

'Awesome! Are you sure it wasn't a dream, Grandad?' Joel asked.

'Yes, I might have thought I'd become delirious and was hallucinating,' Grandad continued, 'but, when I came to, I opened my fingers and there it was – the evidence that I had not dreamt it at all. This small piece – the tip of his horn – must have broken off as he dragged me along the ground. And I've kept it in this box ever since. That is why I've spent so much time reading and researching about unicorns, and it's how I know they really exist, though not necessarily in this world. As for the pin…' Grandad shrugged, 'I have absolutely no idea where that came from. It was on my bedside table, with the psalm, when I woke up on my sixteenth birthday.'

'Hmm, how odd. So anyway, Grandad, what *did* Grandma mean when she said: "What isn't right for a sixty-year-old woman *is* right for a ten-year-old girl?"' Joel asked, curiously.

'Well, you may remember, Joel, that your grandma became very ill with the cancer.'

'How could I forget?' Joel nodded.

'There was nothing more the doctors could do,' Grandad continued. 'I suggested grinding up the horn to make some sort of potion for her to drink – you know – in case it still had some healing properties. Grandma wouldn't hear of it, of course. She said that the note must have meant something to me when I wrote it and that, one day, the riddle would be solved. She was always a very devout Christian; she said it wouldn't be right for a sixty-year-old woman and that if God called her, she must go. She believed that a young messenger would eventually turn up for the horn – and she was right.'

'So, that's what she meant…' Joel murmured thoughtfully.

Grandad smiled affectionately at Joel. 'In any case,' he continued, 'the idea of physical healing properties in a horn for something like cancer is codswallop – a myth! As with all these other false beliefs – like grinding up sea-horses or extracting bear bile, for instance, untold cruelty is executed around the world. All of this is foolishness, which not only doesn't work but endangers whole species with the threat of extinction! Only Jesus has the power to heal incurable diseases – not a piece of horn or any other object, although, Jesus could *use* a piece of horn, or anything else for that matter, to heal someone .'

'You mean, like Jesus used clay and spit to heal a blind man, Mr Jacob?' Peter asked.

'Yes, that's right, Peter, He did. Anyway, it always bothered me about having to give the horn to a young messenger. How would I know when the right messenger came along? I'm so glad it's you, Joel, and I'm in no doubt now, that this was meant to be, now I realise its importance. How I knew all this, years ago and subsequently wrote the note is still baffling, beyond imagination,' Grandad shrugged. 'I don't know how we are supposed to administer it, though.' He leaned forward, took hold of the box and turned it around. 'It's hardly worth…' he was just about to pick up the horn to examine it when, suddenly, he gasped and froze.

'What is it, Grandad?' Joel asked, alarmed.

Grandad slowly turned the box around, towards Joel and Peter. The boys didn't have to look inside it to see the dazzling light exuding from it. Their eyes almost popped out of their heads as they stared at the contents of the box. There, sitting on the soft velvet lining, was the horn, brilliant and sparkling like a jewel in sunlight. The two boys stared at it, speechless.

'Well!' Grandad gasped in amazement. 'For sure, it didn't look like that when I put it in the box. Then, it was just a dull piece of grey horn!'

'Yeah!' Joel agreed, in astonishment. 'That's what fell out of the note...'

'You must be careful not to touch it, lads,' Grandad warned. 'Whoever touches it next will probably absorb the healing power that I believe is meant for Tamara. Keep it safe, Joel. You have the awesome responsibility of getting it to her.' He quickly locked the box again and pushed it, and the key, over to Joel.

'Mr Jacob,' Peter muttered, hesitantly. 'You said that there were no magical healing properties in the horn itself, but that it is just an instrument used to heal. How do you really think I got healed when I touched Storm and how is Tamara going to get healed, using this piece of horn?'

'Good questions, Peter,' Grandad mused. 'Clearly, the healing power was placed supernaturally into Storm's horn and now, this horn, by the only One who can supernaturally heal, who is of course, the Lord Jesus Christ. This horn broke off a unicorn and was used to save my life about 48 years ago; the answer to the riddle in the box has just now been revealed; which tells us that this was all planned many years ago and that only God could have done this. We know through history that God has used people, animals and all manner of things to accomplish His will. He used a donkey to deliver a message; He used a fish to supply tax money. Therefore, it is not inconceivable that He should use a piece of horn to heal a child – on this occasion.'

'Or a unicorn...' Peter added.

'Or indeed a unicorn, Peter, you're quite right,' Grandad agreed. 'But remember, don't make the mistake of attributing any power to the horn itself – that would be sorcery, which the Bible forbids and it would have dire consequences. I believe that the healing power is supernaturally placed there by God, for His purpose.' Grandad could hardly contain his excitement as he stood up. 'It's almost a quarter to two, lads; we'd better get off to the hospital.'

'Wait a minute…' Joel interrupted. 'We can't just waltz into St David's Hospital and dump this on Tamara's head! Everyone will think we've gone potty!'

'Yes, Mr Jacob,' Peter agreed. 'How *are* we going to explain this?'

'Oh – yes – quite,' Grandad rubbed his chin thoughtfully. 'Now, let's think…'

'If it works in the same way as it did with me and Storm, there will be a blinding flash of light,' Peter volunteered. 'I don't see how we could hide or explain that!'

'No, I see what you mean, Peter; that would cause rather awkward and unwanted questions,' Grandad deliberated.

'Unless...' Joel pondered thoughtfully, 'is there some way we can make it look like a short-circuit? You know, make all the lights flash off and on – as if an electrical surge, or something of that nature?'

'Yes, Mr Jacob,' Peter said. 'You know what hospitals are like; they have just about every light on all day!'

'Yes, they do rather think they have first call on the national grid,' Grandad chuckled. 'I can't think of a better idea, lads,' he answered. 'I suppose I could stand near the door in Tamara's room and create a diversion. As you lean over Tamara, I'll flip the light switch off and on and get everyone's attention, then you can slip the horn into Tamara's hand. It's lame, but hopefully everyone will think it's some sort of electrical power surge.'

'Brilliant, Grandad!' Joel beamed.

'Hey, you're cool, Mr Jacob,' Peter grinned.

Grandad chuckled and almost felt like a boy again as he contemplated the adventure.

'Obviously, boys,' he cleared his throat, 'I would not be advocating such a plan if I didn't firmly believe that it was the right thing to do. We're blessed, boys. For some reason, God has seen fit to deliver another miracle of healing for us. We must give thanks and praise to the Lord!'

The two boys sat in silence, guarding the box with their lives, as Grandad drove them to St David's Hospital. Their heads were filled with a whole range of emotions. They felt happy – because Tamara was going to be healed; special – because they had been chosen for something amazing; apprehensive – about the dangerous challenges ahead – and about keeping the secret. However, their immediate concern was that Grandad's plan would work and the whole "horn thing" be kept a secret.

The responsibilities that now rested on their young shoulders were quite daunting; Tamara's life lay in the balance and they had been instructed to return the horn to its rightful owner – whoever that was... Not to mention the mission they must undertake to bring Lilith and Sadler to justice... and the whole incredible thing had to stay a secret. Despite it all though, Joel was overjoyed about seeing his dad again. Knowing that his dad was alright and that he would be able to see him regularly for the next four years was just amazing. Peter was overcome by the wonder of it all, and especially by meeting his natural mother. Knowing that she had not abandoned him, but had fought to keep him and look after him, soothed all the pain of his early years.

Grandad pulled up in front of the hospital.

'You two get out here and go inside, boys. I'll go and park the car and join you in a few minutes,' he said.

Joel gladly stepped out of the rickety old jeep, holding their precious cargo tightly to his chest, as Grandad set off down the car park to look for a space.

'Huh,' Joel tutted as they reached the steps at the entrance. 'Call that a motor? I wish Grandad would get rid of that embarrassing antique and get a motor we could be seen in!'

'It could be worse, Joel. At least he doesn't drive a donkey and cart!' Peter chuckled, trying to be cheerful.

'Well, keep that thought to yourself, Peter,' Joel replied. 'Grandad may just think that's a good idea!'

'How are we doing for time?' Peter asked anxiously.

Joel tilted his wrist to see his watch.

'It's OK, it's only...' Joel didn't get to finish his sentence. Just as he looked down at his watch something was thrust in front of him, tripping him up. He fell onto the steps and, as he did so, he let go of the all-important box. The box went flying up into the air and landed with a thud at the top of the steps, as Joel landed flat on his face.

'Ha! Told you I'd get you, you righteous creep!' Presten laughed loudly, brandishing the stick he had just thrust in front of Joel. He had been hiding behind a pillar beside the steps. 'What's this – the three wise men bearing gifts? Three dozy donkeys, I say!' Presten sneered. Then, seeing the box at the top of the steps, he ran up and grabbed it. 'Oh, you *are* bearing gifts! Bit small for a casket, ain't it Asher?'

'You miserable scumbag!' Joel snarled and rushed at Presten with clenched fists.

'Peter quickly jumped in and stopped him.

'That won't get us anywhere, Joel. We haven't got time; we need to get inside the hospital,' Peter cried. Then he turned to plead with Presten. 'Presten, please, just give us the box back. You don't want to fight now – not with your sister in there…'

Ignoring Peter's plea, Presten rattled the box. 'Oh, there's something inside,' he sneered, as he tried to open it. 'What can it be? A parting gift, perhaps?'

Joel mentally thanked God that the box was locked.

'Where's the key, Asher?' Presten demanded.

'Give that back!' Joel insisted, ignoring Presten's question.

'Give it back, Presten!' Peter echoed in desperation.

'You really want this, don't you…' Presten sniggered. ''What is it?'

'Look, Presten,' Joel urged. 'I forgive you for tripping me up. Just give us our box and we'll be on our way.'

'YOU forgive ME!' Presten shrieked angrily. 'Well, I'm touched, but you see, I don't need your forgiveness – I'm not sorry. I'm the one who's being wronged here! I'm not allowed to see my own sister before she dies! My father won't speak to me and my best friends have been ordered to keep away from me!'

'Presten, we're really sorry for the way things are going for you,' Joel coaxed, 'but that's nothing to do with us and you can't say you didn't bring it on yourself. Now, just let us have our box back, so we can go inside.'

'Sorry? You're sorry? Well, we are charitable today,' Presten snapped, scornfully. 'I get your forgiveness *and* your sympathy! Why should *you* see her when I can't? You're not even family! Well, let me tell you, you're never gonna see your precious box again. I'm gonna break it open and see for myself what's inside it.' He glared at Joel with a look that was full of hatred. This situation had taken his enmity towards them to new depths. Then Suddenly before they could stop him, Presten, with an uncharacteristic burst of energy, jumped down the flight of steps in a single leap – an astonishing and unexpected action for the rather overweight bully. At the bottom, he turned and stared up at them with intense loathing.

'Hey, Asher – I still got the box – loser!' Presten mocked. With that, he ran off down the car park, right past Grandad who was on his way up.

'What was all that about?' Grandad asked anxiously.

'Grandad – he's got the box!' Joel cried, panic-stricken. 'Presten has taken our box!'

'What are we going to do, Mr Jacob?' Peter cried in anguish. Grandad heaved a great sigh and shook his head.

'I should have expected something like this to happen. Why didn't I keep the box on me till we were safely inside?' Grandad mused, bitterly.

'How could you have known, Grandad? It's not your fault,' Joel said, sympathetically.

'Now, it's twenty past two. The blessing starts in ten minutes and it'll probably take about twenty minutes.' Grandad instructed. 'You two had better get after Presten and try to retrieve the box. I'll go inside and endeavour to delay things for as long as I can, but if you're not back by three o'clock, I don't think we've got a chance of saving her, boys,' he warned.

'Oh, I could roast Presten on a spit for this!' Joel spat,

furiously. 'Come on, Peter, that big lump can't have got very far – I'm surprised he has the energy to run at all after leaping down these steps!'

Grandad entered the hospital, while the two boys set off in the direction that Presten had headed. They ran like fury, searching everywhere for Presten, but the podgy twelve-year-old seemed to have vanished into thin air! After a while they stopped, more to scratch their heads than to catch their breath. Joel, being a keen sportsman, was very fit, and Peter – since his healing also seemed to have boundless energy and strength. Presten however, was a different kettle of fish. Just running down the car park would have been enough to completely exhaust him. Joel and Peter just simply couldn't understand how Presten could give them the slip like that.

This is crazy!' Joel exclaimed. 'There's no way Presten could have got this far!'

'Well, there's nowhere he could have turned off – it's a straight road,' Peter said, baffled.

The two boys were suddenly startled by an unfamiliar voice.

'I wondered when you two slow-coaches would twig that "Porky Pie" couldn't have run this far ahead of you,' the strange voice chirped, humorously.

'Who said that?' Joel looked round in surprise.

'Over here…' said the voice.

They both turned in the direction of the voice but there was no one there.

'Where are you?' Joel demanded. 'Show yourself!'

'You're looking at me,' replied the voice.

'Where are you hiding? All we can see is a bird on a gate,' Joel said, looking in the direction of a large raven. Joel stared at the bird. There was something strangely familiar about it. Then, he saw it cock its head to one side and it appeared to raise an eyebrow. Joel gasped – he'd seen that before – only in very dim light. Now he knew it wasn't his imagination.

'Well, it's not the *gate* you can hear,' the voice drawled with a hint of sarcasm.

'It's the bird!' Peter cried in astonishment.

'I know,' Joel agreed thoughtfully.

'It's you, isn't it?' Peter cried, looking straight at the bird.

'Finally!' the raven answered, gazing upward in mock wonder.

'You can talk?' Peter asked in amazement. 'Joel! This bird can talk!'

'Well, not exactly,' the raven explained confusingly. 'You can hear me speak.'

'But, if we can hear you speak, that means you're talking, right?' Peter asked, puzzled.

'Wrong,' the raven continued. 'If I could talk, then everyone would be able to hear and not everyone can hear.'

'Oh,' Peter said, frowning with bemusement.

'Peter,' Joel interrupted. 'Do you remember what my dad said – about the ravens?'

'Oh yes,' Peter said excitedly. 'He said we can always trust the ravens. Joel – this is totally amazing!'

'Well, who are you? And how come *we* can hear you?' Joel asked, curiously.

'Name is Magee,' announced the raven with an air of importance, almost as if he felt they should recognise the name.

'And…' Joel urged.

'I am one of those whom you have already seen,' Magee explained, without explaining anything.

The two boys frowned in confusion.

'Like Charis and Aletheia,' Magee added.

'Oh, you mean you welcome new arrivals, too?' Peter asked innocently.

'Don't be daft!' mocked another raven, as she landed on the gate next to Magee. 'They wouldn't put an angel with his attitude problem in the arrivals job; he'd scare everyone to death – that is, if they weren't dead already…'

'What do you mean – his attitude?' There's nothing wrong with my attitude!' Magee protested haughtily.

'Oh no?' the second raven continued. 'How about

argumentative, sarcastic, pedantic, sorely lacking in tact…'

'Argumentative? Sarcastic? Lacking in tact? My feathers!' Magee reeled, indignantly.

'…and grouchy!' the second raven added.

Magee drew a sharp intake of breath at that last accusation.

'Huh!' he huffed and threw his mate a particularly injured glance. 'The only reason we haven't done reception work, is that we've been seconded onto other important tasks.'

'Excuse me interrupting you two,' Joel cut in, scratching his rather bemused head, 'but what's this all about?'

'Oh, I do apologise for my friend. This is Maggi,' Magee explained. 'She can be a bit of a miserable old trout, but her heart is in the right place.'

'Miserable old trout!' Maggi cawed indignantly. 'Well, of all the…'

'They call us jointly, "The Magi." We have been given the task...'

'Volunteered!' Maggi butted in.

'Yes, all right, Maggi is quite right. We volunteered for the job,' Magee confirmed.

'Job? What job?' Peter frowned.

'Well, the job of protecting you two, of course!' Magee replied, preening himself.

'Oh, of course,' Peter said, with a smile.

'Protecting us!' Joel laughed. 'Well, I hope we don't need protecting when you two are having one of your arguments!'

'There's no need to make fun of us – we are here to help, you know,' Magee retorted indignantly. 'And we've only been ravens this time for a few days. We're still getting used to these bodies.'

'Yes,' Maggi chipped in. 'We've swapped one set of wings for another, again. It's like learning to fly all over again – but with gravity to contend with, you know.'

'Yes, I – I'm sure it can't be easy,' Peter sympathised.

'Anyway, you'll be glad of us when you're trapped in some dungeon and you need someone to come and give you something to eat,' Magee continued haughtily.

'Or – perhaps a key…' Maggi added, comically. 'Really Magee, sometimes I'm sure you think we're still living in the fifteenth century. They don't have dungeons anymore! As to whether these two young boys could end up in one – I ask you!' The raven shook her head in mock despair.

'I'm only trying to illustrate the point, my dear, that they might be very glad of us one day,' Magee insisted.

'I'm sorry, I didn't mean to poke fun at you,' Joel apologised. 'Please continue.'

'Right, well, as angels charged with the responsibility to watch over and protect you,' Magee pontificated, 'it is now our sole purpose...'

'And our duty!' Maggi interrupted again.

Magee shot a stern glance at Maggi. 'Have you finished?' he muttered. Then, turning dryly back to the boys, 'As I was saying – before I was interrupted – it is our purpose, yes and our duty,' Magee threw Maggi a sideways condescending glance, 'to keep you two out of trouble and harm's way. You see, unlike humans who pass on the sin nature, inherently as they reproduce, we are all individually created – not born. So, with free-will, we choose to do God's will, unquestioningly; rather like soldiers following orders in an army, because we love and adore God.'

'Well, there was one…' Maggi muttered quietly.

'Oh yes, the evil one, Lucifer as was – now renamed Satan – the chief devil who started the rebellion and introduced sin to man.' Magee shuddered. 'We don't like to talk about him. Anyway,' he quickly changed the subject, 'we also have every raven at our disposal.'

'Wow!' Peter said. 'Does that mean you could summon every raven to come here?'

'Technically speaking, yes, but that would be a terrible waste of resources,' answered Magee.

'It would also spook the locals and they would probably start shooting at us,' Maggi added, with a frown.

'Yes, quite… not a good idea,' Magee chirped. 'It's best for us to keep a low profile…'

'Magee, you're waffling...' Maggi interrupted again.

'Have you forgotten why we're here?' she nudged Magee.

'Why we're here? Oh, yes of course – well, it's you who keeps interrupting!' Magee retorted.

'Me? It's you who has delayed it all – we could have told them where the fat boy was hiding, ages ago!' Maggi retorted sulkily.

'You mean, we've been standing here, listening to you two arguing with each other, when all along you've known where Presten is?' Joel snapped, as he realized that precious minutes were needlessly ebbing away.

'Yes, see – I told you, Magee!' Maggi cawed, smugly. 'Now, come on, tell them.'

'There's no need to panic,' Magee crooned, dismissively.

'No need to panic! Don't you know that our friend is about to have her life-support cut off?' Joel shouted angrily. 'I demand that you tell us where he is NOW!'

'Oh, all right,' Magee twittered. 'If you'd taken a bit more time in your search, instead of hastily running off, you'd probably have found him yourselves by now, anyway.'

'Magee!' Maggi cawed sharply. 'You can be so annoying!'

'OK, keep your feathers on,' Magee twittered on. 'If you'd looked properly in the bus shelter outside the hospital, you could have saved yourselves this silly marathon. The boy you seek was hiding under the seat when you hastily ran past with a cursory glance inside. Now though, he's sitting on the bench trying to prise your box open, with a penknife.'

'Oh, you stupid pair of twits!' Joel thundered. 'Now I can see why they call bird talk, twittering! Come on, Peter, let's get back before Presten succeeds!'

'Well, really!' Maggi exclaimed indignantly.

'Oh, he won't do that,' Magee uttered nonchalantly.

'How can you say that?' Joel demanded, in exasperation.

'Well, we can't interfere with human free-will. So we cannot stop the boy from trying to open the box,' Magee explained. 'However, we can affect inanimate objects. He could try until doomsday and still never get that box open. I should hurry back though, if I were you, or the blessing will be finished and you'll be too late.'

Joel and Peter glared at Magee in utter disbelief.

'And you two call yourselves angels!' Joel shook his head. With that, the two bewildered boys set off back to the bus shelter at a fast sprint.

Maggi and Magee exchanged glances.

'He called us twits!' Maggi observed, indignantly.

'I know,' Magee replied. 'Nevertheless, do you suppose we should go and assist?'

'I think we should, Magee.' Maggi agreed.

With that, the pair of ravens flew after the boys.

When Peter and Joel arrived back at the bus shelter, Presten was indeed, still sitting on the bench trying to prise open their box.

'What do you two nerds want?' Presten sneered.

'You know what we want, Presten. Give me that box, now!' Joel demanded.

'Get lost!' Presten snapped, rudely.

'Presten, you'd give that back if you knew what was good for you!' Peter added, a little shakily.

'Or what, Jordan?' What are you gonna do about it?' Presten replied defiantly.

Just then, Maggi and Magee landed on the roof of the bus shelter.

'Magee, how about some of those resources you mentioned?' Joel called to the raven in desperation.

'Who are you talking to now, you soft divvy?' snarled Presten, curling his lip in an ugly smirk.

'No one you know, Presten,' Joel replied, tersly.

'There's no one there!' Presten sneered. 'You surely can't think I'm dumb enough to fall for that false back-up ploy we've seen in hundreds of films, Asher?'

Suddenly, another raven landed on the bus shelter roof, followed by another and yet another. Soon, there were scores of ravens all over the bus shelter, on the ground in front of it, inside it, on the seat near Presten and around Joel and Peter. Before Presten knew what was happening, he was completely surrounded by ravens.

'W – What's going on?' Presten shrieked, suddenly panicking. 'Get these mangy vermin away from me!'

'Give us the box, Presten!' Peter demanded.

'Get out!' Presten screamed, cowering from the ravens.

Joel began to walk slowly into the bus shelter and the ravens parted in front of him, making a pathway to Presten.

'What the heck?' Presten yelled. 'Get away from me – you freak!'

'Give, Presten!' Joel held out his hand for the box.

Without warning, Magee flew into the bus shelter and squawked loudly in Presten's face. Presten, scared witless, threw the box at Joel and crouched down on the ground, covering his head with his hands.

'Agh! Get off me! Go away! Go away!' Presten cried. He was completely terrified.

As soon as Joel caught the box, the ravens flew off in all directions, leaving only Maggi and Magee on the bus shelter roof.

'Thanks, Magi,' Joel grinned up at the birds.

'You're welcome,' came the twofold reply.

'Uh oh,' Maggi nudged Magee, and looked upwards to the sky.

Magee followed her gaze and gulped, hard.

'Just when we thought it was safe to come out of the woods…' Magee murmured and hung his head in a resigned shrug.

'You've done it now, Magee. How are we ever going to get promoted now?' Maggi chastised him. 'You're always getting us into trouble.'

'What is it?' Joel asked, puzzled, following the birds' gaze.

'Look, Joel!' Peter cried, pointing to the sky. 'It's a shooting star!'

Joel and Peter watched the bright light as it traversed the sky, seemingly making a direct path towards them. Judging by the ravens' reaction to it, this evidently heralded impending doom.

'There's nothing there, you morons,' Presten sneered, as he

scrambled to his feet and crawled out of the bus shelter.

'It's not a shooting star,' Magee shrugged despondently. 'We know *exactly* what – or rather who, that is.'

Joel and Peter looked somewhat confused.

'It's Maguff,' Magee said gloomily.

'Who's Maguff?' asked Joel, hardly able to take in all that had happened so far.

'He's our "Super,"' Maggi explained. 'Maguff is the angel in charge of all of us earth-bound-guardians. There's no need to worry though, it's us he'll be mad at – not you two. Oh, and by the way, the fat boy can't hear any of us – or even see Maguff.'

'Who are you talking to now, Asher – your invisible friend?' Presten mocked, scathingly. He was still clearly shaken from the ordeal with the ravens, but was unable to hear the birds' side of the conversation. 'You've got what you wanted. Now clear off, you crazy crackpots! It's your fault my sister is going to die. She should have been at home, not with you two weirdoes.' With that, he pushed past Joel and Peter and ran off down the road.

Joel, Peter and the two ravens watched with trepidation, as the star-like light arrived overhead and drifted down to their level, where it hovered for a few seconds. Then, all of a sudden, it exploded like a firework, bursting with hundreds of starry sparks, which then amazingly merged, transforming into a very large and magnificent golden eagle, throbbing with glowing light. The eagle glared at Magee, tutted patronizingly, shook its head, then turned to Joel and Peter.

'Maguff, at your service.' Maguff spoke with authority and gave a noble bow. 'I'm the senior angel in charge of the Magi. Ordinarily, I only get involved in matters requiring urgent management action – or – as in this case…' Maguff threw Magee a displeased glance, '…matters of a disciplinary nature.'

The starchy eagle began to pace up and down with the air of a Major General addressing the troops, while Magee's neck appeared to stretch considerably, which made the poor raven's weak, nervous gulps sound even louder. Meanwhile, Maggi hid her face under a wing, occasionally peering out, forlornly.

'What were you thinking of, Magee?' Maguff launched at the defenceless raven. 'Summoning *every* raven in the vicinity! Of all the irresponsible, cockeyed, dumb stunts! What were you trying to achieve – mass target practice for the locals? Or, were you simply showing off?' the eagle's eyes narrowed as he stared accusingly at Magee. 'I can have all your power revoked, you know, Magee. How would the pair of you like to spend the next five hundred years as sewer rats?'

Maggi looked up and gasped. 'Maguff – I – I'm sure Magee sorely regrets…' Maggi began to wail.

'It wasn't Magee's fault, Maguff,' Joel interrupted, coming to the raven's defence. 'It was me! I insisted on the ravens being called here; Magee had no choice.'

'One always has a choice, Magee,' Maguff retorted, with authority.

Magee hung his head dejectedly.

'Maguff,' Joel intervened, 'don't be too hard on Magee. He was just trying to help. Our friend is about to have her life-support cut off; Magee had to act quickly – we all make mistakes, don't we, unless you can claim otherwise, regarding yourself?'

'Oh, well, erm,' Maguff stopped pacing and cleared his throat. 'I suppose this is a very unusual case.' He turned back to Magee with sudden, unexpected compassion. 'All right, Magee, as your charge has spoken up for you, I'll take his plea for mitigation into consideration and overlook the misdemeanour on this occasion.'

Maggi sighed so hard she almost fell off the roof.

'But!' Maguff added. 'Please, be more sensible in future, Magee; one more dumb, risky incident and I'm afraid I'll have to have your wings – both of you.' He flashed a glance at Maggi.

Maggi squeaked faintly.

'Yes, thank you, Maguff,' Magee humbly nodded

'Well, what are you standing there for?' Maguff boomed at Joel and Peter. 'It's almost three o'clock! Hadn't you better get yourselves down to that hospital P.D.Q.? You've got a life to save!'

'Yes, we certainly do! Thanks, Maguff,' Joel grinned,

clutching the box. 'Come on, Peter. Let's hope and pray that we're in time!'

The two boys swiftly set off in the direction of the hospital.

CHAPTER ELEVEN

A Blessing and the Gauntlet

One by one, Tamara's close friends and relatives said their goodbyes with kisses and tears. Reverend Matthews had just finished the blessing service at her bedside and the doctor was in attendance, ready to switch off the life-support machine.

However, two very close friends were absent – Joel and Peter had failed to turn up for their last goodbye. Grandad kept looking at his watch throughout the proceedings and then, in a final attempt to stall the switch-off, he asked if he could say a private prayer at Tamara's bedside. He was kneeling at her side, praying for the boys to turn up with the box while the doctor's hand hovered over the switch, when suddenly…

'Wait!' Joel shouted, as he and Peter came bursting breathlessly through the door.

Everyone looked round in surprise.

'Praise God!' Grandad muttered with relief, as he saw the box clutched in Joel's hand.

'W – we haven't said goodbye,' Joel blurted out, anxiously. The doctor lowered his hand.

'Alright, boys,' agreed the doctor. 'Two minutes; I'm sorry but I have other patients waiting for me. You really should have been here half an hour ago.'

'Thank you, doctor – sorry,' Joel breathed a sigh of relief while mentally praising God that they weren't too late, after all. Grandad stood up as Joel and Peter approached Tamara's bedside. 'You cut that fine, Joel, lad,' he murmured quietly, as he moved to the doorway where the light switch was.
Grandad winked as he and Joel exchanged glances.

'Bright in here, isn't it,' he remarked, flicking the light switch. As Grandad did this, Joel stood over Tamara and flipped open the box. As the brilliant light from the horn flooded the room, he quickly tipped the horn into the palm of her hand closing her fingers over it, whilst Grandad diverted everyone's attention, gasping and clutching at his chest. Immediately, everyone turned their attention from Tamara to him.

'Mr Jacob!' Mrs Goodchild shrieked. 'Doctor – quick – I think he's had an electric shock!'

'Or a heart attack!' added Mr Goodchild.

The blinding light pulsated for a few seconds, then the room returned to normal daylight. Everyone crowded around Grandad, except Joel and Peter who were grinning from ear to ear at Tamara, who was sitting up in bed looking rather confused at the commotion.

'Where am I? Eoow – Mum! Where did this vile dress come from? Where are my jeans?' Tamara cried. 'What's the matter with Mr Jacob?'

There was a sudden stunned silence, as everyone in the room turned to look in astonishment at Tamara. Grandad meanwhile, seemed to make an astonishingly speedy recovery.

'Tamara!' cried Mrs Goodchild, rushing over and hugging her so tightly that Tamara had to plead for air.

The horn, having now turned dull and grey again, fell out of Tamara's hand onto the bed. Joel discreetly retrieved it and replaced it in the box, turning the key firmly.

'Well, this truly is a blessing!' Reverend Matthews announced, exchanging delighted glances with Joel and Peter. 'Praise the Lord!'

'Amen, vicar!' Mr Goodchild exclaimed, shaking Matthews so vigorously by the hand that the Reverend almost felt as if his arm might be disjointed.

It then seemed as if everyone started talking at once, with claims of a second miracle in one week. Grandad and the two boys did their best to play down the *miracle* theme. The last thing they wanted was a crowd of reporters sniffing around.

Joel and Peter started showing Tamara all the cards and presents she'd been sent. She was horrified to find out how close she'd been to "handing in her riding boots," and declared that she couldn't wait to get back on Cherokee and have a good gallop. Then she announced that she was absolutely starving and begged for a plate of chips with tomato sauce, which the bewildered hospital staff were only too pleased to rustle up.

'So, what's been happening then?' Tamara asked Joel and Peter. 'I bet I've missed loads of exciting stuff?'

Joel and Peter exchanged knowing glances.

'What? In this village?' Joel shrugged. 'There's been nothing happening here, has there, Peter?'

'Oh, huh – here?' he answered. 'That's a laugh…'

'Yeah, I suppose that was a silly question,' Tamara chuckled. 'I mean, what could possibly happen in this sleepy old place?'

'The boys have spent most of their waking hours here, Tamara love,' Mrs Goodchild explained, unable to contain her excitement. 'They've been trying to wake you up with wonderful stories about unicorns...'

'Unicorns!' Tamara interrupted. 'How is Storm?'

Grandad gave the boys a warning glance.

'Oh, you know what Peter is like – always making up these fantasy stories,' Joel forced a laugh.

'The foal is perfectly well now, Tamara love,' Grandad said, reassuringly. 'He was collected yesterday and is now safe and well in his rightful home.'

'Oh,' Tamara sounded a little disappointed. 'Well, I'm glad he is well anyway. Has he gone far – will I see him again?'

'He has gone quite far, Tamara. Whether we will see him again or not is quite imponderable,' Grandad murmured.

†

The doctor wanted to keep Tamara in the hospital for a couple of days for tests, but she refused point-blank. She'd already missed half of the Easter holidays and wasn't going to be detained a minute longer than absolutely necessary.

'I was nearly dead but now I'm as alive as ever; you can't keep me a prisoner in here any longer. I want to get out and start living!' Tamara insisted.

'Well, we can't argue with that, darling,' Mrs Goodchild

agreed, beaming from ear to ear. She was so thrilled to have her darling daughter back, that she'd have agreed to just about anything.

'It's great to have you back, Tamara,' Joel grinned at the feisty ten-year-old.

Everyone nodded in agreement.

The doctor insisted on giving Grandad a full examination before he left the hospital, and then called out the electricians to check the lights. Grandad felt really guilty; it was such a waste of everyone's time when there was nothing really wrong with him or the lights at all. However, he reckoned it was a small price to pay to see Tamara up and well again.

†

That evening, after a good meal, Joel and Peter collapsed in exhaustion on the couch in Grandad's lounge, while Grandad flopped into his rocking chair. They'd all missed a lot of sleep over the past few days and the strain was catching up with them. Now that relief had come, all they wanted to do was sleep.

Joel picked up Grandad's Bible from the table by his chair and turned to the last page of the book of Joel. He smiled at Peter as they both read the last line. Then, he placed it back on the table.

'You were really cool today, Grandad,' Joel murmured proudly, unable to stifle a yawn.

'Yeah, you're the best, Mr Jacob,' Peter agreed, catching the yawn.

His feeling of relief was so immense that words could not express that Grandad just gave them a satisfied but humble smile. The boys finally crawled into their pyjamas and into their beds, and were fast asleep a moment later.

†

At daybreak, the familiar call from Cedric awakened Joel and Peter. They had a comfortable feeling that all was well. Tamara was better, Storm had been safely returned and life was back to relative normality – except that life would never be "normal" again, as far as Joel and Peter were concerned, at least not until they were sixteen.

'Are you awake, Peter?' Joel whispered, propping himself up on his pillows.

'Unfortunately I am now,' Peter yawned, sitting up.

'I was just slowly coming round to the idea that it was all over' Joel mused, thoughtfully. 'Then I realised – it's far from over, isn't it, Peter? It's only just beginning,'

'It really happened then – I mean, your dad and everything?' Peter replied.

'Well, astonishing as it all is, if we'd any thoughts that maybe we dreamt the whole thing, I think they have been well and truly bashed on the bonce by those quarrelling Magi yesterday. We couldn't possibly have both dreamt them up as well!' Joel chuckled.

'Hey, they were something, weren't they?' Peter giggled. Then, suddenly serious, he asked, 'So, what do you think we should do, Joel?'

'You mean, shall we take on the mission or forget the whole thing?'

'Yeah, what do you want to do, Joel?'

'Put it this way, Peter. I'd not seen my dad for four years. If I've got the chance of seeing him again, even if it's only until I'm sixteen, I'm going to take it. I don't care how dangerous this mission is. I'm not a kid anymore; I'll be a teenager this Summer. My dad has work for me to do; he's counting on me and I'm not going to let him down. Whatever it takes, I'm going to do it,' Joel declared with determination. 'What do you say, Peter?'

'You don't think I'd let my best mate face all that danger and excitement without me, do you? Of course I'm going to do it! I'm right there with you, pal, every step of the way,' Peter agreed, with conviction.

'But, what do we tell Tamara?' Joel asked, with concern. 'She's going to want to come up to Zionica with us. We don't want it to look like we're leaving her out, do we? But, there'll be times when we'll need to be on our own, to discuss and plan things; how can we do that without hurting her feelings?'

'I know, especially after what she's been through,' Peter sighed. 'Remember though, what your dad said about time up there; it felt like we'd been up there for hours, but when we got back we found we'd only been gone a few minutes!'

'Yes, and that was only because we watched some real-time stuff on the Vista,' Joel added.

'I'm sure we'll work something out, Joel. Don't forget, Tamara spends a lot of time with the pony,' Peter pointed out.

'Yes, Peter, I suppose you're right. We'll just have to play it by ear for a while. Talking about the pony, let's get up and wrestle that manic cockerel for some eggs. If my hunch is right, someone will be turning up for Cherokee any time now...'

'Your grandad will miss the pony; he's developed quite a fondness for her.'

'Grandad gets fond of anything with four legs and a tail. You know what he's like – soft as mush.'

†

Sure enough, before they'd finished their breakfast, the feisty Tamara arrived, full of beans. She joined them at the breakfast table and pinched some of their toast soldiers, dipping them into the boys' eggs.

'What are we going to do today? Have you made plans?' Tamara inquired, eagerly.

'No, er, we – er thought you'd want to take Cherokee out for a ride. We didn't think you'd want to bother with us until you'd told her how much you'd missed her at least a hundred times,' Joel teased.

'Very funny, Joel,' Tamara replied, with a raised eyebrow. 'We can spend the rest of the day in Zionica – after my ride, can't we?'

'Yes, great idea, Tamara,' Joel agreed. 'You can spend the

morning with Cherokee and we'll do stuff this afternoon.'

'You're not trying to get rid of me, are you, Joel?' Tamara asked suspiciously.

'Of course not!' Joel exclaimed. 'You go and enjoy yourself, Tamara.'

'OK then, this afternoon you can tell me all about Storm and who came for him. See you later.' With that Tamara jumped up and went outside.

'Good. That will give us a chance to go back to Dad and find out exactly what the plan is,' Joel said excitedly to Peter. The two boys packed some food to leave in the tree den for lunch, then they made their way to Zionica.

'We can't delay this any longer, Peter,' muttered Joel, seriously.

'Yes, I agree. I wonder if we'll have to wait for rain and a rainbow every time we go up?' Peter mused curiously.

'That could be a little inconvenient to say the least,' Joel replied, anxiously. 'Dad said if we didn't return within three days, our memories would be erased. I'm not risking that happening. The sooner we go the better.'

'I guess there's only one thing for it then, Joel,' Peter nodded a little nervously.

The two boys left their things in the den then made their way to the plateau. They stood at the edge and glanced at each other hesitantly. Then, trembling with excitement, they gripped hands and stepped onto the plateau together.

CHAPTER TWELVE

A Beautiful Spanish Mentor

Unexpectedly, they didn't have to wait at all. The second their feet hit the plateau, Joel and Peter were scooped up by the light, which carried them through the Fugue tunnel, just as before. They could see the bright light at the top and, before they knew it, they were looking up into the beautiful smiles of Charis and Aletheia.

'Hello again, boys,' Charis beamed. 'We were expecting you, and so are Nathan and Anna. We're all so glad you decided to join us.'

Charis and Aletheia took the boys' hands and helped them up.

'Thanks, Charis,' Joel grinned happily. Then, turning round, he saw Nathan and Anna waiting for them. 'Dad!' he cried.

'Welcome back, boys,' Nathan greeted them delightedly.

'We knew you'd come,' Anna beamed.

'What *is* that?' Peter asked, looking round in amazement. 'I remember beautiful singing last time we were here, but this is something else!'

Peter was referring to the myriad of angels floating and swooping around; they all seemed so excited and were singing with exquisitely sweet voices and calling to each other. They were beautiful, elegant beings, all between two and three metres tall. They each had six white wings: one small pair covered their glowing faces, another small pair covered their feet and a larger pair was used for flying. Soft light ebbed all around them, and they carried gold and crystal sceptres.

'Oh, that's the seraphs,' Nathan explained. 'They're celebrating. Every time there's a new Kairos member confirmed, they rejoice and sing like that. It's such a joy when one such child is found, but on this occasion we've got two together! That's a first for us here in the Zionica zone and good reason to celebrate.'

'We are really happy to be here, Dad,' said Joel, emotionally.

'And your friend, Tamara, is perky as ever, I believe?' Nathan smiled broadly.

'Yes, everything fell into place and it all made perfect sense,' Joel replied, gratefully. 'It was a bit scary though, when Presten stole the box,' he added.

'Hmm, the Magi helped you, did they not?' Nathan asked, with a knowing smile.

'The Magi!' Joel whistled. 'Those quarrelling ravens are a little testing, to say the least!'

'Oh, I see, they were on top-form, as usual?' Nathan grinned.

'Top-form! You mean, that's a regular double act?' Joel frowned, a little exasperated as he remembered the ravens' idiotic arguments, while Tamara's life lay in the balance!

'I'm afraid so, Joel.' Nathan nodded. 'They've been together for a very long time – thousands of years; in fact they're rarely apart and even then, only for very short periods – "joined at the wing" you might say.'

'But you can trust them with your lives,' Anna came to the ravens' defence. 'They would protect you at all costs.'

'Yes, they did come through in the end, Joel, didn't they?' Peter added.

'That they did, good-style – and you did warn us about them, Dad,' Joel nodded. 'Oh, that reminds me, I've got something I need to return, with grateful thanks.' He took the small piece of unicorn horn from his pocket and opened his hand; the horn was now glistening like a precious jewel.

Cheyiea appeared instantly next to Joel, and bent his head down, nudging him. Joel was startled at first but then noticed the jagged edge of Cheyiea's horn. This reminded him that, not only had the unicorn's horn been used to save Tamara's life but it had also been used to save Grandad's life at the age of twelve! Without it, Mum, and Joel himself, would not even have been born! With heartfelt thanks, he replaced the small piece at the end of the unicorn's jagged horn, where it belonged. Immediately, the small piece melted into the horn, making it like new, as if it had never broken off in the first place. Cheyiea nodded his head and his horn shone and glistened like crystal.

'There you go, Cheyiea, as good as new!' Joel grinned. 'You've had to wait a long time for that, haven't you? We're all so grateful to you. We really can't thank you enough!'

Cheyiea blinked and shook his head. Then the unicorn looked up, as if pointing up high, and floated off.

'Cheyiea is directing the glory to God. Just remember, boys, it was the healing power of Jesus that healed Tamara, not the horn itself. The horn was just a tool. It was the same with you also, Peter,' Nathan explained.

'Of course we knew that, Dad, didn't we Peter…' Joel gently nudged Peter.

'Yeah – sure –' Peter nodded. 'Like when Jesus mixed mud with His saliva to heal blind Bartemaus.'

'That's right, Peter. I'm glad you've been studying your Bible,' Nathan replied. 'God has a plan, boys, and it's all based on the work of Jesus Christ at the cross, don't forget that. Without the cross there is no healing – Jesus bore all infirmities at the cross, as well as all the sins of the world.'

'Yes, Dad, we won't forget. So, what happens now?' Joel asked eagerly.

'Come, follow me,' Nathan beckoned. 'Blessed is He,' he smiled at the two reception angels as he led the boys away.

'Blessed is He,' the two angels cried in unison.'

†

Joel and Peter floated after Nathan, while Anna again followed. They continued up the Hall of Archways to the Welcome Room 159, with the pearl-and-gold chairs. Here, the four of them sat down together.

'Now,' Nathan began, 'for every job you first need some basic training, and boys – you're in the army now! You need to know what you're up against and the resources that are available to you, to carry out your missions. So, to ease you into the roles you've been chosen for, who better to show you the ropes than an experienced old-hand? Boys, meet Maria Teresa – or Maité, as she likes to be called.'

Suddenly a beautiful, young Spanish girl emerged from one of the archways off the welcome room and she floated up to them confidently. Her face lit up as she flashed a smile, her dark compassionate eyes framed by her silky black hair.

'Maité, this is Joel and Peter,' Nathan introduced them. 'Maité is from the Spanish arm of the Kairos based at Morisco, where they have several members. She has very kindly offered to help us with your training, as there are currently no other British Kairos members. She is very experienced and is the longest-serving member in the Kairos at the moment, having many successful missions under her belt. She will help you adapt to being part of the Kairos but you'll have to learn fast; it's her sixteenth birthday on Saturday so she will be leaving the Kairos on Friday.'

Maité looked the two boys up and down curiously, with slightly raised eyebrows. Then she spoke in fluent English with a heavy Spanish accent.

'So, you are the two whelps to be weaned from mother's milk?' she teased. Maité spoke as if a seasoned professional to a couple of clueless, wet-behind-the-ears apprentices.

Joel leapt from his chair with great indignation but, thwarted by the lack of gravity, found himself catapulted several meters above, narrowly avoiding head-butting a passing angel. From this position he looked down in acute embarrassment as Maité, stifling a giggle, glided up to him. She held out her hand in order to pull him back down but, recovering his composure, Joel cleared his throat and gripped her hand firmly.

'Good to meet you, Maité. I'm looking forward to getting my teeth into something a little more solid – a little rare beef perhaps?' He looked at her with a twinkle in his eye.

'Hmm – touché maestro.' Maité nodded playfully. 'I think we'll get on just fine,' she replied with a grin.

Joel thought that there was something unusual, enigmatic even, about the young Spanish girl, and his heart seemed to miss a beat.

The pair then floated down to join the others.

'It takes some getting used to...' Maité said, with a smile, 'weightlessness, I mean.'

Peter alighted from his chair more sedately, and gulped as he stared at Maité. He was used to girls fussing over him but he'd never met one quite as cool and confident as Maité before.

Both the boys gave Nathan a look that was almost a plea for help and Nathan, amused by this comic encounter, gave them a knowing smile.

'Now,' he continued, 'the first thing boys, is to present you with your number-mark.'

'Number-mark?' Joel asked, curiously. 'What's that, Dad?'

'It's your unique number in the Kairos. All the Kairos children have a number between one and one hundred and fifty. There's no swearing-in or declaration of oaths in the Kairos, simply because you wouldn't have been chosen and your number-mark would not accept you, if your heart wasn't committed,' Nathan explained. 'This commitment was confirmed when you said the prayer of salvation with Reverend Matthews the other day. Your number stays with you all the time you're in the Kairos. Then, when you leave, you pass it on to another child.'

'Oh, so we don't just become a hundred and forty-nine and a hundred and fifty?' Peter asked.

'Oh no, that's not how it works, Peter. You take on the number of the member you replaced. I have your numbers here. Peter, this is yours.'

Nathan held out his hand and, balanced between his fore-finger and thumb, was a small, white light, about the size of a thumbnail. The light was in the shape of "K 18," like the pin that had been in Grandad's small box, except that this wasn't a gold pin; in fact there was no substance to it at all – it was just pure light! Nathan placed it on Peter's forehead and Joel watched, open-mouthed, as the light seemed to be absorbed into his skin, yet, strangely, it was still faintly visible.

'K-18,' Peter smiled, astonished. 'I felt that, Mr Asher – it felt good.'

Nathan grinned and turned to Joel. Between his finger and thumb was another similar light; this one was K119. Joel, too, felt the light dissolve into his forehead.

'You're right, Peter, it does feel good,' Joel agreed. Then he looked at Maité and noticed, for the first time, a small glow on her forehead. 'You're Kairos 121, he said to her.'

Maité nodded.

'That's right,' Nathan confirmed. 'Now you and Peter are truly both Kairos and you will be able to recognise other Kairos children, and they you.'

'Cool! Hey Dad, what number was Grandad?'

'Oh, let me think – 87. Yes, Grandad was Kairos 87,' Nathan replied.

'Grandad has a gold pin of his number,' said Joel.

'Yes, that's right. All the Kairos children are presented with a gold pin of their number when they leave us. Although they don't remember its significance, they do all treasure it; they know in their hearts it's special,' Nathan explained.

'What was Mum's number, Dad?' Joel asked.

'23,' Nathan replied, without hesitation.

'Psalm 23?' Joel muttered.

'Yes, son, Mum was psalm 23,' Nathan blinked. 'You've taken me seriously. You are learning fast.'

'I'm my dad's son,' Joel replied proudly.

'Yes, I can see you are,' Nathan smiled affectionately. 'Now, I'm going to leave you for a while in Maité's capable hands. Anna will stay with you, too. I believe they've organised a small exercise for you – just to get your feet wet…' Nathan exchanged grins with Maité.

'Wow!' Peter exclaimed. 'A mission – already!'

'You will be back, Dad?' Joel asked anxiously.

'Of course. Don't worry, we'll have plenty of time together. We'll be working closely together for the next four years, son. But now, you should pay attention to Maité. She can give you invaluable help.' Nathan put a hand on each of their shoulders.

'Remember, boys, you have the best defence ***in*** you…

'The Belt of Truth,
the Breastplate of Righteousness,
the Shoes of preparation of the gospel of peace,
the Shield of Faith,
the Helmet of Salvation,
and the Sword of the Spirit, which is
the Word of God.'

With that, Nathan vanished before their eyes.
Joel and Peter glanced at Maité and gulped nervously.

'O.K. SOLDIERS, ATTENTION!' Maité boomed, just like a drill sergeant.
This caused the two boys to jump, as the unexpected command shattered the silence. They both stared at her with open mouths. Maité could keep a straight face no longer, and she dissolved into giggles.

'You should see your faces; they are a picture,' she exclaimed! still giggling. Then, with an effort she recovered from her mirth and beckoned them with her fingers (and a teasing smile) to follow her. 'Come, come, come,' she urged quickly and without waiting, she glided back through the archway into the main hallway.

'I don't know which is worse…' Joel muttered to Peter with a tut '…quarrelsome ravens or the Sergeant Major here!'

'Well, you've got to admit, Joel, she's by far the prettiest,' Peter whispered back. 'Actually, she's quite fun. I think we're going to enjoy this.'

'What?' Joel exclaimed in exasperation, as if Peter had gone slightly mad.
Peter grinned and pushed off to glide after Maité. Joel shook his head and reluctantly followed.
Maité, accompanied by Anna, led them through the turquoise archway to the Vista, where she adopted a more serious attitude. The boys soon discovered that, despite her cheeky sense of

humour and embarrassing teasing, Maité was a true and dedicated professional. Having been a Kairos child for almost six years, she was fully committed to her faith, her missions and the Kairos. She was certainly a worthy mentor to emulate; always putting others' safety before her own.

First of all, with the aid of the Vista, she gave the boys a potted history of some of her own endeavours, ranging from leading searchers to lost children, to providing Spanish police with clues to the whereabouts of a dangerous killer. Many people, who would have been his future victims, walked the earth oblivious of the fact that they were living lives they would have lost, but for the obedience of this brave young girl. Joel and Peter were astonished and amazed at the Vista, which could show them the past as if watching a movie.

'Satan – the devil, had a plan to destroy those people but God's plan prevailed. I cannot stress to you strongly enough, my friends, how important is our work in the Kairos,' Maité explained, gravely. 'We are fighting a very dangerous foe. Satan has armies of evil-doers at his command. We cannot fight him in our own strength – he would slaughter us! The only way we can defeat him – our only defence against him – is the Christian armour described by Nathan, against which Satan is powerless, because the Christian armour is all based on what Jesus did at the cross. It is the Lord Jesus Christ who defeated Satan and it is the Lord Jesus Christ and only Him who has made deliverance from evil possible. The end is already planned for Satan: he will be thrown into the lake of fire, especially made for him – and those who do his evil work will join him. This "hell" was not designed for man, but Satan, that old devil, wants to take as many with him as he can deceive into following his evil ways. Yes, it's true that the Son of God has triumphed over all evil, but the battle for souls still rages on and many are deceived. My friends, it is only in Jesus Christ that any of us can defeat the enemy. The Father has put all evil under His feet.' Maité paused to let these profound facts sink in; it was critical that the boys understood that they could do nothing in their own strength. Then her face softened and she smiled at them. 'So, any questions – before we go into specifics?'

Maité knew the boys would have lots of questions and she was right. There were many questions whizzing around in their heads but they just stared at her, mesmerised and speechless. Then Peter nudged Joel.

'No – no – um – we're with you so far, Maité, aren't we, Peter?' Joel mumbled, feeling utterly stupid.

Peter nodded. He didn't have one sensible question in his head, just a lot of mixed-up ones.

'Yes, let's go into specifics, Maité,' Joel continued, hoping the specifics would clear up the confusion in his head.

'Good, good, this is good, you understand everything, hmm?' Maité nodded, waving her arms in a teasing flourish. 'Then, I have a question for you.'

Joel and Peter exchanged anxious glances. Joel could feel the heat rising under his collar; he was as far out of his comfort zone as if he was trying to ride a bike underwater.

'Which of you two boys can explain to me,' Maité asked them, 'how we get from here into – shall we say, New Scotland Yard – without raising any kind of suspicion?'

'You should have warned us you were going to ask questions, Maité. We'd have made notes,' Joel answered in a blasé attempt to appear cool, when inside he was feeling more like a boiling kettle.

'Of course, you cannot answer that question – I have not explained it to you yet,' Maité cocked her head to one side, smiling confidently, but Joel surprised her – and himself!

'I would have thought the answer to that question is rather obvious, Maité,' Joel replied, with a forced confidence.

'Oh, a smart guy. Go on then, Joel. Give it to me.' Maité grinned.

'The answer is simple: we can't. Whether you have explained it to us or not doesn't change the fact – none of us could appear in New Scotland Yard without raising some form of suspicion,' Joel answered, assertively.

'Hmm, a really smart guy,' Maité replied. 'You knew that was a trick question?'

'I just used the laws of common sense,' Joel shrugged.

'Pretty good; you'll do well,' Maité announced, agreeably. 'O.K. Now, in order to carry out the very important work we are chosen for, it is necessary for us to be able to travel at speed – in short, we need to be able to appear and disappear at will. Supposing there was an emergency in the city, Joel, how long would it take you to get there from your Grandad's place?'

'Oh, yawn…' Joel murmured, sarcastically. 'About a hundred years, the way Mum and Grandad drive!'

'Exactly – several hours,' Maité went on. 'That would be unacceptable in an emergency. But, we can get there instantly!' she explained, with another grand flourish.'

'How?' Peter asked, incredulously.

'Well,' continued Maité. 'You came here through the Fugue. That is a shaft of light able to transport you across the dimension of time and eternity. I must warn you from the start, the Fugue may not be used for general travel but only to and from your home base – in your case this is the plateau in Zionica. General travel, we do through the Vista.'

The two boys stared at Maité, hardly able to believe what was happening; it all seemed so surreal.

'Now, for a simple trial,' she continued, unabated by their evident wonderstruck expressions. 'Where would you like to go, Joel?'

'How about Grandad's barn?' Joel, taken by surprise, replied without thinking.

'Great choice, Joel,' Peter muttered under his breath with a hint of sarcasm.

'Hmm, interesting,' Maité teased. 'You are given a choice of anywhere in the world. Personally, I would have chosen a beach in the Caribbean, but – grandfather's barn – where you could go any day... Oh well, so be it,' she shrugged playfully, obviously taking great delight in teasing the boys.

Joel started a little indignantly, but then realised that to back-pedal now would make him look even more foolish. He felt the colour rising in his face, as his dumb, unimaginative gaffe sunk in.

Peter gave him a sympathetic look. It seemed to him that the beautiful Spanish mentor had a rather mischievous side – in a playful kind of way.

'Let me show you,' Maité demonstrated. 'First, you face the Vista and think of your desired destination. In this case –' Maité teased with an exaggerated sigh, "Grandfather's barn." Her eyes sparkled as she turned to look at Joel – eyebrow raised.

Joel registered that this was something Tamara did when she was teasing and thought that maybe all girls did this. He made a mental note to be wary in future of girls who raise one eyebrow – it means they're up to something.

They all watched the Vista intently, as Grandad's barn appeared in view. Then, as the Vista pushed inside the barn, they saw that Grandad was there.

'Oh, what a shame,' Maité grinned mischievously. 'This is the beauty of the Vista: you can see if the coast is clear, which demonstrably, is not the case here. As Grandad is in the barn, we'll have to take choice B – the Caribbean beach. Oh n – no... Wait a minute.' She was really enjoying this.

They continued to watch, as Grandad picked up a bale of hay and then went outside.

'... Ah, you're in luck, Joel,' Maité continued, with a grin. 'The coast is clear, after all!' She held out her hands to the two boys. 'Come.' Then, glancing over her shoulder, she addressed Anna, who had been quietly watching the proceedings. 'Anna, you will watch the Vista, yes?'

'I'll be here, Maité,' Anna affirmed, with a nod.

Hearts pounding with excitement, Peter and Joel took Maité's outstretched hands.

'Just glide into the Vista, boys,' Maité directed them.

The three of them stepped simultaneously into the Vista and, before the two boys knew what was happening, they were in the middle of the barn – gravity and all.

'Wow!' Peter exclaimed. 'How awesome is that! How did we get here?'

Suddenly, they heard the sound of a horse's hooves outside, and then Tamara's voice calling.

'Hello, Mr Jacob, is it alright to leave Cherokee in your barn for a while?'

'Of course it is, Tamara love. Put her in her usual stall,' came Grandad's jovial reply.

'Thanks, Mr Jacob,' Tamara called, cheerfully.

'Quick, it's Tamara; she's coming in here! How do we get back?' Joel cried.

They saw the latch move on the barn door. Maité raised a hand in front of her and they saw a schism appear in mid-air, like an ethereal curtain opening. The three of them walked through it and it immediately closed behind them. Suddenly, they were gliding out of the Vista and into Heaven again.

'It's as simple as that,' Maité grinned.

'Phew, that was a close call! Tamara almost bumped into us!' Peter whistled.

Joel, meanwhile, merely gazed at Maité in open-mouthed amazement.

'You must take care when travelling through the Vista.' Maité began. 'No one must ever see you arrive or leave. Now, let me go over the rules. First, you must check thoroughly on the Vista that there is no one about, before you travel. You cannot just suddenly appear before someone in the world, for obvious reasons.'

'What if someone does accidentally see you, Maité – I mean if they just arrive as you do?' Peter asked, innocently.

'Well, Peter, we may be in Heaven now, but we are still human which means that no matter how careful we are when travelling there is always the possibility of making mistakes. Fortunately, people are very good at dismissing things as "just their imagination." Have you ever thought that you had seen someone, then looked again and found that they were not there?' Maité shrugged.

Both boys looked a little stunned.

'These double-takes may be nothing at all, but then again... All I'm saying, my friends, is be as careful as you can,' Maité advised. 'Now, as you have seen, using the Vista is simple. You think of the place where you want to go and it will appear before your eyes. Then, you simply glide into it. Remember though,' she warned, 'you will be transferring suddenly into the world's gravity and similarly, the reverse when you return. I've seen kids come – how do you say in England – a cropper?' she sighed. 'Now, as you go through the Vista, a schism opens. To get back, you simply hold up your hand anywhere in the close vicinity of your arrival place, as I did in the barn, and think: Vista. The schism will open up for you and you just walk into it. If for any reason you cannot return to your arrival place, you must still hold up your hand and think: Vista. When you travel the Vista, there should always be someone up here watching you. The watcher will get your message and will create a schism for you. You must *never* travel the Vista without someone watching. In no circumstances are you to attempt to bring anyone up through the Vista who is not a Kairos; it would mean certain death for them. Remember, this is normally a place where people come only when they die. You are enabled to come and go for a reason, and only because God allows it; you have been called for a very special purpose. Any flouting of the rules would result in the instant erasure of your memory of this place and a return to your pre-Kairos life.'

'You mean, I'd forget about seeing my dad?' Joel asked.

'Correct,' Maité stated firmly. 'Also, no objects – coins for instance – only the clothes you are wearing will be accepted by the Vista. A limited amount of paper money is permitted as it is sometimes necessary for missions.' Maité paused to let this sink in. 'Are you still with me, boys?'

'Sure,' Joel replied, coolly.

Peter glanced at Joel and then back at Maité. 'Yeah – sure…'

'Good,' she continued. 'Now, please remember this very important rule. You can go anywhere in the present, but in no circumstances must you ever attempt to go back to the past or forward to the future, this is absolutely forbidden! Only God can change time, because He created it. In the whole history of the world, as far as we know, He has only ever done this once. That was when He made time stand still for about a day, to help Joshua defeat the Amorites.'

'What about Hezekiah and the sundial?' asked Peter, pointedly.

Maité was taken aback at Peter's evident knowledge of the Bible.

'Well – of course, yes,' Maité reflected. 'You know the word of God, Peter – and of course, you have passed the paying attention test. God did indeed make the sun go back ten degrees on the sundial; this is true. I stand corrected. Like I said earlier, we humans are not infallible. Anyway, this was all a very long time ago, even before Jesus came down to the world.' She paused thoughtfully. Peter's evident knowledge of the Bible seemed to have an immediate effect on her view of the two boys standing in front of her; maybe these new recruits weren't as "green" as she first thought.

Joel stared at Peter, open mouthed.

'It's the most fascinating book, Joel – the Bible; you should read it,' Peter said, with a modest shrug.

'The Bible is truly filled with mystery, intrigue, drama and excitement,' Maité agreed. 'The notion that the Bible is boring and full of stiff rules is a complete myth, perpetrated by the enemy because he doesn't want people to know the truth.'

'I see,' Joel nodded thoughtfully.

'Anyway,' Maité continued, 'getting back to the subject of time. This is the mighty power of our Creator. Aren't you glad we're on the winning team!' Maité grinned. 'So, the past cannot be changed; it has already happened. The future is a dynamic arena which does not yet exist and it is an empty void, although God knows everything. Such notions as time-travel are strictly for science-fiction – if it were possible people from the future would have come back to the present to tell us. No, attempting to go to the future through the Vista would be disastrous for you. There would be no return – it would be a one-way ticket to oblivion. The consequences would be so dire that I dare not utter them – *comprende*?'

'Crystal clear, Maité,' Peter assured her.

'Ditto,' Joel shrugged.

'Good! Now, Peter, you take us somewhere,' Maité instructed.

'Me?' Peter asked, surprised.

'Anywhere you like – within reason. Just remember that there are built-in safeguards to stop the Vista from being abused; you will not be allowed into the girl's changing-rooms, for instance.'

'Neither of us would attempt something so unworthy,' Joel retorted indignantly.

'I know, just kidding,' Maité answered and smiled apologetically.

Peter took Maité and Joel by the hand and all three looked into the Vista. Then, right before their eyes, there appeared a view of an idyllic and deserted, white, sandy beach with palm trees, a cloudless sky and kingfisher-blue sea. Suddenly, they all felt the warm sand under their feet and a soft breeze in their hair. The heat of the sun hit them as if they'd just walked into a sauna, and they heard the sound of the gently lapping, crystal clear sea.

'Wow!' Peter took in a deep breath, drinking in the Caribbean air.

'So, at least, one of you has some taste then?' Maité teased, with a cheeky smile. 'Hmm – every job has its perks.' She kicked off her sandals, threw back her head and ran towards the sea, laughing.

Joel and Peter exchanged glances of sheer astonishment and delight. Then, kicking off their own shoes, they followed in hot pursuit. Soon they were all splashing about in the water. For the boys it seemed like the most fun they'd had in ages, after all the upset of Tamara's accident, and it felt really good to "let their hair down."

After a time of tomfoolery in the water, the three of them lay under some palm trees to dry in the heat. Joel was dozing peacefully, when he was suddenly startled.

'So, how long did you think you could hide *this* secret from me, hey?' Tamara's voice rang out in the stillness.

At first, Joel thought he must be dreaming. Then, he heard it again.

'Did you think I wouldn't notice your sudden suntan?' her voice was all too clear.

Joel opened his eyes and, to his utter amazement, he realised he wasn't dreaming at all! Tamara's face was leaning right over him, staring down at him with that "raised eyebrow" and an amused grin.

'Tamara! W – what are you doing here?' Joel quickly sat up and grabbed his shirt.

Peter also sat up and blinked in disbelief, whilst Maité could not hide her amusement.

'Tamara!' Peter cried, astonished.

'You two know this person?' Maité asked, clearly startled.

'This is our friend, Tamara…' Joel answered, baffled.

Tamara looked at Maité and straight away Maité noticed the faint "K63" on Tamara's forehead.

'Oh, hello,' Maité greeted Tamara, getting up and brushing the sand off her. 'I'm Maité.'

'I know,' Tamara replied. 'Anna sent me to fetch you.'

'Oh – she did?' Maité smiled, a little humorously.

Peter and Joel jumped to their feet, both talking at once, wanting to know exactly how Tamara came to be there.

'I came here exactly the same way you did – through the Vista.'

'So, how long have you been a Kairos?' Joel asked, in astonishment.

'Not quite as long as you,' Tamara replied, amused by their reaction. 'You see, I got fed-up of waiting for you two. I thought that, after my ride, we were going to hang out for the rest of the day, but you seemed to be gone ages. I went down to Zionica and waited, but there was no sign of you – just as if you'd vanished into thin air! Your grandad didn't know where you were, either.'

'Wait a minute,' Joel interrupted with a frown. 'I thought that time stood still – that we could stay in Heaven as long as we wanted, while hardly any time passed in the world?'

'But you're not in Heaven now are you, Joel?' Tamara pointed out with a giggle.

'W – what do you mean? We've come through the Vista – surely…' Joel's voice tailed off as it began to dawn on him.

'No, Joel,' Maité explained. 'Much as this idyllic beach *feels* like Heaven, we're in the world now. The second you step through the Vista into the world, you are subject to earth time laws. This is also the case when you watch events in real time – as they happen – on the Vista. Remember what Nathan said: you've only got me for four more days, so you need to learn fast! We must have been here for at least couple of hours.'

'That's right,' Tamara added. 'I went for my ride on Cherokee, then I put her in your grandad's barn and gave her some corn. Anna showed me that on the Vista. It was very funny – how I nearly bumped into you all, in there. Mr Jacob didn't know your whereabouts so I went up to Zionica, as we'd arranged, and waited for you for about an hour. When you didn't show up I wandered around the field and onto the plateau. I called out your names in frustration and – zap! The next thing I knew, I was hurtling up a tunnel and, well, you know the rest. I've spent ages with Nathan and Anna; they've explained everything to me that they explained to you – and guess what? I've seen Storm! He's grown a lot.'

'We know, we've seen him too,' Peter confirmed with delight. 'This is fantastic, Tamara! I'm so glad we don't have to keep all of this secret from you. We were worried about how we could be in the Kairos without letting something slip and you finding out, weren't we, Joel?'

'Yeah, what a relief...' Joel replied cagily, his enthusiasm did not quite match Peter's. He took hold of Tamara by the shoulders and looked down at her with an anxious frown. 'Are you sure you want to do this, Tamara? It's certain to be dangerous and we don't want you getting hurt again – think what you've just been through!'

Maité looked away awkwardly. She was strangely moved by

Joel's sudden show of concern for Tamara. It began to dawn on her that the more she saw of Joel, the more she saw someone she would like to get to know better and realised that he wasn't that cocky kid she at first thought. However, in four days time she would be sixteen and no longer a Kairos child; she would forget she ever knew him at all.

'Joel, I think it's great that you care,' Tamara laughed nervously. 'But I've never been more certain of anything in my life! You couldn't possibly think that I would let you and Peter do this without me, could you?' She was surprised and a little embarrassed by his open and unexpected concern for her. It did though, give her a glimmer of hope as, for some time she'd been hiding a secret crush on him. She looked him up and down with a cheeky glint in her eyes – and the familiar raised eyebrow.

Joel knew that look; it meant that something potentially embarrassing was about to come from her mouth.

'You know, Joel, you've got a problem,' Tamara teased.

'Oh?' he enquired hesitantly, bracing himself.

'Yes,' she revealed. 'Have you thought how you're going to explain your suntan to your grandad? And you, Peter.'

Joel and Peter both looked down at their bare chests. They'd discarded their shirts earlier and, although they'd not been on the beach for long, the sun was so strong that they'd started to tan already.

'Ooh…' Joel sighed with relief. 'Well, Grandad is as blind as a bat without his glasses; he probably won't notice,' he replied with a dismissive shrug.

They all tipped the sand out of their shoes and shook their clothes. Then, Maité suggested that Peter try opening up the schism for them to return to Heaven. Peter was reluctant at first but, with some encouragement from the others, he slowly put up his hand and, as he did so, he squeezed his eyes shut. Then instantly, the ethereal curtain appeared like a slit in the air. Peter opened one eye hesitantly then, with a look of astonishment he opened the other.

'Well, come on then!' Tamara urged. 'Don't just stare at it!'

'One after the other they all slipped through the schism and immediately they glided through the Vista – into what seemed to be a noisy rumpus. Nathan, Anna and the two reception angels, Charis and Aletheia, were waiting for them, as if a welcoming committee.

There seemed to be some kind of celebration going on. The seraphs had gone batty: flying around in a furore, fluttering their massive wings and swooping down. They were singing even louder than before and calling to each other as they shook their gold and crystal sceptres, spreading tiny droplets of light everywhere, like showers of glitter. Everyone had to keep ducking to avoid the excited seraphs.

'What's going on?' Peter cried, as he and his friends emerged from the Vista.

'The seraphs are rejoicing, Peter,' Anna smiled. She too was beaming with joy and happiness. 'Ever since Tamara received her number-mark, it's been chaos. It's such a joyous occasion when one Kairos child is found but now we have three in a matter of days, this is cause for great joy!'

One of the seraphs flew straight at them, stopped and hovered over them. They looked up and the seraph allowed them to see its beautiful, radiant face. Then, tipping its sceptre, it sprinkled a shower of light over them, which tickled their faces and filled them with a warm, happy glow.

'Thanks!' Joel smiled at the seraph.

The seraph returned the smile, then flew off to join the others.

'Wow! That must be some sort of happy dust!' Peter exclaimed.

'They're showering you with love! That's why it feels so good!' Anna said, laughing.

'Triple wow!' cried Joel, in amazement.

'You all had such a wonderful time,' Anna smiled happily at the children. 'I watched you splashing about in the water. I almost wanted to join you.'

'Can you?' Peter asked. 'I mean, is it possible for you to come through the Vista too?'

'Oh, no, Peter,' Anna replied. 'It is strictly forbidden.'

'Oh! That's a pity.' Tamara screwed up her nose.

'Not really,' Nathan answered. 'God has such amazing blessings for us up here, why would we ever want to swap this, for anything the world had to offer? Unless God sends you back in the same body very soon after leaving it – something He has been known to do on very rare occasions – when you're gone from the world, you're gone,' Nathan explained. 'He will only send someone back if He has a good purpose for them in the world. I have to say though, that no one, given the choice, would want to go back to the world; they would only go if God sent them.' Then, he quickly changed the subject. 'You had fun on the beach didn't you?'

'Yes, Dad, it was great! You must have meant it literally when you said we were going to get our feet wet!'

'We thought you'd like that,' Nathan chuckled. 'It was just a little treat we arranged for you before the really serious work begins. Nathan put an arm around Tamara. 'Isn't it wonderful to have Tamara join the team!'

'Yeah, keeping it from her would have been a nightmare!' Peter chuckled.

Tamara looked up at Nathan with a smile.

Everyone seemed to be making such a fuss of Tamara, no one noticed that Maité, who had been standing quietly by, was drifting towards the archway exit to the great hall.

'Yeah, marvellous,' Joel added, sceptically. 'But, remember why we're here – we're ready for action. What's next, Maité?' Joel turned just as she was about to give them the slip.

Maité turned and shrugged – she had wanted to leave unnoticed. 'I think that is enough for now,' she replied quietly. 'We will meet here, tomorrow, at your English time, ten a.m. We will go on a training mission together. It will be kindergarten.'

'Great! See you then, Maité,' Joel called after her.

*'Hasta pronto.' Maité bowed her head, then glided through the archway.

Turning to Nathan, Joel asked, 'What's up with Maité, Dad?

* See you soon,

She seems quiet, all of a sudden.'

'I think it might have something to do with all this celebrating,' he replied, with a knowing sigh. 'It must remind her that, in only a few days, she will no longer be a Kairos and will have no memory of all this. She's been a dedicated worker for six years. Letting go will be hard for her; the Kairos has been her life.'

'At least the upset will be short lived,' Peter pointed out, candidly. 'When she wakes up on Saturday morning, she won't be upset anymore, will she?'

'No, I guess not,' Joel agreed, looking thoughtfully in the direction Maité had taken.

'You three had better be on your way now, too,' Nathan announced. 'Come on, I'll take you to the Fugue.'

CHAPTER THIRTEEN

The Garden of Lilies

Joel, Peter and Tamara arrived back at the plateau to find another unexpected welcome committee – the Magi. All the food that the children had previously left in the den had been tantalising the ravens, and now had to be eaten. Maggi and Magee were, of course, only too delighted to oblige and the three friends were left in no doubt about the origin of the word *ravenous*, because those ravens certainly could eat!

However, they were all hungry and the birds more than earned their share, as they delighted and entertained their young charges with amazing stories of their heroics in times past – even centuries ago! Tamara loved the Magi and thought they were hilariously funny, particularly when Magee, who had been perched on a branch over Joel's shoulder, surreptitiously leaned over and snuck the ham out of Joel's sandwich while he wasn't looking.

†

Now that everything was back to normal – at least as far as the adults were concerned – Peter decided he'd better show his face at home, if only for one night. Tamara's parents were so delighted to have her back, and so terrified of anything happening to her again, that she also decided she'd better go home. First though, they made their way down to Grandad's kitchen where they found him munching on a sandwich.

'We're back, Grandad,' Joel called cheerily as they bounded into the kitchen.

'Oh, hello kids. You found the boys then, Tamara love? I told you they wouldn't be far away.'

'Yeah, it's not like we've been half-way round the world is it?' Joel mocked, with a big grin.

At this the children all collapsed with laughter, because that was exactly where they had been! Then Joel realised that, although it seemed as if they'd been gone all day because of all that had happened, they had in fact only been gone about three hours. It felt strange not to have to explain where they had been all that time, but they hadn't even been missed!

So, exhausted and bewildered, but very happy, the three friends went their own separate ways for the evening.

†

That night, after Joel had climbed into bed, he picked up the framed picture that he always kept on his bedside table. It was a photo from the last holiday with his parents, before his dad died. He looked affectionately at the picture of the three of them: a happy family together. If only Mum knew that he was seeing Dad again. How hard it was going to be not to tell her, when he was longing to blurt it out – *Mum, I've seen Dad and he's alright.* But to mention it at all would be to lose him again, along with the memory. He knew that would eventually happen anyway, but not for another four years – and he was determined to make the most of that time.

Then he began to realise how Maité must be feeling, now her time in the Kairos was nearly over. No wonder she had suddenly become sad when everyone else was rejoicing. They'd had such fun on the beach that day. Joel was starting to like Maité more than he was willing to admit, despite her constant teasing. Then, with his family photo pressed to his chest, he let his heavy eyelids close and drifted into a dream.

†

Next morning, everyone was refreshed and feeling full of energy after a good night's sleep. Grandad was out on the yard tending his flock and Joel was clearing away the breakfast dishes, when Tamara and Peter arrived.

Peter bent down to fuss Rodney who was lying, as was his habit, at the bottom of the stairs. Tamara leant against the fireplace watching Joel, secretly wishing he would just once notice her – maybe if she was a year older he might – but then she realised that would make her and Presten twins! Eek! This thought, if dwelt on, could ruin her entire day! On second thoughts, maybe when they reach sixteen Joel would… but that was so far into the future…

'I wonder what this training mission will be?' Joel pondered.

'I suspect that we'll be given something easy for our first mission,' Tamara answered, snapping out of her daydreams. 'I can't see them throwing us in at the deep end with this Sadler person. What do you two think?'

'I expect that we'll be given a small test-mission before the big one – something simple, I should think,' Peter mused.

'Yes, I agree, Peter, I mean, Maité did say that it would be "kindergarten," and that means kids' stuff – it'll be easy-peasy,' Joel chuckled.

'Like rescuing a cat from up a tree?' Peter giggled.

'Or, how about a kid whose head is trapped in the school railings?' Joel chortled.

'Or someone's toe stuck in the bath tap…' Peter laughed.

'Oh, do be sensible, you two!' Tamara grumbled. 'This is something to be taken seriously. There are lives at stake!'

'We're only having a bit of harmless fun, Tamara,' Peter protested. 'This isn't like you at all. Of course we're taking it seriously – we're just – just…'

'Boys! Tamara. We're just boys. Being a girl, you wouldn't understand.' Joel's explanation clearly failed to impress Tamara.

'Boys will be boys, you mean? So that just excuses silly behaviour, does it?' Tamara chastised them.

'O.K. we're sorry. Now, can we have the funny Tamara back please?' Joel looked at Tamara with a boyish grin.

'Oh, whatever…' Tamara's frown melted into a smile; she couldn't resist Joel's pleading eyes – the ones she often fell asleep dreaming about.

'That's better,' Joel returned the smile.

Peter rolled his eyes, slightly embarrassed. He had already guessed some time ago about Tamara's crush on Joel, but tactfully never mentioned it.

'Right,' he said, a little hurriedly. 'Let's go, shall we?'

As they skipped over the yard on their way to Zionica, Joel called over to Grandad.

'I've done the dishes, Grandad. Do you want me to do anything else?'

'No, son, you go and enjoy yourself with your friends. You've only got a few more days of the holiday left,' Grandad shouted back.

'Thanks, Grandad, see you later.'

'He's right, you know.' Peter remarked with a jolt. 'So much has happened that time has sped by. I'd forgotten that it's Tuesday! Your mum is coming on Saturday to take you back, Joel!'

'Yes, of course you're right, Peter – I'd totally forgotten!' Joel exclaimed.

'Well, at least you two have had an action-packed Easter holiday!' Tamara blurted, with a hint of frustration. 'I've spent most of the holiday flat on my back in the hospital!'

'Tamara!' Joel cried, in surprised annoyance. 'Look, we're sorry that you feel you've missed out on a little action, but you're certainly making up for it now! Anyway, Peter and I were not gadding around having fun! We were right there in the hospital with you! Stop this self-pitying lark. Don't you get it? This means we've only got four more days to get that case off Sadler and deliver it to Smith – to prove my dad was murdered!'

'Yeah, and don't forget we've only got Maité to help us until Friday,' Peter added.

'Oh, guys – I'm so sorry – I was wallowing in self-pity, wasn't I, and now I feel terrible, prating on so selfishly,' Tamara confessed, apologetically, 'when *I've* got the whole of my life ahead of me!'

'Hey,' Joel turned to Tamara with a sympathetic smile. 'If there's anything you're not, Tamara, it's selfish. You're one of the most caring and unselfish people I know, and *that's* why you're our mate and part of this.'

Tamara looked up at Joel with moist eyes and, biting her lip, she nodded.

'I'm sorry I shouted at you,' Joel murmured quietly. 'Forgive me?'

'Of course,' Tamara returned a weak smile.

'Shucks,' Peter remarked. 'This kind of dashes our easy-peasy theory then, doesn't it? I suspect we're gonna get chucked in at the deep end, after all.'

'Maybe that's the best way, Peter; isn't it exciting? Come on, let's go…' Joel suddenly started to run towards Zionica, shouting, 'We're on a mission!'

Peter and Tamara exchanging grins, chased after him.

†

Maité greeted the three friends at the top of the Fugue.

'Aah, I'm pleased to see you're keen,' she teased.

'Thanks, Maité,' said Joel, looking around, surprised. 'Where are Charis and Aletheia?'

'What? Do you expect an angel welcome committee every time you travel the Fugue?' Maité teased. 'They're having a break – even angels get a break, you know.'

'Oh, sorry – I didn't mean…' Joel looked a little embarrassed as he imagined the two angels, sitting in a celestial coffee shop, talking about the latest new arrivals.

'I'm playing with you, Joel; have you no sense of humour?' Maité grinned. 'Come, amigos, we have much to do.' Without waiting, she glided off up the Hall of Archways.

Joel, Peter and Tamara took off, flying after her. Soon, they all came to a halt at one of the archways. This one had a diamond jewel at its pinnacle and a white light glowing from within. Joel guessed that, had that diamond been in the world, there would not be a king or queen who would have enough money to buy it. Maité turned to face the others.

'This is the first stop for a new Kairos member,' Maité remarked, suddenly serious. 'All new members must visit here before they undertake any missions. You need to see this for your own good.'

'That sounds a bit serious, Maité. Should we be afraid?' Tamara asked, hesitantly.

'No. We're in Heaven remember – there's no fear at all up here. But, you should be prepared,' Maité replied, earnestly.

'Prepared for what, Maité?' Peter pressed.

'For truth, amigo. Follow me!' Maité pushed through the archway.

The others looked at each other with trepidation. Then Joel glided after Maité, followed by Tamara, then Peter. As they emerged from the other end, it was as if they'd stepped outside on a beautiful sunny day in the world. Their feet suddenly hit the ground and they were walking instead of gliding, but the ground seemed somehow to be springy under their feet.

'Gravity!' Joel remarked with surprise. 'Is this another gateway back to the world, Maité?'

'No, no, we're still in Heaven,' Maité replied. 'This is the only chamber up here that *appears* to have permanent, *normal* gravity. It's not real, actual gravity. It's a kind of virtual gravity – simulated for a special purpose.'

'What is that heavenly smell?' Tamara asked, taking in a deep breath of the delicious scent. 'It's the most wonderful thing I've ever smelt.'

'Our lady has been here,' Maité explained. 'It is the sweet fragrance of the white Lily of the Valley. Everywhere our lady goes, she leaves the beautiful fragrance behind, so you always know if she is about.'

'Our lady?' Tamara gasped. 'You mean...?'

'Yes, I mean our blessed lady. She is very often to be found here – it is a passion of hers, naturally. Some say that the lilies are our lady's tears.'

'Oh, why is that, Maité? Where exactly are we?' Tamara asked.

'The Garden of Lilies; it is the nursery, you see,' Maité replied.

'Oh, so, she likes flowers then?' Tamara asked, innocently. Maité threw back her head and giggled.

'No, no! The babes – it is the children. The children *are* our blessed lady's lilies! She nurtures and cares for the children. Where else would the most blessed mother of all be found?'

'Oh, forgive me for being so stupid!' Tamara could have kicked herself for being so dumb.

'It is an easy mistake to make, Tamara, and you're not here because you're smart, - you you're here because you have been chosen,' Maité reassured her.

'Oh, I see,' Tamara replied pensively. 'So, have you seen her, Maité? What does she look like?' She continued. 'Will we see her? Will we recognise her?'

'You would know her instantly. You will never have seen beauty or felt love like it. She radiates beauty and love which is so powerful, it stops you in your tracks. I've only seen a fleeting glimpse of her once, in all the time I've been a Kairos. She is very careful not to be seen by – forgive me – people who are still in the world. You see, she is so beautiful that you would fall in love with her and if you saw her more than once, then you wouldn't want to leave here – you would want to die for her. It's hardly surprising that she is so blessed; I mean, God did choose her to have His only Son. However, remember though, that even this beauty and love, powerful as it is, is dwarfed by the beauty and love of God Himself. There are none in all eternity that compare to Him.'

The mesmerised children gazed at Maité; they all wanted to pinch themselves but they knew that they weren't dreaming.

'Now, you all need to know about this place,' Maité continued. 'What you are about to embark on is not without danger; you should be aware that there are risks. So, if a child "hops the twig," this is where they come.'

'Hops the twig?' Tamara frowned.

'Dies, Tamara; this is Heaven's nursery,' Maité explained.

'Not many Kairos children lose their lives, but it has happened. This is why it is not practical to borrow Kairos children from other countries. If anything happened to me while in England, for instance, how would it be explained to my family? How did I get here? How so fast? Maybe they only saw me half an hour before!'

'I see,' Joel nodded. 'So while you're in the world with us in England, you're at some considerable risk.'

'You learn fast, Senor.' Maité looked at him with a humorous glint in her eyes. 'This is why I can only stay for short periods. The beach excursion of yesterday was a very rare exception. But then we were not on a mission as such, were we?'

The three friends looked intently at Maité, as she paused to let it all sink in to their bewildered minds.

'The mission Nathan has for you is long overdue,' she continued, earnestly. 'Those villains have been targets of the Kairos for a long time but, remember, you are currently the *only* Kairos children in England, and the first for many years. This is why everyone is so excited to have you join us. There have been no English Kairos children to take on the mission – until now.'

The children nodded. They gazed in wonder at the beautiful garden in which they found themselves. It was like a sunny meadow or a park. There were all kinds of exotic flowers, plants and trees, winding streams, rocky pools and waterfalls of crystal clear water that sparkled like diamonds in the light. The whole place was alive with an enormous variety of tame animals and birds and all the colours seemed so much brighter and more vivid than anything they'd ever seen before.

A group of children were playing not far from where the four visitors were standing. Suddenly, a very dark African girl, about thirteen years of age, saw them and ran up to Maité.

'Maité! she cried joyfully.

'Hola, Jean!' Maité greeted her cheerfully.

The two of them hugged.

'Jean, say hello to our new Kairos recruits: Joel, Peter and Tamara, from Zionica, England.'

'Hi,' Jean smiled warmly as she greeted at them.

They all nodded and smiled at her.

'How are you finding everything, Jean?' Maité asked sensitively.

'Oh, it's wonderful, thank you, Maité. I wouldn't go back to the world for a solid gold orang-utan!' Jean laughed.

'Wow, it must be good!' Maité laughed with her.

'Well, I won't keep you, Maité. Blessed is He!' With that Jean ran off, back to the other children.

'Adios, mi amiga,' Maité called after her. Then, turning back to her three "apprentices," she explained, 'Jean hasn't been here very long; she was Kairos 18, but you have taken her place, Peter.'

'What's she still doing up here then? Surely, she cannot be a Kairos anymore if I've taken her place?' Peter asked, rather innocently .

Nudging Peter discreetly, Tamara whispered, 'Jean did not fulfil her final mission because she died.'

'Oh dear! What happened to her, Maité?' Peter asked, sadly.

'She was working on a mission involving a mother and three young children. The mother was suffering severe mental depression, brought on by years of drug and alcohol abuse. Jean was assigned to comfort the children, who were being badly neglected due to their mother's addictions. Also, because the mother was unable to cope with the three children Jean was attempting to help her too. Unfortunately though, the mother's boyfriend, who wasn't the children's father, and who also had a drug habit, didn't want the children and threatened to leave the mother who subsequently saw her own children as an obstacle to her happiness with this man. So, in a moment of sheer madness, she strapped the children into her car, placing a hose from the exhaust into the vehicle. Regrettably, all the children perished from the fumes.'

Joel, Peter and Tamara gasped in horror.

'But, what happened to Jean?' Tamara asked, aghast. 'How come *she* died?'

'Well, of course we all knew what the mother was likely to do – we'd seen it on the Vista. Jean's mission was to comfort the children and to counsel the mother. However, she broke the rules and made the classic mistake of getting too emotionally involved in her mission. When she realised that the mother could not be deterred, Jean's refusal to accept something so terrible drove her to do something irreversibly drastic. You must remember this, my friends,' Maité warned gravely. 'You can make any decision you like about yourself, but you cannot force another to take your choice. All you can do is give them the truth; everyone must make their own choices and decisions. You must not interfere with free will – it is forbidden. Jean did everything she could to talk the mother out of this dreadful act but sadly failed. The distress of the children in the car caused Jean to act compassionately, but impulsively. She jumped into the car with the intention of pulling the children out, but unfortunately the seatbelts were jammed. While Jean struggled to release their seatbelts, refusing to abandon the children, she herself was overcome with fumes. Tragically, she perished in the car with them.'

They were all aghast at this tragic story.

'How dreadful!' Tamara cried tearfully.

'Yes, indeed. The children, all being under the age of accountability, were whisked straight up here, where they will stay, in paradise. Jean was instructed to comfort the children through this crisis, but obviously, not to die with them!' Maité continued. 'Heroic though her actions were, this has had a devastating result for Jean. She took her life into her own hands when she should have trusted God; she knew He would take care of these children. Unfortunately, this action cut short her time in the Kairos and in the world and has caused her to miss the plan for her own life.'

'But Maité,' Peter interjected. 'Jesus Himself said, "No greater love has he who lays down his life for a friend."'

'Of course, Peter and this is absolutely true, and a point in Jean's favour.' Maité replied. 'But Jean's sacrifice made no difference to saving the lives of these children; they were all going to die anyway – it was a senseless loss of her life.'

'How utterly tragic! Poor Jean,' Tamara murmured, sadly.

'Yes, and not just for Jean – think of all the people she may have helped, had she stayed in the Kairos for another two years – not to mention her own future husband and the children that will now not be born! Anyway, the important lesson to learn is to trust God, He has already made the way.'

'The Way?' Tamara asked.

'Yes, Tamara, you would not be here if you did not know the Way.'

'Jesus is the Way,' Tamara confirmed.

'Correct,' Maité smiled. 'Alleluia! Now, you see those children Jean is playing with?'

They all followed Maité's gaze to three young children, laughing and having a wonderful time with Jean.

'They are the ones who perished in the car. See how happy they are?'

Tamara suddenly felt a slight tug at her blouse and turned around. She almost fell over backwards with surprise because standing there was a large cartoon-like duck, as alive as she was. The duck gave a friendly smile. He was about a metre tall, was white all over but for a bright orange beak, and had a cute tuft of feathers on top of his head. He looked at her with big, doleful but intelligent eyes. Half hiding under one of the duck's wings was a small shy looking boy, about five years old.

'Hewo,' said the duck.

Tamara gasped with astonishment.

'My name is Twevor,' the duck continued. 'Will you say hewo to my new fwiend. His name is Wobert. He's new here and he wants to make some fwiends.'

'I'd love to,' Tamara giggled. She bent down a little and peering under Trevor's wing, she beamed a big smile. 'My word!' she said with exaggerated surprise. 'A small boy!'

Robert snuggled closer to the podgy Trevor.

'Hello, Robert,' Tamara smiled. 'My name is Tamara and this

is Joel, Peter and Maité. So, now you've got four new friends already. What's that you're hiding in your jacket, Robert?' Robert turned his face to Tamara.

'I've got a kitten,' he announced proudly, revealing the tiny ball of fluff. 'Do you want to stroke him?'

'Oh yes, please! I love kittens, Robert,' Tamara replied.

'His name is Peepoh,' said Robert, proudly.

'Hello, Peepoh,' Tamara murmured softly, as she stroked the tiny kitten. 'Where did you find him, Robert?'

'The beautiful lady gave him to me. He still smells of her.' Tamara put her nose near the kitten and took in a breath of the lovely scent.

'Mm yes, so he does,' she murmured.

'She's coming back,' Robert said quickly. 'The lady said she would come and see me again.'

'Ooh, I've just seen my fwiend, Tugs the teddy,' Trevor interrupted, guiding Robert with his wing. 'Come on, Wobert, I bet Tugs has got some sweets. Tugs has a very sweet toof. He eats too many sweets, te-he, and he gives a lot away, but his sweetie pocket nevew empties. Let's go and see if he has your favouwite, Wobert. Tugs has evewybody's favouwite.'

Trevor and Robert waved goodbye and made their way across the grass towards Tugs who, by then, was surrounded by children, all shouting out their choice of sweets. Whatever they shouted always seemed to be in Tugs' sweetie pocket.

'Bye, Trevor. Bye, Robert,' Tamara called after them.

'Ice cream?' Maité asked, unexpectedly.

'Ice cream?' Joel echoed, in astonishment.

Maité walked up to a small booth about a metre square, then, she turned to face them.

'What flavours do you want?' she asked.

'What is there?' Joel asked in reply.

'Anything your imagination can conjure up,' Maité replied confidently.

'Oh, right. How about toffee, butterscotch ripples and dark chocolate sauce – with a flake?' Joel suggested, somewhat smugly.

'Would that be hot chocolate sauce or cold, Joel?' Maité asked plainly.

'Oh, hot of course,' he replied with a grin, which soon dissolved into an incredulous stare, as Maité put her hand into the booth and pulled out an ice cream cocktail which was exactly as Joel had described, and handed it to him.

'How did you do that?' Peter cried, with a gasp of amazement.

'I didn't do anything,' Maité smiled. 'There is no lack up here. I mean – it is Heaven, after all. Tamara, what would you like?'

'Ooh um, let me see. How about maraschino cherry and mocha, with a chocolate flake?' she replied.

Again, Maité instantly produced Tamara's request, precisely to order.

'Peter?' Maité asked.

'Can I have a strawberry ice, Maité, please?'

Maité produced a delicious looking strawberry ice and handed it to Peter. Then she pulled out a rather spectacular Nicka-bocka-Glory for herself.

The four visitors sat on the soft, springy grass totally engrossed in eating their ice creams and so not much talking went on as they all thought the ice creams tasted like Heaven. They watched children coming, going and playing. Everyone seemed so happy, full of joy, laughter and fun. When they had finished their ice creams, Maité stood up.

'Now, it's time to continue our journey,' she announced.

The three friends arose and followed Maité to a low-roofed building with soothing pastel colours and cute cherubim around. The little cherubim were chatting and giggling with each other but as soon as they saw the visitors approaching, they became very attentive, greeting them warmly and ushering them inside.

The place was teeming with angels, all beautiful like Charis and Aletheia. Soft, soothing angelic singing was barely audible in the background, whilst colourful crystals twinkled and sparkled everywhere.

'You must be careful in here – what you do and say,' Maité

whispered in a low voice. 'If you speak, then please speak quietly and refrain from sudden movements. These are the new arrivals – it's also the Baby Unit. You should not alarm already traumatised children, you understand? These children have no idea what has happened to them, or why they're here. Some were ill for a long time; some were wrenched from the world by accident or crime. They have been taken from the security of their parents and home. Some of them arrive in a very poor state. But, whatever their state, He makes them perfect. There are lots of angels in this place and you must not get in their way. You are simply here to observe...

'Yes, Maité, we understand,' Joel muttered quietly.

'I must warn you, though,' Maité added, 'you may be asked to help in the Baby Unit as they're always very busy.'

A look of panic momentarily flashed across Joel's face at this last piece of information.

'It's the busiest place here,' she continued, 'due to the large number of terminations that go on all over the world.'

'Oh, how terrible!' Tamara cried, in anguish. Her cry pierced the quiet ambiance of the place and a sudden shushing noise could be heard, as several angels put their fingers to their mouths at Tamara's sudden outburst.

'Sorry,' she whispered, lowering her head in embarrassment.

'This is why there is permanent simulated gravity here, you see,' Maité explained in a low whisper. 'The children and the angels have enough to contend with and – well – weightlessness would only add to their problems. They cannot have babies floating through the air; there has to be some form of order.'

They slowly followed Maité through the building, ending up at the Baby Unit. Here, the lovely aroma of the white Lily of the Valley was particularly strong.

'These are the babes,' Maité whispered, as they stood at the entrance. 'Our lady has been here quite recently. You can tell by the strength of the fragrance.

'Mm,' Tamara took a deep breath of the heavenly scent.

The three friends peered inside and had to stifle gasps. There were rows and rows of little cots containing tiny babies, which seemed to go on forever, as far as the eye could see, with many angels in attendance.

'Phew!' Joel whispered, astonished. 'This makes Charing Cross seem like a church on a Monday!'

'Yeah, how come there are so many?' Peter asked, equally astonished.

'Yes, tragic isn't it,' Maité agreed with a sigh. 'Babies die for lots of reasons but the majority of these are terminations, I'm afraid. Many are drug or alcohol related, unwanted pregnancies – the product of promiscuity, abuse and prostitution. Many of these babies were wrenched alive from their mothers' wombs and left in the hospital sluice rooms to die – cold, hungry, rejected, unloved, crying, never having been cuddled – till they came here. The unfortunate nurses just have to leave them and stand by, as their defenceless little lives expire. Those illegal "drug barons" have a lot to answer for, being one of the root causes of ungodly living, driving people to despair and eventual destruction.'

'Oh, how awful...' Tamara tried to stifle a gasp of horror. 'How can people do this terrible thing?'

'Yes, it is horribly upsetting – the work of the devil,' Maité replied. 'Many people think that life begins at birth or near to birth, but in fact, life is allocated at conception: the moment the seed enters the egg and fertilizes it – that's when each vulnerable little life begins. Take cheer though, Tamara,' Maité added. 'Each one is dearly loved by their Heavenly Father. His heart breaks for every one of these helpless babes, never given a chance to live out the plan He had for their lives. You see, God is not the God of accidents. Each of these babies was created on purpose, because He is the life-giver. And no matter what their state when they leave the world, He makes them perfect when they arrive here.'

One of the supervising angels spotted them standing at the entrance and swiftly approached them, holding a tiny baby in her arms.

'Hello, Maité,' the angel greeted her. 'I'm so glad to see you.

We could use some help.' She turned to Joel, Peter and Tamara. 'Hello, so you're the new Kairos recruits then? Welcome aboard! I'm Arianna and I run the Baby Unit.' She gave them a heart-warming smile.

'Thanks,' the three of them echoed in unison and introduced themselves to Arianna.

Arianna's smile turned to a frown. 'Tuesday is termination day at one of the busiest hospitals.' She shook her Head, sadly. 'So, we are inundated with these babies. Well then, there was a right hullabaloo up here when you were confirmed Kairos! Everyone was celebrating,' Arianna smiled warmly again. 'You're welcome up here any time during the holidays. Just turn up – there'll always be plenty for you to do. We can use all the help we can get.' She placed the tiny baby she was holding in Tamara's arms. 'Here, Tamara, we've called this one Rachel. Her mother was a heroin addict, so Rachel was born addicted to the drug too. She was two months premature – poor thing only lived for an hour.'

'What shall I do?' Tamara asked, a little taken aback.

'Just hold her, cuddle her and speak to her softly. Obviously she's not in pain any more. She's quite comfortable, but she's been through a very painful and traumatic time. She won't be in here for very long; as she gets bigger and stronger she'll be moved to the general area in the nursery, where she'll have oodles of fun with the others. Kids grow-up so fast – time doesn't exist here, you see – you'd be amazed. Next time you see Rachel she'll probably be talking and running around.' Arianna picked up another baby. 'This is Stephen; he was a cot death. It's sad, but it happens. Both his parents were heavy smokers and Stephen's cot was in their bedroom. Smoking parents are really bad news for young babies, even if they don't actually smoke in the presence of their children, they still exhale those poisonous fumes for a long time after their last cigarette. Here, Joel, you take Stephen.'

'B – b but…' Joel stammered, but before he could protest, the baby was in his arms. He turned to Maité with a desperate sort of pleading look in his eyes. 'I – I've never held a baby before…'

Maité smiled at Joel with a glint in her eye.

'Well, you're holding one now, Joel, aren't you,' she replied. 'I'm sure you'll get the hang of it.'

'There's nothing to it,' Arianna encouraged him. Then she turned to a young woman nearby who was nursing a small baby. 'Are you coping alright, Catherine?'

The young woman smiled and nodded, without taking her eyes off the baby.

'Catherine arrived yesterday with her baby,' Arianna explained. 'Her husband was using a mobile phone whilst driving the car; he lost control and hit a tree. The whole passenger side of the car was demolished. He survived, but Catherine and the child died instantly. In these situations, the mother comes here through the Nursery Fugue with the child. It's thought best not to separate the child from its mother, unless of course the mother doesn't know the Lord Jesus, in which case, only the child comes here. Peter, why don't you give Andrew a cuddle?' She picked up another baby and handed him to Peter.

Peter took the baby with a little more confidence than Joel had, drawing on his experience with baby farm animals.

'A bit different from the baby lambs you're used to nursing, Peter,' Tamara giggled nervously.

'Quite a lot different, Tamara,' Peter replied, emphatically.

'Well, we're all God's little lambs, aren't we?' Maité added simply.

'Andrew was six weeks old when he came here,' Arianna continued. 'Unfortunately, the poor little soul was a victim of domestic violence – this again, brought on by drugs and alcohol; he was killed by his father because he wouldn't stop crying. He was just hungry and needed changing, but his mother and father had been on a drugs and alcohol binge; they didn't know what they were doing.'

Suddenly, another angel beckoned to Arianna. 'Arianna! We have new twins over here – three months premature!' the angel mouthed softly.

'Sorry, do you mind if I leave you? I'm needed.' With that, Arianna excused herself and vanished, instantly reappearing next to the angel who had summoned her.

Maité bent down to a cot and picked up another of the babies, rocking it gently in her arms. Joel watched her and attempted, somewhat awkwardly, to copy her.

After they had been in the nursery for some time, Tamara felt that if she stayed a minute longer she would not be able to control her tears. She wanted to run outside as fast as her legs could carry her, but with a supreme effort to stay calm and not alarm the children, she turned and walked quietly outside. The others followed. Once outside, Tamara sat on a bench and hung her head in her hands; she was trying to muster up all her strength not to cry. Maité sat next to her and placed a sympathetic arm around her shoulders.

'You can only stay in there for so long before it gets too upsetting – then it's time to leave,' said Maité, with a heavy sigh. 'Imagine how God must feel; he loves each of those babies like His own son or daughter. I make no apologies for showing you these things. You need to see the devastating results of drug and alcohol abuse because, as you know, your first planned mission is directly involved with combating this evil. It will be dangerous, and you will need to have courage. So much is at stake! If you cannot handle it, then you would be unable to carry on in the Kairos. Nathan would arrange for you to leave and this part of your memory would be erased.'

'Are you alright, Tamara?' Peter asked, concerned.

'I think we'd better take her home, Peter. I knew this would be too much for her,' Joel insisted.

'NO!' Tamara exclaimed lifting her head with sudden defiance. 'Don't you see? Now it's even more important than ever that we do this! I want to do everything I possibly can to stop this evil drug menace! Children like these don't stand a chance with villains like Lilith about. I don't care what happens to me! I might have been dead myself by now but, by a miracle,

I'm not – I'm alive and everything from now on is a bonus! If Jesus can sacrifice His life on a cross for me, then I can devote the rest of mine to *Him*. He has saved me for a reason and somehow, I don't think that reason is so that I can sit back and enjoy my own life just for myself. We've all been called for a purpose!' With that she stood up, wiped her face and turned to Maité. 'Maité, I'm ready. I want to start right now!' Though her voice trembled, she was determined. 'I want to stop that disgusting varmint, Lilith, from destroying any more mothers and children with his evil drugs. I know I'm only a child and can do nothing of myself but, if the Lord God can use me, I am willing.' Suddenly there was a flash of light and Nathan appeared in front of them.

'Dad!' Joel exclaimed.

'Hey, you guys,' Nathan smiled at them. 'Maité was right to show you these things but I'm sorry it was necessary. You had to understand the challenges you face, the risks you would be taking and what's at stake. We cannot allow personal feelings to get in the way of our work. You need to stay focused on your missions and be committed, otherwise things could be dangerous for you and for others. The determination and commitment Tamara has just shown, despite her obvious upset, has confirmed to us that you are indeed all able to continue in the Kairos.'

'We're with you, Dad, whatever it takes,' Joel declared with conviction.

'Yes, I believe you are, son; I'm so proud of your dedication,' Nathan replied, with conviction. 'Let's formulate our plan to blast this brood of vipers out of their stinking pit.' Saying this, he wrapped his golden arms around all four of them and instantly they were transported to the Vista chamber.

CHAPTER FOURTEEN

A Snake in the Grass

Everywhere was bathed in the turquoise-blue hue of the Vista chamber. The children materialised, with Nathan's arms still wrapped around them. Then, standing back, Nathan addressed them seriously.

'Well, children, there's no time like the present. Let's make a start on the plan,' he began, decisively.

'Cool, Dad. We're all with you,' Joel confirmed.

Everyone nodded enthusiastically in agreement.

'Good! Now, I've been watching Sadler for quite some time through the Vista, studying his every move,' Nathan explained. 'He's such a creature of habit; I could follow his routine blindfolded. I know where he goes, whom he sees and even where he buys his socks.'

'That's great attention to detail, Dad, but who cares about his socks!'

'Yes, of course, son, quite right. However, our Mr Sadler keeps his socks in a very interesting place.'

'That's all very well, but where does he keep the case? Mr Asher?' Peter asked.

Nathan gave a wry smile.

'If you had something that was almost as important for keeping you alive as the air you breathe, where do you think you might keep it?' Nathan studied the four faces before him.

'In a safe-deposit box, securely locked away in a reputable bank?' Joel proposed.

'Good, Joel,' Nathan congratulated him. 'That is where you or I might keep something of such importance. However, Sadler, clever as he might be, is completely lacking in discernment and common sense. On the contrary, we believe he is seriously unhinged, which is why this sad and misguided villain keeps the case in a drawer under his bed – underneath...'

'Underneath his socks?' Tamara cried in astonishment.

'What?' Joel exclaimed in disbelief.

'Yes, children, our deluded Sadler keeps the case in his own home, a little town-house in the city. I guess those bed drawers are meant for putting clean laundry in, but Sadler thinks they're the ideal hiding place for critical, damning evidence and dirty moolah!'

'Dirty moolah?' Tamara asked, puzzled.

'Ill-gotten gains which he extorts from Lilith,' Nathan explained. 'Fairly obviously, he cannot put this money in a bank without raising awkward questions and causing investigations. So, he's got the case in one drawer and the dosh – his intended retirement fund – in another. He has bought a lot of socks to bury all the evidence under,' Nathan smirked with a wry smile.

'How funny, people used to stuff money in their mattresses in the old days,' Tamara remarked, with amusement.

'It seems that Sadler is still living in the past,' Joel muttered sarcastically.

'You took the words out of my mouth, Joel,' Nathan grinned.

'At least that makes it easier to swipe, Dad,' Joel chortled humorously.' Then suddenly serious, 'I don't care about the money, I want that case of evidence!'

'Precisely, son. However, this just shows what a careless amateur we are dealing with and while that does have certain advantages, it also makes it all the more dangerous for you,' Nathan warned. 'Sadler is an irrational, loose cannon. He is capable of anything and as you've already seen, he is prepared to kill to get what he wants.'

The children all nodded, gravely.

'The next thing is,' Nathan continued, 'Uz and Buz.'

'Uz and Buz?' Joel, Peter and Tamara repeated in unison.

'Who or what are Uz and Buz?' Joel asked, with trepidation.

'I never said this would be easy, guys,' Nathan replied with a sigh. 'Uz and Buz are the pair of extremely large and terrifyingly ferocious rottweilers that Sadler lets loose in his town house; I mean, they roam the house, freely!'

'Jumping mutts!' Tamara exclaimed.

'So much for easy-peasy,' Joel muttered.

'Not a problem, Joel – just leave the mutts to me,' Peter reassured him.

'Yes, do not be discouraged. God has given Peter a gift with animals, as you probably already know,' Nathan confirmed. 'You've been ideally matched for this mission – all of you. Now, you might say, well, that's OK, we'll just wait till Sadler takes these beasts out for their exercise and then, we'll steal in and swipe the case. The trouble is, Sadler never takes these mutts out himself; that's one of Jethro's roles.'

'Jethro?' the three cried together.

'Oh, this just gets better! Don't tell me – Jethro is a nine-foot giant with a black-belt in karate?' Joel mocked, contemptuously.

'Not quite – but something along those lines,' Nathan replied, calmly. 'You see, it's not enough that Sadler has two permanent round- the-clock bodyguards, paid for by Lilith. He also employs his own stooge to follow him around everywhere he goes – only this is no lamb – more I should say like...'

'A slithering, venomous snake?' Tamara hissed.

'More, I would say, Tamara, like an ostrich that thinks it is a bull – in a china shop!' Nathan laughed.

'Oh! You're so funny, Nathan!' Tamara giggled.

'Great!' Joel cried. 'Now we've got three moving targets to dodge! Is that it, or has Sadler got an electrified barbed-wire fence and shark-infested moat around his house?'

'Well, no, but don't forget Sims and Levi, the two henchmen provided by Lilith. Don't underestimate these two; they eat raw steak for breakfast,' Nathan warned.

'Uh-oh,' Tamara murmured.

'These two reprobates are dangerous men, children. The only lives that have any value at all to them are their own – and Lilith's of course, but only because he pays them well,' Nathan warned, gravely.

'This sounds more like a picnic by the minute!' Joel muttered.

'What do you suggest we do, Mr Asher?' Peter asked. 'How do you propose we get the case?'

'I'm really glad you asked that, Peter. So, you're still keen to continue with the plan?'

'Of course we are! We wouldn't dream of backing out,' Joel insisted, glancing at the others, eager for their confirmation too. They all nodded in agreement.

'I should have known; you've been chosen for the Kairos, therefore, you would never back down from a challenge to fight for good against evil,' Nathan smiled. 'You must remember children, the fight against evil is a spiritual battle, evil men are just puppets of the devil. In Jesus, and Jesus alone, is every victory. So, the fight you are called to fight is the fight of faith.' Nathan warned.

'Yes, guys,' Maité added. 'The Lord Jesus Christ defeated and disarmed all evil at the cross, where the work was finished, and your faith must be anchored in this truth – you cannot fight evil in your own strength but by faith in the Son of God. The devil and his demons are scared of the cross!'

'Indeed,' Nathan agreed. 'Now, in answer to your question, Peter, I think the best way to approach the matter is by the Trojan Horse method. You must be invited into the enemy's lair.'

'What! Oh yeah – sure! Sadler is going to invite us in for tea, so we can steal his precious case!' Joel laughed, scornfully.

'Joel, Joel, why the scepticism? Sadler *is* going to invite you in for tea…' Nathan declared '…and you *are* going to accept! Don't forget, Sadler doesn't know that you know what he's up to – he thinks he's in the clear. Right now, Sadler is wallowing like a hippo in a mud-bath. He couldn't see a light-bulb flashing in front of his face – he has been blinded by his own greed! Let's look at the facts: one, he was one of your father's closest friends and business partners; two, he still is friendly with your mother. This being the case, he is one of the most qualified people you could consult about your deceased father. You were only eight when I died, Joel – too young to ask the kind of questions you might have asked now that you're twelve. It's quite conceivable that you may want to find out more about your dad, and who better to consult than your dad's trusted old friend and business partner? See where I'm coming from?'

'Trusted friend and business partner? Duplicitous, slimy, murdering snake, you mean!' Joel spat.

'Joel, if this mission is to have any chance of success, you've got to get past your resentment,' Nathan insisted. 'If Sadler has one shred of decency, he will be a little sympathetic to your plight and possibly he might even be feeling a little guilty. This is his chance to offload some of that guilt. Joel, you are to pay Sadler a social visit.'

Gasping in horror, Joel stared at his dad.

'You mean – you really expect me to go to the house of the man who murdered you in cold blood, and sit and have tea with him?' Joel cried, trembling.

Nathan placed his hands on Joel's shoulders and looked him squarely in the eye. 'Not only must you do this, Joel, but you will behave as if you believe that Sadler was my best friend and trusted business partner. That is how Sadler will expect you to behave. Should you raise his suspicions, your lives – and this mission – will be in jeopardy! There is so much riding on this, Joel, personal feelings have no place. You're in the army now, son – the army of God – and your weapons are not of the world!'

'Yes, Joel,' Tamara added. 'Remember what we've just seen – all those wasted lives because of villains like Sadler and Lilith?' She put a supportive hand on Joel's arm, and smiled encouragingly.

Joel looked up at his father.

'It's OK, Dad,' Joel nodded bravely. 'I can do it. I know I can.'

'That's the Spirit, son,' Nathan gave him a smile of encouragement. 'I know it's going to be hard for you, but I'm confident that you can pull it off. You can take Peter with you. It would be quite understandable for you to take a friend. Maité, Anna and I will keep watch through the Vista.'

'What about me?' Tamara asked, a little indignantly.

'I'm coming to you, Tamara,' Nathan said affectionately. 'Surely you didn't think I would leave you out, did you?'

Tamara perked up and returned the smile.

'Now, today is Tuesday and every Tuesday is "law night" at Wiggies – that's the bar in the city where the "legal eagles," i.e. the members of the legal profession, gather. Many of the top solicitors, judges and barristers meet up after work for a drink – it's part of the old-boy network – most of them know each other from going to the same schools and universities. Sadler goes to the bar straight from the office and will not be home until late. So, we'll have to wait until tomorrow to put our plan into action. But that's OK because Lilith is off tomorrow, which means that if anything leaks out at New Scotland Yard, Lilith would not hear about it until the following morning, by which time, if all goes according to plan, he will have been exposed – and arrested.'

'Great! So what exactly *is* the plan, Dad?'

'We wait till we see Sadler arriving home from work tomorrow evening – it's usually about six o'clock, after he's been to the gym for a workout. Then, you two boys will go through the Vista and knock on his front door.' Nathan turned to the Vista as he talked. 'I'm sure he'll invite you in once he realises who you are, Joel. I believe Sims will be on duty, keeping watch outside. He'll be in his car, parked in the street at the front of Sadler's house; he'll be listening to sport on the radio – if he's not asleep. I don't think Sims will pay any attention to two young boys paying Sadler a visit, anyway.'

The Vista showed them Sadler's three-storey town-house and zoomed in to the front door.

'Peter, when you're settled in the lounge, you must excuse yourself by asking to go to the bathroom. However, you will go to Sadler's bedroom instead.' Nathan continued to talk them through the plan for their mission.

The view on the Vista went up the stairs, across the hallway, past the bathroom and into Sadler's rather untidy bedroom, settling on his unmade bed.

'Eow,' Tamara murmured. 'Yuck! Peter, you'll need to wear an anti-contamination suit to go in there!'

'Don't worry, Tamara, it won't be like that tomorrow,' Nathan assured her. 'Wednesday is "Edna day."'

'Edna day?' Tamara chuckled, humorously.

'Edna the cleaner; she comes on Wednesdays and blitzes the place. So in the early evening when you go, it'll be like a new pin.'

'Good,' Tamara giggled. 'I wonder how long it stays like that.'

'Oh, probably for about ten minutes after Sadler gets back from work,' Joel hissed, sarcastically.

Nathan threw Joel a mock look of reproof. 'Joel you are not of the world. Sadler is as much a victim as the people he hurts. He has been taken captive by the devil – overtaken by evil.'

'Sorry, Dad. Well, how do we get out with the case?' Joel asked. 'Sadler is hardly going to wave us off through the front door with it, and I don't think Peter would be able to hide it under his jumper!'

'Yeah and we can't take it up through the Vista, either,' Peter added.

'True,' Nathan agreed. 'This is where Tamara comes in.'

Tamara cheered up and grinned, now that her part was finally being introduced.

'Joel,' Nathan continued. 'You will keep Sadler talking in the lounge: about me, him, your mother, your school – I don't know, anything that comes into your head, so that he forgets about how long Peter is taking in the "bathroom." Peter, remember you've got three moving targets to dodge: Uz, Buz and Jethro. Each on their own could spell disaster, so you'll have to keep your wits about you.'

'I'm not worried about the mutts, Mr Asher – but Jethro, I'm not so sure about,' Peter replied.

'You'll be fine, as long as you stick to the plan, Peter,' Nathan answered.

The Vista showed the children the relevant areas of Sadler's house, as Nathan continued.

'You've got to get back down the stairs, along the hallway and into the kitchen, with the case, then slip outside through the back door,' Nathan explained.

When the Vista showed the kitchen, they saw the two dogs and Jethro, who was feeding them on raw steak, which they were ripping apart, snarling and growling like ravenous wolves.

'Eek!' Tamara shrieked, as she watched the ferocious beasts.

'I suggest you wait for Jethro to take the dogs to the park for their exercise, *before* you excuse yourself,' Nathan went on. 'Then, grab the case out of Sadler's bed drawer as quick as you can – every second counts. Are you still OK with this, Peter?'

'Piece of cake, Mr Asher; those dogs will be no problem,' Peter shrugged – but not as convincingly as Joel would have liked.

'Now, Tamara,' Nathan said, at last. You'll be watching through the Vista. As soon as you see Peter enter the kitchen with the case, you focus the Vista on the back yard and step through it, ready to relieve Peter of the case as soon as he opens the back door.'

'Easy-peasy, Nathan,' Tamara grinned with excitement.

'Then, Tamara, you'll have to leave the yard by the back gate and wait in the alley for the boys. As Peter rightly pointed out, you cannot take the case up through the Vista. Then, Peter, you must return to Joel and Sadler in the lounge. If everything has gone according to plan, you must get out of there as soon as possible. Give Joel a signal that everything is OK. If you've succeeded in getting the case to Tamara, you will say, as you enter the lounge: "Do you think we should be going, Joel; we don't want to be too late?" As soon as you hear that, Joel, the two of you scarper. You must not leave Tamara in the alley with the case any longer than absolutely necessary as Jethro could return at any moment and she would be in grave danger if she is found with it. Now, Peter, if for some inexplicable reason you fail to either locate the case or to hand it over to Tamara, you will say to Joel: "Am I interrupting something?" Joel, if you hear that, you'll know there is a problem. Make out that you're upset – that it's all too much for you, and ask if Peter can show you where the bathroom is. Then you both go to the bathroom, where you can regroup and, depending on Peter's information, either take action or, if necessary, abort the mission.'

'That's not going to happen, Dad; a kid of six could snatch that case!' Joel chuckled.

'It can be very dangerous to assume things, Joel. That can make you complacent and forgetful,' Nathan warned. 'However, "assuming" everything *does* go according to plan, you say goodbye to Sadler and leave the way you came in – via the front door. Then, you make your way round to the back, without alerting Sims in any way, collect Tamara with the case and take a taxi and make haste to New Scotland Yard. Once inside New Scotland Yard, you will ask to see Detective John Smith. Don't be fobbed off; stress that it's a matter of utmost urgency and Smith will be curious to see you. As soon as Smith sees the case, he will recognise it and will usher you, forthwith, into his office. Remember that Smith presently thinks that case is at the bottom of the Thames! You must make sure that he opens the case and sees the list of villains. It is crucial that he is aware of Sadler and Lilith's involvement. Then, your mission is accomplished; you must leave the rest to Smith and you must then go to a quiet location, where Maité will come through the vista to make a schism to bring you all back.

'To a hero's welcome, my friends,' Maité grinned.

'Oh, and by the way,' Nathan added. 'You'll have the Magi on hand; they'll be keeping watch outside all the time.'

'Oh, yay!' Tamara cried, joyfully. 'I love the ravens!'

'What? That grouchy pair!' Joel exclaimed.

'Joel!' Tamara frowned. 'You may need those lovely birds one day and you'll eat your words.'

'Sorry, I guess they're OK, really,' Joel muttered.

'Right then, any questions?' Nathan asked.

'Sounds like taking candy from a baby. I just hope all our missions are this easy, Dad. It's lucky for us that Sadler is such a pea-brain!' Joel remarked, dryly.

'Yeah, it looks like you've thought of everything, Mr Asher,' Peter agreed, confidently.

'Don't be too confident, boys – no one who passes the exams Sadler has passed can be a complete pea-brain. It's imperative that you remain vigilant at all times! You never know who or what might be lurking round the corner to trip you flat on your face,' Nathan warned.

They all nodded.

'Now, there's nothing more we can do today,' Nathan concluded. 'So, we'll meet here tomorrow, six p.m. GMT.

†

Peter went back home to the farm that afternoon to help his dad, and it was a good job that he did. One of the cows gave birth to twin calves and help was needed to pull them out and get them breathing. This was a task that Peter knew just how to do, having watched and helped his dad in the past, so, both calves and their mum were saved.

Joel was feeling a little guilty that he had not spent much time with Grandad this holiday so, that afternoon, he helped him to repair a fence. This gave them a chance to have a really good grandfather-grandson talk. Joel actually quite enjoyed the afternoon. Grandad had always been a good talker and he never ran out of interesting stories. However, the whole afternoon was periodically interrupted by Magee, who kept fluttering by, occasionally settling on a nearby branch or even the fence they were working on whilst throwing in the odd humorous comment. This somewhat frustrated Joel as he could not reply and just had to let the raven "rave on" regardless. However, if the truth be known, Joel was beginning to appreciate the old raven's dry sense of humour, which was not dissimilar to his own at times – and he couldn't help but let out the odd chuckle. As Joel and his grandad moved further along the fence, so did the raven.

'Well, this has scotched any plans you might have had of becoming a carpenter, Joel, judging by the state of this fence!' Magee remarked dryly, from over Joel's shoulder.

Joel bit his lip to stop himself answering the raven back as he wanted to, but instead threw him a warning glance.

'Don't worry, pops can't hear me; only you can,' Magee went on. 'Does he know what a straight line *is*? My feathers! And this is *before* his evening tipple!'

Joel laughed at this and tried to disguise it as a cough.

'Joel, are you all right?' Grandad asked. 'You keep chuckling. Do I look funny or something?'

'No, of course not, Grandad, I'm fine. I'm sorry, it must be a tickle in my throat, that's all,' Joel replied, glaring at Magee.

'That raven seems very interested in what we're doing, doesn't he, Joel?' Grandad remarked in amusement, as he stood up to rest his back.

'Oh, really Grandad? I'd hardly noticed,' Joel muttered, throwing Magee another warning glance.

'Beautiful bird, isn't he?' Grandad commented.

'At least someone around here has good taste,' Magee cawed, preening himself.

'You know, Joel,' Grandad continued. 'Ravens have a special affinity with humans.'

Magee nodded, proudly.

'Sometimes, you could swear that they understand what you're saying,' Grandad added.

'Not as daft as he's pudding faced, is he?' Magee observed.

'That's going too far!' Joel snapped at Magee.

'No, seriously, Joel. They can appear to understand us.'

Grandad had thought that Joel's terse remark was directed at him When, in fact, it was meant for Magee.

'I'm sure they're very clever birds, Grandad, but they can be quite annoying at times.' Joel glared at Magee.

'OK, I'm sorry,' Magee chirped.

'Yes, you're right, Joel. Intelligent as they are, they have absolutely no common sense and they can be quite quarrelsome,' Grandad agreed.

'Huh! Indeed?' Magee retorted indignantly. 'You can go off people, you know.' With that, Magee spread his wings and flew off.

'I think that's about it for now, Joel. I don't think my back could stand much more of this today. What do you think?' Grandad stood back to admire their handiwork.

'Well, it's not exactly straight, is it, Grandad? But, as fences go, it's functional…' Joel replied. As he surveyed the fence though, he had to agree with Magee. It was a good job he wanted to be a barrister, like his dad!

†

Whilst Joel had been helping Grandad, Tamara had decided that Cherokee needed her mane and tail shampooing – a job guaranteed to get more lather on Tamara than the pony, especially while holding up the bucket to immerse her tail. She plaited her mane, putting brightly coloured ribbons in it, and polished her saddle and bridle. All the while, Tamara was having a lovely chat with Maggi. Being just outside the barn they were out of earshot of Grandad and Joel, who were being entertained by Magee. This left Tamara and Maggi free to chat all afternoon. Maggi told Tamara that she and Magee had been angels for several thousands of years, and were quite inseparable. She regaled Tamara with wonderful tales of assignments they'd worked on over the centuries. This wasn't the first time they'd been ravens, either. In fact, Maggi and Magee had been ravens forty-eight times. Once, they had kept five people, who were trapped in a cave, alive for two weeks. They'd ferried parcels of food – anything they could purloin – until a Kairos member led rescuers to where they were.

'I know we seem to argue a lot,' Maggi mused, 'but who wouldn't, when they'd been together as long as we have?'

Tamara was concerned that her mum would worry about her, so she reluctantly left the boys to themselves and returned home for the night. Cherokee looked splendid as they set off early, with her finely polished saddle, gleaming stirrups and brightly coloured ribbons bobbing up and down as she proudly pranced out of the yard. As there were only a few days of the holidays left, Peter's parents allowed him go back to Joel's grandad's for the night.

†

That night, when Joel and Peter were fast asleep in bed, Joel suddenly woke up with a start. He looked down his bed, blinking and squinting until his eyes became accustomed to the dark. He thought he was seeing things at first; it looked like a small slit in the air, like the ethereal curtain of a schism to the Vista. He saw a faint shaft of light, as the ethereal curtain appeared to open and shut slowly, as if being wafted by a soft breeze.

'Who's there?' Joel whispered, curiously.

There was no reply.

'Peter, wake up!' Joel urged in a low voice.

'What is it?' Peter groaned, half asleep.

'Peter, there's something strange happening and I don't understand what it is,' Joel murmured.

Peter sat up and, after rubbing his eyes, he looked in Joel's direction.

'It's OK Joel, I can see it,' said Peter. 'I think we might be wanted. It looks like someone has opened a schism for us.'

'Correct, my friend,' Magee's now familiar voice cawed as the raven appeared and perched on the bottom of Joel's bed.

'Oh, it's you!' Joel mumbled, bewildered. He reached for his lantern, switched it on and looked at the clock next to it which said: 11.55 pm. The light of Joel's lantern shone on Magee, creating a large eerie-looking shadow of the bird. 'What is it, Magee? What on earth do you want at this time? It's the middle of the night!'

'Not me…' the bird continued '…it's Nathan. You'd better throw on some clothes. Nathan has opened a schism for you to get up to the Vista from here, so you don't need to go to Zionica. I have to tell you, boys, that this is most exceptional, which tells me that it really is an emergency. So please make haste, boys. There isn't a moment to lose!'

Immediately Joel and Peter leapt out of bed and scrambled into some clothes. Then, they both moved towards the schism.

'Wait!' Magee called. 'You'd better put some padding under your bed covers – in case your grandad looks in.'

'Good thinking, Magee,' Joel replied. 'You've done this kind of thing before, haven't you?'

Magee raised an aloof eyebrow.

The two boys stuffed their dressing gowns and a few other items quickly under their covers.

'Thanks, Magee,' Joel whispered, with a grin.

'Yeah, see you, pal,' Peter grinned.

With that, the boys slipped through the schism.

'Hmm, pal… well, that's progress, I guess,' Magee remarked to himself, with a pleased nod.

†

Instantly, the two boys were gliding out of the Vista directly into the Vista room in Heaven, bypassing the Fugue. Nathan and Anna were there, waiting for them. As they entered in, the heady warm glow of pure love again engulfed them. The love in the air was so tangible, it kind of hit them as if stepping off a plane into a heat-wave. However, it wasn't hot, just glowing and warm, like a blanket wrapped around them.

'Wow!' Peter exclaimed. 'I didn't know we could do that – enter Heaven straight from the bedroom!'

'If your heart is right, Peter, you can enter Heaven from anywhere in the world,' Anna replied with a beaming smile. This was such a treat for her, to see her only son whom she'd not seen since he was a baby.

'Anyway,' Nathan began, with some urgency. 'A young boy is in trouble and your first "test" mission is to rescue him.'

'Oh, wow – a mission – already? That's great, Dad! What do you want us to do?' Joel asked eagerly.

'It's going to be a *real* test for you, son, but I know you can overcome it,' Nathan announced confidently.

'OK…' Joel said hesitantly, suspecting that he wasn't going to like what he was about to hear.

'This boy is a runaway,' Nathan began. 'He thinks that no one loves him or cares about him; he's hurting and lost. His parents had been punishing him for something he'd done; something that had caused really severe consequences, and hence the punishment was also severe. Now though, he is missing and his parents are worried sick about him. The police are out looking for him, but they won't find him because they're looking in the wrong places. They're concentrating on all the bus and train routes; they think he may have run off to the city, but by the time they start to look in the right place, it could be too late. He is hiding out in a derelict mine shaft, but he has fallen through some rotting timber and is currently trapped on a narrow ledge about 60 centimetres wide, above a sheer drop of around a hundred metres. The ledge is not stable; it could collapse at any moment. Your mission, boys, is to get him out and there's no time to lose! You must go to the mine-shaft immediately – every second counts!'

'Of course we'll go, Dad,' Joel replied. 'Just show us where he is and we'll do our best to get him out,' he added determinedly.

'I knew you'd say that, son,' Nathan said, proudly.

They all focused on the Vista as Nathan brought up the view of the disused mineshaft. Although it was late at night, thankfully there was a clear, moonlit sky. The view pushed inside the mine, where it was dark, damp and scary.

'Poor kid!' Peter murmured. 'He must be petrified; it's so creepy,' he shuddered.

As the view progressed down a black, desolate tunnel, the Vista compensated for the lack of light, revealing the rotting timber and the hole through which the boy had fallen. Then, about three metres down, on a narrow ledge, they saw the boy. Both Joel and Peter suddenly gasped.

'Presten!' Peter cried, astonished.

'Yes, boys,' Nathan acknowledged, mournfully. 'I'm afraid it's Tamara's brother. You've got to get him out quickly; one slip and he's gone – and that ledge will not hold his weight much longer.'

Joel stared into the Vista in disbelief.

'Poor Mr and Mrs Goodchild,' Peter muttered. 'They've just got over the upset with Tamara and now this!'

'Yes, we must do everything possible to save him. It's quite dark inside the mine but some moonlight is filtering through. Do you think you can get him out?' Nathan asked.

Joel was still staring in utter incredulity.

'Joel…' Nathan urged.

"Dad.'

"Yes, son,"

"Couldn't God just do a miracle and whisk the pesky little blighter out?"

"Well, of course, Joel, God can do anything,' Nathan answered patiently. 'However, God has chosen to work on earth through man. This is what God has ordained and it is the way He wants it done. God could have done everything on His own, but, He has done the hard part – the part that is impossible for man – that is to provide salvation. God has paid the ultimate and highest price – the blood of His own Son. It is a blessing to serve God, Joel and He has given man the privilege of serving Him in the world. Also you must realise that this is not just a test mission, boys, but a test of your hearts. So, are you ready?'

'We understand, Dad,' Joel replied, knowingly.

'Good! Now the Magi are already there, waiting for you.' Nathan put a hand on each boy's shoulders. 'Be careful, boys, it's dangerous as dangerous can be down there. The whole caboodle could cave-in at any moment.

'We'll be alright, Mr Asher,' Peter reassured him, bravely.

'Joel,' Nathan warned gravely, 'don't do anything foolish – you know what I mean? Without you, the Sadler / Lilith mission is a dead duck.'

'We'll be careful, Dad, I promise,' Joel smiled bravely, trying to conceal his nerves.

'Good lads,' Nathan encouraged them.

Joel and Peter focused the Vista on the entrance to the mineshaft, where they could see by the moonlight that the landing would be on soft grass. They glanced at each other with trepidation, then, gliding forward, their feet touched down with the contrasting heaviness of gravity and the chilly night air.

'Our first mission, Joel!' Peter whispered with nervous excitement.

'Yeah, and it just had to be, saving Presten!' Joel tutted. 'Come on then, let's get the weasel out!'

Joel poked his head inside the entrance to the mine. 'It's pretty dark in here, Peter. Damp and musty too,' he reported, his voice a little shaky. They both edged their way inside then, suddenly, they nearly jumped out of their skins as something flew out at them.

'Aagh!' they both screamed together.

'About time!' a haughty voice echoed loudly. It was Magee! He landed on a beam at the entrance.

'Magee!' Joel thundered. 'Are you trying to give us a heart attack or something?'

'Sorreee…' Magee replied, a little disgruntled. 'I thought Nathan would have told you to expect us.'

'He did!' Joel retorted, sharply. 'He said you'd be waiting for us, not hurtling out at us and scaring us almost to death!'

'There you are, see,' Maggi cawed as she flew out a little more sedately, landing on the beam next to Magee. 'I told you we should have waited outside.'

'Well, how was I to know they'd get all startled!' Magee grumbled defensively. 'I thought we should keep our eyes on the boy what's about to plunge to his death down a hundred-metre mineshaft!'

'*Who*, Magee! The boy *who* is about to plunge to his death down a hundred-metre mineshaft,' Maggi corrected.

'Oh, whatever…' Magee wittered.

'TIME-OUT!' Joel bellowed.

It was the ravens' turn to jump. In fact, they nearly fell off the beam! They both stared at Joel in stunned silence and if ravens had a bottom lip, Maggi's would probably have been wobbling.

'That's better,' Joel uttered, a little more calmly. 'This is not a time for one of your arguments. Now, let's formulate a plan to get the boy out, shall we?'

'Huh!' Magee huffed, indignantly. 'Well, what do you suggest? Of course, a rope would be handy but we don't have one, do we?'

'We need some light,' Joel continued, unperturbed by the raven's apparent injured feelings. 'Magee, how long would it take you to fly to Grandad's house and back, and how strong is your beak?'

'Well, of course,' Magee coughed, 'had I not been in this raven's body, I could get there in no time at all. I could transport myself there instantly and, anyway, angels are supernaturally strong. For instance, if you were trapped under a vehicle…'

'Magee!' Maggi interrupted. 'I think time is of the essence here…'

'Oh, yes, well, if you want me to carry something, I would actually have to fly there and back "on the wing," so to speak.

'What do you want him to fetch,' Joel, Peter asked.

'Dogs *fetch*, Peter!' Magee retorted indignantly. 'Angels, I mean – ravens, purloin.'

'Oh, of course, I'm sorry Magee,' Peter apologised humorously.

'Ahem...' Maggi coughed. 'There is a boy on a precarious ledge here...'

'What do you want me to pick up, Joel?' Magee inquired.

'How far are we from Grandad's place?' Joel asked.

'Not that far, actually, Joel,' Peter said. 'I know this mineshaft. It's about two miles as the crow…

'Ahem,' Magee coughed this time, looking pointedly at Peter.

'…I mean, as the raven flies,' Peter smiled apologetically at Magee.

'Two miles, Magee,' Joel pressed. 'Carrying the lantern from my bedside table. How long?'

'Ten minutes,' Magee estimated promptly.

'Make it five,' Joel insisted.

Maggi and Magee looked at each other, rolling their eyes sceptically. Then Magee instantly vanished.

'Well, of course, Magee can get there instantly but he will have to fly back with the lantern – that's assuming your bedroom window is open, Joel. Magee cannot get your lantern out through a closed window,' Maggi pointed out with a resigned sigh.

'I'm fairly certain it'll be open, Maggi. Grandad is a fresh air freak; he opens all the windows all the time. But even if it is shut surely Magee has the intelligence to open it from the inside with his beak!'

'Oh, well of course,' Maggi answered indignantly. 'We ravens are highly intelligent creatures, not forgetting that we are not merely ordinary ravens but angels.'

They all stood anxiously waiting, in silence. Then broke the silence.

'You know, you really got to him, Joel,' she murmured. 'No one has ever shouted at Magee before, except Maguff – and me. I – I could tell he was upset.'

'I know,' Joel nodded. 'So could I.'

'Look!' Peter yelled, pointing upwards.

They followed Peter's gaze and saw a light, like a shooting star, moving swiftly through the dark sky. As it approached, they could see a black dot flying above the bright light.

'He's here already!' Peter cried, with surprise.

Magee flew up and dropped the lantern into Joel's hand. Then he perched, slightly breathless, next to Maggi at the entrance to the mine-shaft.

'Thanks, Magee,' Joel smiled. 'Well done! Hey, I'm sorry I shouted at you before, pal.'

'Apology accepted.' Magee cocked his head on one side then looked up at Joel. 'I – I never thanked you for sticking up for me with Maguff the other day. It was good of you – especially after the way *I* behaved. I'm sorry too, Joel.'

'Well, I couldn't let you or Maggi spend five thousand years as sewer rats, now could I?' Joel grinned.

'Excuse me interrupting, but what about Presten? He's still on that precarious ledge,' Peter butted in.

'Right, come on then, let's get the weasel out,' Joel answered, leading the way with his lantern.

The two boys felt their way slowly along the wall of the mine, stepping carefully. As they ventured inside, the two ravens kept pace with them.

'Presten!' Joel shouted.

'Asher?' Presten screamed in surprise. 'Is that you?' He sounded quite distressed.

'Yeah, where are you?' Joel replied.

'About five-metres from the entrance! Just keep going straight ahead till you come to a wooden platform… but don't put all your weight on it… it's rotten… I've fallen through it. Hurry, Asher! Get me out of here!' Presten yelled.

Joel and Peter continued with trepidation along the tunnel in the direction of Presten's voice. Although it was creepy, they felt strangely comforted by the presence of their little guardians. Then they saw the platform and its jagged edge, where Presten had fallen through. Joel shone his lantern down and they could just make out his huddled form on the rotten wooden ledge below.

'We can see you, Presten!' Joel shouted down. 'How are you doing?'

'How do you think, dummy!' Presten bellowed back rudely. 'I'm stuck down a filthy, disgusting pit on a tiny, creaking ledge that's about to give way! How the devil did you find me, anyway?'

'Not through him, that's for sure,' Joel muttered.

'So, what's the plan, Asher?' Presten called shakily, standing up. 'How's the big hero going to rescue me now?'

'Describe the state of the ledge you're standing on, Presten,' Joel demanded, ignoring his rudeness.

'It's just a few rotting planks and joists, held up by some sort of rusty scaffolding. Looks as if it's going to fall apart at any minute! I feel like I'm standing on the skin of a rice pudding!

I'm scared, Asher! Get me out of here – and hurry-up!' Presten whimpered.

Joel and Peter looked around.

'Yeah, Joel, what *is* the plan?' Peter whispered in a low voice.

'I don't know...' Joel murmured. '...but we can't tell him that!'

'Well, we'd better think of something, quick!' Peter urged. 'That ledge sounds extremely dodgy...'

'Hm, Presten is pretty heavy as well – too heavy for us to pull him up from that far down,' Joel mused. 'You're taller and lighter than me, Peter. Presten and I could pull you up between us. If I lower you down and Presten stands on your shoulders, I could pull him up over the top. Then, you can stand on his rucksack and Presten and I can pull you up. What do you say?'

'Well, I guess it's a plan, Joel; I can't think of a better one,' Peter shrugged, bravely.

'What are you two chumps hatching?' Presten yelled up. 'Can't you see this whole ledge is about to fall apart? Get a move on, will you!'

'Presten, I'm going to lower Peter down to you. You'll have to grab his legs and help him down. Then, climb onto Peter's shoulders. I can pull you up from there. After that, we'll pull Peter up between us, OK?' Joel shouted down.

'Yeah, yeah, get on with it then, Asher! Get down here, Jordan, and hurry up!' Presten demanded. 'This place gives me the creeps!'

'I don't think you can trust that boy, Joel,' Maggi warned.

'You're right, Maggi,' Joel agreed. 'We can trust him about as much as a starving dog in a butcher's shop – but we ain't got a choice. Come on, Peter, I'll help you down.'

Joel found the strongest part of the platform edge. He broke out into little beads of sweat as, with trembling arms, he helped steady Peter, while he slowly climbed down over the edge.

'I've got a bad feeling about this, Magee,' Maggi murmured.

'Yes, I know, dearest. So have I,' Magee replied, shaking his head.

'Have you got him, Presten?' Joel called, straining with Peter's weight.

'Yeah, you can let go now, Asher,' Presten replied.

Presten guided Peter's legs down to the ledge but didn't take much of his weight. Consequently, as Joel let go, Peter dropped the last metre, landing heavily on the ledge and making it slump. The whole ledge and its supports creaked and wobbled precariously as Peter slipped, grazing his knee on the stone wall of the shaft.

'You stupid moron!' Presten screamed, clinging to Peter. 'Don't bother getting up, Jordan. Let me climb on your back.'

Peter stooped on the tiny ledge, clinging to some rusty piping on the wall. The obnoxious Presten stamped his boot onto Peter's back and climbed up onto his shoulders. Peter winced under Presten's considerable weight.

'Right, get up, dweeb!' Presten demanded, impatiently. 'I can't reach Asher's hands from *this* far down!'

Peter grimaced as he slowly and carefully stood up, keeping his body flat against the wall. Presten clung to Peter in fear.

'Careful, Jordan, careful!' Presten shrieked in a terrified, almost squeaky voice.

When Peter was on his feet, Presten reached up with his hands and found the ends of Joel's fingers. Presten must have weighed about 150 pounds – quite a weight for a twelve-year-old boy.

'Get my hands, Asher!' Presten shrieked, fearfully.

Joel gripped hold of Presten's hands firmly and seemed to gain a supernatural strength as he pulled with all his might. Presten kicked off Peter's shoulders, causing Peter to cry out painfully.

'Agh!' Peter cried.

Finally, Presten scrambled over the top of the platform, aided by Joel, to the safety of the tunnel.

'Peter!' Joel cried. 'Peter, are you alright?' He scrambled back to the edge of the platform and peered over.

'Yeah, don't worry, I'm OK,' Peter called back bravely, as he rubbed his bruised shoulders. 'Is Presten OK?'

'Yeah he's fi…' Joel began.

'I'm peachy,' Presten interrupted as he stood over Joel and shouted down the shaft. 'And I'm touched you care. Now hand me my rucksack, Jordan!' he demanded.

'No!' Joel cried, jumping to his feet. 'Peter needs to stand on it so we can reach him! It's only a rucksack, Presten!'

'Only a rucksack!' Presten screamed with rage, his demented voice reverberating through the mineshaft. 'My most valuable possessions are in that rucksack, you moron!'

'Don't be a fool, Presten! We can come back in daylight with proper equipment to get your beloved rucksack,' Joel urged. 'Help me lift Peter up! We can pull him up between the two of us.'

'Lift him yourself!' Presten snarled and as he did so, he pushed Joel violently. Joel lost his balance and tried to grab hold of Presten but the puffed-up, hateful boy jumped out of the way. Then, in a flash, Joel realised that he was falling over the edge of the platform and there was nothing he could do to stop himself…

'Aagh!' Joel screamed as he plunged headfirst: down, down, down, towards certain death. His last thought as he passed out was about his dad and the mission that had now been thwarted.

'Joel!' Peter cried desperately, watching in horror as his best friend catapulted down the mineshaft. 'Presten! What have you done?' he yelled up in anguish.'

Presten looked suddenly very afraid; he turned and ran out of the mineshaft; leaving the two Kairos boys to perish.

'Magee!' Peter yelled.

Magee was momentarily stunned with shock as his charge disappeared over the edge.

'Magee!' Maggi echoed. 'Do something!'

Magee, seemingly came to his senses and took off like a rocket, in a nose-dive down the shaft, but immediately crash landed onto Joel's back. Peter watched in stunned silence, as Joel appeared to be floating, spread-eagled, back up the shaft! A strange light appeared to glow all around him! Peter's first thought was that Joel must be dead and that this must be his spirit floating up to Heaven… but then why was Magee lying prostrate on Joel's back?

Then, it all became clear as Joel floated past Peter up to the top of the shaft and Peter saw what, or rather who, was lifting Joel. Peter could hardly believe it! Maguff was flying underneath Joel, raising him up on his huge eagle's wings! The glow was coming from Maguff!

Maguff set the unconscious Joel down on the floor of the tunnel. The glowing light coming from Maguff, lit up the whole cavern.

'Maguff!' Peter cried. 'You're a blessed angel! How is he?'

'Joel's passed out,' Maggi called, 'and so has Magee! They're both out cold!'

'Oh, I – I didn't realise that angels could pass out,' Peter called, surprised.

'It's the raven's body that's passed out – not Magee,' Maggi explained, as she dipped a wing in a pool of water and shook it over Magee's head.

'He's just concussed, that's all,' Maguff confirmed.

Magee opened his eyes and groaned. Then, he stood up and shook himself vigorously.

'Thank you, my dear,' Magee teetered a little as though punch-drunk.

Maggi repeated the process of dipping her wing in the water and this time, she shook it over Joel, who stirred and opened his eyes.

'Where am I?' Joel muttered. 'Magee! You saved me!'

'Well, er, it wasn't actually me, Joel.' Magee nodded in Maguff's direction. Joel followed Magee's gaze and gasped in amazement when he saw Maguff.

'Maguff? It was you!' Joel cried in astonishment.

'Yes.' The officious eagle seemed unperturbed by the dramatic events. 'I'm not supposed to intervene in the guardians' cases, but you are an important asset, Joel – a special case. I was ordered to save you.' Maguff looked sympathetically at Magee. 'Good as your intentions were, Magee, I think you might have struggled to apprehend and lift forty times your body weight, falling at great speed. Also you hesitated, which could have lost us the asset.'

'I – I...' Magee hung his head dejectedly. 'It all happened so fast, Maguff. I'm sorry…'

'Well, anyway,' Maguff continued. '*I'm* sorry I knocked you out, but there obviously wasn't time to warn you – and I couldn't take the risk of losing the asset – you understand.'

'N – No, er… I mean yes – of course – I understand, Maguff.' Magee raised his head. 'You saved the day. It was good that you were in the neighbourhood.'

'Yeah, thanks Maguff,' Joel echoed, gratefully. 'You saved my life.'

'Like I said, it was an order. And now I must leave you; I was in the middle of an urgent call-out,' Maguff announced.

'Excuse me…' Peter shouted up. 'Have you forgotten – I'm still on this ledge?'

'Peter!' Joel cried, jumping to his feet. 'Maguff, you can save Peter now!'

'No, I'm sorry, Joel. I'm not allowed to intervene with Kairos missions unless specifically instructed to do so. Rules have to be obeyed! As I said, I'm needed elsewhere now. If I delay any longer many lives could be at risk and this is *your* mission, Joel.' With that, Maguff vanished into thin air.

'I don't believe it!' Joel cried, stunned.

'I'm OK, Joel, ' Peter called, 'but can you please hurry up! I don't know how long this ledge is going to hold me!'

'Stay exactly where you are, Peter!' Joel shouted down.

'Well, I don't think I could go anywhere if I wanted to, Joel,' Peter laughed nervously.

'No, I mean, don't move a muscle!' Joel instructed. 'I need to know exactly where you are! I'm going to get you through the Vista and there's not much landing space – if you get my drift.'

'Joel, are you sure? You could miss the ledge and fall,' Peter cried anxiously. 'The ledge is creaking like billy-o already, so I don't think it's going to hold *me* much longer – let alone you jumping onto it! Don't forget, you've got to survive and get

Sadler! You mustn't risk yourself for me, Joel!'

'It'll be alright, as long as you don't move! Just be ready to jump right back with me through the schism into the Vista.' Joel turned to Magee. 'Thanks for trying to save me Magee. I promise I'll never shout at you again.'

'Just don't go diving off too many cliffs,' Magee answered and then continued with a sense of foreboding. 'Joel – what you're about to attempt is very dangerous! I've never seen it done – or heard of anybody landing on such a precise target from the Vista. I don't think you can be that accurate. If you are even slightly out – if you misjudge it, both of you could fall...'

'I haven't got a choice, Magee,' Joel insisted. 'The Vista is our only chance.'

Magee nodded reluctantly.

'Do be careful, Joel,' Maggi implored.

'Well, go on then, before the whole caboodle caves in!' Magee urged. 'We'll wait here…' he shook his head, forlornly. Then, as Joel hurried back out of the mineshaft to where they had landed from the Vista. Magee muttered under his breath.

'... to pick up the pieces.'

'Such a brave boy...' Maggi murmured morosely, as if doom was inevitable.

Outside the mine, Joel raised his hand to open a schism and dived quickly through it. Nathan was waiting to catch him as he jumped in with some speed.

'Thank God for Maguff; the starchy bird has his uses, doesn't he?' Nathan sighed as he caught Joel. 'You must remember not to leap into the Vista too quickly, son.'

'I know, Dad, but I think my next leap will be even faster!'

'Joel!' Nathan warned seriously. 'Magee is right. What you're about to attempt would be extremely difficult, to say the least, even for someone who was experienced at using the Vista. With your limited experience, landing on a specific spot is almost on a par with a multi-pocket shot! I've never seen it done, either.'

'Evidently no one has ever needed to do it before, Dad. There's always a first time for everything,' Joel smiled courageously.

'You've only got one shot at this, son, and the light from the lantern is not brilliant. If you misjudge this, it could be fatal for both of you. If you both fall, I don't think Magee could pull off Maguff's stunt – certainly not for two of you, anyway,' Nathan warned gravely.

'I know, Dad, but that ledge is going to go. I've *got* to try!'

'God be with you, son,' Nathan smiled proudly. He stood by with Anna, both of them looking very tense.

Joel faced the Vista and brought up the view of Peter, motionless on the ledge. The rotting ledge was creaking and bits of wood were falling down the shaft. With deep concentration, Joel put his hand out in front of him ready to grab Peter. He suddenly glided into the Vista and was instantly on the ledge. Peter immediately grabbed hold of him, as the ledge slumped heavily. Presten's rucksack slid to the edge, almost dropping off. Joel immediately turned around and held up his hand to open the schism. They both made a mighty leap together, just as the entire ledge and its supports came away from the wall with a horrid, creaking sound of twisting metal. Then, the whole lot went crashing down into the depths of the shaft – along with Presten's precious rucksack containing his "valuable possessions."

Joel and Peter glided through the Vista into Nathan's waiting arms. As he caught them, Nathan hugged them both tightly and the overjoyed Anna joined in.

'Well done, both of you!' Nathan beamed with a mixture of joy and relief. 'I'm really proud of you! That was an excellent test mission. You're both true Kairos boys and are now ready for your first main mission.'

'Yes, and there'll be time for celebrating later,' Anna added. 'Right now though, you boys had better get back to bed before you're missed.'

'OK, Anna,' Peter grinned, bringing up Joel's bedroom on the Vista.

'There's just one thing I need to do first,' said Joel, mysteriously. 'You go on, Peter; I'll be there in a minute.'

Peter looked uncertain.

'Go on, Peter,' urged Nathan. 'It'll be alright.

Peter nodded. He was really exhausted and didn't need much persuading to go back to bed. After he had glided through the Vista, Joel brought up Tamara's house.

'Anna,' Joel asked, turning his face away from the Vista, 'could you check Tamara's bedroom and make sure she's in there and dressed?'

'It's OK, Joel,' Anna confirmed. 'The coast is clear. I don't think anyone in the Goodchild household is ready for bed right now, they're all too anxious about Presten.'

'I thought they would be,' Joel replied. He turned back to the Vista and there was Tamara, sitting fully clothed on her bed, looking as if she was praying. Joel glided into the room.

'Joel!' Tamara whispered in surprise. You startled me – what…?'

'Ssh.' Joel put a finger to his lips. 'I can't stay. Presten is...'

'I know. I can't believe he's done this! But, how come *you* know about it, anyway?'

'I can't tell you now. I need to get back. I just wanted to let you know that Presten is on the road by the old mine shaft. Go and tell your dad that Presten may be there because he's always been fascinated by the old mine. If your dad acts quickly, he'll find him near there now.'

'Thanks, Joel,' Tamara smiled, gratefully. 'I don't think my mum could take any more upset after all she's been through. You really are the best friend anyone could wish for, Joel – and after all Presten has done to you and Peter...'

'Don't worry, I'll see you tomorrow,' Joel answered with a grin. Then he raised his hand and disappeared back through the Vista, emerging back into Heaven again.

'You really are a true Kairos, Joel,' Nathan stated, proudly. 'Despite the fact that Presten almost killed you – and certainly left you for dead, you still put your duty to the Kairos first, letting his family know where to find him. Thank you for not letting me down, son. Now, you must to go back to bed. I'll see you at six pm tomorrow.'

'Good night, Dad,' Joel grinned.

'Good night, son,' Nathan smiled.

When Joel returned to his bedroom, it was just as he had left it; even the lantern had been returned to his bedside table.

'Thanks, Magi,' he whispered to himself, thinking they'd be long gone to roost for the night.

'You're welcome,' Maggi and Magee replied softly, in unison.

Surprised, Joel went over to the window, and there they were, perched on the ledge outside.

'What are you still doing here?' Joel asked.

'We're just having a rest, that's all,' Magee replied.

'Oh, so it's not that you wanted to check I arrived back alright, then?'

'We do have a duty, you know,' Magee cawed, 'I mean, it's nothing to do with the sewer-rat threat,' he added hastily.

'Well, good night, angels,' Joel murmured with a smile.

Joel and Peter fell asleep, exhausted but relieved that the evening's episode in the mineshaft was over. They must have been asleep for about half an hour when they were both awoken yet again. This time it was Grandad, who burst into the room and hurriedly switched on the light.

'Grandad!' Joel sat up, surprised. 'What's the matter?'

'Oh, thank God!' Grandad sighed with relief.

'What is it, Mr Jacob?' Peter sat up, yawning.

Grandad sat down on Joel's bed and chuckled. 'Fancy me falling for that!'

'Falling for what, Grandad?' Joel asked.

'You know, boys, I think Tamara's brother is seriously deranged.

'I can't believe that you've only just come to that conclusion, Grandad!' Joel declared with some amusement. 'What's he gone and done now?'

'Well, I've just had Presten's father on the phone,' Grandad began. 'Presten ran away from home this evening, leaving a note saying that he knew that they didn't care for him anymore, so they'd never see him again. Naturally, Mr and Mrs Goodchild were beside themselves with grief, and the police have been searching all evening for him.'

'Oh, poor Mrs Goodchild,' Joel sympathised.

'Yes, well, as it happens, Presten had been hiding in the old disused mineshaft, about two miles from here,' Grandad continued. 'Mr Goodchild picked him up on the road near there only a short while ago.'

'Oh, so he's back home again now?' Joel yawned.

'Yes, but get this!' Grandad continued. 'Presten must be seriously deluded because he swears that you and Peter were also in the mineshaft – only half an hour or so ago! Not only that, but he reckons he saw you, Joel, plunge one hundred metres to your death, down the mineshaft!'

'What?' Joel shrieked, with feigned shock.

'Yes, how ridiculous is that! Also, he insists that you, Peter are still stuck on a ledge three metres down the shaft!'

'Well, I have to agree, Grandad,' Joel giggled, 'the words *deluded* and *deranged* do come to mind. But, as you can see, Peter and I are perfectly safe and well, tucked up in our beds!'

'Yep!' Peter agreed. 'It looks like Presten has finally lost the plot completely!'

'Yes and I'm sorry I woke you guys,' Grandad apologised.

'Oh, not at all, Grandad. It was worth being woken up for the laugh,' Joel grinned.

'Well, I'll go and ring Mr Goodchild and let him know that this tale is the product of his son's overactive imagination. Good night, boys,' Grandad chuckled. 'Praise the Lord!'

'Good night, Grandad,' Joel chuckled delightedly.

'Good night, Mr Jacob.' Peter replied, equally amused.

As Grandad closed the door, the two boys could contain their amusement no longer and stifled their giggles with their quilts.

CHAPTER FIFTEEN

A Bitter Appointment

Sympathy was in short supply the next day, when Tamara told Joel and Peter the outcome of Presten's misadventure. A happy homecoming it was not, although obviously everyone was relieved that her brother had been found. However, Presten was in yet further trouble as a result of the "scare-mongering" stories he had seemingly "conjured up" about Joel and Peter's demise in the mine. Tamara though, was enthralled as the boys explained the real evening's events to her – but completely outraged by Presten's evil behaviour. The three of them had gone up to the den at Zionica, to discuss the recent amazing turn of events.

'Things look pretty grim for Presten,' Tamara informed them. 'Dad is still fuming about it all, and Mum is taking Presten to see a child-psychologist. The silly little twit won't stop wittering on about the two of you being in the mine; he keeps insisting that you are both dead, Joel – despite your grandad confirming that the two of you were in bed at the time and are demonstrably very much alive and well!'

'Yes, thankfully people are bound to think that Presten is making it all up,' Joel chuckled. 'Although I do feel rather sorry for him, really.'

'What?' Tamara raised an eyebrow. 'Joel – Presten tried to kill you!'

'No, I mean it,' Joel added. 'He's a messed-up kid; he's his own worst enemy.'

'Do you think he *deliberately* pushed you over the edge, Joel? I mean, what are the chances that it was simply an accident?' Peter asked.

'It's difficult to say, Peter. It all happened so fast and the light was very dim…' Joel paused thoughtfully.

'I'm scared, Joel,' Tamara frowned. 'If Presten really meant to kill you, that changes everything!'

'I see what you mean,' he mused. 'If killing me was Presten's deliberate aim, then the obnoxious little squirt is no longer just an irritating bully but…'

'Oh no! My brother could actually be a cold-blooded murderer!' Tamara cried in horror.

'Whatever we think of Presten,' Peter added, 'I can't believe that he's a cold-blooded killer – he's just a kid! How could it have been premeditated – he didn't even know that we were going to be there? Then again, he could have made some sort of attempt to pull you back, like a normal person would have done. But Presten just ran off!'

'Maybe he was scared that I might pull *him* over the edge as well,' Joel suggested.

'He didn't go for help, either,' Tamara added gravely, 'which means that he left you to die, too, Peter! Remember, Presten thought you were stuck on that perilous ledge...'

'Yes, but he did eventually tell your parents,' Peter argued, finding it hard to believe that Presten could be that evil.

'Yes, he did, Peter, but only because Tamara's dad picked him up on the road! The question is: would he have reported your plight to the police if Tamara's dad hadn't found him?' Joel asked. 'And just remember this – every notorious murderer was once just a kid!'

'Joel's got a point, Peter,' Tamara agreed. 'He did swear revenge this holiday. Anyway, let's not waste any more time discussing Presten. Let the psychologist sort him out.'

'Yes,' Joel nodded, 'I'm more interested in talking about our mission and the Kairos. Let's go over our plan for this evening again. I don't want *anything* to go wrong.'

†

At five minutes to six that evening, the three friends met at the edge of the plateau in Zionica. Peter and Tamara had their parents' permission to stay over at Joel's grandad's again. This, they felt, would limit the risk of the adults becoming suspicious; chances were that it would be quite late by the time they had chased half-way across London with Sadler's case.

'Have you got some paper money for the taxi, Joel?' Tamara reminded him.

'Yeah,' Joel patted his shirt pocket. 'I always bring some dosh away with me. I don't know why; we never go anywhere to spend it!' He laughed nervously. Then, he held out both his hands to his friends. 'Ready?'

Tamara and Peter smiled excitedly and nodded. They took hold of Joel's hands and all three stepped onto the plateau together. Maité, Anna and Nathan were waiting for them as they emerged at the top of the Fugue. After the usual greetings, they all made their way through the Hall of Archways to the Vista Chamber. After a brief recap of the plan, they were finally ready. The three new recruits were beside themselves with nervous excitement.

'You know, I have never, ever, whatsoever, been so excited in all my life!' Tamara exclaimed.

'I think everybody is feeling just the same, Tamara,' Nathan smiled.

Joel, Peter, Anna and Maité all nodded in agreement.

'So,' Nathan continued. 'On Wednesdays, Sadler always leaves the office early. He goes direct to the gym for an hour, then gets fish and chips for supper. He heads home for the evening and slumps in front of the television with his fish and chips and several cans of beer.'

'Sounds like a sensible lifestyle,' Joel mocked. 'I suppose he's got to put all that weight back on after working it off in the gym!'

'Oh, there's not much working-out done in the gym, Joel; this is a serial couch-potato we have here! No. When Sadler is at the gym, he spends most of his time lazing in the jacuzzi with a gin and tonic! Sadler is lazy with a capital "L."'

'Lazy and stupid, I would say,' Joel added.

'You learn fast, Joel,' Nathan continued. 'By now, he should have finished his supper and be opening his second or third can. Detective Smith is on the late shift; he finishes at ten pm. That should give you plenty of time to purloin the case and get to New

Scotland Yard, before he clocks-off for the night.'

Nathan brought up the view of Sadler's lounge on the Vista. Sadler was sprawled on an easy chair with one of his legs draped over the arm. He snapped the ring-pull off a can of beer. Another can lay empty on the table beside him, along with his screwed-up fish and chip paper.

'Such a creature of habit,' Nathan tutted.

'Such a slob!' Joel muttered in disgust.

The view changed to the street outside. A giant of a man was slumped back in his car, outside Sadler's house, apparently fast asleep.

'That's Sims – it's his shift tonight,' Nathan pointed out.

'Big fella, isn't he?' Joel gulped, a little nervously.

'Yes,' Nathan nodded. 'This isn't going to be a piece of cake, guys. There are many adversaries; these are not amateurs you're dealing with.'

The Vista view changed to the deserted alley down the side of Sadler's house.

'Good, there's no one there. Ready, boys?' asked Nathan.

Joel and Peter smiled nervously and nodded, as they walked towards the Vista.

'God be with you,' Nathan encouraged the boys, as he gripped Anna's hand reassuringly.

'Adios, amigos,' Maité cheered. 'God go with you – and don't forget, soldiers, you are not on milk bottle now, but best steak – and the new wine of the Holy Spirit!'

Joel looked over his shoulder at Maité and smiled. 'Would that be well-done, Maité, or rare?' he teased, with a grin.

'Touché!' she replied, returning the grin.

With that, the two boys glided into the Vista, landing in the alleyway. There was a chill in the air which, combined with their nervous excitement, caused them to shiver and draw their jackets around them.

'Right, there's no turning back now, Peter,' Joel said firmly.

'Are you sure you're OK – seeing this Sadler guy, Joel, knowing that he killed your dad?' Peter asked.

'Well, Peter it's a bit late for that now, isn't it!' Joel replied with a shrug. What I'd really like to do, is punch his lights out and spit in his eye. But… I'm going to be as nice as pie.'

'I know it's going to be hard for you, pal, but we're gonna have the victory in the end,' Peter reassured him.

'Yes, Peter, it's good to know we're on the winning side,' Joel replied. 'O.K., let's go for tea, shall we?'

The boys turned the corner into the street from the alleyway. Sims didn't bat an eyelid as they walked past his car, and then up Sadler's path to his door. Two familiar figures were perched on the fence by the front door: Maggi and Magee were in position. The boys looked up with trepidation.

'I hope you are good at dissimulation, boys,' Magee muttered with a wink.

'Maybe I could answer that, Magee – if I knew what it meant,' Joel replied sarcastically. Then he whispered to Peter, 'I'm sure that raven has swallowed a dictionary.'

'He just means you've got to convince Sadler that you think he's a good guy, when you really...' Peter began to explain.

'...want to smash his face in!' Finishing Peter's sentence, Joel bashed the doorbell with his fist.

Immediately, the two dogs began to bark and growl ferociously, which made the boys jump and sent a chill down Joel's spine. He turned and threw Peter a look of sheer panic. Sadler was one thing, but those dogs…

'Don't worry, Joel. Sadler will have those dogs under control,' Peter assured him, calmly.

'Shut-up!' They heard Sadler growl from inside. 'That's enough!'

The two boys exchanged glances, now both trembling with fear.

'Eek!' Joel uttered in a squeaky voice. 'I don't know whose bark sounds worse, the dogs' or Sadler's!'

'Oh, definitely Sadler's,' Peter whispered back, with a gulp.

The fierce command from Sadler appeared to silence the dogs. Then, they heard a series of bolts rattling and keys turning. Eventually, the door opened slightly and a rather dishevelled

Sadler peered suspiciously through the narrow opening. He was still wearing the tracksuit that he had worn for his visit to the gym and he held an open can of beer in his hand.

Joel had only ever seen Sadler in a smart suit and hardly recognised the unshaven, rough looking figure in front of him.

'Yeah?' Sadler snapped, tersely. He hadn't recognised Joel, either.

'Mr Sadler?' Joel asked.

'Who wants him?' Sadler replied, shiftily.

'It's Joel Asher, Mr Sadler – Nathan Asher's son – and this is my friend, Peter Jordan.' Joel swallowed nervously.

Sadler's jaw dropped and the can he was holding dropped from his hand and hit the ground like a stone, spilling its contents onto the doorstep. He looked visibly shocked. Joel reckoned that it was a conviction of his guilt.

'Joel?' Sadler endeavoured to pull himself together. 'I – I – didn't recognise you – you've grown. W – what are you doing here? Er, is your mother here, too?' he asked, peering over their shoulders.

'No, she doesn't know I'm here and I don't want her to know,' Joel added quickly, clenching his fists at his sides, fighting the urge to punch the duplicitous killer on the nose. But he had to get inside that house! He took a deep breath and smiled.

'I wondered if you could spare me a few minutes for a chat. Only, you knew my dad probably better than anyone else; you were one of his best friends *and* his business partner.' Joel squirmed inside. Having to say all these things to Sadler left a nasty taste in his mouth. 'I was very young when my dad…'

'Had the accident, you mean, Joel?' Sadler finished.

NO! WHEN YOU MURDERED HIM! Joel wanted to scream, but instead he took another deep breath. 'Yes, Mr Sadler. I don't remember much about it but I wondered if you could tell me about my dad,' he squirmed.

Dad and Peter were right; he *was* finding this incredibly difficult. Joel had underestimated how much self-control he would need to be courteous to this vicious murderer.

'Of course, lad,' Sadler wheezed, with more smarm than charm. 'Come in, let me get you something to drink.'

Sadler opened the door wide enough for Joel and Peter to enter. As they stepped inside, the two Rottweiler's emitted low growls through bared teeth.

'Shut up, you two!' Sadler snapped, grabbing the two dogs by their collars. 'I'll put them outside, in the back yard.'

'No!' Joel cried suddenly. Then, he felt the colour rising in his face as he inwardly kicked himself, hoping that he had not blown their cover. He couldn't let Sadler put the dogs in the yard – that was where Tamara was going to arrive!

Sadler looked suddenly startled at Joel's outburst.

'I – er, we love dogs, Mr Sadler,' Joel pleaded. 'Please can they stay with us? Peter is very good with dogs, aren't you, Peter. What are their names?'

Striving to overcome his fear, Joel bent down and forced himself to pat one of the dogs on the head. He looked up pleadingly at Peter, hoping for some help, as the dog looked as if it wanted to take his arm off. Peter bent down to the two dogs and began to stroke their heads, talking calmly to them. Suddenly both dogs went all soft and wimpy, nuzzling up to Peter like a pair of Labrador puppies!

'Well, I'll be doggone!' Sadler marvelled. 'I've never seen these two mutts take to *anybody* like that! O.K. then, they can come with us. This one is Uz and the larger one is Buz.' He let go of the dogs and led the boys into his lounge. 'Funny – they'd kill you as soon as look at you, normally!' he chuckled, with a casual coldness that the boys found quite chilling.

Once in the lounge, Sadler sat the boys down and went to get some lemonade from the kitchen.

'Just keep those brutes under control, Peter,' Joel urged in a low voice. 'They give me the creeps!'

The dogs seemed perfectly happy with Peter, but whenever Joel caught their attention, their lips curled back, displaying their huge, razor-sharp teeth.

Sadler returned with lemonade for the boys and another can of beer for himself. He sat in his easy chair and continued drinking, staring at Joel through narrowed, suspicious eyes.

'Well, you're the last person I expected to see when I opened the door, Joel. You could have knocked me over with a feather!' Sadler drawled with a forced laugh.

Joel wanted to spit at him, *"after all you've drunk, a sneeze would knock you over!"* But his self control won.

'How's your Mum, Joel? She managing alright?' he asked.

'She's fine, thank you – she misses Dad of course,' Joel deliberately slipped that in.

'Yes, I'm sure it must be very hard for her,' Sadler sympathised, shifting uncomfortably in his seat and running a finger nervously round the inside of his collar.

'Mr Sadler, you won't say anything to my mum about me being here, will you?' Joel pleaded. 'She might get a bit upset, you know. Wondering why I didn't ask her, but you know…'

'Of course, Joel, I understand very well. Don't worry, mum's the word, hey.'

'Thank you.' Thanking Sadler really stuck in Joel's throat.

'How old are you now, Joel?' Sadler asked.

'Twelve, Mr Sadler. I was eight when I lost my dad.'

'Oh, yes, I'm sorry, Joel. You must miss your dad a lot.'

I bet you're sorry! thought Joel.

'Yes, Mr Sadler,' he replied

'So you're in high school now, then? Are you following your dad's footsteps into the rugby team?'

'I'm captain of the junior team, Mr Sadler.'

'Captain, already!' Sadler grinned. 'That's the stuff. Your dad was a darn good rugby player, you know, Joel. He would have been proud of you, lad.'

An uneasy pause followed. Then, Peter nervously broke the silence.

'May I go to the bathroom, Mr Sadler?' Peter muttered. 'I think I've drunk too much lemonade.'

'Of course, lad, top of the stairs on the left,' Sadler directed.

Peter stood up and headed for the door.

'If you go too far, you'll end up in my pit – not an experience I would recommend,' Sadler added with a laugh.

'Oh, I'll steer clear of that then, Mr Sadler. Thanks,' Peter forced a cheery reply.

Great, Joel thought to himself. *He's even saved Peter time by telling him where to find his bedroom – the snake-brain! I'm sure it is a pit – a snake pit! Go on, Peter, get that case and let's get out of here!*

'What are you going to do with your life, Joel; any thoughts on a career?' Sadler enquired.

'I want to be a barrister like my dad, Mr Sadler.'

'Fine choice,' Sadler nodded. 'So… now you are here, what would you like me to tell you, Joel?'

'Well, like I said, I was very young…'

'Yes, yes, right,' Sadler squirmed, nervously. 'Well, I knew your dad for many years, Joel. We were at "uni" together; we studied and partied together. Then, we ended up in the same law firm as business partners. He was energetic, funny, witty and popular. The main thing that sticks in my mind is his integrity. You could always count on him to do what he said and he could never be bought. He was one of the best barristers I have personally known; undoubtedly the finest and most honourable man I have ever met. I wish I could be more like him…' Sadler tailed off, pensively.

Joel gritted his teeth, thinking to himself, *yeah, that's something you know nothing about, you two-faced snake: fine qualities, like integrity and honesty!*

'His death was a great loss,' Sadler added, in a sort of daze.

Suddenly, footsteps could be heard. The dogs pricking up their ears, immediately charged excitedly out of the room, only to return with the owner of the aforementioned footsteps, who was holding two dog leads. Uz and Buz were jumping all over him, clearly eager for their exercise. Jethro looked suddenly startled as his eyes fell on Joel.

'Do you want me to take the dogs out now, Guv?' he asked.

'Jethro, this is my late partner's son, Joel Asher,' Sadler explained. Then he turned to Joel. 'Jethro feeds the dogs and takes them out for their exercise. Do you mind if he takes them now, Joel?'

'Of course not,' Joel replied, quite relieved that the slobbering monsters were finally leaving.

'Are you sure? He can take them later if you want them to stay,' Sadler offered.

'No! I mean, I wouldn't want to deprive the dogs of their exercise,' Joel insisted. 'Please, Jethro, by all means take them.'

Jethro attached the leads to the dogs' collars and to Joel's delight, the two vicious brutes towed Jethro away.

'Are you alright, Joel?' Sadler asked.

Joel suddenly snapped out of his private thoughts and glanced at the clock on the mantelpiece. He was shocked to see that it was 6.45 pm. His mind had been drifting for ten minutes! *Where was Peter? He'd been gone for nearly fifteen minutes! What was keeping him?*

'Yes, I'm fine, thank you – just a bit sad that I've missed so much of my dad,' Joel replied.

'Well, you've got your mum to think about, Joel. You're the man of the house now.'

Thanks to you! Joel thought, trying desperately hard not to pull a contemptuous face. He wrung his hands together anxiously.

'Your friend has been a long time, Joel,' Sadler observed, curiously. 'Why don't you go and make sure he hasn't washed himself down the plughole, while I go and get myself another beer.'

Joel's mind began racing again. *The beer would be in the fridge, which would be in the kitchen – where the backdoor to the yard was – where Peter could be right at this moment, handing over the case to Tamara!* He jumped up from his chair.

'Let me get your beer for you, Mr Sadler; you stay there. I'm sure Peter will be alright and he'll be down in a minute,' Joel insisted. He was finding it quite a strain to keep a cool exterior when his mind was in a frantic whirl.

'No, don't trouble yourself, lad. I can get my own beer. You go and check on your mate.' Sadler started to get up.

'No!' Joel put up his hand. 'I mean – if I can't get a drink for my dad's best friend…' Those words almost choked him. 'You stay where you are.' Then, before Sadler could object, Joel was at the door of the lounge.

'OK then, the kitchen is at the bottom of the hallway, the way Jethro has just gone with the dogs.' Saying that, Sadler resignedly sat down again.

The dogs! Joel panicked. *Jethro had taken the dogs to the kitchen! Peter was supposed to wait till the dogs had gone out, before going to the bathroom! Oh no, he went too soon!* Realising this, Joel ambled out of the lounge, then raced down the hall to the kitchen.

Joel stood in the kitchen, scratching his head, wondering where on earth Peter had got to, when suddenly, a hand touched his shoulder. He spun round in fright. It was Peter!

'Peter!' Joel gasped with relief. Then, in a frantic whisper. 'What's happening? I thought you'd have handed the case over and be back in the lounge by now!'

'I've been in here for ages. I couldn't find the key to the back door,' Peter whispered back. 'Then I heard that man, Jethro, coming with the dogs, so I hid behind this door.' Peter moved the door to expose the case hidden behind it. 'I thought I was done for – that the dogs would lead Jethro right to me. But they like me, so the guarding instinct didn't kick in and anyway, they were too eager to get out for their walk. At least I clocked where the key is kept, although it doesn't really matter now because Jethro has left the door unlocked. I was just about to go outside when I heard you coming and thought it might be Sadler.'

'Tops, mate!' Joel grinned. 'I've had about as much of that psychotic creep as I can stand!'

'Have you found that beer, Joel!?' Sadler called.

'Yes – coming, Mr Sadler!' Joel shouted back. He grabbed a can from the fridge and scurried back to the lounge.

'What kept you?' Sadler asked, as Joel arrived back in the

lounge with the can of beer.

'Sorry,' Joel said apologetically, handing the can to Sadler. 'Nice place you've got here, Mr Sadler,' he replied, trying to avoid answering the question.

'Your mate isn't back from the bathroom yet,' Sadler continued. 'Shall we send out a search party?' he laughed.

'Oh, he won't be long now,' Joel said.

Then Peter entered the lounge.

'Are you alright, son?' Sadler asked him. 'You seem to have been a long time.'

'Yes, I'm alright, thank you,' Peter replied. 'Do you think we should be going now, Joel? We don't want to be too late back.'

That was it – the signal! Joel jumped to his feet.

'Yes, Peter. We shouldn't take up anymore of Mr Sadler's time,' Joel replied, with immense relief. 'Thank you, Mr Sadler, I appreciate your time and now we'll leave you to enjoy your beer in peace.'

'Not at all, Joel, any time,' Sadler grinned. He seemed to be as relieved that the visit was over as the boys were. 'Give my best to your mum. Oh, she's not supposed to know. It'll be our little secret. I mean it, Joel – there's nothing I wouldn't do for Nathan Asher's boy.'

Yeah, that's the guilt talking all right… Joel thought. *Well, you're going to have plenty of time to repent at the Crown's pleasure, when you're nicked, Mr Dan Sadler!*

'Thanks again, Mr Sadler.' Joel made a hasty retreat to the front door, closely followed by Peter.

Sadler showed them out of the front door. As soon as they had passed Sims's car, they scooted round the corner into the alley, bursting through Sadler's back gate into his yard, where they came to an abrupt halt. Tamara was there alright, clutching the case, but – she was frozen petrified in the corner, hemmed in by the viciously snarling and drooling Uz and Buz!

Suddenly, the back gate slammed shut behind them! Joel and Peter wheeled round to face a sneering Jethro, who wielded a gun which he was pointing right at them!

'Is that it now, or are there any more of you little blighters running around?' Jethro snarled. 'I don't know what you three are up to, but I'd guess that it's no good. We'll see what Mr Sadler has to say about this, shall we?' Saying this, he opened the back door and pushed them all inside.

†

Sadler was slumped, half asleep in his chair as Jethro shoved the three children into the lounge, keeping the gun trained on them.

'Boss!' Jethro grunted. 'These kids are up to something!'

'Jethro...' Sadler replied humorously. 'What in the world are you're doing? These are just kids! Put your gun down before you hurt someone!'

'Kids or not, there's something suspicious about that case!' Jethro continued with urgency, pointing to the case in Tamara's hand.

'What case? Jethro…' Sadler began to get irritated. Then, suddenly he gasped; his jaw dropped and his face twisted into a ferocious scowl as he recognised the case in Tamara's hand! 'That's *my* case! What the devil is going on?' he shrieked. 'Jethro! Where did this girl come from and what is she doing with *my* case?' Then he peered in complete astonishment at Joel and Peter. 'What are you two boys doing back here?'

'Maybe we should find out, Guv,' Jethro suggested, smugly.
Sadler walked up to Tamara and glared at her.
Bravely, she glared right back at him, screwing up her nose in defiance.
Then, he snatched the case out of her hand and hurriedly opened it to check that the contents were intact, which of course they were. Breathing a sigh of relief, he closed it and placed it on the floor next to his chair.

'Good work, Jethro,' Sadler smirked, still in a state of bewilderment.

'Yeah, good work creep-face!' Joel muttered.
Jethro's smug smirk dissolved into a contemptuous scowl, aimed

in Joel's direction.

'Is this all of you or are there any more?' Sadler demanded.

'Far as I know, it's just these three, Guv. I think I've caught them all,' Jethro interjected, gloating pridefully.

'Where did the girl come from? How did she get in?' Sadler snarled.

'The blonde boy was hiding in the kitchen, Guv, when I took the dogs out. I didn't know he was just a kid at that point so I pretended I hadn't seen him. I went outside, intending to come back in through the front and take him by surprise. I took the dogs out of the back gate but, as I shut the gate, I heard the back door open then I heard voices. So I peered through a gap in the gate and saw that it was these two kids: the girl and the blonde boy. I don't know where the girl came from; I guess they both must have been hiding in the kitchen. The boy went back inside and left the girl in the yard with the case. I didn't know what they were up to but I guessed it was no good. So, I burst back into the yard with the dogs and nabbed her. Then I waited, figuring that the boy would come back for her, but the two boys turned up – after you let them out at the front. That's all I know, Guv.'

'Sorry…' Tamara apologised dejectedly to the boys.

'It's not your fault,' Peter muttered. 'I went too soon to the bathroom; I was supposed to wait till the dogs went out.'

'Went too soon!" Sadler repeated incredulously. 'It sounds like a covert SAS operation – who planned all this?'

'Yes, you got that right, snake-face – like *you* planned to murder my dad!' Joel spat.

'Shut up!' Sadler snapped. 'I need to think!' He began to pace up and down the room, becoming more agitated by the second. 'I need to know who's behind this.' He suddenly wheeled round and glared at Joel, scarily. 'You really had me fooled, kid. Who sent you?' he demanded.

'Frosty the Snowman!' Joel answered, contemptuously.

'Who's codename is that?' Jethro asked stupidly.

'No one's, you fool, Jethro! The kid's just trying to be smart!'

Sadler barked. 'Who sent you, and who else knows about this case?' he snapped at the boys.

Jethro stepped forward and placed the gun next to Tamara's head. 'You've got five seconds!' he snarled menacingly. Something told the boys that Jethro was mean and stupid enough to pull the trigger.

'Detective John Smith of New Scotland Yard knows – and he's coming to get you – you murderer!' Joel threatened.

'What? *Smith*? How the devil...?' Sadler gasped in a confused panic. Then he added suspiciously, 'Wait a minute. So, the police have resorted to using kid detectives now, have they? What is this, Scotty Yard's version of downsizing? Metropolitan cut-backs? No one knows you're even here, do they? But, how did you know about the case?'

'That's none of your business,' Joel replied with disdain. Sadler paced up and down again, rubbing his chin and trying to make some sense of this very peculiar situation.

'If Smith thought there was anything dodgy going on, he'd be here himself with a posse of cops. No, there's someone else behind this...' Sadler mused, shrewdly, 'and there's one way to find out!'

Sadler hastily grabbed the phone and dialled New Scotland Yard.

'Give me Detective John Smith!' Sadler requested with a forced charm. 'Tell him it's Dan Sadler.' He smirked at Joel as he was put through. 'Ah John – not bad thanks – yourself? Uh huh – Oh, I was just wondering if there was anything coming up I should be aware of. You know, any *cases...'* he threw an evil grin at Joel, '...to prepare for in my schedule? Oh, him. Well, we all know he'll end up in the slammer... anything else? Well, you know, you don't get to be a Senior Partner by letting the grass grow, John. Yes, OK, call me.' Sadler replaced the receiver.

'So Smith knows, does he?' Sadler drawled sarcastically. 'I knew there was something not quite kosher about you, Joel.' Sadler poked Joel in the shoulder, then turned to Jethro.

'Jethro, take our amateur sleuths down to the basement and lock them in. I'll deal with them later.'

'A pleasure, Guv,' Jethro replied with a smug smirk. 'Come on, you! Move it!'

'Give yourself up, Mr Sadler,' Tamara cried bravely, 'while you've still got a chance! You'll get caught – you're being watched, you know!'

'Oh really, and who's watching me? The rest of your school?' Sadler laughed, sarcastically.

'Move it, I said!' Jethro poked his gun in Tamara's back and gave her a push.

The children were herded along the hall, through a heavy door and down some stone steps into the musty cellar. Ordering them to sit on some wooden chairs, Jethro tied their hands behind their backs with rope.

'There's no point in screaming. No one is going to hear you down here – and if you do make a noise, I'll come back and shut you up,' Jethro sneered menacingly. With that, he slammed the wooden door shut and turned the key in the lock, sealing them inside their prison.

'Nice one!' Joel quipped. 'What shall we do for an encore?'

'It's not as bad as it looks,' announced Maité, stepping through the Vista right in front of them.

'Praise the Lord!' Peter exclaimed with relief.

'Yes, amigo,' Maité replied with haste, as she began to untie the rope around Tamara's hands. 'We haven't much time. Sadler will not let you go; he intends to kill you all! You must all come back with me now through my schism. The mission is aborted.'

Joel stamped his foot in frustration.

'I've blown it!' he exclaimed bitterly. 'I've let everyone down; I'm so sorry.'

'It's not your fault, amigo,' Maité answered graciously as she began to untie Joel, while Tamara untied Peter. 'These things happen all the time. There'll be other opportunities.'

As the boys' ropes fell to the floor they jumped up out of their chairs.

'Come on, we must hurry! Jethro could be back any minute,' Maité urged.

'I'm not leaving without that case!' Joel insisted. 'Who knows what Sadler might do with it now. What if he destroys it? The evidence would be gone forever!'

'How are you going to get out of this room unless you come with me now? Think this through, Joel!' Maité reasoned.

'Yes, Joel. I don't think you have a choice,' Tamara pleaded.

'Yeah, come on mate, there's always tomorrow,' Peter added. 'Sadler won't destroy the case, remember – it's his insurance for safety against Lilith.'

'I said no noise!' Jethro bellowed. Then, they heard the sound of his footsteps coming back down the stone steps.

'Quick! Now!' Maité grabbed Joel with one hand and put up her other hand to open a schism. All four of them dived through, just as they heard the key turning in the lock. The four friends emerged through the Vista into Heaven at some speed and suddenly became as light as feathers as they left the world's gravity behind. Nathan and Anna were easily able to catch them. Once through the Vista, they all turned around to watch it. Jethro was standing in the middle of the cellar scratching his head, obviously baffled by their disappearing act.

'Quick, show me Sadler,' Joel cried. 'What's he done with the case?'

A view of the lounge appeared on the Vista. Sadler was pacing up and down in a state of great agitation and the case was still there – next to his chair. Then, Jethro came running into the lounge.

'They're gone, Guv!' Jethro wailed, breathlessly. 'The kids – they've escaped!'

'What?' Sadler screamed. 'You buffoon, Jethro! How could you be such an imbecile?'

'I – I – I'm sorry, Guv. I tied them up real well and locked them in just like you said,' Jethro stammered helplessly.

'Well, evidently not well enough!' Sadler snapped.

'I'm going back!' Joel declared.

'Don't be a fool, Joel!' Maité cried. 'Can't you see what you're up against here? These people are professional killers! They have no scruples!'

'Maité is right, Joel,' Nathan agreed. 'It would be crazy to go back now. The mission stands aborted.'

'No!' Joel argued, quietly determined. 'What's at stake is too important – more important than me. This might be the only chance to get that evidence. If Sadler decides to destroy it, it's all over. Tamara and Peter can stay here, but I'm going back.'

'You can't go on your own, Joel,' Peter protested. 'What if you run into the dogs? They'll eat you alive! No, if you're going, then I'm coming with you.'

'Well OK, that makes sense,' Joel conceded. 'Peter comes but Tamara stays.'

'Ah but…' Tamara started.

'That's the deal!' Joel interrupted, determinedly. 'I'm not taking any chances with you, Tamara. I wouldn't be as effective if I was watching out for you as well. Besides, we may need you later. You're more useful on standby up here.'

'OK,' she nodded, a little reluctantly. 'Just, please, don't do anything crazy…'

'Mama mia!' Maité exclaimed, throwing her arms up in exasperation.

'Joel must do what he believes is right, Maité,' Anna reminded her gently. 'He must make his own choices.'

'That's right,' Nathan smiled. 'I'm proud of you, son. You're willing to put doing what's right above your own life. This is the true calling of a Kairos. God go with you.'

Joel tried to swallow the lump in his throat as he looked at his dad. These were words he had thought he would never hear from him again.

They all turned their attention back to the Vista where Jethro was receiving the brunt of Sadler's wrath.

'Three kids escape from a *locked* cellar – where they had been *tied* to chairs? They get up the stairs, past the two of us *and* the dogs and then just slip outside, vanishing into thin air?' Sadler snarled at Jethro. 'What did you tie them up with – liquorice shoe laces?' Sadler gave a chilling laugh as he glared at Jethro with contempt. 'Maybe you forgot to lock the door, or – maybe you deliberately let them go! Are you going soft on me, Jethro?'

'I'm really sorry, Guv,' Jethro whined pathetically. 'I was sure I'd locked them in – honest!'

'You ignoramus, Jethro! Go and take the dogs out! It's about all you seem capable of!' Sadler spat.

'Yes, Guv.' Jethro skulked out of the room.

Sadler slumped into the easy chair and snapped open yet another can of beer. He looked nervously at the case by the side of his chair and tapped his fingers impatiently on the table.

'Now is our chance, while Jethro is out with those two brutes,' said Joel, gritting his teeth determinedly.

'What are we going to do?' Peter cried, perplexed. 'He could keep that case next to him all night!'

'But, look at Sadler's clock – it's a quarter past seven! We've got to get to Smith before ten!' Tamara added anxiously.

'Oh no! I'd forgotten about the time...' Joel answered with annoyance, 'and what about Grandad? We've got Tamara staying with us tonight. He'll be looking for us soon.'

'Believe me, boys, the rate Sadler is knocking back those beers, he's surely going to have to go to the bathroom soon; that'll be the time to act,' Nathan reassured them. '...and don't worry about Grandad; I had one of our angels visit him with a present.'

Joel, Peter and Tamara looked at Nathan curiously. He nodded towards the Vista and as they looked, they saw a view of Grandad. He was sitting in his rocking chair with a bottle of malt whisky and a small glass on the table next to him. He was out for the count, snoring loudly.

'Good old Marcus,' Nathan grinned. 'He never could resist a drop of best old malt whisky. Just a little tot and he's off like a baby and he sure deserves it after all that fencing today, doesn't he, Joel?'

'Yes, Dad, I guess he does,' Joel agreed, with a grin.

The Vista view returned to Sadler's lounge. The villainous lawyer looked decidedly rough. Several beer cans lay scattered around his chair. Then, as Nathan had predicted, he staggered to his feet.

'There he goes,' said Nathan.

Sadler lurched out of the room and grabbed hold of the stair banisters as he made his way to the bathroom.

'Good,' said Joel. 'We can steal in now, while he's in the bathroom – if he makes it that far without collapsing. He looks in a bad way. Come on, Peter, now's our chance – a two-year-old could snatch that case!'

'Yeah, I think you're right, Joel. I've never seen anyone in such a mess!' Peter agreed, in disgust.

Without a further thought, Joel leapt impetuously through the Vista. However, as the gravity of the world pulled him down, he landed with a heavy thud which caused him to fall over, twisting his ankle. In his eagerness, he'd forgotten to glide through the Vista and had taken off like an rocket. Hastily, and feeling rather foolish, he hobbled to his feet and anxiously looked around. He hoped in vain that Maité had not seen him land as his arrival had not been as stealthy or as cool as he had intended.

By way of contrast, Peter landed sedately, and in control, right next to him.

'Are you alright, Joel?' Peter whispered with concern. 'You jumped through the Vista so fast, I thought you would shoot straight through the wall and wind up in the alley!'

'Yeah, so did I,' Joel muttered with embarrassment. 'I'm OK; just twisted my ankle, that's all. I forgot I was jumping into the world's gravity. Anyway,' he grinned as he picked up Sadler's case, 'I guess now, it's an open-and-shut case. Come on, let's get out of here.'

As they couldn't take the case up through the Vista, they made their way out of the lounge and down the hallway towards the front door. Joel was leaning on Peter for support as he hobbled his way along.

'Funny,' Peter whispered. 'It always used to be you

supporting me, Joel, before I was heal…'

'Well, if it isn't the Snoop sisters! I think you'd better stop right there, lads!' Sadler interrupted. He sounded surprisingly sober, considering the amount of beer he had consumed.

The boys' hearts sank as they turned to face their adversary, who was levelling a gun at their heads!

'I'm sorry, Peter,' Joel murmured. 'It's my stupid fault for being so carelessly noisy.'

'It's not your fault, mate. Don't blame yourself,' Peter tried to console him.

'You two couldn't have made more noise if you'd arrived on stampeding bulls and blowing trumpets!' Sadler sneered with a high-pitched laugh. 'So, you were hiding in the house all along.' His face twisted into an evil scowl. 'I knew you'd give yourselves away sooner or later. Get back in the lounge!' he demanded, tipping his gun in the direction of the lounge. With his hair flopping over his face, his half-crazed staring eyes and that laugh, he cut quite a scary figure – a mixture of evil and lunacy.

Joel limped into the lounge, supported by Peter.

'Where's Miss Snoop, then?' Sadler barked, as he snatched the case from Joel.

The boys stood silently and glared at Sadler, wondering what this deranged lunatic was going to do next.

'Huh! Oh well, she won't get far – the dogs will ferret her out,' Sadler scowled. Then, glancing at his clock on the mantelpiece, he yelled, 'Jethro! Where the devil are you!' He sighed impatiently and muttered, 'Where is that idiot?'

They heard the back door slam shut.

'Jethro!' Sadler bellowed again.

Jethro came running into the lounge like a well-trained dog.

'What's going on, Guv?' he asked breathlessly. Then, he saw the boys. 'You! Where did you find these two, Guv?'

'Never mind! I've got my case; that's all I care about,' Sadler snapped.

'So, whatya gonna do with 'em now, Guv?' Jethro asked.

'It appears, Jethro, that these two Columbos are late for their appointment with DEATH!' Sadler sneered coldly. Then he turned to the boys with an evil, piercing stare. 'How do you two know about this case? Tell me who sent you?'

'The Easter bunny,' Joel spat contemptuously.

'Right!' Sadler hissed, placing his gun next to Peter's head. 'You've got precisely three seconds to give me a straight answer, or blondie gets it!'

'All right!' Joel shouted, his brain racing like an express train. He had to come up with something plausible quickly and – fairly obviously – the truth would not be perceived by Sadler as a straight answer. 'Lilith!' Joel blurted out. 'We're here because of Lilith.'

Open-mouthed with shock, Sadler lowered the gun, in fact he almost dropped it, as the very mention of Lilith's name gripped him with intense fear.

'Lilith?' he gasped. 'No! Lilith isn't crazy enough to pull a stunt like this – using kids?'

'I suppose the kid must be talking the truth, boss,' Jethro mused. 'How else could they possibly know about Lilith?'

'Anyway, isn't it Lilith's stock-in-trade – making his fortune out of exploiting kids?' Joel added.

'Shut up, you!' Sadler barked, then he began to pace up and down, with increasing agitation. 'What's he playing at?' Sadler muttered, panic written all over his face. His hand was shaking as he picked up yet another can of beer and ripping off its ring-pull, he poured its contents down his throat. Then, crushing it like an eggshell, he flung it onto the floor. Staggering a little, he struggled to make sense of the situation. The sad drunkard looked a far cry from the smart barrister he posed at the office.

'Lilith will not be happy now – he's out to get you!' Joel continued.

'I said shut up!' Sadler screeched. 'Jethro, tie these clowns up again – do it properly this time – and make sure you gag 'em tight!'

'Right, Guv, you got it.' Jethro ran off to the kitchen and was back in seconds with a roll of wide, brown parcel tape. He yanked the boys' wrists roughly behind their backs and proceeded to wrap tape tightly around them.

Sadler flopped down into his chair, sinking his head into his hands; he had broken out into little beads of sweat as even the mere mention of Lilith's name made him quiver like a jellyfish. Joel decided to milk the situation, before Jethro gagged him, while Sadler was confused and unable to think clearly because of the amount of beer he had consumed.

'And, what's more,' Joel added, 'if we don't report back by ten o'clock, Lilith will come here *personally* to get you!'

'What?' Sadler's voice trembled in sheer horror. 'What does he want?' He slowly rose from the chair and staggered across the room. Towering menacingly over Joel, he screeched hysterically, 'TELL ME WHAT HE WANTS!'

'I would have thought that was obvious,' Joel answered, glaring defiantly up at the villainous Sadler. 'He wants your case of evidence.'

'Does he now?' Sadler smirked. 'Well, he's not going to get it – I'll shoot everyone first!'

'Steady on, Guv,' Jethro entreated him, nervously. 'It ain't that bad!' Evidently, Jethro didn't trust Sadler either.

'Not that bad!' Sadler screeched hysterically. 'It couldn't possibly be worse, you cretin! I thought I told you to gag these wretched kids! What are you pussyfooting around with that tape for? I don't want them to get away this time!'

Sadler grabbed his case and was just about to make a hasty exit – probably to pack a bag and do a runner with the money – when they heard the doorbell ring. Sadler gasped in fright and froze! Despite their perilous situation, Joel had to fight the urge to shout BOO! at Sadler, who was very quickly unravelling into a complete nervous wreck.

'No! Oh no, oh no...' he whimpered pathetically. 'He's here, already! What am I going to do?'

'You don't know it's him,' Jethro whisperd. 'The kid said, "by ten o'clock." It won't be Lilith yet, Guv. Let me take the kids through to the dining room while you go and open the door, ignoring it will just raise suspicion. You never know, it may just be Jehovahs Witnesses – those loons are always knocking on doors.'

Sadler threw Jethro a glance of mixed scathing and astonishment.

'Yes, yes, you may be right, Jethro – for once.' Sadler muttered. 'OK, keep those brats quiet. 'Where are the dogs?' he asked quickly, starting to pull himself together.

'I've shut them in the backyard, Guv,' Jethro replied.

The doorbell rang again, and again Sadler jumped. He put down the case, smoothed his dishevelled mop of hair and hurriedly kicked the empty beer cans out of sight under his chair.

Jethro grabbed the roll of tape and pushed Joel and Peter through a set of double doors into the dining room. Shutting the doors, he pulled out two chairs and placed them facing the doors.

'Sit!' he ordered.

taking a deep breath, Sadler headed for the front door.

Joel and Peter sat on the chairs and glared up at Jethro, who was standing guard over them with his revolver.

'You've been spending too much time with the dogs, Jethro,' Joel goaded defiantly. 'You've turned into a lapdog yourself! Woof, woof!'

'Shut your mouth!' Jethro retorted angrily. He ripped some tape off the roll and plastered it over their mouths. 'One sound from either of you and you're both toast!'

Hearing voices coming from the lounge, Jethro pressed his ear against the door to listen. Straining to hear, Joel and Peter could just make out the conversation between Sadler and his visitor.

'I was a bit concerned, Dan,' the visitor began. 'After your rather rushed, and might I say odd, telephone call, I began to suspect that all was not quite as it seemed.'

Joel and Peter exchanged glances. They both came to the same realisation that the visitor must be Detective John Smith, and that he was bound to see the case and recognise it. Joel had met Smith a few times and he was sure it was his voice. This gave the boys a glimmer of hope. Thank God, Smith should get the case after all and now would be able to rescue them.

'No, John – really…' Sadler forced a laugh. 'Everything is fine – there's nothing to worry about at all. I – I just thought it was a while since we spoke – you know how it is…'

Then suddenly, they heard a thud.

'What's this?' Smith asked in surprise.

Great! Joel thought. *Smith has stumbled over the case!*

'Er, I can explain, John…' Sadler squirmed.

Go on, Smith! Arrest him! Joel thought eagerly, anticipating the sound of handcuffs. There was silence for a few anxious seconds. Then, the double doors were suddenly and unexpectedly flung open, sending Jethro flying and narrowly missing knocking the boys off their chairs.

'FREEZE!' Smith yelled with authority and promptly got the shock of his life. As he stood in front of them, gun levelled, Smith almost dropped his gun as he recognised Joel – clearly the last person he expected to see behind those doors! 'Joel...?' he gasped in complete astonishment.

Jethro groaned as he picked himself up off the floor, throwing Smith a sinister scowl.

Smith called over his shoulder. 'I knew something was wrong, Dan. It's a good thing I followed through my hunch,' he said, quickly ripping the tape off the boys' mouths. 'You're OK now, kids. I'm the law.'

'Not around here, Smith!' Jethro's scowl had been replaced by a triumphant smirk, as he looked over Smith's shoulder.

Then, they all heard a click as Sadler cocked his gun.

'Not so fast, Smith,' Sadler drawled smugly, holding his gun at Smith's head. 'Drop it – now!' he demanded.

Smith dropped his gun onto the floor and Jethro quickly snatched it up, grinning malevolently.

'Nice one, Guv,' Jethro smirked.

'Tie him up, Jethro,' Sadler sneered.

Jethro handed Smith's gun to Sadler and began to tape Smith's wrists behind his back while Sadler frisked him.

'This is the kind of thing I pay *you* for, Jethro, but I end up having to do everything myself!' Sadler whined. 'We'll put them all down in the cellar while I decide what to do. Damn it! Now we've got three bodies to dispose of.'

'Four, with the girl – when we find her, Guv.' Jethro added.

'Yeah, she must be around somewhere. We'll use these as bait. We can't have Miss Snoop running around shouting her mouth off,' Sadler chillingly replied. 'Now, get down to the cellar. Find out where these meddlesome kids got out last time and block it off!'

Jethro obediently scurried out of the room to the cellar, while Sadler pushed Smith down onto a chair. If the boys had doubted Maité's earlier claim about Sadler's intentions, they were in no doubt now. It was clear that the man had no scruples; children or not, he intended to kill them – and Smith too!

Joel felt the blood drain from his face. He and Peter stared at each other as the horror of the prevailing circumstances began to painfully dawn on them – because they were forbidden to use the Vista in the presence of a stranger – in this instance, Smith – Tamara and Maité would be powerless to help them. They were going to die!

CHAPTER SIXTEEN

Lambs to the Slaughter

Unfortunately the two boys now found themselves in the ironic situation whereby, the very man they had hoped would be able to rescue them was now, unwittingly, actually preventing their rescue! Joel gulped nervously as he continued to stare at Smith, his tongue sticking to the roof of his exceedingly dry mouth.

Sadler paced anxiously up and down in a sweat, while he waited for Jethro. Meanwhile, Joel and Peter sat dejectedly contemplating their fate.

'You won't get away with this, Sadler,' Smith warned. Then he looked at the boys and winked – as though he knew something that no one else knew.

'Just watch me!' Sadler spat.

'Anyway,' Smith continued, ignoring Sadler's comment. 'What are you doing with a couple of kids? They're harmless! At least let the kids go; where are your scruples, man?'

'He hasn't got any scruples, Detective Smith,' Joel blurted out, scathingly. 'He murdered my dad!'

'Shut up!' Sadler hissed.

'What exactly are you doing here, Joel?' Smith asked, curiously. 'How on earth did you come to be in this den of iniquity? Aren't you supposed to be at your grandad's place, miles away in the back of beyond?'

'I said, no talking!' Sadler screeched.

Then, suddenly, Joel heard a slight creaking noise to his left. He was sitting nearest the door that must have led to the kitchen. Joel suspected that someone was hiding behind the door, listening to them and endeavouring to slowly open it. He tried to look covertly, moving his head as little as possible, scared that it may have been one of his friends and he didn't want to give them away. He leaned over to his right and whispered in Peter's ear.

'Bogey at nine o'clock.'

Peter – and Smith, who had also heard the creaking, glanced

furtively in the direction of the door, just in time to see the barrel of a gun poking through the opening. This definitely wasn't a friend! Peter tried to stifle a gasp, which caused Joel and Smith to look at the door too.

'DUCK!' Peter cried, and rolled off his chair onto the floor. Joel and Smith also dived onto the floor as the door burst open. Sadler suddenly froze with fear as a huge man barged into the room wielding the firearm. It was Sims – all formidable twenty stone of him!

'What the devil is going on, Sadler?' Sims demanded.

'Sims!' Sadler squeaked in terror, expecting that at any moment, Lilith would be right behind him.

'There's been something suspicious going on here, tonight, Sadler!' Sims bellowed. 'I've just spoken to Lilith and he's instructed me to find out what you're up to. What's Smith doing here? Are you making a deal with the law?'

'Lilith?' Sadler whimpered, gripped with fear at the mere mention of the ruthless gangster's name. 'Sims…' he continued in panic. 'You've got it all wrong – I'd never make a deal with the law! What, me – double-cross Lilith? What would I stand to gain?'

'*Lilith?*' Smith echoed, in astonishment, picking himself up off the floor. 'What's Lilith got to do with all of this?'

'Lilith is the "Black Mamba", Detective Smith. He and Sadler feed from the same trough!' Joel winced grimly, struggling to stand up on a swollen ankle and with his hands tied behind his back.

Smith stared at Joel in utter open-mouthed bafflement. 'But – Lilith is a top crust at Scotty Yard!' he retorted incredulously.

'Which makes him ideally placed, don't you think, Smith?' Sadler screeched in a high-pitched hysterical laugh.

'Enough!' Sims barked. 'Sadler, tell me what's going on, before I run out of patience; Lilith is waiting for my call!'

As Sadler was pleading pathetically with Sims, Jethro – unbeknown to any of them – having heard voices, crept up to the door behind Sims. He saw Sims pointing his gun at Sadler and –

typically, without thinking, Jethro burst into the room.

'…And you just ran out of time, moron!' he bellowed insanely, as he coshed Sims on the head with the butt of his gun. The burly Sims crashed to the floor like a Dibnah chimney stack. Jethro leaned down, checked Sims and snatched his gun, while Sadler stared, mouth gapes wide open, hardly able to believe what was happening.

'He's out cold, Guv,' Jethro confirmed.

'Jethro! You imbecile! What have you done?' Sadler wailed.

'What d – do y – you mean, Guv?' Jethro stammered wimpishly. 'That moron had a gun on you!'

'That moron, for your information, Jethro, is Sims!' Sadler wrung his hands in anguish. 'Lilith's top henchman!'

'Oops...' Jethro winced and scratched his head. 'What a mess!'

'Mess doesn't cut it, Jethro! It's the worst *ever* case scenario, by miles!' Sadler lamented.

'Oh, well, I suppose we could dispose of all the bodies in convoy – we'll never get this many bodies in the car at once – especially Sims!'

'Jethro!' Sadler almost burst a blood vessel, as he screeched at Jethro. Grabbing a hunting whip from a hook on the wall he attacked Jethro with it, swiping him across the shoulders. Everyone tried to duck as Sadler cracked the whip over his pathetic sidekick, who by now was crouching in a corner. 'How stupid are you?' Sadler continued to rant. He threw down the whip and slapped his forehead in frustration. 'Do you ever engage that pea-sized brain of yours? We can't kill Sims! He's one of Lilith's best men! Lilith would hunt us down like animals! If Sims doesn't report back to Lilith soon, I – *WE* – are DEAD MEN!'

Jethro slowly stood up and gulped; the colour drained from his face as he realised his bungling gaffe.

'Yes, you idiot!' Sadler raged on. 'Of all the people you had to cosh! A twenty-stone, psychotic robot – with a brain just as stupid as yours! Jethro, how many times have you seen Sims?

How could you make such a mistake?'

'I'm really sorry, Guv,' Jethro muttered, gazing sheepishly down at his feet. 'I – I just didn't recognise him. I just saw the gun and...'

'Your miniscule portion of grey matter took over,' Smith interrupted dryly.

'Shut up!' Sadler spat. 'Anyway, you're very chirpy – for someone under a death sentence, Smith!'

Jethro pushed Smith back down onto the chair.

'…and you two twerps can sit down, too!' he ordered.

Peter climbed back onto his chair, while Joel hobbled back to his.

'You've done it now, Jethro,' Smith quipped. He immediately tried to avert their attention from Joel, by goading Jethro. 'You'll have to go and stand on the naughty mat!'

'I said shut up!' Sadler snapped again.

'Yeah, button it!' Jethro sneered.

'Jethro – watch these three, while I try to revive Sims.' Sadler barked.

'If you haven't killed him already!' taunted Joel. 'Or maybe you've damaged his "pea-sized" brain and he won't remember who he is! You'll be in trouble then, Sadler…'

'All of you, just shut up!' Sadler yelled, hysterically. He was so gripped by fear that he was almost in tears.

Sims started to groan and Sadler threw himself down and began to shake Sims, slapping him about the face.

'Sims – I was just joking…' Sadler whimpered pathetically.

'Jethro, did you discover how these nuisances escaped?'

'Well, I think so, Guv. I mean there's only one possible place they could have squeezed out – a narrow window high up at the back of the cellar. I'm amazed they got through it though. Anyway, I've blocked it off so there's no way they could escape now.'

'Good. Take them and Smith down there and lock them in.'

'Oh, finally, we're being shown to our quarters. What's that Jethro, en-suite bath and TV?' Smith seemed bizarrely amused by it all.

Sadler narrowed his eyes and looked at Smith suspiciously.

'You are too cool by far, Smith, for a man who is about to DIE,' Sadler hissed.

Joel was also curious; he too thought Smith was surprisingly cheerful for a man who was about to be murdered – in cold blood. It was almost as if Smith was enjoying the show...

'Are we missing something here?' Joel whispered to Peter. 'Either, Smith knows something that we don't, or he really is a super-cool dude.'

'...or he could be plain stupid, Joel' Peter reflected.

The two boys looked at each other; they were simply baffled. Joel felt dazed and confused – as if he was a member of an audience watching a play that would soon be over, and then they'd all clap and go home. If only that were true!

'Well, it's like this, Sadler,' Smith replied calmly. 'I just can't help being amused by your incredibly incompetent bungling.'

Sadler threw Smith a look of contempt.

'Jethro! Get these clowns out of my face!' he screamed.

'Yeah – move it!' Jethro demanded, poking Smith in the shoulder with his gun. 'And you two!' he snarled at the boys.

'Once again Peter and Joel were unceremoniously herded, this time with Detective Smith, down to the cellar.

'Home, sweet home,' Joel remarked dryly as Jethro pushed them, for the second time, down the stone steps into their makeshift dungeon.

'Well, don't get too comfortable; this ain't a long-stay hotel,' Jethro sneered. 'If you know any prayers, Smith, now's a good time to say them.'

'I think it's *you* who needs the prayers, Jethro,' Joel retorted.

'Yes, you'll get *life* for child abduction and murder!' added Smith. 'Why don't you let these two boys go and shop Sadler. We'll do a deal – maybe reduce your sentence from life to – say, fifteen years – give or take.'

'You think you're so smart, don't you, Smith?' Jethro spat. 'If I shopped Sadler, there'd be nowhere on this earth I could hide – I'd be a dead man.' With that, he slammed the door shut and turned the key, locking them into their tomb.

Smith turned round and presented his back to Joel.

'Here, Joel, back up to me and see if you can jiggle this tape off my wrists,' he instructed.

Joel did as he was bid and began tugging and tearing at the tape, as best he could with his own wrists taped. While he was doing this, he and Peter told Smith about Sadler and Lilith's nefarious collaboration. They told him everything about Nathan's murder; what had happened to the case; the double dealings and double-bluffs between Sadler and Lilith; about Sadler blackmailing Lilith and the squealers and also the dirty money in the drawers under Sadler's bed. Smith listened in quiet amazement. Then, when the boys had finished, he looked at them quizzically.

'How do you know all this, Joel? How did you become involved and what does your mother think of it all – or does she even know you're here? How did you get here, when you are supposed to be staying with your grandad?'

Smith was far too inquisitive; these questions were altogether too awkward for comfort. Joel was, however, a little surprised that Smith knew that he was staying at Grandad's – why or how on earth did he know that? He must have *seen* Mum, but why? Finally, Joel managed to yank the last bit of tape off Smith's wrists and swiftly turned to face him.

'My mother doesn't know I'm here, Detective Smith, and she must not find out! Promise me that you won't tell her!' he insisted. 'I mean, if we ever get out of here alive – I need your word on that, Detective.'

'OK, son,' Smith agreed with a smile and a shrug. 'If it means that much to you.'

'Thanks, Detective Smith,' Joel breathed a sigh of relief.

Smith quickly ripped the tape off Joel's wrists.

'May I know your name, lad,' he asked, as he ripped the tape off Peter's wrists.

'It's Peter, Detective Smith,' Peter answered. 'I live near Joel's grandad.'

'What in Heaven are you two doing here?' Smith persisted.

If only Smith knew how close to the truth he was! It was indeed through Heaven that they happened to be there. However, they couldn't let Smith know that. Joel was suddenly lost for words. In his eagerness to give Smith the low-down on Sadler and Lilith, he hadn't thought how he was going to explain to him just how he and Peter happened to have all this information. For sure, he couldn't tell Smith that his dad had told him – that would mean a one-way ticket to Nuttersville! And, just as surely, they couldn't tell a lie.

'Sadler…' Peter came to the rescue. 'He – he caught us earlier – in fact he was gloating, wasn't he, Joel.'

'That's right, Detective Smith,' Joel nodded. 'I believe Sadler thinks the police are stupid and easily fooled.' Joel hoped that this remark would galvanise Smith, without telling a lie, and take his attention off their all-too-thin explanation – especially, how they came to be there in the first place!

'Oh he does, does he?' Smith muttered. 'Well, that didn't take long,' he added, casting the tape contemptuously onto the floor 'Thank heavens we're dealing with amateurs. Now, how did you two *really* get out of here last time?' Smith asked, as he looked up, doubtfully, at the tiny, boarded-up window at the back of the cellar.

Joel and Peter looked up at it too and they realised immediately that a starving whippet would struggle to get through that tiny window, never mind the two of them! As they pondered over how they could explain their previous escape, suddenly a familiar and very welcome voice saved the situation.

'Room Service!'

The boys recognised immediately the unmistakeable, wry tones of Magee.

'Up here!' Magee called, 'the ventilation hole.'

They turned their gaze to the side and saw a grille, high up near the ceiling, about one brick's width and three high. Joel rushed up to the wall, dragging a chair. Then, climbing onto the chair, he found himself face to face with the cheeky raven, who was clinging by his huge claws to the grille. In his blessed beak was a very pleasing sight indeed – a key!

'I'm not one to say I told you so…' cawed Magee as he pushed the key through a hole in the grille… but…'

'What would we do without you? Bless you!' Joel grinned, taking the key from the raven's beak.

'Without who?' Smith asked. Obviously unable to hear the raven speaking.

Joel jumped off the chair with an enormous grin and held up the key in his hand.

'The key, of course!' Joel beamed. 'As you said, Detective Smith, it's lucky we're dealing with amateurs.' He handed the key to Smith.

'I don't believe it!' Smith shook his head in amazement. 'What a classic! Come on, let's get out of here.'

'You won't leave without the case, will you, Detective,' Joel urged, anxiously.

Smith turned and looked curiously at Joel.

'Why are you so concerned about the case, Joel?' he asked.

'Because there's something in it that will prove Sadler murdered my dad,' Joel replied, solemnly.

'Oh?' Smith coaxed.

'The chloroform-soaked handkerchief! Sadler stuffed it in the case with everything else, the night he killed my dad!' Joel replied, shuddering with loathing.

Smith pulled a silver pen out of his top pocket and, putting an arm around Joel, he showed him the pen.

'Joel, do you know what this is?' Smith asked.

'Looks like a pen, Detective Smith,' Joel replied, mystified.

'Looks like a pen, Joel, and writes like a pen – but do you know what else it is?'

Joel shrugged, wondering where all this was leading.

'This, son, is our "get out of jail free card,"' Smith continued with a satisfied grin. 'This baby is also a bug! Not the creepie-crawlie type, but a very sophisticated, hi-tech recording device which is connected by satellite, direct to Scotty Yard – oh, the marvels of technology!'

It was Joel and Peter's turn to gasp, open-mouthed, at Smith.

'Yes, lads,' the detective beamed. 'Everything that has been said here tonight by you, Sadler, Jethro and Sims, has gone straight to the Yard. Every word – including what you've just said about the handkerchief.' Smith sat down on the stone steps by the door. 'Not only that, but this baby has the finest tracking device you could imagine. You don't think I came to this viper's den alone, do you?' Smith chuckled. 'No Siree! The Yard knows exactly where I am and furthermore, lads, this whole house is surrounded by armed cops.'

'Wow!' Peter exclaimed. 'I thought we were done for! I couldn't understand why *you* were so cheerful. That's pretty cool, Detective Smith.'

'Thank you, Peter,' Smith grinned. 'I've had my suspicions about Sadler for some time; I knew he was up to no good. He has far too much money to throw around. I've been watching him and those lamb chumps who follow him everywhere he goes. Only these lambs aren't as white as snow. It doesn't take a boffin to work out that a normal barrister would not need three bodyguards! What's he got to guard? I had no idea though, that two of them were paid by Lilith, and as for Lilith being the "Black Mamba" – well, none of us had an inkling! This is a major breakthrough! Lilith will probably have been picked up by now and taken to the nick.'

'Good!' Joel exclaimed.

'When Sadler phoned this evening,' Smith continued, 'alarm bells started to ring in my head. I had a nasty feeling that something was about to break. Then, I had an unusual visitor.'

'Oh, who was that, Detective?' Joel asked curiously.

'Well, I don't exactly know, Joel,' Smith went on. 'A young girl – she can't have been more than about ten or eleven – walked right into my office – unannounced, she never went past the front desk! How she got into Scotland Yard with all of its security is baffling, to say the least.'

'What did she say?' Joel asked hesitantly, knowing full well it could only have been Tamara.

'She said, that I couldn't trust Dan Sadler and that I must go immediately to his house and take some back-up with me. If I didn't, she said... ...innocent people were going to die. Then, she left the room and disappeared. It's a mystery how she got in and it's a mystery how she got out – no one saw her arrive and no one saw her leave. She just simply vanished, into thin air! I tried to follow her out of the room but my attention was momentarily distracted by, of all things, a raven! This huge bird was tapping furiously on the window with its beak – like a stupid woodpecker! It almost seemed as if it was trying to get my attention on purpose! How crazy is that?'

'Ahem! Is that the thanks we get for saving your butt!' Magee cawed, still clinging to the vent. 'Such a thankless task!' he muttered, shaking his head.

'Well, I don't know what you're so uppity about, Magee,' Maggi chirped as she landed on a pipe next to the vent. 'It's me he's just called stupid!'

'Well, my dearest Maggi, whoever insults you, insults me,' Magee insisted.

'Oh, really, Magee?' said Maggi, bashfully. 'Well, I – I don't know what to say…'

'Anyway,' Smith continued, oblivious to the ravens' banter. 'By the time I had shooed the silly raven away, it was too late. The girl had disappeared without trace.'

'Huh!' Silly now, am I?' Maggi retorted.

'Do you want me to peck his nose, dear?' Magee offered.

'I don't think that's a good idea, Magee. Maguff may come and clip our wings!'

'Oh, all right,' Magee conceded, with a sigh.

'You know, kids,' Smith mused, 'I think I was visited by an angel! She was certainly very pretty – just like I would imagine an angel to look…'

'Oh, what a nice man! All right, he's forgiven,' Maggi cawed, preening herself.

'I think he was talking about Tamara, dear,' Magee explained.

'…blonde hair and lovely blue eyes,' Smith added.

'Yes, that's definitely not you, is it Maggi?' Magee blundered on, tactlessly. 'Anyway, as an angel, your forgiveness should be unconditional.'

'You know, Magee,' Maggi retorted. 'Sometimes I think you're a miserable, tactless old – gerbil! I apologise to all gerbils!' With that, she flew off.

Peter looked up at Magee who was still clinging to the vent.

'I think you've done it now, mate,' he whispered, sympathetically.

'What? What have I done now?' Magee hung his head. 'Me and my big beak! It seems every time I open it, I put my great big clodhopping claw in it! Now I suppose I'll have to go and eat worms…' he murmured with a tut.

Joel and Peter looked at each other, and finally were unable to stop themselves from bursting out laughing at the amusing ravens.

'Oh, go on then,' Smith sighed. 'Call me a nutter and laugh at me if you must. Everyone at the yard did, when I told them.' He hadn't heard the raven's funny banter and so thought the boys were laughing at him, which made the boys giggle even more.

'OK, fine, laugh, but the fact remains that my suspicions were sufficiently aroused to bring forward "Operation Shepherd" and it's a good job for you that I did!' Smith reminded them.

The boys snapped out of their mirth and both looked at Smith, with intrigue.

'What's "Operation Shepherd," Detective Smith?' Joel asked.

'Well,' Smith continued. 'I had a hunch that Sadler was into something big, involving the underworld. I just didn't know what, and I had nothing of substance to go on. I figured, if I watched him like a hawk, sooner or later there'd be a proverbial banana skin and I'd get him. I formulated a surveillance strategy to find out what he was up to. "Operation Shepherd" is the code name for this initiative. Like I said, this place is surrounded with police and they are waiting for my signal to round up this little flock of villains.'

Smith spoke into his pen. 'The shepherd and sheep are safe –

although, we seem to have acquired some lambs! Round up the wolves!' With that, he turned to the boys. 'That's the green light,' he explained. 'Oh, and by the way,' he spoke into his pen again, 'these boys were never here – just like my angel visit never happened...' Smith grinned at Joel and Peter as he held up the key. 'Shall we go, boys?'

'I'll certainly be glad to get out of this place,' Peter said, with a shudder.

'Ditto to that,' Joel agreed, heaving a sigh of relief.

As Smith unlocked the cellar door, they heard an almighty crash, followed by the sound of running feet and shouting, as the front door was battered down. Then, within seconds, everything became quiet and by the time Smith and the boys reached the lounge, Sadler, Jethro and the dazed Sims were all handcuffed and under arrest.

A uniformed officer approached Smith.

'A job well done, Sir. All sheep present and counted,' the Sergeant announced, congratulating Smith.

'What about Lilith?' Smith asked quickly.

'Oh, don't worry about him, Sir. We picked him up alright; he's in custody.' The Sergeant turned to Joel and Peter. 'Well done, you two! The Commissioner asked me to thank the two boys who helped bring down these evil villains. May I know your names?'

Joel and Peter certainly did not want to answer that question. Joel panicked at the thought of their names being in the newspapers or something. How would they explain this to Mum and grandad?

'What about the money in Sadler's other bed drawer?' Peter reminded Smith ignoring the Sergeant's question.

'Oh, yes!' The Sergeant replied, then he hurried out of the lounge.

'Don't forget this, Sergeant,' Smith called after the him as he picked up Sadler's case and followed him. 'It's important evidence.'

The boys quickly exchanged glances once Smith had left the room.

'This must be about the spot where we came through the Vista, Peter,' Joel whispered. "Quick – before they come back!'

'Yes, before we have to answer that awkward question,' Peter replied.

Joel raised his hand to open a schism and they both slipped through it. Instantly, they were gliding into Heaven to the most tumultuous applause. Nathan, Anna, Tamara and Maité had been watching these events through the Vista, which was still running. Joel and Peter turned around to watch it, too. They saw the Sergeant coming back into the room with Smith.

'Where did those two go?' The Sergeant scratched his head, baffled.

'What two, Sergeant?' Smith rubbed his chin with feigned nonchalance.

'The two boys, Sir! Where did they go?' the Sergeant asked, perplexed.

'What boys? There were no boys here, were there, Sergeant?'

'No, Sir, none at all,' the Sergeant conceded with a shrug, although clearly mystified.

'There are a few unanswered questions, Sergeant, but I guess there are just some things that we are not meant to know. Anyway, well done! A good clean arrest and "the Black Mamba" is snaffled! That's the important thing, isn't it?'

'Yes, Sir. Well, good night, Sir,' said the Sergeant.

'Good night, Sergeant,' Smith smiled. 'Oh – you found the moolah in the bed drawers, didn't you? I suspect that *was* real.'

'It was there, Sir,' the Sergeant replied.

Nathan closed the Vista and turned to face the young heroes.

'Congratulations on a very successful mission, all of you; I couldn't be prouder of you! What you've achieved here will benefit countless people!'

The children were a little overwhelmed by it all, but felt an enormous sense of relief. Sadler and Lilith had both been exposed and caught; their reign of crime, corruption, misery and exploitation was now well and truly over.

'Now, you must go home before Grandad awakes and realises

that you're missing,' Nathan added. 'First though, I have something for you.' He presented each child with a cube of light, no bigger than a large marble. As he gave Maité hers, he squeezed her hand affectionately.

'The last one, Maité,' he said. 'You know what this is?'

Maité closed her fingers around the cube of light and nodded.

'Thank you so much for helping us to get the new recruits up to speed,' Nathan continued, softly. 'I know you're upset about leaving, but you're going to have a wonderful time on Friday – and a great future, so be happy.'

*'Adios, Compadré,' Maité murmured. Then, with moist eyes, she set off for the Fugue.

*'Amiga mía!' Joel called, as he flew after Maité. Landing at her side, he held out his right hand and smiled, *'Muchas gracias.'

'You've been taking Spanish lessons, Joel.' Maité took his hand and returned the smile, but quickly looked away so he didn't see her eyes fill up. She wiped her moist cheek with her other hand.

'I've learned a little Spanish – but I've learned a lot of other things, thanks to you, Maité.'

'You do your father proud. *Adios amigo,' she murmured, turning to leave.

*'Hasta pronto,' Joel called, as he watched her float away.

'Thanks for everything, Maité,' Tamara called. Then, turning back to Nathan, she asked, 'What *is* this?' as she inspected her cube of light.

'It's your invitation, Tamara,' Nathan explained, 'to the Ball.'

'A Ball!' Tamara cried, excitedly.

Peter looked at Nathan and Tamara in surprise.

'What Ball, Mr Asher?' Peter asked.

'Here, this Friday evening at seven pm, your time. It's your welcome celebration and Maité's passing out,' Nathan explained.

On hearing that, Joel flew back over to the rest of the group.

'So, we'll see Maité again, Dad?'

*Goodbye good friend, *My friend! *Thank you very much. *Goodbye friend. *See you soon,

'Yes, son, she'll be here. It will all be hosted here and you will meet the rest of the Kairos. When you get home tonight you will be able to read your invitations, but as soon as they've been read, they will automatically dissolve back into the light. Come, you must go back now. God be with you.'

Seconds later, Joel, Peter and Tamara found themselves standing once again on the plateau in Zionica, their first major mission having been a complete success. Although the air was a little chilly, they were too excited to feel cold. They still felt wrapped in the wonderful, warm glow of Heaven.

The weary friends were astonished to discover that, after all that had happened, it was still only just after nine o'clock. The sun had set and they could hardly believe, as they looked up at the dark, star-speckled sky, that they had been right up there – in Heaven itself.

The dark night meant that they would easily be able to read their invitations, which they could hardly wait to do. The excited friends held up their light cubes and, as they opened their fingers, they watched incredulously as the glowing cubes appeared to unroll themselves open into squares. Then, droplets of light fell away from them like fireflies, which dissolved into the air. These were the spaces in between the letters.Eventually, all that were left were the letters themselves, suspended in the air, forming easily readable words which spelled out the invitation:

Welcome to the Kairos!
You are cordially invited to the
Easter Kairos Celebration Ball.
To be held at the
Andance Regis Ballroom, Heaven.
Friday 7.00 pm GMT
Come Hungry! Gowns will be provided...

'Wow – how amazing is that!' Tamara cried. As she spoke, the glowing golden letters dissolved, just as the spaces had done.

'Awesome!' Peter blinked.

'I wonder what we'll be doing?' Joel mused, apprehensively.'

'I wonder what the gowns will be like!' Tamara sang, dreamily. 'I just can't wait!'

'I guess we'll all just have to wait till Friday to find out,' Peter answered, with a shrug.

'Oh, come on, you two!' Tamara cried excitedly. 'Aren't you just a little bit excited?'

Joel frowned as he noticed one of Tamara's eyebrows twitching.

'Maité will be there, Joel…' she teased, annoyingly.

'It's getting chilly. Let's get back before we're missed.' Joel sighed, deliberately ignoring her comment. Pulling his jacket around him, he set off for the house.

'Yeah, come on Tamara,' Peter urged, with a reproachful frown. 'I'm hungry.'

'I'm sorry, that was unfair.' I didn't think...' Tamara muttered apologetically.

'Tell Joel – not me…' said Peter, as they set off in silence after him.

†

They found Grandad still asleep in his rocking chair. The bottle of whisky was on the table, just as they'd seen it on the Vista. He'd hardly had a drop; the bottle still looked almost full and yet he was fast asleep, snoring loudly as he nursed a small glass on his lap.

'Your dad wasn't joking when he said one glass sent your grandad off to sleep, was he,' Peter chuckled.

Joel gently lifted the glass from Grandad's fingers and as he did so, Grandad stirred.

'Oh, hello,' Grandad yawned. 'I must have dropped off. An old friend came for a visit and brought me this fine bottle of old malt whisky. What time is it, Joel?'

'Nearly half-past-nine, Grandad,' Joel replied. 'Who was your friend?'

'Oh, old Scobie,' Grandad smiled. 'He's a man of the road. He quite often pops in on his travels from village to village and we always have a good chat. I usually sit him in the kitchen and give him a meal. But, tonight he couldn't stay – said he had urgent business. Someone evidently had given him this whisky, but he doesn't drink so he gave it to me.'

'That was kind of him, Mr Jacob,' said Tamara.

'Yes, Tamara, love. He is very kind,' Grandad agreed. 'So, what have you three been up to? You've been out for a long while – sun went down some time ago.'

'Oh not much, Grandad, just messing about in Zionica, you know,' Joel replied, casually. 'I'm starving! Shall we make some sandwiches for supper?'

'Oh yes, good idea, Joel,' Grandad agreed. 'I'm a bit peckish myself. There's some of that lamb in the fridge and some roast beef – and chicken legs too. Oh, and Peter's mum came round with another gooey chocolate cake.'

'Yum!' Joel enthused, rushing into the kitchen. 'Tamara, you can butter the bread. Peter, you get the meat and I'll slice the chocolate cake!'

'I bought some fresh doughnuts from the bakery today as well, in case you're still hungry after all that!' Grandad grinned as he joined them.

A short while later they were all sitting round the kitchen table, munching a veritable feast. Then, suddenly, they were startled by a gentle tapping on the window and all looked up in the direction of the noise. The Magi were perched on the sill outside, staring in at them through the window.

'Look, Joel!' Grandad chuckled. 'Is that the raven that was watching us fencing earlier?'

'Oh, it looks like it, Grandad, doesn't it.' Joel jumped up and opened the window. 'He's brought his mate with him.'

'Did someone mention a feast – perchance?' Magee inquired, nonchalantly.

'I think they're hungry, Grandad. Can we give them something to eat?'

'Of course, son, I wouldn't want any of God's creatures to go hungry – especially ravens.'

'Now you're talking. I'm glad to see someone is getting their priorities right!' Magee chirped. 'Now, I fancy some of that beef. How about you, Maggi?'

'Well, yes, it would go down a treat,' Maggi agreed, coyly.

'Beef it is then,' Joel whispered with amusement.

'Um… you couldn't cut it up into shreds for us, Joel dear, could you? Only we've just got beaks,' Maggi asked politely.

'No teeth!' Magee added.

'Well then, Magee. Perhaps you'd like me to chew yours for you, too?' Joel whispered in amusement.

'Hmm!' Magee huffed, with mock indignation.

Joel put some shreds of beef on a saucer with some pieces of bread and placed it on the window ledge for the birds.

'Room Service!' Joel cried, humorously. 'Enjoy your meal, friends.'

'Thank you very much, Joel dear, and thank your grandad, too,' Maggi cawed.

'You're welcome,' Grandad said cheerily.

The three children gasped and stared at Grandad, whilst Maggi and Magee, shreds of beef hanging from their beaks, paused, staring goggle-eyed – Grandad wasn't supposed to be able to hear the ravens speaking!

'What did you say, Grandad?' Joel asked.

'Oh,' Grandad chuckled. 'I assumed the birds would be grateful for the food – and that *if* they could speak, they would say thank you! So, I said, you're welcome! I was just being jovial, that's all.' Grandad, explained – with a curious twinkle in his eye.

They all laughed at this, and a jolly good feast was had by all.

CHAPTER SEVENTEEN

The Preparation

So much had happened over the last couple of weeks and it suddenly hit Joel with a shock, when he woke up the next morning, that it was already Thursday! In two days time, the Easter holiday would be over and Mum would arrive to take him home. He contemplated glumly the prospect of returning to the "normality" of school, homework and studying. He wasn't ready for that; things had only just begun. He had many questions; he longed to spend time with his dad – to find out what his next mission would be. How could he concentrate on schoolwork with such an exciting development? How could he look Mum in the eye, knowing what he knew? He was sure that he would feel awkward; would she suspect anything? And would he ever see Maité again? He really liked Maité but, at their age, a gap of three years and three months between them seemed an insurmountable gulf. How could she really be interested in a boy so much younger than herself? She would be sixteen on Saturday and he wouldn't be thirteen until July – he wasn't even a teenager yet! In her eyes he was just a kid and yet Joel felt that, despite the age difference, there was a special bond between them. After all, his own dad had been three years younger than Mum – it didn't seem to matter once you became an adult.

†

Peter and Tamara came over after breakfast and Tamara could hardly contain herself! She was positively bubbling over about the forthcoming Ball and couldn't stop talking about the gowns they were to be given. It was all the boys could do to keep her quiet about it in front of Grandad so they whisked her off to Zionica for the day, where she could fantasise to her heart's content.

'Just think of it!' Tamara exclaimed, as they made their way to their tree. 'We're going to be given *heavenly garments to wear* – clothes that are not of this world! How completely amazing is that! I cannot begin to imagine what they will be like, can you?'

Ordinarily, Tamara would have driven Joel barmy, but now though, he actually found that her excited babbling gave him some respite from his preoccupation about Maité – and the upsetting prospect of never seeing her again after the Ball.

Without waiting for an answer, Tamara continued. 'I've never been to an *actual Ball!* Oh, it's like Cinderella coming to life! I'm so excited I could burst! I don't know how I'm going to get through the next few hours; I simply can't wait!'

Peter and Joel chuckled, in amusement. They'd never seen Tamara – or anyone else for that matter – as excited about anything! Then, as they reached their tree, Tamara suddenly stopped and gasped.

'Joel!' She took hold of Joel's arm and looked up at him. 'Do you think we'll see… I mean, what's the possibility that we might actually meet – Jesus Himself?' she breathed with an air of awesome wonder.

'Well, I er…' Joel thought for a moment. 'Tamara, I just don't know. How can any of us possibly know that?'

'Heaven is His home, isn't it? That's where Jesus lives!' Tamara persisted. 'The Bible says that He ascended into Heaven – to sit at the right hand of His Father.'

'I suppose, based on that, there must be every chance that He'll be there – somewhere. Although, how He would show Himself to us we couldn't really say,' Joel mused. 'For sure, it's certainly an amazing thought, though.'

'That would be sooo cool, wouldn't it? To meet Jesus and talk with Him,' Tamara continued.

'You can talk to Jesus any time you like, Tamara; you don't have to be in Heaven to pray,' Peter explained. 'Heaven might be His home but He also lives in the heart of every believer.'

'I know that!' Tamara retorted. 'But this is different! I mean, how many people get the chance to visit Heaven – and come back again!

They reached their tree and all climbed up to the den.

'I wonder if we'll be able to choose where we sit, or if our places will already be decided for us?' Tamara pondered, dizzily.

'Now, that I think is an easy one,' Peter answered. 'Our places will be reserved for us – if it was left to us to decide, there would be chaos I should imagine.'

'Oh, why do you think that, Peter?' Tamara looked puzzled.

'Well obviously, given a choice, everyone would want to sit next to Jesus – if He's there in Person,' Peter replied.

'Wow!' Tamara swooned. 'Do you actually think that Jesus might be there – *in Person?'*

'I suppose anything is possible, Tamara,' Peter replied. I mean, would you have believed a few days ago that you would even be attending a party in Heaven this weekend?'

'That's a bit of a daft question to ask Tamara, Peter!' Joel laughed. 'It's only because of a miracle that she's still with us in the world!'

'Oh, of course it is!' Peter chuckled, seeing the funny side of his question.

The three friends spent the day in Zionica, doing the kind of things they used to do before the "Kairos." The pond was teeming with life. The tadpoles no doubt were happy to be free of their jam-jar prisons, but by the time they become baby frogs, Joel would be back in the city with Mum, Naomi and school.

However they tried to amuse themselves though, none of them could concentrate on anything much apart from the forthcoming Ball in Heaven and the mission adventure of the previous evening. So, as they whiled away the day in their tree den, they marvelled at how they had been rescued from the brink of death, and how glad they were that the villains had been caught. In short, the children were all a little overwhelmed by the phenomenal circumstances in which they had become involved. Tamara had to keep pinching herself to remember that she was awake and not still in a coma, dreaming all of this. They marvelled at the ingenuity of Smith's hi-tech pen. Joel and Peter praised Tamara for her quick thinking in paying Smith a visit, and fell about laughing at the idea that Smith thought he had been visited by an angel – although Tamara was quite flattered by his description of her. They giggled helplessly at the ridiculous notion that Grandad might have heard the ravens speaking.

Tamara, of course, kept fantasising about the imminent Ball in Heaven. 'It's terribly sad that Maité has to leave, just because she's sixteen on Saturday, when she so wants to stay on in the Kairos.' She looked at Joel, anticipating some sort of reaction. They were all going to miss Maité; they had become fond of her, but Joel, who had not been able to keep secret the fact that he had a crush on the beautiful Spanish girl, was finding it harder than the others to accept that, after the Ball, he may never see her again. Tamara was feeling a little fazed by Maité's alluring personality and looks, as she herself had for a long time had a crush on Joel, but *she'd* managed to keep her affections secret – at least from Joel, although Peter was not so easily fooled.

'She's so good, too,' Peter agreed. 'All that experience – it's such a waste!'

'I know, but isn't that what life is like?' Joel began. 'I mean, you spend your life learning stuff and gaining experience then, when you hopefully get to some great old age like ninety or something, and you have a wealth of knowledge and skill in whatever you spent your life doing – bosh! There it goes – you hand in your clogs and it's all over – gone to dust!'

'Oh, dear...' murmured Tamara, her voice quavering a little. 'That wasn't a very nice thing to say, Joel.'

'I'm sorry, Tamara,' Joel shrugged. 'But that's what happens. We're all going to hand in our clogs sooner or later. I mean, *you've* just had a stay of execution, but eventually, some day, those riding boots of yours will become redundant!'

'That's horrible!' Tamara burst into tears. 'I can't believe you've said that.'

'Yeah, that was a bit harsh and tactless, Joel,' Peter muttered. Joel looked suddenly remorseful at his own thoughtless words. Tamara stood up and reached for the rope swing, but in her haste to run off, she tripped over Peter's outstretched legs as he was sitting between her and the rope. Missing the rope, she stumbled, falling backwards over edge of the den. Joel saw her trip and, as if by some supernatural means, he leapt up like a bolt of lightning and grabbed her round the waist. Tamara's terrified face stared up at him. He felt a sudden strength in his arms as they became like rods of steel. By a miracle he pulled her up, saving her from falling to the ground. He held onto her, very tightly, hardly able to believe that he could have spoken such stupid and tactless words, that had put her within inches of her life.

Peter, who had been temporarily frozen with fear as he watched, open-mouthed, suddenly scrambled to his feet and pulled the pair of them back into the den.

'I'm so sorry,' Joel murmured, gently, still holding onto Tamara.

Tamara was momentarily too shaken to speak. Her eyes were glazed with fear, as she stared up at Joel, contemplating how close she had just come to the fulfilment of his tactless prophesy.

'It's a good job Joel is a strong rugby player, Tamara. I wouldn't have been quick or strong enough to do that. I think we've just witnessed yet another miracle.'

'Well, thank God,' Joel sighed with relief. 'Are you all right, Tamara? I can't believe I allowed my self-pity to hurt you like that and put you in such danger. Can you forgive me?'

'Of course I forgive you, you great big oaf!' Tamara replied with a forced cheerfulness – although she was clearly still shaken by the incident. Breaking free from him, she continued. 'I – I thought for a minute your horrid prediction was coming true – but thank you for saving my life – again!'

'We're friends then?' Joel smiled, a little anxiously.

'Yes, you can't get rid of me that easily, Joel.' Tamara replied, bravely, returning the smile. 'It was just a careless comment – forget it.'

They all sat down again.

'You know, you're wrong, Joel,' Peter pointed out. 'We've been privileged to witness the fact that it's not all over – turned to dust – as you quoted; that is not the case at all. It must require great skill and experienced judgement to run such an important organisation as the Kairos. Your dad's experience during his life on earth has very definitely not all turned to dust. In fact, he's putting all that he learned while on the earth to very good use. O.K. our earthly bodies may very well turn to dust but our souls and spirits live forever; we passed from death to eternal life when we accepted Jesus as our Saviour.'

'Yes, Peter, you're right!' Tamara agreed, cheering up. 'You know what I think? This life must be a training ground – a "life school," and we'll all be given jobs to do in Heaven according to what we've done with our lives down here.'

'Of course,' Joel agreed, this life could be the preparation for greater things to come!'

'Maybe that's what Jesus meant in the parable of the talents,' mused Peter.

'So this life must be boot camp!' exclaimed Tamara.

'Yes, I suppose, in a way – he who is faithful with the few talents he is given and puts them to good use, will be given greater responsibility and he who squanders and wastes what he has been given will lose it all. Maybe part of the "greater responsibility" that Jesus was talking about, is our employment in eternity.' Peter pondered.

'Well, I'm going to do the best I can because I want a good job when I get to Heaven. I don't want to spend eternity removing chewing gum from pavements,' Tamara declared. 'I want to live in a mansion and have lots of horses.'

'I doubt that there's chewing gum in Heaven, Tamara, remember those Celestial pavements are made of gold!' Peter answered. 'But we do know the Bible says that all Jesus' disciples get mansions in Heaven and we know for a fact that there are horses in Heaven – and that we will be riding them, it says so in the Book of Revelation: chapter 19 and verses 11 to 14. I know what you mean, though. You only get one chance and we need to make it count.'

'Some people think they come back again and again and have more chances, don't they?' Tamara remarked.

'Yes, Tamara, but it's not true,' Peter answered seriously. 'You only get one life and you've got to learn and do what you can, while you can. This is not a rehearsal, as they say; this is the real deal! The Bible clearly says that it is appointed once for man to die and then judgement.'

Their impromptu Bible study was abruptly halted by the appearance of Maggi, who settled on a nearby branch.

'Hello, children!' she cawed.

Then Magee landed beside her. 'Any food lying around, perchance, kids?' he enquired.

'There's loads of food, Magee. We're all too excited to eat, so help yourselves,' Tamara offered.

'Excited, really?' Maggi asked. 'You don't *sound* excited, Tamara. Is there something wrong, dear?'

'Tamara has just had a very scary moment, Maggi,' Joel explained. 'It's my fault. I said something stupid and she almost fell out of the tree.'

'But Joel saved me,' Tamara added quickly. 'I don't know how – it was a miracle! He leapt up and stopped me from falling.'

'Oh, you poor dear! What a terrible fright! Are you all right?' Maggi asked, sympathetically. The raven immediately flew to a branch next to Tamara and rubbed her head gently on her cheek.

'I'm O.K. now, Maggi, thank you,' Tamara smiled up at the raven. 'Joel needs your sympathy more than me, though. He's lamenting the prospect of never seeing Maité again when she leaves the Kairos after Friday's Ball.'

'I thought we would *all* miss Maité,' Joel said defensively. 'Anyway, we'll all eventually have to leave the Kairos, when we reach sixteen.'

'At least you won't remember Maité then, Joel,' Tamara pointed out.

'You'll be the last to leave, Tamara and then you'll have to keep it all secret from us,' Joel answered.

'Yeah, that's going to be soooh hard…' Tamara pondered, thoughtfully. 'For two years! It isn't easy keeping a secret from you for two minutes, let alone two years!'

'Yes, I'm sure it isn't, Tamara. I wonder what Maité will write in her note,' Joel mused. He really couldn't get Maité out of his head and he supposed that, now the "cat was out of the bag" regarding his now-not-so-secret crush on the beautiful Spanish girl, it was a waste of time trying to deny it.'

'She might tell you, Joel, if you ask her tomorrow night,' Tamara teased, raising that suspicious eyebrow again. 'You've really got a crush on her, haven't you? You're in lurve!'

'Do give it a rest, Tamara!' Joel retorted, awkwardly. He felt his face turning the colour of beetroot, and quickly looked away.

'There's no point denying it, Joel. It's as obvious as a lamp-post on your head!' Tamara giggled. 'You light up whenever you see her.'

'I like her – but we all do, don't we?' Joel protested.

'Of course we do,' Peter answered.

'Well, what's this then?' Tamara asked, pulling a book from Joel's pile and holding it up. "Learn Spanish!" Got a sudden desire to learn Spanish, have you, Joel? Going on holiday? Wouldn't be to – Spain by any chance or Morisco, more specifically?'

'Oh, I don't know what that's doing there,' Joel said quickly, snatching the book from Tamara.

'Yes you do – I've seen you reading it!' Tamara giggled.

'So what!' Joel challenged, defensively.

'Oh, whatever,' she laughed mischievously. 'Anyway, I happen to know she likes you, too,' Tamara teased, twisting a lock of hair around her finger.

'You do!' Joel took Tamara's bait, then quickly realising, he added coolly, 'I mean, do you?'

'Yes, girls know these things,' Tamara continued, 'and that girl definitely has a twinkle in her eye for you, Joel, just as you do for her.'

'Oh, whatever, Tamara,' Joel replied, mimicking her. Then, rising to his feet, he snatched the rope swing. 'Anyway, I'm going back to the house. Are you coming, Peter?' With that,

Joel swung to the ground.

'I'll be right down,' Peter called. Then he turned to Tamara.

'You shouldn't tease him like that, Tamara. It's very unfair. It's not as if he's ever likely to see Maité again, is it?' he breathed quietly. 'Tomorrow night might very well be the last time. Think how you'd feel if that was someone you were fond of!'

'Oh…' Tamara whispered softly. 'I was only having a bit of fun – I didn't mean anything by it. I feel dreadful now.'

'And so you should, but I bet you don't feel half as bad as he does. Wait till you get older and have the *hots* for some boy, then you'll know what it feels like. Anyway,' Peter urged as he took hold of the rope and handed it to her, 'it's getting late, let's go.' Tamara took the rope. She knew full well what Peter was talking about; she didn't have to be older to experience what he was describing. She felt like that at the end of every holiday, when Joel went back to the city.

'Huh – humans!' Magee exclaimed, as the children made their way back to the house. 'What complicated lives they lead. Now, my little gooseberry, let's get started on this veritable banquet; all this excitement has made me very hungry indeed.'

'Typical, Magee – always thinking of your stomach!' Maggi shook her head. 'OK then, perhaps a little ham.'

CHAPTER EIGHTEEN

I'll Lead You All in the Dance, said He

The cat was out of the bag! It now seemed to Joel that the whole world knew about his crush on Maité. He decided that there was no point brooding over it and that he would focus instead on the Kairos. Oh, how Joel had missed his dad; he had thought that he would never see him again, but now, he was so happy he couldn't wait for Friday evening when he really would see him again.

After what seemed like an eternity, the evening of the Ball arrived. Joel asked Grandad if they could take a feast up to the den and have their supper up there by lantern-light. This would excuse them from having to eat a big meal in front of him so that they could go to the Ball hungry, as instructed, and leave all the food in the den. There would be no problem with time, as they would not be going anywhere through the Vista but would be in Heaven all evening. This meant that they would be able to stay at the Ball as long as they wanted, without much time passing in the world. They wore jeans and casual tops – anything else would have aroused Grandad's suspicion. Anyway, as gowns were to be provided, it didn't really matter what they wore.

With a hint of nostalgia, Grandad agreed to the feast in the den and, as he watched them running excitedly down the yard to the field, he found himself almost wishing that he was twelve again, so that he could join them.

The three children positioned the lanterns in the den under the watchful eyes of the Magi, who, typically seemed more interested in the contents of the picnic basket.

'Having a little picnic again, are we?' Magee chirped, peering eagerly at the basket of food as if trying to x-ray it with his eyes.

'You have a food-seeking antenna for a beak, don't you, Magee?' Joel remarked with a grin. 'Well, it's your lucky day. All of this food needs to be eaten and *we* can't eat any of it because we're going to the Ball!'

Magee's eyes lit up.

'Oh yes, the Kairos Ball, as if I could forget that!' Magee cawed. 'Maggi has been driving me batty, reminiscing about it all day – especially the scrumptious food!'

'Oh, and the gowns…' Maggi swooned dreamily, as she swept into the den, spreading her wings in a curtsy.

Tamara giggled with delight at the funny ravens. 'I suppose you have both been to many of these Balls, Maggi?'

'Oh yes my dear, we've been to *hundreds* of Kairos Balls!' Maggi chirped, with a grand flourish. 'There might only have been three generations of Joel's family in the Kairos, but the group has been going for many centuries!'

'And we haven't been Kairos earthbound guardians forever,' Magee added. 'We used to be regular angels!'

'Wow! So there's a Ball at the end of *every* school holiday?' Tamara asked, excitedly.

'Of course, dear,' Maggi replied.

'Oh how marvellous!' Tamara cried. 'But, why didn't you tell us about this before! Tell me about the gowns, Maggi, what are they like?' she urged.

'Oh, I couldn't possibly tell you that, Tamara my dear. I don't want to spoil it for you by telling you beforehand. It's so much more exciting if you don't find out till you get there. You cannot conceivably imagine some of the things in store for you up there, children. It's like nothing on earth,' Maggi smiled.

'Especially the food…' Magee reminisced.

'Well, never mind, Magee,' Tamara giggled happily. 'You two can feast away to your hearts' content on this little picnic. I suppose it'll be quite romantic by lantern-light,' she mused.

Maggi bowed her head and blinked bashfully, while Magee stargazed aloofly.

'Angels don't bother with that sort of thing, Tamara. I'm sure the lighting will be quite adequate,' Magee muttered.

'Magee, we happen to be ravens at the moment!' Maggi pointed out. 'But *you* seem to be behaving like a cold fish! Anyway, come on now, children, you must get there in good time. It wouldn't do to arrive at the last minute,' she urged them.

The three friends said their farewells to the Magi and made their way excitedly to the plateau – although for Joel, the excitement was mingled with trepidation.

Magee held up a wing, inviting Maggi to snuggle up.

'Come here, Petal,' he cawed softly.

Maggi sidled up under his wing and the pair of ravens watched them go.

It was a clear night and the sky was peppered with many stars. A fresh breeze swirled around Zionica and served to exhilarate the excited children even more. As they approached the grassy plateau, they turned to wave to the Magi, who were silhouetted by the lantern light. Then, holding hands, the trio stepped onto the plateau and were immediately swept up by the Fugue.

At the top of the Fugue, they were met by beautiful, soft angelic singing but, instead of Charis and Aletheia, they were welcomed by two seraphs. The seraphs didn't speak but hovered over the top of the Fugue, smiling tenderly and shaking their sceptres over all the Kairos arrivals.

'Ooh, that's lovely!' Tamara positively glowed as the droplets of love fell on her face like glittering stardust.

'They're showering us with love again,' Peter exclaimed excitedly, as a warm flush enveloped him.

'I should use that sparingly over Jo… oops…' Tamara suddenly realised the insensitivity of her comment.

Joel looked around a little embarrassed, as Peter chastised her with a frown.

'Sorry… there goes my mouth again,' she winced.

The three friends fell in line, as a steady stream of excited Kairos members arrived. There were a few regular angels flitting about greeting the children in the normal way.

'Just keep going to your right. Blessed is He,' beamed a beautiful angel, as the trio from Zionica passed by.

They glided off to the right up the Hall of Archways with all the other children. Soon, they noticed an archway on the left that they hadn't noticed before. They guessed that this was the venue of the Ball because this archway was not just glowing, but exuded an explosion of colour which seemed to be flashing and sparkling, as if a brilliant firework display was going on at its entrance; this all added to the awe and excitement of the evening. Angels guided the flow of excited children forward and two cherubim angels could be seen, one on either side of the entrance to this sparkly archway. Unlike the tall, elegant, six-winged seraphs, the cherubim were much smaller. The cherubim appeared to have the role of checking that all the children had the seal, which was the seal of God. Having done this they smiled and politely ushered the children through.

'Thank you,' Tamara leaned down and smiled at the cherub on her right.

The little cherub gave Tamara a cute smile and held up a flower in its tiny hand.

'You're supposed to take it,' a Chinese boy whispered from behind.

'Well, thank you, again,' Tamara beamed at the cherub and took the flower. She put the delicate blue rose to her face and smelt the heady fragrance. 'Mm, this is lovely!' she murmured. The cherub gave her a heart-melting smile.

'A blue rose,' the Chinese boy remarked quietly. 'That's special!'

The children glided through the archway and as they did so, their feet hit the ground with an unexpected jolt. However the floor was slightly springy, which rather lessened the impact. There were several angels waiting to receive the children as they glided through.

'Gravity?' Peter exclaimed, surprised.

'It's only simulated gravity,' one of the angels explained, with a giggle. 'It takes everyone by surprise the first time. The springiness takes a while to adjust to, but you'll soon get the hang of it.'

Meanwhile, regular angels were handing out garments to the children and calling, 'Girls to the right and boys to the left, everyone.'

'These are yours, Tamara,' an angel announced as she handed

Tamara her garments. 'Please go into the changing rooms and put them on. You will not be allowed into the banquet unless you're wearing the right garments.'

'Oh, thank you. I'm so glad you've got mine, but how did you know my name?' Tamara asked.

'It's on your forehead, dear – your Kairos number,' the angel replied, pointing to the gold embroidered number 63 on her garment.

'Wow!' Tamara cried gleefully. 'That's so clever!' Then, taking the garment, she hurried into the changing room.

Moments later, she emerged in her new tailor-made and perfectly fitting attire. She was wearing a beautiful gown with a fitted violet velvet bodice, which matched the colour of her eyes. A golden lion was embroidered, along with the number 63 – her Kairos number – on the right by her shoulder. It had a full-length violet silk skirt, with delicate gold and silver beading around. A floor-length silver cloak was attached to the shoulders by golden epaulettes. On her feet she wore glittery slippers.

Tamara immediately spotted Joel and Peter and hurried to show them her gown. The boys wore an almost knee-length blue tunic of fine linen, over white fine linen trousers. The tunic had a wide gold belt and gold insignia on the chest, displaying a golden lion and their Kairos number. They each wore a knee-length purple cloak which was attached to their shoulders by golden epaulettes. On their feet they wore soft white boots.

'Wow, look at you! You two look so different!' Tamara cried excitedly. 'I feel like a princess!' 'Well, the Bible does say that we are all royal priests and kings, Tamara,' Peter whispered.

'Well, step this way, your majesty,' Joel chuckled and gave a short bow.

Tamara giggled, nervously.

They all gazed around in wonder, as the room filled up with children. It seemed that just about every nationality was represented – from Aborigines and Zulus to Eskimos. All the boys were dressed the same and all the girls' gowns were the same, except for the colour of the bodice of their dresses which in every case exactly matched the colour of their eyes. Altogether, it made a spectacular scene!

As the children surveyed the gathering, they were quite overwhelmed by the dazzling array of colour and the awesome atmosphere of the occasion! The enormous banqueting hall seemed to be bursting at the seams with all manner of brightly flashing colours, with crystals and jewels sparkling and glowing everywhere. This must have been what had caused the firework-effect that the children had seen as they glided up the Hall of Archways.

There was a host of angels on a platform at the top of the room, singing softly and playing musical instruments. Along the two long sides of the room were small archways which were obscured by a mist within: seven along each side. Seventeen large round tables were dotted around the room. Each table had nine chairs and nine place settings of silver and crystal. There were five gold taps, with no handles, suspended around the middle of each table. At the top of the room was a long table set with seven place settings, all facing down the room.

Most of the other children seemed to know each other and were chatting excitedly. Several regular angels were circulating around the room, welcoming the children and putting them at ease – although they were all so excited that seemed to be an impossible task. Some cherubim also seemed to be on duty, checking tables and darting in and out of the misty archways, making sure everything was in order.

Joel, Peter and Tamara were overcome with awe and wonder as they looked around them. Tamara was so awestruck that she was almost floating, despite the gravity. Joel smiled at Tamara slightly bemused.

'Tamara is so excited, I think she may actually spontaneously combust!' Joel murmured, with a grin.

'Are you sure I woke up from that coma, Peter, or am I dreaming all this?' she asked in amazement.

'We'll compare our dreams tomorrow, Tamara, and see if we both dreamt the same thing,' he replied. 'But, you're right. It is totally awesome!'

'Peter, can you see Jesus?' Tamara asked. 'I want to see Jesus!'

'Well, I suspect, Tamara, that we would know if He was in the room in person,' Peter replied thoughtfully. 'Because that would be where everyone would be gathering – you know, "wherever the body is, there the eagles will be gathered together." I suppose there would be a very bright light, too. He is the Light of the world, after all!'

'Yes, I suppose you're right,' she agreed. 'You always know everything, Peter.'

'Maybe He'll turn up later, Tamara, after everyone else has arrived,' Joel suggested.

Charis and Aletheia appeared and congratulated them on their successful mission.

'Everyone is talking about it!' Charis enthused, beaming with joy. 'Praise God for this victory!'

'Yes, it's a wonderful success. Nathan has been after those villains for quite some time. He's been waiting for the right Kairos members in England for this work, but of course, it's the Lord who does the appointing,' Aletheia pointed out.

'And the Holy Spirit does the anointing!' Tamara chipped in.

'How very inspired, Tamara,' Aletheia added with a smile. 'Well, we're all so excited to have you three on board, aren't we Charis?'

'We certainly are, Aletheia!' Charis replied.

Suddenly, Joel felt a light tap on his shoulder and he turned round to find himself face to face with Maité. He swallowed nervously as he noticed immediately how beautiful she was. The colour of her gown bodice, like Tamara's, perfectly matched her big, amber Spanish eyes. With her glowing olive skin and her face framed by a flock of rich dark hair, she looked a vision of loveliness.

For some inexplicable reason, Joel found himself blushing so profusely that his head felt like a giant tomato. At the same time, his heart seemed to give a bit of a hoppity-leap all on its own and his tummy kind of fluttered. It was all very strange; he'd never experienced feelings quite like these before. He just hoped that Maité – and everyone else – would just think his face was reflecting all the vivid colours that were flashing all around them.

'What do you think of it, so far?' Maité asked, with a grin.

For a moment, Joel felt a little tongue-tied. 'Well – um – it – it's – it's all so awesome, Maité,' he managed to reply. Then, with an effort, he pulled himself together. 'But, I guess you must be used to all this by now.' No sooner were those insensitive words out of his mouth than he realised the clanger he had dropped – if only he could recall those words – that they would slip silently back into his mouth and not be uttered at all because, of course, this was the *last* Kairos Ball that Maité would be attending. 'Oh, I – I'm sorry, Maité – I didn't mean…'

'It's O.K. Joel. You never get used to something this wonderful,' she replied graciously. 'It's a precious experience every time, and a fantastic opportunity to meet other Kairos children. It's good to be able to talk freely about our work, which we obviously cannot do in the world. I wonder who the special guests will be this time. You know, there are usually three or four Patron Saints invited. They sit at the top table with Nathan and Anna.'

'Patron Saints?' Tamara cried excitedly.

'Oh, yes, usually related to children's causes. You know, like the Patron Saint for abandoned children – that sort of thing,' Maité replied.

Joel nodded. He was trying to look intelligent and attentive in a cool sort of way, but inside he was as tense as a coiled spring.

'We're all saints, Tamara,' Peter explained. 'Everyone who trusts in the Lord Jesus and what He did at the cross for their salvation is a saint. You're a saint!'

'I'm a saint?' Tamara asked in surprise.

'Of course you are!' Peter continued. 'You would not be here otherwise, Tamara. Whosoever believes that Jesus died on the cross to take the punishment for their sins and that He rose again from the dead, is a saint and we all have everlasting life!'

'Peter's right, Tamara,' Nathan affirmed as he suddenly appeared, seemingly out of thin air, by their sides. 'ALL people who are true believers in the one true gospel of the Lord Jesus Christ are saints – even those still living on the earth. You don't have to physically die to become a saint. Neither do you need to be canonised by man to become a saint. If you trust in Jesus' sacrifice at the cross you qualify!'

'Wow, I really am a saint...' Tamara repeated, dreamily.

'That means then, that all these Kairos children are saints!' Joel uttered in amazement.

'Yes, Joel, every single one of them,' Nathan replied. 'We're all one big community, the whole company of Heaven and earth: all the saints, the angels, the archangels, everyone who has ever come to know Jesus; whether they're here or still in the world.'

'That is so amazing!' Joel murmured.

'Yes it is,' Maité agreed.

'Excuse me,' Nathan interjected, 'I'm needed elsewhere – the guest saints are arriving.' With that, he vanished instantly.

Then, to Joel's horror, Tamara leaned over to him with that cheeky look on her face. He recognised the look: mouth twitching; one eyebrow raised. He felt the hairs rise, prickling the back of his neck and before he could do anything, out of her mouth it came:

'Maybe St. Valentine will be here, Joel; that would be convenient, wouldn't it?' she giggled, teasingly. 'Perhaps he will have one or two arrows in his bow...'

Joel's mouth became suddenly dry and the colour rushed to his face again. He began to open and close his mouth in a fish-like manner, as Tamara continued embarrassingly.

'Oh my, Joel – your face is like Rudolf's nose!' she giggled.

Joel didn't know whether he wanted to throttle Tamara or flee from the room as fast as his legs could carry him – or both! However, while Peter gave Tamara a look of reproach, Maité came to Joel's rescue.

'Isn't it amazing, how the different coloured lights reflect all around up here, Joel?' Maité murmured, softly. Then, turning to

Tamara, she peered into her face, scrunching up her nose. 'Tamara, your face is suddenly the colour of Joel's cloak.'

'What?' Tamara cried. 'But, his cloak is purple!'

'Yes, Tamara, it is,' Maité grinned, cheekily. 'I'm afraid your face looks like an aubergine.'

Joel and Peter tried to stifle the urge to burst out laughing as Tamara huffed indignantly. Maité however, ignoring Tamara's indignation, continued to explain.

'The invited special guests sit at the top table with Nathan and Anna'

'Boot's not very comfortable on the other foot, is it, Tamara?' Peter muttered in her ear.

'Just Nathan and Anna?' Joel asked, surprised. 'What about everyone else's guardians?'

'Everyone doesn't have their own guardian with them in the Kairos, Joel,' Maité chuckled.

Joel stared at her blankly.

'Oh – you really don't know, do you?' she continued, quite astonished.

'Know what?' Joel blundered, naively.

'I assumed you knew – that Nathan is assigned to lead the Kairos group; he's in charge of all Kairos activities and responsible only to our Lord, the King of Glory, Who, obviously, is the Head; Anna is Nathan's deputy.'

The three Zionica recruits stared at Maité in surprise. They had all assumed that Nathan and Anna had been there merely because they were Joel and Peter's guardians!

'My dad – in charge of the Kairos?' Joel marvelled.

'It's purely coincidence that Nathan happens to be your earthly dad,' Maité explained. 'It's the same with Peter – a coincidence that Anna is his birth mother. What? Did you think everyone was given their missions by their own guardians? In that case, did you not wonder where Tamara's guardian was?

'Yes, I did wonder,' Tamara replied, hesitantly.

'My dad, in charge of the Kairos...' Joel repeated incredulously.

'Uh-huh. He's a vet., too,' Maité continued.
Joel looked stumped and he didn't quite know what to say. He felt that perishing fish impersonation coming back and that he had made bungling gaffe after bungling gaffe, and wondered that Maité wanted anything to do with him at all.

'You know…' Maité explained, 'a veteran – of the Kairos. In fact, to date, Nathan has the reputation of being the bravest Kairos child ever and holds the record for the most successful missions. His exploits are famous, so it was inevitable, I guess, that when he came here for good he would take over the post of running the group. Your dad is quite a hero, Joel – but only because he has been totally submitted to God and consequently put all of his great faith in the Lord Jesus. This enabled the Holy Spirit to work the mighty power of God in him to accomplish his missions. You know, none of us could be used by God at all, if our faith was not solely in what Jesus has already done – that is, the finished work at the cross that gives us every victory. Anyone who starts to think their success is of themselves gets very quickly brought down to size. We owe our success to the Divine supernatural power that is behind us and indeed, in us, keeping us upheld.'
The three friends listened in awe.

'This means, Joel that, unfortunately for you, once it gets out whose son you are, all eyes will be watching you – great things will be expected of you,' Maité sighed, with a glint in her eye.

'No pressure then, Joel,' Peter muttered.

'You've a lot to live up to, my friend,' Maité continued. '...and you've "*fuelled the fire,*" with your death-defying leap in the mine-shaft! The story has leaked out already and everyone is talking about it. So, expectations have already been set.'

'Wow, and they still don't know who you are, Joel! Think what they'll say when they all find out you're Nathan's natural son!' Tamara blurted out.

'You're Nathan's son?' an Arab boy gasped loudly, as he overheard Tamara. This, in turn, caused several heads to turn around and stare in their direction.

'Well done, Tamara,' Peter muttered sarcastically. 'I guess there's nowhere you can hide now, Joel, mate.'

Joel looked round, in some trepidation, at the sea of faces staring at him as this news was whispered, with the inevitability of a tsunami wave, throughout the entirety of the room.

'Oh, bother!' Tamara giggled. 'Sorry, Joel.'

'You've been giving me a glowing report, Maité,' Nathan grinned, as he appeared suddenly at their sides again.

'Not at all, Señor. It is not glowing enough,' Maité replied, smiling.

'What was your Kairos number, Dad?' Joel asked.

'119, the same as you. Now that is not a coincidence, but an ordained sign. The issuing of Kairos numbers is not a lottery; every child's number is specially chosen for them – it's their destiny.'

'For you, Joel, a legacy,' Anna added with a smile, as she appeared by their sides. 'The legacy of Nathan's reputation, which I'm sure you will have no problem living up to.'

Joel gulped, nervously. There was altogether too much to take in. How could he live up to his dad's amazing track record? Then Maité suddenly gripped his arm.

'Oh, look! Joel! There's St. Nicholas!' she cried. 'If there's something you specially want for Christmas, now is the time to mention it. Remember what Christmas is all about; it's a time for giving and receiving gifts. This tradition was started by our Heavenly Father, when He gave the greatest gift of all – His own Son!' She sped off, with Joel in-tow, towards a tall figure with a long, white beard.

'Saints alive!' Tamara exclaimed in astonishment.

At this, several children and angels turned to look at her.

'Oops… sorry…' she murmured, sheepishly. At ten years of age, Tamara had not yet mastered the art of tact.

Everyone circulated around the room, greeting each other excitedly, while the cherubs seemed to be busily flitting about. Then, after some time, a trumpet sounded. The room was suddenly silent and everyone stood still, facing the front.

Nathan was standing at the centre of the top table. Anna and five guest saints were seated with him, three on either side. A really cute cherub hovered at the side of the table, holding the silver trumpet which he had just blown. He looked a little nervous, but obviously thrilled, as though it was the first time he had been honoured with the responsibility of blowing the trumpet.

'Welcome, and thank you for coming to the End-of-Term Kairos Celebration,' Nathan began. 'Blessed is He who comes in the name of the Lord!'

'Blessed is He!' the whole assembly cheered.

Suddenly, one hundred and fifty-three brightly coloured balloons appeared, suspended over the one hundred and fifty-three chairs around the seventeen tables in the ballroom. Each balloon had a gold number which corresponded to the one hundred and fifty Kairos numbers, except that three of the numbers appeared twice, accompanied by a letter.

'Now, as usual, everyone has been allocated a seat,' Nathan announced. 'This is merely a formality,' he continued, 'just to show that you all have your rightful place here. So, I trust everyone's garment fits,' he chuckled. The top table guests chortled slightly at Nathan's attempt to kick the proceedings off with tongue-in-cheek humour. However, the children were all so excited that his humour went over most of their heads. 'Most of you know the drill but, for the newcomers, you are free to wander around the Regis Ballroom and mingle while you eat. You may even swap seats if you wish. As usual, we've invited some Patron Saints and I'm pleased to introduce them to you.' He waved an arm in the direction of the guests seated alongside him who, each in turn, stood and took a bow as they were introduced. Each announcement was met with enthusiastic applause.

'Maria Goretti – Patroness of Youth and Women Victims of Violence.

'Jerome Emiliani – Patron of Abandoned Children.

'Charles Lwanga – Patron of African Youth.

'Anna, of course, my assistant here on my right.

'Nicholas of Tolentino – Patron of Animals and Babies.

'And, last but not least, Nicholas of Bari – commonly associated with Christmas time.' There was a loud cheer as this last saint was introduced, leaving no doubt about his popularity among the Kairos children.

Anna leaned forward and whispered something to Nathan.

'Oh yes,' he continued. 'Three of the numbers on the balloons are repeated. Most of you will know that when members leave us, their replacement joins at the same time. We welcome four new members, and sadly say farewell to four, although unfortunately, only seven of those eight are here tonight. The seven children in question will find their initial, as well as their number at their seat.' He paused a moment before explaining: 'I'm sure you all must know by now that Jean has left the Kairos prematurely… So – there is one less seat than would normally have been the case.'

There was an audible silence at this announcement. Nathan cleared his throat, then, continued. 'Unfortunately, because of Jean's method of exit from the Kairos, she will not be able to join us here. Sadly her life was cut short during her last mission which is a great loss to the Kairos. Let this be a reminder to you children, of the dangers that you may face in your missions, and make you aware of the importance of discernment and not *taking matters into your own hands*. You're all mighty warriors in the Lord and you should be expeditious in your missions in accordance with *instructions'*. Nathan paused briefly then continued.

'You all know from your own experiences that our work in the Kairos can be tough and you cannot carry out your missions in your own strength. Wisdom – children – get wisdom!'

'Alleluia!' proclaimed Charles Lwanga, the saint sitting on Nathan's left.

'Yes, quite,' Nathan murmured in agreement. 'Anyway, today you're here to have fun and enjoy yourselves.' Another wave of his arm caused the mist that had obscured the entrances to all the little archways down both sides of the ballroom, to clear. This occasion, children, is a celebration of the very important and sometimes dangerous work you undertake on behalf of the Kairos. You'll find every culinary delight imaginable – and then some! A veritable feast for your eyes and your taste-buds: from the Chinese Lantern to the American Diner; the Ice-cream Parlour; the Sombrero; Bella Pasta; the Soda Fountain; French Confection; Indian Curry Tent; the Swiss Chocolate Chalet; and the Cheese Mountain, to mention just a few. I personally recommend the hot chocolate sauce in the Ice-cream Parlour. So, without further ado: enjoy!' With a beaming smile, Nathan sat down.

Immediately, the whole assembly began to chatter again as they moved in waves around the ballroom, disappearing into the archways and emerging with platefuls of the most delicious-looking food. Most of the children were too excited to sit down, preferring to mingle with each other while eating. However, Joel noticed that more and more eyes seemed to be following his every movement.

'Am I becoming paranoid, Peter, or is everyone staring at me?' Joel whispered faintly to his friend.

'Pretty much everyone,' Peter replied plainly.

They saw the Arab boy again, talking to a group of children who all turned and looked at Joel.

'Yes, Joel, it seems that Shariq has started the rumour that everyone...' Maité was suddenly interrupted.

'You're Nathan's son!' A small, pale, blonde girl blurted, as she stood in front of Joel, gazing up at him.

'All right, there's no need to tell the entire assembly, Hilda,' Maité muttered, with a sigh. Then, taking Joel by the arm, she swiftly led him away. 'Let's go in Bella Pasta and try some heavenly spaghetti, Joel.'

'Mm, perfect choice, Maité,' Tamara agreed, as she started to follow them. 'Hey, did you ever see Lady and the...?' This time Tamara was interrupted – by Peter.

'You should try some savoir faire, Tamara,' he said quietly, taking her arm and leading her in the opposite direction.

'Ah but…' Tamara began to protest. Then, suddenly, 'Oh,

what's "savoir faire," Peter? Some sort of savoury dish?' she asked, inquisitively.

'It's tact, Tamara,' Peter mumbled, under his breath.

'Oh – bother…' Tamara tutted, as she watched Maité and Joel drift off happily in the direction of the Italian Pasta archway.

†

'How are we supposed to get to know all these people?' Tamara asked Peter, as they emerged from the Spanish Flamenco archway with plates of the most scrumptious paella ever seen or tasted. 'Most of them are foreign – or do they all speak English, like us?'

'Mr Asher gave his introduction in English,' Peter mused, 'So I suppose, up here everyone must understand English.'

'No, he didn't!' a black, curly-haired girl interrupted.

Peter and Tamara turned around to see the girl who had spoken. She was jet black and grinning an extremely white, dazzling grin.

'You *heard* Nathan speak in English,' the girl informed them. 'You're new, aren't you? You have much to learn,' she gestured, with a knowing flourish.

Peter and Tamara were a little taken aback by this forthright young girl.

'My name's Topsy,' the girl introduced herself boldly. 'From Jamaica. Who are you and where are you from?'

'Hello, Topsy,' Peter smiled, 'I'm Peter and this is Tamara.'

'Oh!' Topsy almost squealed. 'You're the new Zionicans, aren't you? Everyone's talking about you, you know.'

'Really?' Peter muttered in surprise.

'Yeah! You've hit the ground running: the unicorn horn miracles; the mineshaft leap; then you go and bag some real big-hitter drugs baron – and all this in your first week!' Topsy marvelled. 'That's some record – I wouldn't count on keeping a low profile; you're pretty famous already. Where's your mate – the good-looking one?'

Tamara was quite astonished, as the excitable young Topsy

surveyed the room. Evidently, she regarded Joel as "the good-looking one." Peter was fine with that but Tamara couldn't help but feel a twinge of jealousy at the thought that this Topsy may be after Joel.

'I suppose he's gone off with that Spanish beauty. Oh well, some girls have all the luck!' Topsy breathed with a sigh.

'What did you mean, Topsy,' Peter asked, 'when you said that we "heard" Nathan speak in English?'

'Let me make it easy for you, guys.' Topsy explained. 'Everyone speaks in tongues up here. It's our heavenly language and we can all understand it – up here. Down there though, in the world I mean, it sounds like gobbledegook! But up here, it's our *local vernacular*.'

Tamara stared at Topsy blankly, and Peter cleared his throat a little uneasily. Then, sensing their bafflement, Topsy continued.

'Let me explain. When you speak in the heavenly language up here, everyone *hears* as if it's their own language.'

'How fascinating!' Tamara marvelled. 'So, what is vernacular and how do we speak it?'

'You're already speaking it, Tamara,' Topsy laughed.

'You two might think this is funny, but everyone is being perfectly horrid to me! First, I've been told I look like an aubergine, and now I'm talking some kind of gobbledegook!'

'Vernacular means your *native language*,' Peter said, softly. 'The language that you speak down in the world – in our case, it's English.'

'I *know* my native language is English, Peter, and I always speak it,' Tamara retorted, a little impatiently.

'I guess what Topsy is saying,' Peter explained, 'is that there is a native language up here too, and while we are here this is our native language because we are born again of the spirit into the Heavenly kingdom.'

'Exactly, and we can speak it down in the world too, although down there we don't understand it, but God does,' Topsy added. 'The ability to speak in tongues was given to you when you were baptised in the Holy Spirit, after you were born again, it's a gift.'

'Well, what's the point of speaking a language you don't understand?' Tamara asked.

'Because when you speak it in the world, you are not speaking to man, you are speaking to God. Unless God has given you a message in tongues for man, in which case He will provide the interpretation to someone,' Peter replied.

'Oh. So, you mean to say that we're speaking in a foreign language, right now?' Tamara continued, astonished.

'Yes, I suppose you could say that, but it's not foreign to you here, Tamara,' Topsy explained.

Tamara still looked a little puzzled. Topsy, sensing that Tamara was struggling to understand this language concept, smiled kindly. 'Here, take Ashok, for instance. Now, he can't speak a word of English. Ashok!' she called and beckoned to an Indian boy who was standing not too far from them.

The handsome Indian boy came over to them, smiling.

'Hello, Topsy. How are you?' Ashok greeted her cheerily. 'Congratulations, by the way, on saving that toddler from drowning last week. That was real quick thinking.' He turned to Tamara and Peter. 'Topsy threw a stick into a river to land next to a toddler who had fallen through the railings of a bridge, into the water. A huge Labrador dog bounded into the river after the stick and swam back to the bank with the stick in its mouth and the toddler clinging to its neck.'

'How astonishing!' Tamara exclaimed.

'It just seemed the obvious thing to do,' Topsy muttered, modestly. 'Anyway, Ashok, let me introduce Peter and Tamara – two new Kairos members from Zionica, England.' She turned to Peter and Tamara. 'Ashok is a seasoned Kairos, but unfortunately, he'll be leaving us when he turns sixteen this summer.'

'Welcome aboard! It's good to meet you.' Ashok flashed a dazzling grin as he shook their hands. 'I've just been talking to your fellow Zionican: Joel. We're all very impressed with the mineshaft leap. Everyone's talking about it. We didn't know it was possible to use the Vista with such pinpoint accuracy – and that ledge – it must have been held up by cobwebs and prayer! You were the one stranded on the ledge, I presume, Peter? You must be very brave.'

'I didn't exactly have a choice in the matter,' Peter nodded.

'And you must be the young girl brought back from the brink of death, Tamara? Maité told me of your terrible accident and how you were miraculously revived. It's wonderful that God knows everything, isn't it. He knew about your impending accident all those years ago, when Joel's grandad was a young boy and fell into the icy pond. God put measures in place to revive you, before you were even born! How amazing is that! God has a great plan for your life, Tamara; you've been saved for a purpose – for such a time as this...'

This statement touched Tamara deeply; she had not thought about it like that, but she now knew that Ashok was right. All of this revelation was making her a little emotional, especially being reminded of how close she had come recently to "handing in her riding boots" for good, and that only by the grace of God was she alive at all! She wanted to speak, but felt tears welling up in her eyes and she thought that if she opened her mouth, she might actually start to cry. So, she bit her lip as she awkwardly attempted a smile. Thankfully though, she was rescued by the diversion of Joel and Maité's return, carrying bowls piled high with tasty looking treats. They seemed to have the giggles; the slightest thing set them off laughing.

'Oh, aren't you having so much fun – I don't want this night to end!' Maité beamed.

Joel's face totally echoed Maité's comment. They were both determined that they were not going to think about it ending; they were just going to enjoy it.

Suddenly, Nathan reappeared at their sides again, followed by Anna.

'I'm so happy to see you having such a good time, all of you. However, it's only just beginning; there's so much more to come,' he proclaimed, joyfully.

'There's more? It's already mind-blowing, Mr Asher,' cried

Peter.
Topsy giggled and Peter looked a little awkward.

'There's no Misters up here, Peter; everyone uses Christian names in the Kairos,' Anna explained.

'Peter, I'd like you to call me, Nathan,' he smiled at him.

'O.K, Mr Ash… I mean, Nathan,' Peter grinned, sheepishly.

'Oh, does that mean I have to call you Nathan, too, Dad?' Joel asked.

'Technically speaking, yes, Joel. I'm not here as your dad or your guardian, I'm here as Chief of Staff of the Kairos. Mr Asher no longer exists. I'm Brother Saint Nathan, now,' he answered, smiling fondly. 'However, I think that maybe we can make an exception in this most unusual case, Joel, and allow you to call me Dad while you are in the Kairos, if you wish. In fact, I think I would like that. I must tell you though, you can only call me Dad, as a term of endearment, you must not call me father. We have one Father – our Heavenly Father, the great Jehovah.'

'Yes, Dad, I understand,' Joel answered, with a grin. He looked around at the sea of different coloured faces. 'I've never seen such a varied mix of nationalities, Dad,' Joel marvelled. 'Is everyone here a Christian?'

'Of course!' Nathan replied with some surprise. 'You know that He is the Way, the Truth and the Life, Joel. No one can come to the Father unless through the Son – the Lord Jesus Christ and because of what He did for us at the cross. No one could be here if they were not believing and trusting in Jesus and His finished work at the cross.'

'There are children representing many nationalities here,' Anna explained, 'but despite their religion or culture at birth, one way or another, they've all come to know Jesus. Isn't that marvellous, how God's grace reaches people in all nations? Take a look around you,' she continued, waving an arm. 'There's Alon; he was born a Jew. Oh and Mia, she was born a Buddhist; Hassan and Armad; they were born Muslims; and Noor was born a Hindu. Everyone here has one thing in common – we've all fallen in love with Jesus and accepted Him as our Lord and

Saviour, trusting in His finished work at the cross for our salvation. Obviously that is a pre-requisite of being in the Kairos but even after you're sixteen and your memory of all this is erased, you will continue in your personal relationship with Jesus. When you leave the world and come here for good, you'll see Him as He really is – the glorified Son of God.'

'I'll say Amen to that,' Nathan smiled. 'All this fighting in the world over religion is all so pointless, because there *is* only one Heaven. This is it and there's only *one* way to get here. Anyway, I must be getting back to the guest saints now. Don't forget to try that hot chocolate sauce will you – it really is worth sampling!'

'Yes, come on, eat up, Joel,' Maité urged. 'I want to take you to the Ice-Cream Parlour! You cannot leave a Kairos banquet without tasting rich hot chocolate sauce dripping over cold peaks of vanilana ice-cream – it's the best!' Then, without waiting, she grabbed Joel by the hand and charged off in the direction of the highly recommended Ice-Cream Parlour.

'Vanilana?' Tamara asked, quizzically.

'Yes, it's not vanilla and it's not banana, but it could be either or it could be neither,' Topsy announced with a grin.

Tamara gave Topsy a look of perplexed exasperation.

'We've already been to the ice-Cream Parlour. How about we try the Candy Mountain next, Tamara?' Peter suggested, tactfully steering her in the opposite direction to the one taken by Joel And Maité.

'Sounds good to me!' Tamara replied, enthusiastically.

The Ice-Cream-Parlour proved to be the most popular archway of the evening. There was every flavour and variety of ice-cream imaginable – and more – all manner of treats and decorations: marshmallows, various sprinkles, chocolate, sweets, biscuits and a host of sauces and creams.

There were so many people to meet, wonders to see and delicacies to taste, hardly anybody sat down, most preferring to meander around while they devoured the heavenly mouth-watering delights. Only after all the children had eaten their fill did they begin to find their seats, unanimously proclaiming that the delicious food surpassed anything they had ever tasted before.

'Hey, Joel! You're here next to me!' Maité pointed to a balloon with 119J on it. 'You're next, Tamara, 63T, and then Peter, 18P – oh,' she hesitated for a second, 'you must have taken over Jean's number, Peter...'

The four of them took their appointed seats, along with the other five children on their table. They placed their empty dishes on the table and all marvelled as the dishes instantly vanished before their eyes.

'Wow!' Tamara giggled. 'That was neat!'

'Yes, Tamara. Aren't you glad there's no dishwashing in Heaven?' giggled a young girl sitting opposite her.

'Of course. Um – excuse me asking, but how did you know my name?' Tamara inquired.

'You're kidding, aren't you?' the girl replied with a bemused frown. 'Everybody here knows your name; your miraculous recovery from death's door is the talk of the party!'

'...along with your two friends and other exploits,' a boy on their table interjected. 'You new Zionicans have made the most high profile entrance to the Kairos since any of us here have been involved – you're big news!'

'Yeah,' the first girl continued. 'I'm Bindu by the way, This is and this is Col, pleased to meet you.'

The boy, Col nodded ha greeting.

'Most kids slip in under the radar,' Bindu continued. 'With much longer basic training, real low-profile stuff, hardly getting a whisper of a mission for quite some time. But you and your team on the other hand have made the biggest splash since Flipper! Within a week you're setting records; receiving astonishing miracles; taking on and successfully completing difficult and dangerous missions! You've got the buzz! Everyone is waiting to see what happens to you next – I mean this is real exciting business!'

'Well – I – um...' Tamara appeared a little overwhelmed. 'I guess it is kind of amazing, isn't it.'

'Yes, indeed, praise God. It's a good thing your grandad kept that piece of horn until the appointed time, Joel,' Maité remarked. 'Imagine if he'd ground it up into powder to give to your grandma!'

'God knew your grandad would keep it safe, otherwise He would have left it with someone else,' Peter remarked.

'Yes, doesn't the Bible say that God has seen the end from the beginning?' Joel added.

'Well said, Joel!' Maité remarked in surprise. 'You've been studying more than just Spanish, my friend. I'm impressed!'

Joel smiled a little bashfully, but his heart was thumping so hard he wondered if Maité would actually hear it beating. But now, he no longer cared because Maité had said she was impressed with him! That fact filled him with a warm, tingling glow.

'Hey, I could do with another drink,' Peter muttered, clearing his throat.

'That's what these taps are for, Peter,' explained another girl. She held her glass under one of them and liquid started to pour from the tap. 'It's like the ice-cream booth in the Garden of Lilies; you just think of the drink you want and hold out your glass ready.'

Peter held his glass under one of the taps and it immediately began to fill with blackcurrant juice.

'Thank you, er…' Peter started.

'Juanita,' the girl smiled.'

'Oh, where are you from, Juanita?' he asked.

'From the Philippines,' Juanita replied. 'My dad was taken into prison five years ago, when I was only seven. I had to go and live with him there, in the prison because there was no one to look after me.'

'How dreadful!' Tamara exclaimed with genuine shock.

'Yes, it was,' she answered. 'I was there for six months until the Christians took me in and I came to know Jesus.'

'Where is your mother, Juanita?' Tamara asked.

'She died giving birth to me. Unless you are wealthy, medical facilities are not as available over there as they are in England.'

'Oh dear, it must have been terrible for you – losing your

mother *and* having to live in prison!' Tamara gasped.

'I'm one of the lucky ones,' Juanita explained, sadly. 'Some kids have been there for years; some don't even remember the outside world, because they were so young when they went in – some were born there! I have friends still in there; I pray for them every day. I can't see them but I cannot forget them.'

'How shocking! How long is your dad's sentence – does he have much longer to go?' asked Tamara.

'I don't know. His case hasn't even been heard yet. The legal system is very slow over there, so it could be several more years before it gets to trial.' Juanita sighed.

'You mean, he has to stay in prison, even though he may be innocent?' Tamara was so alarmed – she couldn't believe it.

'Oh yes, I believe my dad is innocent,' Juanita stated firmly.

'Well, I hope and pray that he is found innocent and released soon, Juanita,' Tamara said, encouragingly.

'Thank you,' Juanita answered, with a smile.

'Hey, Joel. Why don't you try these cool taps?' Maité suggested. As she held her glass under one and sparkling fuchsia-pink lemonade poured out.

'Yes, Joel,' Tamara added cheekily, turning to him with a glint in her eye and that dreaded *raised* eyebrow again. 'Maybe you'd like a passion fruit crush…'

Joel glared at Tamara as his face started to turn the colour of Maité's drink.

'I think you should have a bitter lemon, Tamara,' Peter suggested.

'Or, maybe even some prune juice!' Maité added, with a knowing look.

Joel meanwhile, wanted to sink under the table and hide but seemed to be frozen in his seat. Suddenly though, he was saved by a loud trumpet blast and the room instantly became silent, as everyone turned their attention towards the top table where Nathan was standing at the centre, with the special guests either side of him.

'I trust everyone has had their fill?' Nathan began with a grin, knowing full well that the food in Heaven was like nothing ever tasted in the world.

A loud cheer resounded, indicating the unanimous consensus.

'Good,' Nathan continued. 'Now, I'm not going to make you sit through a long speech. I've sat through too many boring speeches myself to risk subjecting you to one. However, I would like to review our successes, introduce four new members and say farewell to the loved and trusted members who are leaving us this time. New members first, please stand briefly.

'Mwafu from Masaka, Uganda.'

Mwafu stood and bowed his head. There was some mild applause, then he hurriedly sat down again.

'Peter, from Zionica, England.'

Everyone clapped loudly and turned to look at him, as Peter half-rose from his seat and, feeling awkward, quickly sat down again.

'…And back from the brink of death: Tamara, from Zionica, England,' Nathan announced.

Everyone clapped again, even louder and with accompanying cheers and whistles, as Tamara pushed her chair back and stood up, smiling coyly at everyone before returning to her seat.

'Last but not least, my own earthly son: Joel, also from Zionica, England,' Nathan proclaimed proudly.

There followed a thunderous applause as Joel barely left his seat, then promptly sat back down. This was followed by a whispered hush throughout the ballroom.

'Well, Joel,' Peter said in a low voice, 'If anyone hadn't heard the rumour yet, they certainly know now!'

Nathan tapped the table loudly and raised a hand for silence.

'Yes, well, thank you, and welcome to the Kairos, all new recruits. You've got an exciting few years ahead of you and we wish you every success in all your missions,' Nathan smiled. 'Now, will the three leavers present please stand up.'

The three leavers each rose from their seats, as Nathan called out their names.

'Phillipe from Taize, France; Nicolau from San Luis, Brazil; and Maité from Morisco, Spain.' There followed bursts of joyful applause as each child rose from their seat then Nathan continued. 'Thank you for the wonderful years you've given us. The selfless dedication with which you have bravely carried out your missions has been an inspiration to others. God bless you in your future ventures in the world, till we all meet again with the great cloud of witnesses.

The three leavers returned to their seats again amidst further applause, cheers, whistles and banging on tables.

'Now for a review of some recent Kairos missions,' Nathan announced, and, as he did so a huge Vista appeared behind the top table. There followed a montage showing glimpses of various Kairos missions over the Easter holidays. There was one of Maité descending down a deep, narrow and extremely muddy pothole where a small child had slipped in and been trapped for several hours. No adult could get down the hole as it was too narrow, and any digging could have buried the child. Maité located the child and the two of them emerged triumphantly, covered in black, slimy mud and looking exhausted but thankfully alive and well.

Another mission concerned a woman in Africa who had been walking with six children for several days, without food or clean water. She had become quite desperate and hadn't realised she was very close to a missionary camp, with fresh water and food. A young African Kairos called Wolisso led them to the camp, and the woman cried as she was greeted by the missionaries.

'Finally,' Nathan announced excitedly, 'I'd like to mention the successful first mission of the new recruits from Zionica. These three pulled off a very dangerous mission with very little notice and a fast-track training programme. Their brave efforts have ensnared a group of evil kingpins of crime, putting an end to their illegal and corrupt drugs organisation.'

A scene from Sadler's lounge appeared on the Vista. It was of the villains being arrested, cuffed and led outside by the police.

'Well done, Zionica team,' Nathan beamed, 'and a huge thank you to Maité, who put herself at great personal risk, outside of her own Country Zone, to mentor our three newcomers. This was

a tremendous achievement; well done all of you.'
Everyone cheered and clapped again.

'Remember,' Nathan continued, 'these villains are just one branch of an evil perennial weed. Unless we take action, other shoots will sprout. I'll be talking to you next holidays about this. Now, a moment you've all been waiting for. I'd like to finish with a groundbreaking *fait accompli* from the new team: a jump through the Vista with the precision landing of a jump-jet on an aircraft-carrier. This life-or-death action by Joel had never before been attempted by anyone, and was all the more amazing because of his limited experience in using the Vista. As you can see on this Vista, Peter was stranded on a rapidly disintegrating ledge in a mine-shaft – the only thing between him and a thirty metre drop. There was no time to lose. Joel glided through the Vista with pinpoint accuracy. Landing next to Peter, he grabbed him and they both leapt back through Joel's schism into Heaven. The moment they took off from the ledge it collapsed and hurtled in a cloud of dust, down the shaft. A brilliant manoeuvre, executed with nerves of steel! Praise God!'
Everyone cheered again, applauding enthusiastically.

'You have *so* set a precedent, Joel,' Maité whispered into Joel's ear. 'There will be nowhere for you to hide now. Everyone will be expecting such heroics from now on, especially now they all know that you're Nathan's son. Expectations have been set!'

'And now, we have another treat for you,' Nathan announced cheerfully. 'I'm sure you'll be delighted to hear that the Melanesian Boys have agreed to give us a show. So please give it up for the spectacular Melanesian Boys!' He sat down again.
The boys appeared in a kind of rugby scrum circle, on the raised platform where the Vista had been. Evidently the Melanesian Boys were very popular, judging by the applause. They wore grass skirts and strings of feathers and shells around their arms, ankles and necks. They began their show with a prayer, which they chanted as they huddled in the scrum; this was to dedicate the song and the dancing to the glory of God. Then, they all leapt up and began to sing, dance and play an assortment of musical

instruments: bongo drums, maracas and pipes, to name a few. The whole atmosphere was infused with tremendous energy, and many of the Kairos kids jumped up and danced around their tables, worshipping God. It was a very joyful affair indeed! At the end of their show, the leader of the Melanesian boys shouted, 'Give the glory to God!' then they all disappeared in a cloud; they didn't wait for applause – all the praise was for God.

Everyone cheered and clapped again.

Nathan stood up. 'Wasn't that fun – praise God!' he grinned. 'Now, it's time, for the final dance – the *girls' choice dance.* This is when all the young ladies present may choose a partner for the final dance of the evening. I have to remind you, boys, that this is not optional. If a lady asks you to dance, you may not refuse – even if you feel that you have two left feet – and the first invitation must be accepted; girls must not ask a boy who has already been asked by another.'

Joel sank deep into his seat, in the vain hope that this would somehow make him invisible to all the girls – except Maité. However, because Maité had been in the Kairos for six years, there were, Joel thought despondently, bound to be other boys she would like to share her final Kairos dance with. For her, it really was the final; this would be her very last Kairos Ball...

Suddenly, all the girls stood up and it seemed to Joel that they were all swarming towards him from every conceivable direction, as if he was some sort of girl-magnet. He cringed even lower into his seat, wishing that the artificial gravity could suddenly be switched off so that he could leap out of the way.

Then, as Tamara looked incredulously at the sea of girls heading for Joel, she decided to jump in first. Ideally placed, sitting on his right, she had a distinct advantage and tapped Joel on his right shoulder.

Joel slowly turned his head and, looking at Tamara, his heart sank in resignation. He didn't believe he stood a chance of having this dance with Maité and supposed that he may as well dance with Tamara – at least that would rescue him from the troupe of girls that were moving like a tidal wave towards him – as if he was the

centre of a vortex, drawing all females in the room.
Peter was also dreading being asked to dance too because he couldn't dance for toffee. He suspected though, that Joel's preference would be Maité and not Tamara, so he decided to give the two of them a chance by distracting Tamara. Anyway, if he had to make a fool of himself by stepping on someone's toes, it didn't matter so much if the toes were Tamara's! With this thought in mind, Peter jumped up and took hold of her arm, turning her to face him, before she could ask Joel to dance.

'I'd love to dance, Tamara,' Peter heard himself blurt out.

'Peter!' Tamara whispered in annoyance. 'But…' she began to object. Then, realising the futility of that, she sighed in compliance and allowed Peter to lead her away – for the second time.

Joel watched Peter and the reluctant Tamara disappearing in the direction of the dance floor and braced himself for the inevitable scrum... Then, he cringed as he felt a tap on his other shoulder. With a feeling of impending doom, wondering which of the swarming girls had got there first, he slowly turned back his head, expecting some spotty, goofy, strange girl to be standing there. However, his jaw dropped what seemed like a mile when he saw whose hand it was!

'Dance with me, Sẽnor?' Maité offered him her hand.

Joel felt a strange mixture of relief, surprise and delight as he stared, open-mouthed, at her. He had been convinced that by now she would have sped off to some older, more accomplished boy and that he'd be left sitting next to an empty chair. Now though, the chair on his left was demonstrably not empty but thankfully, very much occupied. Quickly recovering, he gulped and took Maité's hand. Then, to Joel's acute embarrassment, there was an audible hushed 'Oh!' of disappointment as the other girls saw him take Maité's hand and realised that they were too late – at least for this dance, anyway. Joel's relief though was short lived, as he then remembered that he couldn't dance!

Beautiful, soft music began to play as a group of angels gathered on the high platform and began to sing sweetly.

Joel and Maité stood up together, and joined the other boys who had been asked to dance by one of the girls. An area cleared to the side of the tables in the enormous ballroom and they all converged onto it for the dance.

'I hadn't realised how much competition I had for your attention, Joel,' Maité teased softly. 'You seem to be much in demand.'

"*You've got zero competition, Maité*," Joel thought, without daring to say so.

'Actually, Maité,' he replied, modestly. 'I think they were all heading for Peter; he's the one the girls usually buzz around.'

'He's right,' a fair girl confirmed as she drifted past them. 'I was going for the blonde one.'

The dark boy she was with gave her a look of mild indignation.

'Oh, but I'm glad I chose you, Rojerhat, of course,' she added quickly.

Joel felt, as he normally did in Heaven, as if he were floating on air. Maité looked down and giggled, he followed her gaze to their feet and was astonished to notice that they *were* both actually floating – skimming the floor a couple of inches above it, as if they were really dancing on air. The artificial gravity was still clearly switched on, because, as they looked around at the others, they noticed that they were the only couple floating!

'We're not working within the physical constraints of the natural world here, Joel,' Maité explained. 'We're operating in the supernatural, spiritual realm, which is not governed by science and physics. Despite the gravity, we're floating because the Holy Spirit is holding us up – our spirits feel light and free because we're happy together. Up here, we can expect the unexpected! You know, Joel, maybe we are soul mates.' Saying that, she threw back her head in delighted laughter.

'I expect I shall wake up at any moment and find that I'm in the middle of a very strange dream,' he replied. Joel was perplexed – was Maité teasing or was she being serious – about being happy together? He had no idea what her feelings were for him. All he knew was that Maité lit up the room and he was very happy to be with her and he was "a prisoner of hope" on many levels.

The two of them laughed together and Joel felt unexpectedly relaxed as they swirled around the floor. It was as if they were the only couple on the dance floor and they didn't realise, until the dance was nearly finished, that they *were* the only couple left dancing! All the other couples had stopped in astonishment to watch Joel and Maité floating! However, as soon as he noticed they had an audience, Joel became suddenly self-conscious, and stopped dancing. Immediately, he dropped to the floor. Maité followed suit and almost fell into his arms as he steadied her.

'Thanks,' she breathed, smiling up at him.

'You're welcome,' Joel muttered softly. Suddenly he didn't care about the apparent audience they had attracted; he was in fact, in actual perfect Heaven – but then, alas, another trumpet sounded.

Everyone returned to their seats and Nathan rose to his feet once again. After they had taken their seats, Maité and Joel exchanged sideways glances and smiled.

'Those who are leaving us,' Nathan announced. 'I'm told it is now time for your exit meeting.'

This announcement turned the hoppity-skip of Joel's heart to a sudden stab, at the thought that Maité was now to be taken from him, just as he was coming to the realisation that what he was feeling may have been love. *Could he actually be falling in love with her,* he wondered, *is this what love felt like*?

Instantly, a new archway appeared at the top of the ballroom to the left of the main table. There were three brightly shining seven-point stars on either side of the archway and one at its pinnacle. Two very large, tall and elegant pearly-white angels emerged from the archway, emitting a glowing aura of light. They hovered for a moment, then, one after the other, spread out a pair of huge white wings and began to fly around the banqueting hall. Each angel had a wing-span of about four metres. They flew a lofty circuit around the perimeter, then closing in, they swooped majestically over the children's heads.

The children gasped at this wondrous sight and watched, wide-eyed, as the angels came to rest again on either side of the new archway, where they closed their massive wings by their sides.
A cloud formed within the archway with a seven-tongued flame that burned steadily in front of it. Immediately, a breeze seemed to emanate from the cloud and everyone could hear the sound of a rushing mighty wind, and the effects of it were clearly visible as it gently swirled around the room, blowing their hair and filling everyone it touched with a sense of warmth, comfort and wonder.

'Wow!' Peter gasped.

'Totally awesome!' Tamara whispered.

Three smaller angels emerged from the archway, each carrying a small pole with a flame burning at its top. These angels wore small white hats, rather like sailor's hats. One of them came straight over to Joel's table and hovered with the burning flame over Maité, while the other two did likewise over the other two leavers. Maité stood up to follow the angel back out through the archway.

'Maité!' Joel murmured, and caught her arm.

'Don't worry, Joel,' she reassured him. 'I'm not leaving yet – I'll see you before I go. The flame is the signal for my private meeting with the Saviour. I am to receive the gifts from the Holy Spirit that will stay with me all my earthly life and will help me to serve the Lord in the world – when I no longer remember the Kairos.' She smiled, then nodded at the angel hovering over her as it led her through the archway of the flame. As soon as the three leavers had passed through the archway, it closed up behind them.

'The rest of you may mingle until the leavers return, then we'll close for the term, recommencing our Kairos activities in July during the Summer holidays,' Nathan announced, before sitting down again to talk with the guests. The Kairos children immediately rose from their seats and began to chatter excitedly.

After a while the Joel and Peter noticed a man, clothed in white, who appeared to be talking to Tamara. They couldn't see His face because He had His back to them, neither could they hear what He was saying. They assumed that He was a guest saint, or perhaps an angel.

'Y – y – y – yes,' Tamara appeared to whisper softly. Her eyes looked somehow mesmerised – in fact, she rather looked as if she was melting into a pool of bliss!

'It's a pleasure,' Tamara murmured. 'I – I want to do everything I can to help.'

Then, the man seemed to vanish as quickly as He had appeared. Joel and Peter immediately approached Tamara to ask who it was and what He had said to her that had given her such a dreamy look.

'Who was that?' Joel asked curiously. 'What did He say to you?'

'He said that His mother had asked Him to thank me for all the extra help I've given in the nursery, particularly in the new baby unit. He told me that Arianna is always grateful for extra help and that His mother has a great passion for the babies, as does His Father.'

'Who did you say it was?' Peter asked, staring at Tamara as though she'd just stepped off a spaceship. Which crazily would not appear outrageous, in the circumstances.

'I er – He was – He was – He had the most beautiful eyes I've ever seen.' Up until this moment Tamara had long believed that Joel's eyes were the only eyes that could cause a girl to melt and that she could never get tired of gazing into them. Now though, those eyes she used to dream about had been overwhelmingly surpassed. 'So beautiful – I'll never forget them as long as I live!' Tamara murmured, in a dreamy daze. She had a kind of luminous glow about her and her face positively shone, her eyes sparkled and even her hair had a kind of glittery light about it.

'Well – who's His mother then?' Peter asked innocently.

'Isn't it blindingly obvious?' Joel replied, pointedly. 'Who takes a special interest in the nursery?'

Peter gasped. 'But I thought He was having private meetings with the leavers,' he remarked with a confused frown.

'Yes, He is, Peter,' Nathan confirmed as he suddenly appeared next to them. 'He is having individual meetings with all of them. He is also with all those people in the world who call upon His name, giving them all His attention and listening to every prayer; every heartbeat of even every sparrow. You should know that the Lord is omnipresent – everywhere at once; and omniscient – all-knowing; and omnipotent – all-powerful.'

'Wow!' Peter marvelled. 'But – what's happened to Tamara? She's suddenly gone all weird.'

'That's not weird, Peter,' Nathan explained, joyfully. 'She's different. What you see is a reflection of the One she's just been with. You see, no one can be with Jesus and remain the same. Everyone who meets Jesus like this falls deeply in love with Him and it's a lasting love, for eternity. What Tamara has just experienced is the essence of pure, undiluted love because God is love.'

'Wow!' Peter repeated. 'Joel, we've just seen…'

'But we've only seen His back,' Joel interrupted with an air of disappointment. 'Anyway, Tamara, exactly when have you been giving all this extra help in the nursery? You're always with us!'

'No, not always, Joel,' Tamara answered, softly. 'I can be up here for several hours but only be gone from the world for a few minutes; you know that.'

Joel pulled a face – of course he knew, and he was embarrassed to have been reminded of it by Tamara, who was still only ten!

'Cheer up, Joel,' Nathan grinned affectionately. 'One day you'll get to see the Lord, and you'll see Him just as He is. That's a promise in the Bible to all true, faithful believers, but until then, diligently run the race set before you.'

'I just thought you might have told us, Tamara – I mean, we may have gone with you,' Joel insisted a little peevishly. He knew full well as he said it that he would not have wanted to go.

'Oh,' I see,' Tamara replied, with a wry smile. 'You would have come, would you, Joel – to rock and cuddle all those babies?'

'Well, er, no, probably not,' Joel conceded, feeling rather silly. 'Well, at least this shows that you *can* keep secrets from us,

Tamara, which is good, I suppose, as we'll reach sixteen two years before you will!'

'Now, there's a thought, Tamara,' Peter quipped. 'You'll be coming up here for two whole years after we've forgotten all about it.'

Tamara's brow furrowed as she considered the prospect of two years of missions without the boys – never mind not being able to even *discuss* the Kairos with them.

Suddenly, a flurry of excitement announced the return of the leavers to the ballroom. Maité rushed excitedly up to Joel. Her face too was shining just like Tamara's. She was glowing all over and emanated a new, different kind of beauty, which caused Joel's heart to skip a beat. In fact, it was as if she was exuding a powerful and irresistible force, which seemed to hit him like a thunderbolt! He had never experienced a feeling quite like it, and he found himself realising finally that *this was what love felt like*?

'Oh, Joel, Joel, I'm so happy!' Maité bubbled over with excitement. 'I'm ready to go now.'

'Go?' Joel initially panicked. 'Go where? But – how will I find you?' In an instant, his cool image got its coat and left. Despite being the tender age of twelve, he felt like he'd found the love of his life and he had no intention of letting her go without a fight.

'You will forget me, Joel,' Maité sighed. 'You're young – there are too many years between us; I'm sixteen tomorrow! You must go back to school, work hard and be that great barrister you're meant to be. Anyway, you've got important Kairos work to do; you would not have time for me.'

'So, what's a few years?' Joel persisted. He was conscious of an audience, as Peter, Tamara and even his dad were in earshot, but he didn't care. The cool image abandoned, he continued. 'There were four years between my mum and dad; it didn't stop them!'

'So, Tamara, you've been a big help to Arianna in the baby unit…' Nathan put his arms around her and Peter's shoulders and tactfully led them a short distance away. Meanwhile, Joel and Maité continued their discussion.

'But I bet both your mum and dad were adults when they got together,' Maité suggested gently, not wanting to be the cause of his upset and possible later embarrassment.

'But, Maité, I'm nearly thirteen – in three months...' Joel persisted. 'There's only three years between us and I know of many couples with much larger age gaps than that!'

'It is best this way, amigo. For you, it is only a schoolboy crush. Tomorrow, I will no longer be in your head,' she continued, brushing aside his protests. 'If you came to Spain, I would not know you and when you leave the Kairos, you will not remember me, either.'

'We got to know each other once, so what's to stop us doing it again – for real in the world.' Joel knew she felt something for him, but she was denying it to him and to herself.

'Joel, let's see what life has in store for us. Follow your destiny; what will be will be. Remember, God has a plan for our lives and that is the plan we must follow. Now, I must say goodbye.'

'I'm sorry to interrupt,' Anna murmured gently, as she appeared next to them, 'but it really is time. Everyone is starting to leave.'

'Yes, Joel,' Maité teased, endeavouring to bring some light humour to the situation. 'These outfits dissolve on the stroke of midnight. Imagine how embarrassing that would be!'

'What?' Joel spluttered, turning red. 'Really?'

'No!' Maité laughed. 'I was joking, of course!'

'Oh, well, I suppose I should have realised that,' Joel sighed.

'Adios, amigo,' Maité offered her hand to Joel.

'Adios.' Joel took her hand. He was normally so in control but at that moment, he felt like a fish out of water. He wasn't ready to handle all the confusing emotions that kept taking him by surprise. With great reluctance, he let go of her hand.

Maité said her goodbyes to the others and, as she set off, Joel called over to her.

'Maité!'

She turned and glanced his way.

'Hasta pronto!'

'See you too – maybe…' she replied.

'Dad,' Joel turned suddenly to Nathan.

'Yes, son,' he replied.

'When you left the Kairos – when you were sixteen, what did you write in your note to yourself?'

'To find and marry Elizabeth Jacob, your mother, son,' Nathan answered, without hesitation.

'Thanks, Dad,' Joel grinned, as he felt a little spark of hope inside. 'So, what's…?'

'…Your next mission?' Nathan interrupted, already suspecting what Joel was going to ask. 'You're not to concern yourself with that now, Joel. It's important to concentrate on your school-work. The Kairos is non-operational during school term-time. You'll find out about your next mission when you come back in the Summer.'

'I can't believe I'm not going to see you all term. Can I come and visit you, Dad?'

'I'm afraid not, Joel. That would be flouting the rules. The Fugue is not for personal use. Your future with the Kairos would be jeopardised by any such violation. You're very special, Joel. I cannot tell you anything more yet; in the Kairos, information is shared strictly on a "need to know" basis. Be patient: *Let patience have its perfect work*, as the word says. Come on, I'll take you to the Fugue.'

Joel, Peter and Tamara returned their gowns and put on their own clothes. Then, as they passed through the archway and out to the main Hall of Archways, they became weightless again. They thanked the cute little cherubim on their way out and, to Tamara's delight, a surprise was waiting for them: Storm and Cheyiea.

'Storm!' she cried excitedly.

'They are inviting you to take a ride to the Fugue,' Nathan grinned. 'Storm's real name up here was Farga. I say *was*, because he has decided to change his name permanently to Storm, in honour of the victory of your mission and to thank you for looking after him during his stay in the world.'

'Oh my! What a wonderful tribute! Thank you, Storm.' Tamara threw her arms around Storm's neck and hugged him, pressing her cheek against his soft mane as he nudged her affectionately with his nose.

'Well, I'll say goodbye here, then, and let Storm and Cheyiea escort you to the Fugue,' Nathan murmured, a little emotionally. 'It's been wonderful having you three join the Kairos and I'm really excited about our future missions. You're all very important to our work. We'll meet again in the Summer. Till then, God go with you, children.'

Tamara floated up onto Storm's back.

'Goodbye, Nathan – see you in the Summer! Come on, Storm, let's go!' she urged.

Storm took off at speed and Nathan shook his head in amusement. Tamara was an experienced rider, but even if she did fall off, Storm could easily circle around and pick her up again as she floated in mid-air. Peter gave his mother, Anna, a hug and floated up onto Cheyiea.

'Are you coming, Joel? There's plenty of room on the back, isn't there, Cheyiea?' Peter grinned.

Cheyiea gave a half-rear and snorted.

'I'll tell you what, Peter, I think I'll pass. No offence, Cheyiea but I'd prefer to float right now.'

With that, Cheyiea and Peter set off for the Fugue, rather more sedately than Tamara and Storm.

'Goodbye, Dad, I'm so happy that we're going to spend time together again.'

'I couldn't be happier, Joel.' Nathan agreed as he hugged Joel and gave him a kiss on his forehead. 'Will you pass that kiss on to Mum, Joel?'

'Yes, Dad, of course I will.'

'She needs looking after. She's too young to be on her own and I approve of her choice.'

'What do you mean, Dad? What choice?' Joel asked, with a confused frown.

'You'll find out when she's ready, son. It's her place to tell you, not mine. I just wanted you to know that I approve and it would make me happy if you accepted it and supported her choice, too.'

'OK, Dad, whatever you say,' Joel replied with a shrug.

With his head in a spin, wondering what all *that* was about, Joel made his way to the Fugue – still dancing on air...

CHAPTER NINETEEN

Deliverance in Time

Knowing that hardly any time would have passed at all because they'd stayed in Heaven, the children were astonished that the Magi had still managed to make a thorough job of demolishing the food they had left in the den. Despite the fact that it felt as if they had been gone for hours, the children discovered that it was still only just after seven o'clock in the evening. To Maggi and Magee though, it seemed as if they'd only just waved the children off to the Ball and that the night was still young. Consequently, the two ravens were not the least bit tired and they were keen to hear all about the Ball in Heaven.

'Don't leave anything out!' Maggi cawed eagerly. 'I want to hear *every* detail.'

'Yes, every detail,' Magee echoed, pecking away at a beef sandwich. 'Did you try the *melt-in-your-mouth* Italian meat balls, covered in cheese?'

'Tell us about the gowns,' Maggi pleaded. 'What colour were they this term?'

'No, tell us about the mission montages!' Magee spluttered, as he turned his attention to an enormous pork pie. 'That's much more exciting!' he chomped.

'Did you go in the ice-cream parlour?' Maggi asked them.

The children sat and regaled the ravens with details of the evening. Then, after about an hour, Tamara began to yawn.

'Oh, I'm simply exhausted! It's all been sooo exciting!' she sighed. 'I think I'll say goodnight.'

'Look!' Magee suddenly exclaimed, and flew onto a higher branch for a better view of the plateau.

'What is it?' Joel called up.

'A visitor...' Magee exclaimed curiously.

'A visitor?' Joel asked, in surprise.

'It's not Maguff, is it!' Magee asked with trepidation as she joined Magee on the high branch.

Joel, Peter and Tamara leaned over the edge of the den to try to get a better view. They could barely make out the silhouette of a figure walking towards them, but it was too dark to clearly identify the mystery visitor.

'It's your Spanish friend,' Magee called. 'Oh my, is she in trouble – using the Fugue like a personal taxi service!'

As Maité approached, they all recognised that it was indeed her.

'Joel – Magee is right – it is Maité!' Peter gasped, astonished.

'Maité?' Joel murmured, hardly able to believe his own eyes. He quickly grabbed the rope swing, slid to the ground and landed right in front of her, startling her as their eyes met which caused Joel's heart leap. That very moment he knew, as he gazed into her eyes that she was the only girl for him, no one else would do.

'Maité! What are you doing here?' he breathed.

'I know – it's crazy, and totally not allowed. I may be shot at dawn if I'm discovered,' she laughed a little awkwardly. 'But I had to come! I had to see you one more time – to say goodbye, before my memory of the Kairos – and you – is erased.'

Joel's heart melted as he listened to her – was he dreaming or was the love of his life actually standing there, in front of him, confessing that she felt the same about him? This was a different Maité, one he had never seen before. Her normal faultless self confidence had got its coat and left, leaving a vulnerability that endeared her to him even more. He was taken aback at this apparent chink in her usual super-cool armour. Clearly, she felt more for him than their conversation at the end of the Ball had indicated.

'At midnight,' Maité continued, 'in just under four hours, I won't remember anything of my precious time in the Kairos – or of you – and I'm scared, Joel...' she hesitated. 'I'm scared of not remembering.' Her voice trembled a little with emotion and her tear-moistened eyes glinted in the moonlight. She looked away, biting her lip, as a glistening tear rolled slowly down her cheek. She hastily wiped it away with her hand. 'I'm sorry, I shouldn't have come. This could get all of you into trouble; I should leave straight away.' She turned to go, but Joel gently took hold of her arm, his fumbling nervousness had finally been replaced with a surge of confidence. He had a strong urge to put his arms around her but, conscious of a mesmerised audience, he resisted.

'No, you're here now. Stay, for a while at least,' Joel urged. 'Hey!' he added, with a grin, 'the glass is half-full, not half-empty; we've got almost four hours! Come on up!' He motioned to the ladder.

Maité smiled and, accepting his invitation, climbed up to join the others in the den. Joel wanted to punch the air and shout a victorious "yes!" However, he contented himself with an, almost silent, whispered "yes!" and a grin as he followed her up.

'Hello, Maité, dear,' Maggi greeted her cautiously, as she emerged at the top of the den.

*'Buenas tardes, Amiga mía,' Maité replied, and sat next to Tamara.

Joel settled down next to Maité.

'What a surprise!' Tamara bleated, with a forced cheerfulness. 'I hope you're not going to get into trouble, Maité. I mean – how did you manage to *sneak* into the Vista chamber at this late hour?' Tamara purposefully put an emphasis on the word, "*sneak*," implying that Maité was sneaky, then she immediately felt guilty and wished she hadn't.

'Yeah, Maité. We're not supposed to use the Vista without someone in Heaven watching,' Joel added, with genuine concern.

'She didn't use the Vista,' Magee stated, bluntly. 'She Fugue-hopped.'

'Fugue-hopped?' Joel echoed, none the wiser.

'Yes, Maité simply jumped from her Fugue in Morisco direct to this one, here in Zionica,' Magee explained. 'It can be done – if you know where the Kairos entry points are – but it's risky, very risky, and there'll be big trouble if she's found out.'

'Oh, so we'd better hope that Maguff isn't in the locality, then,' Peter quipped.

'Huh?' Magee almost fell of the branch, at the mere sound of Maguff's name. 'Maguff! Oh dear, oh dear! I Maguff got to hear about this, the sewer rats assignment would be like a picnic

* Good evening, my friend,

in the dark – I – I – mean p – p – p – p – park!'

'Oh dear, I think Magee is having a turn,' Maggi squawked then added, 'and it's not without danger, children. Only a very experienced Fugue traveller could possibly attempt Fugue-hopping and, even then, it's a perilous thing to attempt – perilous!' she warned them, shaking her head. 'Maguff had better not find out; I dread to think what he would do if he heard about it,' she shuddered. 'We're supposed to be responsible for you, children…' she added, morosely, hiding her head under a wing.

'He'd hang us out to dry – by our beaks!' Magee gasped.

'Oh no!' Maggi shrieked.

'Yes, not so much for Maité coming here per se, but because now, Joel knows about Fugue hopping – right at the beginning of his Kairos journey! This would be likened to putting a piece of steak in front of a starving dog then telling him not to eat it – for sure, that steak was already eaten the moment the dog saw it!'

'I'm so sorry!' Maité apologised as the seriousness of her rash act began to dawn on her. 'I've put you in a rather compromising situation, you're all at risk – because of me!'

'We understand your being upset, my dear,' Maggi whispered sympathetically. 'Six years with the Kairos as your main focus in life must be extremely difficult to give up.'

'Nevertheless,' Magee added. 'Give it up you must. This is why your memory of the Kairos will be erased at midnight tonight, to limit this upset, otherwise you would be unable to function in your God given plan and be no use in the Kingdom.'

'What if Maité loses her memory of the Kairos while she's here? How would she get back to Morisco?' Joel asked.

'By conventional travel, Joel,' Magee answered. 'Plane, train or boat, I'm afraid.'

'But her parents would report her missing!' Tamara cried. 'They would think she had run away – or been kidnapped! My parents went through torment when Presten disappeared.'

'I'll be O.K. as long as I'm back before midnight,' Maité reassured them. 'That's when I turn into a pumpkin…' she muttered, sadly.

There was an awkward pause – no one knew what to say. Then Peter broke the silence.

'Hey, but it's great to see you, Maité, isn't it, Joel?' Peter declared, endeavouring to cheer her up.

'Yeah, of course.' Joel replied, attempting to sound cool, although inside he felt anything but cool. He was thrilled, of course, at this unexpected chance to see Maité one more time. Nevertheless, he was feeling a little foolish about pleading with Maité earlier at the Ball in front of everyone! This, together with genuine concern for Maité, somewhat deflated his joy at seeing her.

Magee nudged Maggi. 'Well, my little gooseberry,' he muttered to her, with a furtive nod of the head. 'I think it's time to make ourselves scarce, hitherto the aforementioned eagle lands.'

'I was just thinking the same thing,' Maggi agreed. 'If we're not here, we cannot report the alleged misuse of the Fugue. Of course, now you've told Joel about Fugue-hopping, you've just made our job a whole lot more difficult, Magee; he'll probably try it, first chance he gets!'

'I suppose you're right, Maggi – for once...'

'Huh!' Maggi gasped indignantly. 'I'm always right, Magee; if you don't know that by now, after six thousand years, it's about time you learned it!'

'In hindsight, that wasn't very clever, was it?' Magee agreed, but ignoring her indignation the old raven turned his attention to Joel. 'Now listen, Joel,' he warned. 'Once you step into the Fugue, you are not operating within the constraints of the natural world, governed by science and physics. You are entering into the supernatural realm, my dear boy. The only boundaries in the supernatural world are good and evil. You must consider in your heart your motive for using the Fugue. If this is rooted in a selfish desire, you could be giving the enemy a foothold and I must emphasise most earnestly that footholds can turn into strongholds! Strive, with all your might, not to give the enemy any footholds in your life. Everything has consequences, Joel.

You are in a war; you are fighting against principalities and powers of which you have no knowledge and the only way you can win is to rely on the weapons of warfare which are mighty in God – the cross of Christ, the blood thereupon shed and the name of Jesus, which is above every other name. Remember the Sword of the Spirit, which is the word of God – memorise it and praise God, for these are powerful weapons and will give you victory over the devil who wants you to fail! Selfish motives will be a hindrance to all that has been planned for you. Listen to me! You have a responsibility, Joel, that is greater than you could possibly imagine; your path is already ordained – don't stuff it up with momentary lapses – heed this warning!'

Joel looked suddenly very serious.

'Joel, dear, you *must* ensure that Maité returns well before midnight,' Maggi added. 'If not, the consequences could be dire!'

'Oh, the impetuosity of youth!' Magee cawed. Slapping one of his wings over his eyes he shook his head, in despair. 'Come Maggi, let us make haste,' he urged. 'Good night, children.'

Immediately, the two ravens vanished.

With Magee's words echoing through his mind, Joel looked gravely at Maité; a cold shiver ran down his spine. Much as he wanted to see her, he didn't want anything bad to happen to her.

Maité's bottom lip began to tremble.

'I've made a terrible mistake!' she cried. 'I'm so sorry! I've put everyone in danger because of my selfish action,' Maité confessed, tearfully. 'I should leave immediately.'

'We can't let you go like this, Maité. You're here now,' Joel answered desperately. 'Maybe you could just stay for a few moments longer – then I'll walk you to the plateau.'

'Well, I'm shattered,' Peter announced, standing up. 'Shall we go back to the house and ring your dad, Tamara, to let him know you're ready for him to come and pick you up?'

'Sure. I am rather tired. Do you want a lift home, Peter?'

'That would be good, thanks,' he smiled, then turned to Joel. 'I'll be seeing you before you leave, Joel. Your mum is coming tomorrow, isn't she?'

'Yes,' Joel replied. 'See you tomorrow, Peter.'

'Adios, Maité,' Peter smiled. 'And cheer up. I'm sure your reason for coming here was motivated by something more powerful than the enemy understands.'

'Thank you, Peter,' Maité replied, with a faint smile. 'Go with God, my friends.'

'What do you mean, Peter, more powerful than the enemy understands?' Tamara whispered.

'Love, Tamara,' Peter answered. 'That's something the enemy knows nothing about.'

As the reality of Peter's words sank in, Tamara glanced at Joel, who was totally engrossed with Maité, and realised with a stinging heart that her secret crush on Joel was in vain and that her dreams of romance were all but doomed.

Peter took hold of the rope and swung to the ground. Then, as she took the rope, Tamara turned to Maité.

'Thanks for all your help, Maité…' she smiled weakly.

'I pray that all your dreams come true, Tamara,' she replied, with a knowing look. Although Tamara had managed to keep her crush on Joel a secret from him, Maité wasn't fooled; she knew full well about Tamara's secret passion.

'Oh, wait a minute, Tamara.' Joel reached into a nearby box and pulled out a small packet which he handed to her. 'I nearly forgot. Happy Birthday – it's next week, isn't it!'

'Ah, thanks Joel – you remembered!' Tamara beamed.

'Yes, you'll be a whole year older next time we meet,' Joel threw her a cheeky grin.

'This is true, but so will you, Joel,' Maité pointed out, squashing Tamara's momentary rush of hope.

'Yes, I'll be a teenager in July'? Joel affirmed with delight.

'The seventeenth, to be exact,' Tamara added. 'And I'm eleven next week!' She unwrapped the package Joel had just handed her and her expression changed to one of pure delight as she took out the gift. 'Joel, this is just fantastic!' It was a framed photograph, the one that Grandad had taken of the boys with Storm, the day they returned him, when Tamara was in hospital.

'You couldn't have given me anything better. Thank you! Maité, don't stay too long – you wouldn't want Joel to see you turn into that pumpkin, would you?' Then with a cheeky giggle, she slipped down the rope, after Peter.

After the others had gone, Joel was able to relax, not having to be on his guard against embarrassing teasing from Tamara, or perhaps Peter thinking he had gone soft. Nevertheless, he was a little nervous as he found himself alone with Maité for the first time ever, with not even a raven in sight.

The pair sat and talked as they'd never talked before. Time seemed to evaporate as they enjoyed each other's company and they didn't notice how late it was. Maité shivered a little.

'Here.' Joel took a woollen blanket out of a chest and wrapped it around her shoulders.

'Thanks,' Maité murmured, as she snuggled into the blanket. 'I'll have to go soon. I can only use the Fugue until midnight and Spanish time is about an hour ahead of English time.'

Joel nodded, looking as if he wanted to say something.

'What is it?' Maité asked him.

'Oh, nothing really,' Joel muttered hesitantly.

'Go on, you were going to say something,' Maité urged.

'I just wondered – er, what you wrote in your note to yourself. You don't have to tell me if you don't want to,' he added hastily.

'I thought you might ask that, so I brought it with me,' Maité smiled and, taking the note out of her pocket, she handed it to him.

Joel took the note and unfolded it nervously, and read:

> *If you find a rugby-playing barrister,*
> *don't dismiss him out of court. He may*
> *be worth a try.*

A bubble seemed to rise up from Joel's stomach and it travelled all the way up to his mouth, so that he had to stifle a gasp. There was no question about it, now. She *did* like him, after all! His hand quivered slightly as he passed the note back to her.

'That's smart,' he chuckled.

Maité took the note and unexpectedly ripped it into two pieces, handing one half back to him. 'You keep half and you never know, the two halves may meet up one day and become one again.'

Joel's heart raced as he read his half. He couldn't quite believe what he'd just heard her say! He thought he must be dreaming – this was as good as a "be my boyfriend" ring.

playing, barrister,
out of court. He may

'That's going to really bug you tomorrow, Maité,' Joel remarked, slightly overwhelmed. 'It simply won't make any sense at all.'

'I know,' she giggled nervously. 'But, I'll know it's special and one day – who knows – it might make perfect sense…'

Their eyes met briefly but then they both looked away, a little awkwardly. Maité snuggled down with her head on Joel's shoulder and he carefully pulled the woollen blanket around her. He nervously used the opportunity to put his arm around her shoulders, half expecting her to throw a fit, but she just sighed contentedly. Joel felt that this was a really special moment; he didn't want it to end although he knew that it must, but the memory of it would stay with him throughout his Kairos journey.

†

Joel wriggled uncomfortably – he couldn't feel his left arm! He had that weird sensation of his arm having "gone to sleep" and he had no control over it, as if it was not attached to his body. Yawning, he opened his eyes and suddenly gasped as he saw something black and hairy on his chest. Then, he realised that it was Maité's head! He couldn't see his watch and he couldn't move his arm because it was completely numb! With a struggle, he gently reached over Maité with his right hand and grabbed his left wrist, tilting it to look at his watch. Fortunately, the lamps were still burning – just – and gave off enough light for him to read it – he gave another gasp as he realised that his arm evidently wasn't the only thing that had gone to sleep. They had both been asleep for nearly two hours – and the time was now ten minutes past midnight! Grandad must have had some of that whisky and fallen asleep too, otherwise he would have been down to the den to get him before this late hour. Thank God he hadn't – how would he explain where Maité came from?

Joel began to panic! What if Grandad came now and saw Maité? What on earth would he say? Then, like a thunderbolt, a much worse fear hit him – how on earth was Maité going to get home?

'No!' Joel cried.

Maité stirred and looked sleepily up at Joel. Then, suddenly, she sat up and stared at him, strangely. He saw fear and a heart-breaking lack of recognition in her eyes; she didn't know him at all! Maité evidently didn't have a clue where she was, either! She leapt to her feet, looking around her. Then she began to rant in Spanish.

*'Qué es esto? *Hay un problema – *tenemos qué Ilamar a la policía!' She was clearly very distressed.

'Maité – please – calm down!' Joel cried, as he grabbed at his limp left arm, rubbing it to restore the feeling.

'English?' Maité cried, with a confused frown. *'Estoy Mareada! Who are you? Where am I?'

It was quite apparent that Maité didn't even realise that she was in another country, but presumably assumed she was being held hostage in Spain! Joel's arm now tingled with pins-and-needles as thankfully, the feeling began to return. He rose to his feet slowly, not wanting to alarm her even more.

'How do you know my name?' Maité continued to bombard Joel with questions, now in English. 'What am I doing here?

Have I been kidnapped? My family have no money! You're wasting your time!'

'We – er fell asleep…' Joel tried to explain.

'I would not!' Maité shrieked, indignantly. 'I would never fall

* What is this? There is something wrong. We must call the police. *I feel dizzy.

asleep with a strange boy I've never met – and – and – in a tree!' Maité looked around the den in disgust. 'I insist that you release me, immediately!' she demanded defiantly.

'Maité, I can't release you because you're not a prisoner! Please – just sit down for a moment and let me explain,' Joel pleaded.

'I will not! HELP! HELP!' she began to scream.

'You stupid boy!' Joel heard the stern voice of Maguff and looked up to see the golden eagle perched on a branch above them. Maguff glared down at him with just about the *most* angry look Joel had ever seen in his life.

'Maguff!' Joel sighed with relief. 'Thank goodness! Can you help us?'

'Who's that you're talking to now?' Maité cried, looking around her. 'I can't see anybody!'

Of course, Maité could not now hear or see Maguff at all.

'You've drugged me, haven't you!' she continued. 'I'm not staying here with you – you crazy psycho!'

'Maité…' Joel pleaded again in desperation and he took a step towards her.

She immediately backed away from him.

'Get away from me!' she screamed, not looking where she was going. Too close to the edge of the den, in the darkness of the night, she stumbled; her foot slipped and in a terrifying moment, she toppled over the edge, letting out a piercing scream as she fell. 'Aaaagh!'

There was a horrid thud as she hit the ground – then, silence.

'Maité!' Joel cried. He leapt onto the rope swing, dropping to the ground beside her like a stone. 'Maité!' he whispered in anguish, leaning over her unconscious body. 'What have I done? I should have let you go straight back...' A terrible feeling of déjà vu grieved him to his soul, as he remembered leaning over Tamara's unconscious body on the road, only two weeks previously. Then, Maggi's words echoed painfully through his mind. *"You must ensure that Maité returns well before midnight. If not, the consequences could be dire!"*

'She's only unconscious – luckily for you! She hit her head in the fall but it's not serious – as it was with your other friend. She'll just have a bad headache when she comes round, that's all. It's a good job the ground is soft and spongy round here,' the eagle muttered, reproachfully. 'No sign of those pesky Magi, I see!' he tutted. 'Where are those twittering ravens anyway? Skiving off, I suspect, when they're supposed to be watching YOU!'

'It's not their fault, Maguff. We – er didn't want them to stay here tonight, that's all. We wanted some privacy. Look, getting angry and looking to apportion blame isn't going to help, is it?' Joel suddenly found himself speaking up against the somewhat bombastic eagle. 'What are we going to do about this dreadful mess?'

Maguff looked aghast. He was used to being top-eagle! No one normally dared stand up to him. 'Do you realise who you are talking to, dear boy? *We* are not going to do anything about it – this is *your* mess, boy and *you* can sort it out!' The eagle wagged his head vigorously. 'If you soldiers keep flouting the rules, you will have to face the consequences which, in this instance, happen to be quite dire. I suppose the girl will have to stay here tonight as she'll be concussed and not fit to travel. Then, in the morning, your grandad will have to put her on a plane back to Spain. Of course, her parents *and* the Spanish authorities will have to be informed as obviously she will not have a passport on her... Yes, Joel, you summed the situation up quite accurately – it truly is a dreadful mess...'

Joel gasped, painfully aware of the seriousness of the situation.

'But, you saw what she was like, Maguff! She's sixteen now, remember. How am I going to explain to her how she got here? She thinks she's been kidnapped! There's no saying what she'll do when she comes round! And – what about Grandad?' Joel pleaded. 'What on earth would I tell him?'

'Well, if you're lucky, your grandad may get off with a caution. Kidnapping is a criminal offence, you know,' Maguff droned pompously. 'Interpol may be involved. There could be a major international incident – perhaps it will even be splashed all over the papers and television… I dread to think what your mother will say about it all..'

'Interpol! Television! My mother!' Joel wailed. 'Maguff, you cannot be serious – you know my grandad is not a criminal!'

'I'm sorry, dear boy, but my wings are tied. Rules are rules, you see…' Maguff shrugged his wings, nonchalantly.

'Oh, stuff the rules Maguff!' Joel cried, angrily.

Maguff gasped and glared at Joel intently, at this outburst.

'Surely you can make exceptions.' Joel continued desperately pleading with the eagle. There *must* be something you can do! Can't you do anything off your own bat, or is your head just one big, silly rulebook? How long have you been doing this job, Sergeant Major?' he mocked. 'Maybe you've reached your limit – promoted to your level of incompetence, as my dad used to say about people stuck forever in a job beyond their capabilities!'

'Well!' Maguff huffed. 'Quite a little hot-head, aren't you? May I remind you, Joel, that it was *"stuffing the rules"* that got *you* into this mess in the first place, my boy! And I certainly don't have to stay around to be insulted. If that's your attitude, I might as well leave right now!'

Just then, Maité stirred and began to groan.

'Oh, please, Maguff – she's coming round!' Joel pleaded. The warning Magee gave him as the raven departed, was now ringing like a clanging church bell in Joel's head.

> *"Everything has consequences, Joel. You are in a war; you are fighting against principalities and powers of which you have no knowledge and the only way you can win is to rely on the weapons of warfare which are mighty in God – the cross of Christ, the blood thereupon shed and the name of Jesus, which is above every other name. Remember the Sword of the Spirit, which is the word of God – memorise it and praise God. These are powerful weapons and will give you victory over the devil who wants you to fail! Selfish motives will be a hindrance to all that has been planned for you...*

'Maguff, I'm truly sorry! I didn't mean to insult you, please forgive me. I'm completely at fault and I'll take all the blame, but please, just help me to get Maité home now; then I am willing to accept my punishment.'

Suddenly, Maguff began to glow with that warm golden light that enveloped the angels in Heaven; then, after a few seconds, he returned to normal.

'Well!' Maguff boomed. 'You must carry some clout, my boy! Talk about having friends in high places! There must be something really big planned for *you*! I've just been given instructions regarding this matter; your confession and acceptance of guilt has been accepted. However, I must warn you, Joel that what is about to happen can only come from the Highest Authority and it must not be taken lightly. You must see things in a different light from now on – remember that! It seems that you have, yet again, a *"get out of jail free" card.*' Maguff shook his head, gazed upward, and vanished in an instant.

†

Joel felt suddenly very dizzy and opened his eyes with a start. He was back in the den! The cramp in his arm had just awakened him and Maité was sleeping soundly with her head resting on his chest. Quickly, he snatched his wrist to look at his watch, then he let out an enormous sigh of relief. The time was five minutes past ten! He was overcome with awe – time had been turned back for them! It was at that moment that Maguff's words concerning the importance of what must lie ahead really began to dawn on him! Whatever it was, it was so important that it called for time itself to be changed! He looked up in wonder towards the sky.

'Thanks,' he whispered.

Maité began to stir. 'What did you say, Joel?' she murmured.

'You'd better wake up, Maité, it's time to go,' he replied softly.

'What time is it?' she asked, with a start.

'It's all right, Maité. Everything is OK. It's only just after ten,' he smiled reassuringly. 'We just dozed off for a short while, that's all, but you don't want to risk falling into a deep sleep.'

'I guess so,' she reluctantly agreed, getting to her feet. 'It wouldn't do to be an alien with amnesia in England.'

Joel smiled knowingly and nodded.

'Yeah, how would we explain that to my grandad and your parents!' he replied, with a grateful upward glance.

They made their way to the edge of the plateau and turned to face each other.

'I guess this is i…' Joel began, but wasn't able to finish his sentence because Maité had leaned forward and – before he knew it – she had planted a kiss on his lips! 'Wow!' Joel murmured as their lips parted.

'I wish I could say I will never forget you, Joel, but I know that in less than two hours I will no longer be fifteen and will not even remember your name,' Maité murmured sadly, stroking Joel's cheek.

'I wish you'd told me about this Fugue-hopping before.' He replied, his voice a little shaky. 'Hey, I could hop back with you and you could show me where you live in Spain,' Joel suggested. Barely had those words left Joel's lips when suddenly and without warning, a dazzling fork of lightning struck a nearby tree, severing a large branch which crashed to the ground. This was immediately followed by an almighty clap of thunder and the heavens opened as torrential rain began to fall in sheets. Joel realised instantly the folly of what he had just suggested, even though it was said in jest, and he remembered Maguff's warning:

"it must not be taken lightly.
You must see things in a new light, Joel."

'No, Joel!' Maité insisted. 'Your own missions are paramount now; you must forget about me. Please don't try it – and don't try to find me; I should never have come here! If you come to Spain, I will not know you – I really must leave, now.' Saying this, she turned to face the plateau. *'Hasta la vista, Joel,' she called.

*'Adios, my friend,' Joel replied.

Maité tuned her head and smiled at him through the beating rain, then she stepped onto the plateau and was gone in a blinding flash.

'That was some flash of lightning, Joel,' Grandad exclaimed, his voice barely audible above the rain.

Joel quickly swung round and there was Grandad, approaching with an umbrella and Joel's coat over his arm. Which flash of lightning was Grandad referring to? Joel wondered. The actual lightning or, could it be that Grandad saw the Fugue flash? Anyway, even if he did see the Fugue flash, Joel reasoned, he would have thought it was actual lightning.

'Come on, lad, get this on and let's get back to the house before you catch a chill. There's a roaring fire in the grate and some hot cocoa waiting,' Grandad urged tenderly, whilst helping Joel on with his coat.

Joel almost skipped back to Grandad's cottage; he now understood the expression "walking on air." In fact, he felt pretty much as if he was floating in Heaven; the memory of his dance with Maité at the Ball and the incredible risk she had taken to see him one more time, made him glow inside. Despite her emphatic instructions not to look for her, Joel now knew that she had feelings for him – and that was enough for now.

Back at Grandad's cottage, Joel nestled sleepily into the cushions of the settee with a warm drink of cocoa and wallowed in the memory of the evening. Suddenly, he was brought back to earth with a bump as Grandad reminded him of the reality of normal life.

'Your mother is coming tomorrow,' he announced.

Joel detected an air of anxiety in Grandad's voice.

'Are you all right, Grandad?' Joel asked. 'You seem a bit edgy. There's nothing wrong, is there?'

'No, no, everything is fine,' Grandad reassured him, rather unconvincingly.

* See you around, * Goodbye

'It's all gone so quickly, Grandad, hasn't it?' Joel continued, hoping that Grandad would reveal what was on his mind.

'Tempus fugit – time waits for no man, Joel,' Grandad agreed. Joel chuckled to himself. If only Grandad knew that this very thing – reversal of time – had actually occurred just moments before!

'I've been thinking, Joel,' Grandad continued, hesitantly. 'There's no need to tell Mum about any of this unicorn business and miracle healing, is there, son?'

'Not if you don't want to, Grandad.' Joel shrugged. *So that's it*, he thought, that's why Grandad appeared to be anxious. Joel was inwardly relieved because he didn't want to have that discussion with Mum, either.

'It's not that we want to keep anything from her, deceitfully, Joel, but we don't want her thinking we've gone soft in the head, either. You know Mum; we don't want to alarm her and we don't want awkward questions, do we, son? What a nightmare we could be facing, you know how these things can get out of hand. Why, before we knew it, we'd have all manner of psychiatrists and analysts digging around…' Grandad shook his head, huffing and puffing at the very idea of it. 'Even television crews!'

'Yes, Grandad, I know exactly what you mean,' Joel nodded in agreement.

'So we'll keep mum, shall we? Excuse the pun,' Grandad added, with a chuckle.

'That's fine by me,' Joel agreed, yawning. 'I'm tired now, Grandad, so I think I'll go to bed. Goodnight.'

'Goodnight, son. I'll not be far behind you. I'll just have a little night-cap – it helps me sleep.'

'Well, don't fall asleep down here, Grandad,' Joel sighed, as he climbed the twisty stairs.

'No, I'll be doing that tomorrow night when your mum is here,' Grandad replied.

Joel climbed into bed with Maité's note in his hand. Sinking back into his pillow, he frowned. He was looking forward to seeing Mum next day but, at the same time he was apprehensive.

Would he be able to act normally, knowing what he did? Would he feel deceitful, having to hide the fact that he'd seen Dad, and would Mum see through him and suspect something? He was aching to tell Mum that Dad was alright, but to do so would be to lose him again and Dad had made it very clear that, he could not tell a single soul about the Kairos.

With all of these thoughts swirling around his head, Joel was too exhausted to think clearly. He placed his half of Maité's note under his pillow and smiled at the thought of her waking up next morning and finding its utterly confusing other half by her bedside. Now he really did feel special! He was overwhelmed by the evening's events. The Ball in Heaven had been amazing and – as if that had not been astonishing enough – time had been changed for him! And, of course, now he was no longer just a boy; he'd had his first kiss! With a contented smile, Joel switched off his lantern and fell into a deep sleep.

CHAPTER TWENTY

A Shock Announcement

On Saturdays, Grandad always made a special lunch – bacon butties – crispy bacon and plump, meaty sausages in freshly-baked bread! Peter arrived just in time to join Joel and Grandad for this veritable feast, which was followed by Mrs Jordan's delicious chocolate cake that Peter had brought with him – and another for Joel to take home, together with an angel cake for Grandad, which his all-time favourite cake!

After they'd eaten as much as they could possibly manage, they flaked out in the lounge, whilst waiting for Joel's mum to arrive. However, by tea-time there was still no sign of her, so Joel and Peter went outside for a wander around the yard, which gave them the opportunity to talk in private.

'I guess I won't see you now till the Summer holidays, Joel. It seems so far off,' Peter remarked, sadly.

'Yes, but, Peter, I don't know if I can wait that long to find out what the Kairos has in store for us,' Joel answered. I feel as if I could actually burst if I don't find out soon. I cannot imagine how I'll get through the next three months.'

'I know what you mean. In a way, I wish we could speed up time, cut out the school term and get straight to the Summer hols!'

'Yeah, you and just about every other kid!' Joel glanced away for a second. Peter didn't know about the time-changing incident with Maité and Maguff, because Joel hadn't had a chance to tell him yet, but time had indeed just been changed. 'You're not going home yet, though, are you, Peter? Can you stay for supper?'

'Sure, that'd be cool,' Peter replied with a grin.

'Hey, and don't take any more nonsense from that weasel Presten either, after I'm gone,' Joel chuckled.

'No worries, Joel. Presten's rule of tyranny is history now, mate.' Peter assured him.

Finally, after Grandad had made the evening meal, Joel's mum arrived in time to eat it. The sound of tyres could be heard turning into the yard and, leaping up from his chair at the kitchen table, Joel hurried over to the back door. Grandad, on the other hand, who would normally be eager to go outside and greet Mum, strangely busied himself at the cooker, stirring the simmering stew.

'Mum is in a different car!' Joel remarked, puzzled. 'I wonder what's happened to hers; I hope she hasn't broken down – maybe that's why she's late.'

Grandad continued vigorously stirring the stew, furtively endeavouring to hide a slight grimace. Joel sensed that Grandad was trying to avoid telling him something.

'Grandad?' Joel questioned, suspiciously. 'Grandad, is there something you're not telling me?' He was beginning to suspect that something was horribly wrong. 'You know something, don't you, Grandad.'

It didn't take long for Joel to discover the reason for Grandad's odd behaviour. As the car pulled up in the yard, he opened the kitchen door and stepped outside. Mum got out of the passenger side and immediately threw open her arms, as she always did whenever they had been apart for more than a day or two. Now though, Joel was nearly thirteen and found this a little embarrassing.

'Darling, I've missed you so much,' Mum cooed. 'I really need a big hug!'

Not wishing to upset Mum, he responded with a very brief hug and, as he looked over her shoulder, he gawped with astonishment! The driver's door opened and the identity of Mum's chauffer was revealed; Joel could hardly believe his own eyes and went into immediate panic-mode as he recognised the man who stepped out – it was none other than Detective John Smith!

Joel gulped, as the word *Traitor!* rang in his head. He thought the cat was out of the bag – that Smith had gone back on his word and told Mum everything! *What a double-crossing traitor! Oh no, how on earth was he going to explain his recent presence in London to Mum? Oh, things couldn't go more horribly wrong!* This was a hole that even Houdini couldn't dig his way out of!

'Oh, darling, you remember Detective John Smith, don't you?' Mum piped, cheerily.

There seemed to be something different about Mum; she was full of the joys of Spring. Joel couldn't remember the last time he had seen her looking so happy – radiant even*! If Smith had told Mum about London, she would certainly not be full of the joys of Sprin but very anxious to know what Joel had been doing there – and more to the point – how on earth he got there!* Now Joel was really confused! However, he did detect a hint of trepidation in Mum's manner, as if she too was hiding something. Joel sensed that some impending bombshell was about to explode and he was bracing himself for the inevitable third degree, about Sadler's house and the City. He would though, never have guessed what this bombshell really was!

'Er – er…' Joel stammered, lost for words.

'Of course he remembers me, don't you, Joel,' Smith held out his hand. 'It's not that long since we've clapped eyes on each other, is it?' he boldly announced, with a teasing smile.

Joel tried to suppress a gasp as Mum, thankfully, turned her attention to Grandad, who was standing in the doorway, warily keeping his distance – could that be because of the possible fall-out from the suspected impending bombshell?

'That's supposed to be funny, is it?' Joel muttered in a low voice, scowling at the detective as he took his outstretched hand.

'Remember, mum's the word,' Smith replied with a slightly amused look, as he squeezed Joel's hand.

One thing Joel had noticed about Detective Smith was his odd sense of humour. He seemed to find mirth in situations that other people might find distinctly uncomfortable – such as this one. Joel certainly didn't find anything even remotely amusing about this situation. In fact, he thought that Smith was rather annoying. However, it appeared that Smith evidently hadn't told Mum about their experience in the city. This then posed the question, what in the world was he doing there? Joel was so confused he couldn't think straight; he just whispered frantically to Smith while Mum and Grandad greeted each other.

'What are you doing here, Detective Smith? You haven't said anything to Mum, have you, about...?'

'Of course not!' Smith whispered in mock indignation. 'My word is my word, young man.'

Joel's relief was marred slightly by trepidation, wondering why Smith was even there at all. All kinds of nightmarish questions began to whirl around Joel's head – had the police identified him and Peter? Had their finger-prints been discovered in Sadler's house? Had they identified Tamara from her popping up at New Scotland Yard? Were they going to be arrested as Sadler's accomplices? Would they have to go to court? Surely, Smith would not come all this way if he was merely informing Mum of Sadler's arrest, which Mum must have seen in the news anyway! And why is Mum being so aloof?

'Come on, you two!' Mum called from the doorway. 'Supper's ready!'

Before any explanations could be given, Joel and Smith felt obliged to make their way inside. Grandad was already at the stove, ladling out the stew, and Joel introduced Peter as though he and Smith had never met. Then the boys had to endure polite conversation over supper, before all was astonishingly revealed.

'You're not wearing your callipers, Peter!' Mum remarked with some surprise. In all the years they had been visiting Grandad, she had never before seen Peter without them.

'No, the doctor said I don't need them anymore, Mrs Asher; must be something I've grown out of,' he shrugged.

'So, John, did you have a good drive down from the city?' Grandad enquired, anxious to divert attention from the subject of Peter's healing.

'Yes thanks, Marcus,' Smith replied. 'It's a terrific long way though, isn't it? I mean, at the very least a full day's journey, unless of course you have…' he looked curiously at Joel, '…wings or something…'

Joel shifted uncomfortably in his seat and exchanged glances with Peter, before glaring, piercingly at Smith in the hope that this would discourage him from saying anything revealing.

'This is a "proper stew,"Marcus,' Smith remarked, with a timely pun. 'Are you enjoying this stew, Joel?'

'Grandad's stew is ok,' Joel grunted warily.

Ignoring Joel's grunts, Smith turned to Mum.

'This one is delicious, isn't it, Elizabeth?'

Mum smiled at Smith and nodded, too polite to answer with food in her mouth.

Elizabeth! Joel thought indignantly. *What happened to Mrs Asher?* Joel was becoming increasingly alarmed, not just by Smith's presence but also his evident familiarity with Mum! What was going on? Why was Mum a passenger in Smith's car? Joel sensed a degree of tension in the room; it seemed as if everyone was "treading on eggshells." He just wished that they would get on with it, instead of pussyfooting around.

Following supper, they all moved into the lounge, where Grandad put his old black kettle on the hearth to make some tea. Joel was trying not to look worried but was very anxious to know what had brought Smith all this way, as soon as they were all seated in the lounge, he could wait no longer.

'So, what are you doing here, Detective Smith?' Joel blurted out, suddenly.

'Joel!' Mum exclaimed in embarrassment at Joel's forthright question.

'It's all right, Elizabeth,' Smith reassured her. 'I think your mother had better explain that, Joel,' he answered.

'Come and sit here, darling.' Mum smiled at Joel, patting the settee cushion next to her.

Joel looked anxious, as he hesitantly sat next to Mum.

'What is it, Mum? Are you in trouble? Am I in trouble?'

'Oh gracious, no!' Mum cried. 'You didn't think I was under arrest, did you, Joel? I thought you looked a bit worried. No, dear, it's nothing like that, but I do have something to tell you, that you are going to find upsetting, love – something of a shock.'

Joel was feeling rather strained; he thought he knew what was coming, but he wasn't supposed to know. Presumably, Mum was going to tell him of the recent discovery that Dad had not died in an accident but that he had been murdered. Somehow, Joel would have to act surprised and shocked, as though hearing it for the first time.

'Joel, evidence has come to light…' Mum bit her lip and with a trembling voice, continued, '… you won't have heard, not having television here, but it's in all the papers; all your school friends will know. I told Grandad on the phone but I asked him not to say anything to you about it before I got here. Joel, darling, it seems that your dad didn't fall asleep at the wheel. In fact, he didn't die because of an accident. Joel – Dad was murdered!'

This explained Grandad's state of anxiety the previous evening, and odd behaviour during the day. He was obviously in shock, having heard the devastating news. Joel didn't have to worry about acting shocked, though. One look at Mum's face, with tears brimming in her eyes, was so heart-rending. He couldn't bear to see her so upset and took hold of her hand. He knew that he should ask her if they had caught the villain responsible, but he couldn't bring himself to ask because he already knew the answer. However, after a brief pause to pull herself together, Mum continued.

'They've caught the man who did it, Joel,' she explained, with a trembling voice. 'Do you remember that creepy man who used to come to our house with Dad occasionally – his former partner at the practise?'

'Dan Sadler!' Joel snarled, grimly.

'Yes, darling, his concerned visits to us since Dad's death must have been guilt trips,' Mum remarked bitterly, 'because he deprived me of a husband and you of a father.'

'The scheming snake!' Joel snapped.

'It emerged that Sadler was caught up in some organised crime racket, involving drugs and blackmail,' Smith volunteered.

'We've caught the ring-leaders; they'll be going to prison for a long time and Sadler will go down for murder, too.'

'Good!' Joel spat. Trembling, he bit his lip. Although glad to hear that justice was being served, it was obviously no compensation for losing his dad.

Smith was, of course, aware that Joel already knew what he was telling him, but the well-meaning detective evidently wanted to spare Mum the ordeal of explaining it all herself. Joel inwardly sighed with relief. So, Smith was evidently just there to help explain about all of this, but why? Joel's relief was brief because he was still slightly confused. Why would the detective need to come all this way, to explain what Mum could have explained herself? Something just didn't add up and Joel began to feel uneasy about what might be coming next – although he honestly didn't have a clue what that could be.

'John was the man responsible for leading the investigation, Joel, and the subsequent arrest of the culprits,' Mum added.

Oh, so it's John now! This is cosy – Joel thought – Mum on first name terms with the detective.

'He's been a tremendous support through all of this,' Mum continued. In fact, I don't know what I would have done without him.' Then, to Joel's utter astonishment, she stretched out her other hand to Smith, who was sitting in the easy chair next to her and, taking his hand, *squeezed it* and smiled at him!

Joel was completely taken aback by this apparent display of affection, and even more so when he saw Smith actually place his other hand on top of Mum's hand and return the warm smile!

'And well, you see, darling,' Mum continued with another smile in Smith's direction, 'I didn't want to spring it on you, Joel, but we've been seeing each other for some time now and, with this latest development, John was worried about me driving all this way while I was so upset. So he decided to drive me himself. The thing is, darling, we have fallen in love. John has asked me to marry him and – well – I've said yes. We're engaged!'

Joel was suddenly speechless! Grandad's kettle began to whistle its head off as it came to a rapid boil, providing a fitting audible climax to this flabbergasting news! Joel felt like his head was about to explode in competition with the kettle and imagined steam coming out of his ears too! All this time he had been extremely anxious, wondering what on earth Smith had really come for, panicking that he might be asked to explain his recent presence in the city when he was supposed to be at Grandad's, in the country. Now though, he realised that Smith wasn't just there to help explain about Dad. He was there as Mum's boyfriend – fiancé even! So, that's what Dad meant when he said he approved of Mum's choice! Dad was talking about her choice of marriage partner!

Joel gasped in utter astonishment. This wasn't just a mere fish impersonation moment. No, this was much more serious! It wasn't going to be Joel, Mum and Naomi anymore – it was going to be Joel, Mum, Naomi – and Smith! Oh no – the annoying Detective Smith was to be his step-dad! How could this happen? Grandad, anxious to avoid involvement in any fallout, busied himself with the kettle and the making of the tea.

'Oh, you're shocked, Joel. Of course you are,' Mum murmured, a little awkwardly. 'I'm sorry I had to tell you all that about Dad… It's a terrible business, I know. We would have preferred to have announced our engagement in happier circumstances, but unfortunately this terrible discovery has only just come to light. At least the villains have been caught and Dad can rest in peace now.'

This reminded Joel of the kiss Dad gave him for Mum. He endeavoured to pull himself together and leaned forward, planting the kiss on Mum's forehead, just as Dad had given it to him – kind of, passing the kiss. 'I'm sure he can, now, Mum and if he was here he would give you a kiss, so that was from Dad. I believe that he would approve of your decision.' Then he kissed her again. 'And this is from me. Congratulations!'

'Thank you, Joel darling.' Mum smiled with relief and seemed to cheer up instantly. The drained look vanished from her face and she was once again radiant.

'Congratulations, Detective Smith.' Joel stood up and offered his hand to Smith.

'Thank you, Joel,' Smith replied, humbly. 'It means a lot to have your approval, and please call me John, now we are to become family.' Saying this, the detective shook his hand.

Grandad gave an audible sigh of relief and patted his face with his handkerchief. Now that this news had been delivered and amicably received, he too became much more cheery and also offered his hand to Smith. 'Great news, John! She needs someone to keep her in line – been on her own too long. Welcome to the family.'

'Thank you, Marcus. Well, perhaps now might be an appropriate time for this,' Smith announced, 'now that we've been given the family approval.' Taking a small box out of his pocket, he flipped open the lid, took a diamond ring out of its cushion and held it out to Mum.

Mum was still wearing her wedding ring from Dad and she looked at it for a second, hesitating, almost reluctant to finally remove it. Then, she slowly slipped it off her finger and allowed Smith to place the new engagement ring in its place.

'It's beautiful, John,' Mum breathed, a little overwhelmed. Then, she turned to Joel. 'Joel darling, I want you to keep this. You never know, one day you may like to give it to a young lady.'

Joel took the ring and placed it in his shirt pocket. Unknown to them, he already knew whose finger he would like to place it on one day.

'Now, tell me about your stay with Grandad.' Mum enthused. 'I've missed you, sweetheart. What exciting things have you been doing?'

'Oh, there's not much to tell really, Mum,' Joel shrugged, 'is there, Grandad?'

'No, it's very quiet here in the country, Lizzy,' Grandad agreed. 'I'm afraid you're barking up the wrong tree if you're expecting excitement. You should know that; you grew up here yourself! Tea, anyone?'

CHAPTER TWENTY ONE

The King of Glory is in the House!

Grandad slept on the couch for the night, as he usually did when Mum stayed, so that she could have his bed. After all the excitement and revelation, culminating in saying farewell to his friends, Joel came down to earth with a bump at bed-time that night when, instead of his friend Peter, he found himself sharing his room with Smith! Of course, Joel had been relegated to spending the night in Peter's camp bed while his own bed was occupied by the detective!

'You don't snore do you, Joel?' Smith chuckled as he snuggled down in Joel's bed.

'I could ask you the same question, Detective,' Joel answered, dryly.

'Do call me John. I would feel much better knowing that you think of me as a friend, Joel, and not just a detective – or Mum's fiancé. I do love your mother, you know.'

'I know, John,' Joel answered blandly. 'I have it on good authority.' He felt slightly uncomfortable using the detective's Christian name, but supposed that he would get used to it in time.

'What do you mean by that, Joel,' the detective enquired, curiously. 'Whose authority?'

Joel immediately realised his gaffe; he had let that slip out and was annoyed at himself for not being more careful.

'Oh er, if Mum thinks you're cool, that's fine by me, John,' Joel answered, quickly. 'Mum rules, you know.'

Smith grunted but did not seem convinced; he continued to stare at Joel with an air of suspicion. 'There's something different about you, Joel – something mysterious, but I can't quite put my finger on what it is,' he muttered.

'It's just your imagination – probably your detective mind running wild,' Joel replied. 'Go to sleep, John, we'll talk tomorrow, it's late.' Joel hoped that Smith would forget about this conversation by the morning. He knew that his Dad approved of Smith and he rather liked the detective himself, too, despite Smith's rather annoying sense of humour and nosiness. Accepting Smith in the role of dad though, was going to take some getting his head around. He lay in bed with an ache, deep down in his belly, which seemed to be connected to the moisture filling his eyes. He missed his dad so much and now he knew that he was also going to miss Maité. *Why did life have to be so complicated?*

After lying there for about an hour, sleep still seemed far away. All Joel could think about was the Kairos, his dad and the "something big" that was planned for him. This "something big" was important enough for time to be changed! How amazing was that! Only God could change time! This meant that God had a plan for him. Suddenly, Joel had an overwhelming yearning to know what this plan was. He could not endure the whole Summer-term at school without knowing more; he simply *had* to know now! A quick glance at his clock told him that it was a quarter-past-midnight. He checked Smith, who was sleeping like a baby, then, turning to the window he noticed that it was a clear night; the light of the moon spilled in through a chink in the curtains. Suddenly, he felt an irresistible urge to get out of bed. He rose slowly and quietly, careful not to wake Smith. He put on some clothes and slipped through the door. Stealthily tip-toeing downstairs, he missed the steps that he knew were the creakiest. Once in the kitchen, he put on his shoes then went outside. Before he knew it, Joel was striding over the field to Zionica. He felt strangely compelled, as if drawn by some irresistible force. With an excitement in his heart, he took a deep breath and stepped straight onto the plateau before he could chicken-out. He wondered if the Fugue would snatch him up or whether it wouldn't work, now that the Kairos was officially closed for the term. But there was no delay; he was instantly caught up!

At the top of the Fugue, Joel floated out and looked around. Beautiful, soft music and angelic singing could be heard in the background but otherwise, the Hallway of Arches appeared surprisingly deserted.

Heart pounding, Joel closed his eyes. '*Which way*?' he quietly muttered to himself. He'd never actually ventured to the left of the Fugue, as the couple of rooms he had been allowed in previously were both to the right. When he opened his eyes, Joel felt that he should set off in the direction of the Vista Chamber, which he knew, hoping that he might be able to find some answers to his burning questions there. Joel floated along the hallway, gazing wondrously at all the different coloured archways. Some were sparkling and twinkling and some ebbing soft colours. Everything was light and bright; there was no darkness at all. As he drew near to the Vista chamber entrance, he heard a deep rumbling sound as if from a distant thunderstorm. It seemed to be coming from a large archway further up the hallway on the opposite side to the Vista. The irresistible drawing force seemed to be compelling him towards it and he was curious to investigate the source of the thunder-like sound. Joel thought that it possibly was a thunderstorm – he was in Heaven after all – maybe all thunderstorms originated there?

Joel floated up to the large archway and, as he did so, the rumbling noise became louder. He hesitated at the entrance, expecting one of those mighty men to leap out and stop him, but there was no one there. As he peered in, not knowing what to expect, Joel felt the pounding of his heart competing with the sound coming through the archway. Cautiously, he pushed through a spectrum of different colours – not a material curtain, but literally tangible colour just hanging in the archway like an ethereal curtain. He floated through the entrance, carefully moving the colour aside, and found himself in a high, wide tunnel. The thundering sound became increasingly louder and now seemed to be mixed with shouting, as Joel pushed on through the waves of colour. After only a few seconds, he could see the end of the tunnel which seemed to open out to an intense light. He peeped excitedly through the final veil of colour. What he saw took his breath away and he almost fainted but with a gasp, he caught his breath! There were myriads of riders on white horses, so many that they were uncountable! The riders were assembled in rows, which extended further than the eye could see. The riders were dressed in radiant white garments and armour, and light shone brightly all around them. The whole place appeared as if lit by floodlights – but the light seemed to be coming from the mounted army – a vast celestial cavalry of light, positioned in blocks. There were rows of angels hovering "in flank," some of whom were singing, while others had silver trumpets which they sounded intermittently. Joel crept as close to the tunnel end as he dared.

Then, as if this wasn't awesome enough, Joel saw the most wondrous of sights: a brilliant Soldier, millions of times brighter than all the others. He also was dressed in white, and was riding a magnificent white horse. However, He was not merely shining brightly like the other riders but He was the light! He was so bright that He was the *actual source* of the light, which illuminated the whole place and it was His light that the whole army reflected! Although He appeared to be a real person, even His garments and armour seemed to be made of light! This brilliant Soldier was galloping up and down the rows, shouting and waving his arm triumphantly. He seemed to be really enjoying Himself. All the other riders were watching Him, excitedly saluting and honouring Him with cries of "Allelulia!" "Glory to the Lamb!" "Honour!" and "Blessed is He!" His horse was almost dancing as it swerved, leapt in the air, swung around and reared up. Joel had never seen anyone handle a horse like it, ever – not even Tamara, and she was a superb rider! As Joel watched in awe, he just wanted to join in with all the ranks and shout in adoration of this brilliant Soldier! So overcome was he, that he momentarily forgot where he was – and that he shouldn't have been there. As he hovered at the edge of the tunnel, Joel caught his breath. Unfortunately though, his gasp alerted two mighty men who were stationed either side of the archway end. They both instantly turned to face Joel, crossing their enormously long swords in order to bar his way. Joel froze! Suddenly the brilliant Soldier pulled up, turned and galloped full-pelt in Joel's direction. He was holding a bejewelled sceptre of light which He seemed to be pointing at Joel, as if he was going to joust with him. Joel's heart leapt in his chest. Swifter than an eagle, the brilliant Soldier appeared right in front of them. Leaping off His horse, He thrust His sceptre up over the crossed swords of the mighty men and pointed it at Joel. He stood before them at the entrance to the tunnel, like a mighty tower. He was altogether glorious and awesomely amazing and He wore a spectacular bejewelled crown. Even though it looked as if Joel was done for and he thought he might even die, all he wanted to do was fall at the feet of this brilliant Soldier and worship Him. He couldn't do that though, because he was frozen: unable to move a muscle, suspended between the crossed spears of the mighty men.

'It's alright,' the brilliant Soldier spoke with authority. 'He's with Me.'

'Yes, Commander,' the mighty men uttered obediently. Immediately, they stood at ease, their swords returned to the scabbards by their sides, and Joel was suddenly released but, due to the lack of gravity, he floated sedately down.

Joel gulped, his mouth was very dry as he gazed up, transfixed, at the brilliant Soldier, wondering who this was and how he was going to explain his presence there to this evidently very important Person. Joel expected that he was in *big trouble* – and wondered what the Commander would do with him!

Then, the brilliant Soldier grinned at Joel and immediately Joel's heart melted as waves of pure joy swept over him – even though Joel thought he was in heaps of trouble, he couldn't feel afraid if he tried. Who was this amazing Person? Whoever He was, He must be very important indeed! Suddenly the curtain of colour parted behind Joel, and Nathan emerged in a flurry.

'Lord, Majesty, I'm so sorry!' Nathan apologised earnestly.

Then he turned to Joel. 'Joel! What are you doing here?'

Joel was lost for words; he actually couldn't think of one single thing to say. All he knew was that he didn't want to take his eyes off this brilliant Soldier who had been addressed by the mighty men as Commander and who, Joel believed without doubt, had all authority.

'Nathan, friend, there's no harm done,' the Commander reassured him. 'I was expecting Joel.'

'Huh?' Joel found his voice – just.

'My Father drew him and I knew that he would not be able to resist the call. That's part of why he's been chosen – for such a time as this,' the Commander announced.

'Of course, You knew. How silly of me,' Nathan muttered. 'Thank you, my Lord. Come, son, let me take you back to the Fugue, at once.'

'No!' the Commander insisted. 'Anyone who comes to Me, I will by no means cast away, especially the children.' He turned to the great army who were waiting silently behind him, and waved his arm. 'Exercise over for now, brothers!'

The entire army faded into invisibility before Joel's very eyes, causing him to gasp yet again and he pinched himself so hard it hurt.

'Oh, don't worry, they're all fine. They've all gone to their mansions; they'll be back,' the Commander explained. 'It's the *preparation*; we're all getting ready for the big day. There's so much to do before that day can happen, though, Joel.'

'Oh, I see,' Joel gulped, nodding. 'What day are you preparing for, Commander? Are you going into some sort of battle?'

'Come, Joel,' He replied. 'Let us sit for a while and I will answer you, and show you great and mighty things that you do not know.' The Commander looked around. 'A courtyard, I think.' He spoke with authority and immediately a small table and three chairs appeared, along with a quaint fountain and a few trees and shrubs, making a very attractive little courtyard.

'Whoa!' Joel cried, awestruck that this Commander caused things to appear, just by speaking! There was creative power in His very Word; it seemed as if the Commander imagined in His head how He wanted the courtyard to be and commanded it to be so with His voice.

The three of them sat at the table by the cool fountain. A small tree was situated behind Joel; its leaves looked thicker than any leaves he had seen before and he could not resist squeezing one of them. He was surprised to find that when he pressed it between his finger and thumb, it immediately sprang back again like a firm sponge as he let it go. Even more amazing was the fact that it gave a little squeal as he pinched it! Then a cute cherub appeared and served them drinks in sparkling goblets. Joel was just about to take a sip of his when he noticed some rather peculiar looking fish in the fountain that the Commander had just created out of nothing. The fish were upright in the water and had small defined faces and *hair,* which was blonde and silky, and they actually appeared to be talking to each other – even having some sort of heated discussion under the water!

'Wow!' Joel exclaimed, as he studied the fish. 'What extraordinary fish!'

To Joel's surprise, one of the fish popped its head up out of the water and, addressing the Commander, it asked Him a question!

'Excuse me, oh Mighty One, which of us praises You the most? I say it's me, but…' preened the fish, when he was suddenly interrupted by the other fish popping up out of the water.

'And I say it's me! Oh King of Kings,' the other fish piped.

'So, which of us is it, Oh Lord of Lords?' the first fish warbled, persistently.

The commander smiled at the two fish, answering them in a gentle voice. 'It's neither of you – if you're going to argue about it.'

The two fish looked startled. Then, suddenly understanding, they turned to each other.

'I'm sorry, Bernie,' the first fish sobbed.

'So am I, Gumf,' the second fish uttered with a wobbly voice. 'Friends?'

'You bet!' Gumf beamed, placing a fin around Bernie.

'Now, you are both praising Me,' the Commander chuckled.

'Thank you, oh Wonderful Counsellor,' Bernie bowed.

After a joint bow, the two fish sank under the water and swam off together, around the fountain.

Joel stared, open-mouthed, after the fish. Was he in bed, dreaming all of this, or had the Commander just had a conversation with two weird looking fish?

'I thought you would like those,' the Commander answered Joel with an amused chuckle. 'Anyway,' he continued, suddenly serious, 'the big day, Joel, that we are preparing for is certainly not a battle, but a victory march! Now, Joel, it's a good job I saw you first and raised My golden sceptre for you, signalling that you are accepted. Otherwise, the outcome may have been something that none of us would have wanted. Take this as a warning, you cannot just wander around Heaven when you are still earth-bound; you could get yourself into real trouble and you've already caused a bit of a stir last night, haven't you?'

'Oh, yes, I'm so sorry…' Joel began, with a sheepish look. He understood that the Commander was referring to the time-changing incident with Maité, at the tree den in Zionica. 'I'm ready to take my punishment,' he asserted. 'It's all my fault; Maité is not to blame at all.'

Nathan hung his head in his hands; whilst Joel was in the Kairos, he was Nathan's responsibility. But the Commander leaned forward and, placing a finger under Nathan's chin, He gently lifted his head back up and smiled at him.

Joel suddenly caught his breath with a gasp. He could hardly believe his eyes! As the Commander lifted Nathan's chin, Joel noticed a scar on the Commander's hand, as if a big, long nail had been driven through it!

'Nathan, my friend, there is no condemnation here,' the Commander reminded him. 'I'm overjoyed that Joel is here with us at last. How long have we waited for this stage of the plan? Joel has a seeking heart. He has been made for the role; we've just got to knock off some of the rough edges – refine him a little here and there, that's all.' The Commander threw Joel a teasing smile.

'Yes, Majesty,' Nathan replied. 'Thank you.'

As Joel looked into the Commander's eyes, he suddenly understood what Tamara had said at the party in Heaven. There was an indescribable quality in the Commander's eyes that seemed to draw Joel, as if he was falling into a pool of something totally irresistible. Joel knew from that moment onwards that he was somehow connected to the Commander by an inseparable bond, so strong that he would even lay down his life for Him.

'Joel,' the Commander continued. 'Your confession and remorse has been accepted and the punishment already paid – I paid for all your misdemeanours, over 2000 years ago. You are free; your sin is no longer remembered. This is the Divine Exchange that My Father set in motion: the principle of substitution by grace, through faith.

'Thank you, Commander,' Joel murmured, slightly dazed, as he remembered what the Vicar had taught him about Jesus paying the price for all sin, on the cross. Could this really, actually be…?

'Although still children until they are sixteen,' the Commander continued, 'we regard all the Kairos children as responsible young adults, because they all have the light and know the truth. You are a mighty warrior in Me and,' turning to Nathan, He added, 'we have much planned for Joel, have we not, Nathan?'

'We have, Lord,' Nathan agreed, with a grin. 'Keeping him on the plan though is not going to be easy; he tends to be little headstrong at times.'

Joel was completely overwhelmed by the amazing Commander. First, He appeared as the Commander of the great army, ready to rule and reign with a rod of iron. Then, the next minute, He was gentle as a Lamb! Also, He was wearing a magnificent crown and Dad had just referred to Him as Majesty! He must be a King!

Then Joel looked at the Commander with a frown.

'Hmm,' the Commander murmured. 'I sense a question coming. What would you like to ask Me, Joel?'

'Well,' Joel began hesitantly. 'I don't understand something, Commander.'

'You want to know why we have guards with swords in Heaven, don't you, Joel?'

Joel was suddenly taken aback as he realised that the Commander could hear his thoughts and knew what he wanted to ask.

'I was wondering – why on earth – I mean in Heaven – do You need guards? I thought Heaven was supposed to be paradise with no crime.'

'You know, that's a good question, Joel – and because you've asked it, I'm going to give you an answer,' the Commander replied. 'You see, Joel, although Satan was thrown out of Heaven for his rebellion, he still knows his way back and does occasionally attempt to come and make a nuisance of himself – mostly by accusing My people on earth of all kinds of misdemeanours. He rants on to My Father about every little thing, hoping My Father will give him the authority to punish them. The guards are there to restrict his movements and prevent him from entering where he shouldn't. Satan has no power or authority of his own and My Father only allows him to do what He can turn around for good. I disarmed the devil and his workers of evil at the cross.'

'Wait a minute,' Joel quickly asked. 'So – You – paid for every sin – on the cross?'

'Yes, that's correct, Joel,' the Commander replied. 'I came down to the earth and was born as man for the specific purpose of sacrificing My life on the cross, to pay for the redemption of the souls of men. My blood is the new covenant which was shed for the sins of the world and it will never lose its power.'

'Wow!' Joel exclaimed. 'So You're...' he could hardly speak.

'Yes, Joel, that little baby born in a manger, to a young woman who did not know any man intimately but obeyed God and submitted to the power of the Holy Spirit.'

Joel bit his lip.

'What is it, Joel?' the Commander asked softly.

'I'm sorry, Commander – I was rude to Maguff when Maité fell out of the tree.' Joel shook his head in remorse. 'He was just doing his job and we were in the wrong. I guess I was still mad at him for abandoning us in the mineshaft, with Peter's life in the balance on that ledge,' he admitted.

'Apology accepted – but you already apologised to Maguff,

didn't you, Joel?' The Commander smiled. 'It was forgotten the moment you repented of it – you're forgiven. Now, Nathan, let's have a Vista – over here, I think.'

Surely the Commander could easily have created the Vista Himself but, for some reason, He wanted Nathan to do it.

'Of course, right away, Lord,' Nathan replied with a grin. Immediately, a large Vista appeared.

Joel was so overcome with awe that he wondered – could he possibly still be asleep in bed? He pinched his own arm and flinched.

'Yes, it's real, Joel, you are not dreaming,' the Commander answered him, evidently knowing what was on his mind.

'So, what should I call You?' Joel asked, hesitantly.

'All My names and titles are mentioned in the book that was written about Me,' the Commander continued. 'You can use any of them.'

'The Bible?' Joel breathed incredulously.

'Yes,' the Commander replied assuredly. Then He continued as they all turned to look at the newly appeared Vista. 'There's something I want to show you about Maguff, Joel. That night, in the mineshaft, he was doing something for Me. Angels cannot intervene in human affairs unless specifically commanded to do so, by the Most High,' He explained. 'Maguff had no choice in the matter; he was on his way to another very serious situation when suddenly, I diverted him to the mineshaft to save you. Maguff told you that this was then your mission. The mineshaft situation was a test for you, Joel. I'll now show you why Maguff could linger no longer to save Peter, after saving your life.'

Joel watched the Vista intently. A speeding train, full of people, was hurtling towards a bridge over a huge ravine. A close-up of the bridge showed that a critical bolt in the middle of the bridge had become loose and fallen out, leaving the bridge perilously close to collapsing.

'Joel, that bridge would not have stood the weight of the approaching train.' The Commander explained. 'Maguff's orders that day were to prevent the deaths of everyone on the train –

which happened to be in India, and this was where Maguff was heading when I diverted him to save you, which was why he could not linger another moment in the mine shaft.'

They continued to watch and, at the precise moment the train mounted the bridge, Maguff appeared. The huge eagle spread his magnificent wings underneath the bridge to support the full weight of the bridge and the train. Maguff held everything up as the train rattled over it to the safety of the far side of the ravine, where it continued on its journey. All on board were safe and oblivious to the peril they had so narrowly escaped. This allowed precious time for a Kairos child to bring the problem to the attention of the railway company, so that they could make the bridge safe.'

'Wow! That is astonishing!' Joel exclaimed.

'Yes, there were 500 people on that train, Joel and only 53 of them knew Me,' the Commander nodded. 'Had Maguff tarried for one more second at the mineshaft, the entire bridge would have collapsed and all 500 people onboard the train would be dead – 447 of them would have been lost forever, in eternal Hell. Now though, those 447 lost souls have more time to come to know Me and be saved.'

Joel gulped in humility, as he realised how he had misjudged the grumpy old eagle.

The Commander continued. 'Joel, Maguff may appear a little abrasive at times but the gold is not just on his wings, you know, it is also in his heart. You were capable of rescuing Peter from that ledge and did so very successfully. This challenge was part of your training, Joel. Lean not on your own understanding – you need to see things from My perspective; I am working everything together for good.'

Their attention turned again to the Vista. Joel watched as view after view flashed by. Each view was a scene from the world: crowds of people of every tribe and tongue. Multitudes of people, all going about their daily lives: working, eating, studying, playing, travelling and getting married…'

What on earth is all this? Joel thought to himself. *Why am I being shown all these people?* He was utterly confused.

'I know you are confused, Joel,' the Commander continued patiently, 'but it will become clear to you. You see, son, I love all these people. I died for each and every one of them and yet the vast majority of them do not even know My Name – indeed many use My Name wrongly, cursing and blaspheming My holy Name. My Father loves these people and He is heartbroken that His friendship with man was cut off because of their sin. You see, Joel, sinful man cannot stand in the presence of God, because the perfect Holiness of God would burn them to a frazzle. Only a perfect, sinless man can possibly stand in God's presence, but there are none born from Adam who are righteous. When Adam committed the first sin, the sin nature became part of mankind's DNA and consequently the curse of sin has been passed on to the entire human race, so everyone cannot help but sin because it's in their nature. This meant My Father had to separate mankind from Himself for their sake. He is a righteous Judge and so He has to punish sin. If He didn't, then He would be condoning it which is impossible for Him to do. The wages of sin are death and eternal separation from My Father. Every man's soul is created to live forever; those who are without sin come up here when they die, and those who are not without sin go down to the unimaginable blackness and darkness that is hell. Since we have already established that there are no sinless people because all have sinned, this would be the fate of everyone, and would mean a lost eternity for the whole of mankind, forever separated from love and comfort, because God is love and the God of all comfort. The final destination of every man is not determined by how many or how bad their sins are, because the only sin that would banish a person from My Father's presence is the sin of rejecting the grace of the price paid by My blood, on the cross, for their salvation.

'So, it's not people who live good lives that come to Heaven then?' Joel asked.

'No, Joel, far from it. There is no way for people to earn their way to Heaven – that is impossible. The only way to come to

Heaven is by grace, for by grace you are saved, through faith in the Son of God who loved you and gave Himself for you, because there are none who meet the standards of a Holy God,' the Commander answered. 'An impossible problem for man to solve, but it has been solved because God provided the answer Himself – each person must be born again with a new spirit, created afresh without the curse of sin. So, how can that happen? A substitute! One person: pure, spotless, holy and righteous, must be the "fall guy" and pay the penalty for everyone's sin, because God would accept the selfless sacrifice of such a person, not deserving of death, in full payment for the penalty of all sin. But where could such a person be found? The penalty demanded to wipe out the stench of sin is death for all men – because none are righteous. So, who is there that is innocent who could or even would take upon himself the whole penalty so that the human race could go free and still satisfy a Holy Judge?'

'Well, Commander,' Joel answered. 'It seems that the only one good enough, who is totally without sin, is God Himself. But God can't die, can He, because He is God.'

'Correct on both counts, Joel,' the Commander agreed. 'This is precisely why God's own Son was the *only* possible answer to provide this atonement to redeem man. God's Son had to go down from Heaven, to the earth that He created, and be born as a man – God in bodily form on earth, conceived not of the seed of a sinful man, but miraculously by the Holy Spirit of God. Therefore the woman had to be a virgin who had not know a man intimately. *Only* this deliverer – the Messiah – the Son of God, who became the Son of man in the flesh, could be the perfect, sinless Lamb of God who takes away the sin of the world and whose sole purpose from birth was to be that sacrifice by giving his life on the cross. This was the ONLY acceptable payment for all sin – a sacrifice that God would accept. God has shown acceptance of His Son's sacrifice by raising His innocent Son from the dead. Jesus was the ONLY man ever born who did not deserve death. Anyone who believes and trusts in this great act of mercy will receive the grace of forgiveness: a free pardon from

My Father, no matter what they have done,'

'This is why, *without the atonement of God's Son on the cross there is no salvation*!' Nathan agreed. 'All who reject this grace are destined for a lost eternity in Hell – with no exceptions. That, my son, is why there is only one sin guaranteed to separate man from God, forever to abide in the torment of Hell – the sin of rejecting the Lord Jesus Christ which is the *most insane* decision any person on earth could ever make! The decision, Joel,' Nathan continued, sombrely, 'to accept or reject the Lord Jesus as Lord and Saviour, has to be reached on earth before death occurs, because once a person dies there is no chance of ever changing that final destination. Salvation is only available *before* death. All men were condemned to eternal Hell because of sin, but God decided, because of His great love for all men, that man should have a choice – to either accept grace and mercy through the sacrifice of Jesus Christ as their Lord and Saviour before they die, or meet Him as judge on their death.'

'Woah!' Joel gasped. 'So, Commander, You really are…'

'Yes, Joel,' the Commander answered. 'Before Abraham was, I am: the One who was and is and is to come. I was here with My Father from the beginning. I went down from Heaven and was conceived in the virgin Mary, not by the seed of sinful man but by the sinless seed of the Holy Spirit of God. I was born to go to the cross; this was My Father's plan from the beginning. I endured the wrath of God for all. Then, after I had been dead and buried for three days, it was the same Holy Spirit of God who raised Me from the dead; My Father was satisfied that all sin had been paid for, it was dealt with at the cross and there it was finished! My blood was the ransom God paid to redeem men – to give man that choice. I am the way, the truth and the life; no one comes to the Father except by Me. I am the resurrection and the life. He who believes in Me will receive eternal life, but he who rejects Me will suffer eternal death.'

'So, God will now let everyone into Heaven, regardless of what they've done, because You died in their place?' Joel asked.

'In theory, yes, God the Father has promised to let everyone into Heaven, not on the basis of any goodness in themselves but on the basis that they believe by faith that I paid for their sins, on the cross,' the Commander answered. 'They lay all *their* sin at the cross, where the Divine Exchange takes place – that is, I give them *My* righteous nature. Then, through Me, they become "born again" into everlasting life. Just as My Father raised Me from the dead, He makes their spirit alive again. The cross is the birth canal into new life – a new creation – a new person who can come into God's presence.'

'That is so amazing!' Joel exclaimed, mesmerised. 'Why did You do that? Why did You suffer that awful death for all those people, some of whom even blaspheme Your Name?'

'Because God is Love, Joel,' the Commander answered. 'I saw the tears of My Father's broken heart – a heart breaking because of His enforced separation from all His people due to their sin, and broken also because of the terror suffered for eternity that is the fate of all people who die without a Saviour. I could not bear it and the pain of the cross was preferable to seeing the pain in My Father's heart. What kept Me resilient and strong to bear the cross and the humiliating rejection by My people, was the thought of the joy that this saving path back to My Father would bring to Him and that, trusting Him as I did to raise Me from the dead, I would soon again be enjoying the glory that I had with Him before and sharing that joy with all of My true believers – all born-again Christians.'

'The problem is solved now, then?' Joel asked, pensively. 'Why then do I sense that a *but* is coming, Commander?'

'Well, wouldn't that be just perfect, son,' the Commander replied, with a melting smile. 'Sadly, even though I did everything for all people and the work was finished at the cross, it's not quite *all* over.'

'Oh?' Joel asked the Commander. 'What else is there to be done? Why am I here and why did You show me all those people on the Vista?'

'I am glad you asked that, Joel,' the Commander continued. 'If only everyone knew that blessed truth and believed it! 'You see, Joel, salvation is received through grace – of God, by faith – believing without seeing. This is why I have my servants preaching the gospel to all the world, so that everyone may have the chance to hear it. Sadly though, many of my servants have gone astray and preach strange doctrines instead of what I commanded them to preach – which is the cross!'

'This has the most terrifying consequences for those preachers, Joel, Nathan added. 'All the preachers in the world who are not preaching the cross – Jesus Christ and Him crucified, are like the pied piper of Hamlin, tragically leading those they preach to into the pit and make no mistake about it, son, those preachers will find themselves in that very same pit and the blood of all those they have led astray will be upon their heads!'

'My people are perishing for lack of knowledge,' the Commander continued. 'Joel, if you were terribly poor and spent your last pound on a lottery ticket, and your ticket won several million pounds, what would you then be?'

'Well, I would be very rich!' Joel grinned.

'Correct – in worldly terms, you would be rich indeed. However, if you failed to take your ticket back to the shop to claim your prize but just left it lying around, because you didn't believe that such an amazing blessing could be given to you freely, what would you be then?'

'Still terribly poor – and a complete idiot!' Joel answered.

The Commander nodded and smiled.

Joel grinned; he was in complete awe of the Commander – but, he wondered where all this was leading.

'It is a tragic fact, son,' the Commander sighed deeply, 'that the spiritual equivalent of this happens every day. People are dying and perishing in darkness because they have failed to believe that such a free gift is possible for them, neither do they believe that this is the *only* way to My Father and to Heaven.'

'God will never allow the Lord Jesus' suffering on the cross to be bypassed.' Nathan added. 'Anyone who thinks that they can earn eternal life for themselves, is viewed by God as *trampling on His grace* and that is an evil abomination in His eyes.'

'Many believe that they can earn their way into My Kingdom and foolishly proclaim themselves good. But, Joel, no one but God is good. What I did at the cross is the only way of salvation. To be born again one must repent of their sins and accept that I redeemed them by My blood on the cross. Whosoever believes this and calls on My name, shall be saved. I am the *only* Mediator between God and man but many people are deceived into thinking that *some men* can fill that office of mediator, but that is a lie. Man has a very real enemy, the devil and his demon spirits, who appeal to man's pride and prowl around looking for ways to kill, steal and destroy the people. One of the ways he attempts to do this, very successfully so far, I might add, is to confuse and deceive them into following a false religion – of which there are many on earth, Joel. My true servants proclaim My gospel and tell people that I love them. But beware, Joel, there are many false shepherds – wolves in sheep's clothing, who entice My people into false religions. You can spot them by their behaviour and the message they deliver – if their message is anything but Jesus Christ and Him crucified for the sins of the world, then they are false preachers. If they do not show My love to My people by preaching what I did for them at the cross, then they themselves are not My people and will perish.'

Joel nodded gravely as this vital truth was sinking in.

'There may be many "faiths" on earth, Joel, but there is only one truth,' the Commander asserted. 'No one comes to the Father except by Me. This is too serious a matter to get wrong, because it has eternal consequences – the end result is for *all* eternity! All that people have to do is come to Me, just as they are and to accept Me into their hearts as their Saviour and Lord. Then I will shower salvation upon them and give them eternal life. It's such an easy choice but the road to destruction is broad and many go down it. My Father created souls to live forever. Souls do not die, only the body dies; an eternity in Hell is an everlasting death from which a soul in that state will never be released. My Father raised Me from the dead and I am alive forevermore. The cross was planned, Joel, and it was the *greatest victory* in all eternity.

My Father fooled the devil and provided the way by which any soul who believes this would not go to hell, but instead would inherit eternal life. This is an inheritance that the devil will never see; he is destined for the lake of fire and eternal torment, because it is the devil who caused the fall and who is behind every evil deed on earth.'

Joel rose from his chair and knelt at the Commander's feet. He worshipped and loved this wonderful Mediator between God and man, Who gave so much for so many.

'You are Jesus; the Christ, the Son of God; the promised Messiah; the Light and Saviour of the world,' Joel worshipped Him. 'You are called the King of Kings and Lord of Lords, but I say that You are also the Hero of Heroes and the Bravest of the Brave. What an amazing plan! Thank you, Jesus for all that You have done for me. Tell me what Your plan is for me, Lord and I know, by Your strength, I will accomplish it.' Trembling with a mixture of excitement, trepidation and adoration, Joel committed his total allegiance to the Commander.

'Yes, I am the King of Glory; Jesus, the Bread of Life; the Living Manna from Heaven; the Root of David; and the Bright and Morning Star,' the Commander affirmed. 'You do not know how glad your commitment makes Me, Joel. I will be returning to the world soon. The first time, I came offering grace for salvation, not to condemn the world but to save it; to deliver people from the bondage of sin by paying the penalty on the cross for the world's sin. The faithful church is My bride and I am longing to bring her to Me. I will be doing this soon by way of the rapture, when I call up my faithful and true believers. I will meet them in the air and they will forever be with Me. However, I will not visit earth in person at this time. Some time after that, I will return to earth and all of My true believers will be with Me. My next actual visit to earth will be as Judge and I will deliver judgement to those who have rejected My grace and the whole earth will be full of the knowledge of My glory! Before these two events happen though, Joel, a mighty move of God will take place for all peoples of every tribe and nation – a mighty outpouring of My Spirit such as the world has never seen before; I will pour out My Spirit on *all* flesh. You were chosen long ago for such a time as this, Joel. My Spirit is *in* you. You are the house – the temple of the Holy Spirit of God – I am the King of Glory and I am sending you to the lost sheep of Israel. I am giving them a final opportunity to come to Me before I rapture My saints. Those who reject My grace will endure the terrible tribulation that is about to come upon the world. In the judgement, there will be no excuse for rejecting My grace. I am Jesus, the Lamb that was slain. The world thinks that I have forsaken My people, Israel, but **I am still The Lion of the Tribe of Judah!** My people rejected Me and so have been veiled from the truth whilst the rest of the world had an opportunity to hear the Gospel and be saved. Now, that veil is about to be removed. Joel, I have shown My people how they will be delivered and saved through the blood – My blood which was shed for them. I opened the way for their deliverance through the Red Sea when it seemed that they had nowhere to go and Pharaoh's armies were almost upon them. The Red Sea is not so-named by coincidence – it is symbolic of My blood, shed at the cross. The children of Israel passed through the midst of the Red Sea by the path that I made for them. This was a foreshadowing of what will happen at the end of the end times. My people will come again to a place where they have nowhere to go and their enemies will almost be upon them, to annihilate them. Then, their blind eyes will be opened and they will see that their true salvation is not through the Red Sea, but through the blood – My blood which was shed for the sins of the world. They will call to Me and repent of their unbelief and then I will return to the earth and I will save them; I will be gracious and merciful to them.'

Joel was dumbfounded. The Commander was truly the most awesome person in the universe and Joel's mouth-of-the-fish impersonation was way surpassed!

'Just remember though,' the Commander continued seriously, 'the work I have prepared for you is no bed of roses; you will be opposed and there will be times of great struggle and difficulties.

At times you may even be tempted to give up and think that I have abandoned you. But, Joel, I will never leave you or forsake you. I have inscribed you in My hand. Do not believe the lies of the enemy. Stay in Me; you can do nothing of yourself. Only in Me will you find strength, because *I am* your strength.' Saying this, the Commander put His hand on Joel's head and proclaimed, 'Be filled with My Spirit. Receive the *fire*!'

Joel instantly felt a rush of power flowing into him, flooding his whole being with energy and light, as he was filled with the Holy Spirit.

'I give you a double portion of My anointing, Joel,' the Commander spoke, gently but with complete authority. 'Remember this warning though: Anything you try to do apart from Me will fail. I am the Vine; you are only a branch.' The Commander stood and, taking hold of Joel's hands, He raised him to his feet. 'God promised Abraham, Isaac and Jacob that He would bless *all* the families of the earth through their seed – and God always keeps His promises. The King of Glory is in the house!' the Commander announced, and blew softly on him. Joel felt himself falling over backwards as if he was blissfully floating in slow motion into a huge mound of feathers.

†

When he awoke, Joel was glowing! He could hardly believe the amazing feeling of peace and joy he felt, as if bathed in glory. He thought that the sun must be streaming in through the windows, as if on a hot, midsummer's day. Then, he opened his eyes and was suddenly brought to earth with a bump as his gaze fell on Smith, who was towering over him with his hands on his hips, still in his pyjamas! There was no sun streaming through the windows, there was barely enough light in the room to see anything; the curtains were closed and the light was switched off!

'Oh, you're awake now, are you, Joel?' Smith muttered. He sounded slightly suspicious which, Joel was starting to realise, was *normal* for Smith. Perhaps this was how all detectives were

– suspicious by nature. Joel blinked and, rubbing his eyes, he looked around to reassure himself that he was actually in his bedroom, and yes, he was in the camp bed that Peter had been using; of course, Smith had slept in Joel's own bed.

'Have I overslept or something?' Joel murmured.

'No, but I couldn't help noticing, when I went to the kitchen for a drink, that your shoes were drenched...' Smith replied, somewhat curiously. 'Do you sleepwalk, Joel? It looks like you've been traipsing round the field half the night!'

Joel decided that it probably wasn't a "detective" thing, after all; Smith was just plain nosey. He ignored Smith's question and hid under his quilt, hoping to regain that lovely warm glow. But it was no use; Smith, determined to keep talking, continued to waffle on about how Joel's shoes could have become wet whilst he was supposed to be asleep in bed. Joel was about to come to the conclusion that he may as well just get up – if for nothing else to escape Smith – when thankfully, Smith conceded defeat.

'OK, we'll talk about this later. Don't be too long, because you need to have your breakfast and get ready so we can leave early for home,' Smith muttered resignedly, retreating to the bedroom door. 'By the way, you had better switch off that torch – it's bad for your eyes to read by torchlight under the covers. Don't bother denying it, you're caught red-handed! I can see the light.' With that, he left the room and closed the door.

'Tut... if only he *could* see the light,' Magee lamented from the open window.

'What torch?' Joel murmured, utterly confused.

'It's you!' Magee answered him. The raven, who had been perched on the window ledge outside, hopped in and landed on Joel's camp bed, peering at him curiously. 'You're glowing like a belisha beacon – it's because you've been with Jesus.'

Joel looked slightly alarmed as he stared at Magee.

'You can't be in the presence of the Lord of Glory,' Magee explained, 'without reflecting some of His glory. 'Don't worry, it will have faded by breakfast time,' Magee reassured him.

'Oh, right. Thanks for the explanation,' Joel answered, still somewhat confused.

Mum and Smith were planning to set off back to the city straight after breakfast. So even though Peter and Tamara came over to say goodbye, they did not have very long but promised to keep in touch until the next school holidays. Joel was bursting to tell them about the previous evening but the opportunity did not arise. As he sat in the back of the car waiting, Grandad had some very important last-minute instructions for Smith about the "valuable cargo": his daughter and grandson. Joel looked up and noticed the two ravens perched near the gate; he had grown fond of the amusing birds and he was going to miss them, too. Magee gave him a surreptitious wink and Joel remembered that he had seen that wink before… on the night he arrived at the beginning of the holidays... when he had nearly fallen out of his bedroom window… *So, I didn't imagine it, after all,* Joel thought to himself, *I knew something pushed me back inside – it can't have been just the wind!*

'Look, Joel!' Grandad exclaimed. 'There's that pair of ravens again!' He pointed to the Magi, who just stared blankly at him.

'Yes, Grandad, so it is,' Joel replied, chuckling to himself as he imagined the sort of dry banter that would be going through Magee's head as he surveyed the proceedings.

'I'll miss you, son,' Grandad muttered, blowing his nose.

'I'll miss you too, Grandad,' Joel answered, smiling back at him.

Peter and Tamara stood by the gate and waved as Smith's car cruised out of Grandad's yard. With the Easter holiday officially over, it would be the school Summer holidays before Joel would see them again. How far off that seemed, but how excited he was about the prospect of resuming the Kairos activities then; he could hardly wait for the Summer. Then, a hint of sadness came over him as he remembered that Maité would not be there and he wondered if he would ever even see her again.

Changing gear, Smith sped off down the lane. Then, Joel was brought painfully back to the present as he realised that he was going to be shut in the car with Mum – and Smith – for several hours! What on earth would they talk about? Would Smith start asking awkward questions that Joel simply could not answer? Joel felt the safest option would be to pretend to be asleep. Then, he would have the entire journey to bask in the memories of precious moments with Dad; his successful missions; the funny ravens; the fabulous party in Heaven; Maité – and that kiss! Then, the most wonderful of all – the truly *amazing* experience of the previous evening, after everyone else had gone, when he went back up the Fugue. There, in Heaven, he had met with the most important and magnificent Commander: the King of Glory Himself, Who had told Joel some of the plan and purpose for his life! This must be the "something big" that Maguff had referred to – something that was important enough for time itself to be changed! Wow, what a responsibility! He had not even had an opportunity to tell Peter and Tamara – they knew nothing of any of this – not even the time-changing incident with Maité. Would he be up to the task and how, he wondered, was he supposed to do it? Then, he remembered what the Commander had said: '*You can do all things through Me. I strengthen you.*'

He suddenly felt a tremendous relief as he realised that he did not have to rely upon himself, but that the Lord of Glory would give him all that he needed to fulfil the tasks ahead. Joel became suddenly very excited as he remembered Maité's words following the leaked news about him being Nathan's earthly son: "*Expectations have been set.*"

Then he heard a still, small voice speak to him.

"Just remember, son, I will never leave you nor forsake you. I have inscribed you in My hand; He who is in you is greater than he who is in the world. The King of Glory is in the house!"

Phew! What a confirmation – the work had already been prepared for him, along with all that he needed to accomplish it. So, no problem then... The only problem was, how on earth Joel would be able to get through the new school term with all of this excitement. He couldn't wait till the Summer holidays when he could resume his activities in the Kairos!

What does it mean to be Born Again?

Would you like to be saved – for the *Divine Exchange* to apply to you, and to have a special relationship with the Creator of the universe, which means that God is your Heavenly **Father** and not your **Judge**? Not only would this mean that you would go to Heaven when you die, but that God the Holy Spirit would help you throughout all of your life! Who on earth would not want the power of God helping them? To me it's a no-brainer – why would I want to struggle with the problems of life myself, when the Creator of the universe knows so much better than me how to deal with everything? I'm so glad that I'm saved – Born-Again!

God has judged all sin, past, present and future, by punishing His own Son, Jesus Christ, on the cross – even though Jesus never sinned Himself at all. Whether you believe it or not does not alter this truth. To be saved – Born-Again – means we accept that Jesus took the punishment Himself for our sins and that all who ***believe*** and ***trust*** in His Sacrifice of His own blood, on the cross, can receive a free pardon and be forgiven of all their sins and are 'accepted in the beloved' (Jesus) and will go straight to Heaven when they die. This is salvation by grace through faith. Those who reject that grace will be judged for their sins and have to pay the penalty themselves when they die and will spend eternity in Hell – which is much worse than anyone can possibly imagine!

The Bible says that we were 'purchased at a price,' meaning that God paid this price – the blood of His own innocent Son (Jesus) on the cross. Jesus was innocent and not deserving of death and so God the Father raised Him from the dead, thereby showing that **all who believe in what Jesus did at the cross for them,** are seen as innocent by the Father and receive everlasting life immediately as God makes their spirit alive. This is what is meant by being Born Again – it's not a physical birth but a spiritual birth, which enables them to enter Heaven when they leave this world. **How wonderful and amazing that God did this for us –** no matter what we have done! Forget Batman, Superman, etc – Jesus Christ truly is the ultimate Super-Hero and none can compare to Him!

A place in Heaven cannot be earned; it can only be received freely, by grace. The Bible says that none are good enough in themselves but ALL fall short of the standards of a Holy and perfect God. Of course, we know that Jesus is the Son of God because He was placed, by God the Holy Spirit, in the womb of His mother, Mary, who was a virgin and had never known a man intimately. So how could Jesus have got there, if not by God? We know that Jesus rose again from the dead because all the scoffers had to do was produce His body and no one ever did, but there are records that hundreds of people saw Him alive after He had been crucified and died on the cross.

No one knows when they are going to die, but we all do die eventually – some, sadly, well before their time. However, even a long life on earth is a very short time when compared to eternity – which is never-ending! God created our souls to live forever and once your body has gone, it's gone – there's only your soul and spirit left. Since it is being Born Again that makes your spirit alive, without this transformation you would remain spiritually dead. Your soul though – which is your mind, will, emotions, memory and everything that makes you who you are – will continue on for all eternity. So you want to make sure you arrive in the right place, because there's no changing your mind and going back once you get to eternity; it's a one-way ticket and the decision has to be made in this life. Hell is the most gruesome place and there is no way out, and yet, there are millions there right now because they thought that they were good enough in themselves. If you think about the great price that God paid to save us – the sacrifice of His only begotten, perfect and innocent Son, you would know that there was no other way to Heaven. Jesus said: 'I am the way, the truth and the life, no one comes to the Father except by Me.'

This is final, friend. God the Father will not allow anyone to bypass what His Son did at the cross. **No one** can earn their way to Heaven. The Bible says it is by **Grace** (of God, not our own efforts) through **faith** (believing God has purchased our souls with the **blood of His Son, shed on the cross**). So, whoever you are and however good a person you think you are, you cannot make it without our Saviour, Jesus Christ, because no one is good enough in themselves to reach the standard of a Holy God. Furthermore, there's no in-between place – you're either saved (from the wrath of God's judgement) by Jesus Christ and what He did at the cross or, the alternative is an eternity of torment in Hell. God has done everything to save us from this terrible fate and because He loved us, He gave His only Son. Only an innocent person could be our substitute for this sacrifice. This is why Jesus is called the sinless Lamb of God who takes away the sin of the world, because He was a sacrifice. Since all have sinned and fallen short of the glory of God, no man ever born from the original Adam has been qualified for the task – until **God gave Mary a pure innocent seed (a Son, Jesus)** Who did not come from the corrupted seed of man with the curse of sin, but from our Holy and perfect God.

You can be saved now, this very moment, by accepting Jesus Christ as your personal Lord and Saviour. Then you will be Born Again – a new creation in Jesus Christ (the beloved). **Salvation is free!** ***If*** you say the following prayer on the next page, to God, and **mean it in your heart**, that's all you have to do! **God then writes YOUR name in the Lamb's book of life in Heaven, because Jesus stood in your place and paid the penalty that was yours to pay, so you go free!** You haven't got to be good or perfect or sinless, because Jesus was and is all those things and when you confess Jesus as your Lord and Saviour, he cleanses you from the inside and gives you eternal life. This means that all your sin is washed away by His blood, shed at the cross and when you do die you will arrive in the right place and live forever in glory! Praise God!

Remember this serious warning though: salvation is based on forgiveness – God forgiving all of your sins when you repent. You MUST do likewise and **forgive others**, no matter what they may have done to you because if you do not forgive others then Father God **cannot forgive you** of your sins either, and you will not be saved! Please, say the prayer overleaf and become saved.

PRAYER OF SALVATION

Heavenly Father, thank You for sending Your Son, Jesus, to pay for my sins, on the cross. I believe that You raised Jesus from the dead because He was innocent. I'm sorry for all of my sins. Please forgive me. Jesus, come into my heart and into my life and wash me of all my sin. As You have forgiven me, I forgive all others. Please fill me and baptise me with Your Holy Spirit. Thank You that I am now a new creation in Christ Jesus and I am Born Again! **Amen.**

If you meant that, you have crossed over from death to eternal life already! There is rejoicing in Heaven because your name has been added to the Lamb's book of life! **Luke 10: 20**

Start to read the Bible: the King James Version or the New King James Version; it really is an exciting book and is God's word – living and active, and the Creator's instruction manual for the human race!

Tune your TV to Sonlife Broadcasting Network (SBN) available on Sky and Free-view or sonlifetv.com, where you'll find marvellous Holy Spirit anointed teaching, preaching and wonderful anointed music to lead you into the presence of the Lord, and you will be blessed!

Tell someone else – do not be afraid to tell people that you have given your heart to Jesus. The Bible says that if you are ashamed of Jesus before other people, He will be ashamed of you before the Father – and you don't want that to happen!

Start to pray – **in the name of Jesus** – He is the way to God. If you want your prayers to be answered, don't leave Jesus out because no one comes to the Father unless by Him.

Bibliography

Although the Kairos is a fictional story, it is written against a factual backdrop of the Gospel of Jesus Christ, on the basis that the Bible: King James Version or New King James Version, is the inspired Word of God. The description of Heaven in the story however is the author's imagination of what Heaven *could* be like, for the purpose of the story. If you have enjoyed reading The Kairos, why don't you get a Bible and look up the following references and refer back to the relevant pages of the book which should be a very enjoyable and fruitful exercise. If you really want a greater understanding of the Word of God, you may also like to try the Jimmy Swaggart Expositor's Study Bible, as it has extensive notes; there is also a Crossfire version of this for young people, which you can obtain through SBN.

Page No.	**Bible Ref bk / chap / vs**	**Page No.**	**Bible Ref bk / chap / vs**
Chapter One		9	Rev 21: 4
7	Rev 4: 3 & 6	9	John 15: 13
7	Rev 21: 10 – 14	13	Psalm 125: 1
7	Rev 21: 18 - 25	13	Heb 12: 22
7	Rom 8: 11	13	Jam 1: 17
7	Eph 3: 16 – 19	13	Rev 14: 12
7	Rev 7: 14 – 17	13	Gen 1: 26
7	1 John 4: 8	17	John 12: 36
8	Psalm 91: 10 – 1	17	Psalm 91: 11,12
9	Isa 25: 8	30	Gen 9: 8 – 17
9	Rev 7: 17		
Chapter Two		42	1 John 4: 14
38	Luke 2: 7	42	Acts 4: 10 - 12
38	Heb 2: 4		
Chapter Three		48	Gen 3: 1 – 5
48	Gen 1: 1, 4, 10, 12	48	Gen 3: 17 - 19
48	Gen 1: 16,17,18	49	Rev 12: 3
48	Gen 1: 21, 25, 31	49	1 Peter 5: 8
48	Psalm 100: 3	49	Eph 6: 12

Page No.	Bible Ref bk / chap / vs
Chapter Eight	
117	John 6: 44
117	Rev 4: 1
117	John 14: 5, 6
117	John 15: 16
117	Matt 20: 16
117	Jerem 29: 11 – 13
118	Gen 28: 10 – 19
118	Deut 30: 15 – 20
118	Luke 15: 7
118	Col 2: 14, 15
118	Isaiah 46: 9 – 11
118	Isaiah 53: 4 – 6
118	John 10: 9
118	John 14: 21
118	Matt 7: 21
119	Hos 4: 6
119	Isaiah 5: 13
119	Col 1: 12 – 14
119	Col 1: 19 – 21
119	John 8: 36
119	Rev 12: 12
119	2 Corin 10: 3 – 5
119	Eph 2: 8 – 10
119	Rom 3: 10 – 12
119	Rom 3: 23 – 25
119	Acts 4: 12
119	Eph 6: 12
120	2 Corin 10: 3 – 5
120	Rev 12: 9
120	Matt 25: 41
120	2 Peter 3: 9
120	Isa 53: 4 - 6
120	Gen 7: 15, 16
120	1 Thes 4: 16

Page No.	Bible Ref bk / chap / vs
120	Rom 11: 25
120	Rom 6: 23
120	Heb 9: 27
120	Joel 2: 11
120	Mark 1: 14, 15
120	Matt 24: 6 – 14
120	Rev 20: 10 & 15
120	Rev 19: 20
120	Jude 20 – 23
120	Matt 13: 37 – 43
120	Joel 2: 28, 29
120	2 Peter 3: 3
120	Acts 2: 15 – 21
121	John 10: 10
121	Rev 12: 10
121	2 Corin 10: 3 – 5
121	SoS 2: 15
122	John 8: 32
122	Isa 58: 6
122	Galat 5:1
122	Matt 18: 3
122	Psalm 131
122	Matt 19: 14
122	Isa 46: 9, 10
122	Jerem 29: 11
123	John 15: 13
123	1 Corin 13: 8
123	John 15: 16, 17
123	1 Corin 13: 13
123	Heb 7: 25
123	Col 2: 9
123	Matt 28: 19
123	Matt 10: 29 – 31
123	1 Cor 1: 24
123	Isa 24: 23

Page No.	Bible Ref bk / chap / vs
Chapter Eighteen	
309	Matt 22: 11 – 14
309	Ephes 6: 10 – 17
309	Rev 1: 5 – 6
310	Rev 5: 9, 10
311	Matt 24: 27, 28
311	John 9: 5
311	Acts 9: 3 – 5
312	Act 9: 32
312	1 Thes 3: 13
313	John 3: 16
313	John 6: 28, 29
313	John 5: 24
313	Heb 12: 1, 2
314	Matt 28: 18
315	Philip 3: 9, 10
315	1 Corin 2: 5
315	2 Tim 1: 8
315	Psalm 18: 35
315	Isa 41: 10
316	Psalm 119
316	John 3: 16
317	Psalm 118: 26
317	Heb 12: 1
318	Prov 4: 1 – 7
318	Rev 19: 1
320	Acts 2: 4
321	Mark 16:17
321	Acts 19: 6
321	John 3: 3
321	John 3: 5
321	John 1: 12, 13
321	Ephes 2: 1
322	Acts 2: 4
322	Acts 2: 6 – 8

Page No.	Bible Ref bk / chap / vs
322	Acts 2: 16
322	John 1: 32 – 34
322	John 3: 11
322	1 Corin 12: 10, 11
323	Ephes 1: 4
323	Jer 29: 11
323	Esth 4: 14
323	1 Corin 6: 19, 20
323	Ephes 2: 8 – 10
324	Matt 23: 9
324	John 14: 6
324	Acts 4: 10 – 12
324	Matt 16: 16 - 18
325	Heb 11: 6
325	1 John 3: 2
325	John 14: 6
325	Gal 2: 16
326	1 Corin 2: 9
326	Psalm 150
326	Ephes 2: 8 – 10
327	Isa 46: 9 - 11
328	1 Thes 5: 17
328	Luke 18: 1
332	2 Sam 6: 14, 15
332	1 Peter 4: 11
333	Job 4: 4
335	Zech 9: 12
335	Rom 5: 5
336	Rev 1: 12 - 20
336	Matt 17: 2
336	Matt 17: 5
336	Psalm 29: 7
336	Acts 2: 2 – 4
336	John 1: 29
336	Rom 11: 29

Page No.	Bible Ref bk / chap / vs
Chapter Twenty One	
374	Rev 1: 17, 18
374	Esther 4:11
374	Esther 5: 2
374	Rev 1: 17
374	Prov 18: 10
374	Josh 5: 14
374	Phillip 4: 7
374	1 John 4: 8
374	1 John 4: 18
374	Matt 28: 18
374	1 Tim 6: 12 – 16
375	James 2: 23
375	John 6: 43 – 45
375	Esth 4: 14
375	Col 2: 2, 3
375	John 6: 37
375	Matt 19: 14
375	John 14: 2
375	Matt 9: 37, 38
375	Joel 2: 11
375	Ephes 6: 13 – 17
375	Acts 2: 20
375	Jer 33: 2, 3
375	Heb 1: 1 – 4
375	Rom 4: 17
375	Gen 1 - 31
375	Mark 4: 39 – 41
376	Rev 19: 16
376	Psalm 150: 6
376	Isa 9: 6
377	Col 2: 14, 15
377	Esth 5: 2
377	Psalm 3: 3
377	Romans 8: 1, 2

Page No.	Bible Ref bk / chap / vs
377	1 Corin 2: 2
377	Jer 29: 13
377	Matt 7: 7
377	Ephes 2: 10
377	1 Peter 1: 6, 7
377	Psalm 66: 10
378	1 John 4: 8
378	John 15: 13
378	1 John 1: 9
378	1 Corin 6: 20
378	Ephes 1: 7
378	Romans 8: 2
378	John 8: 36
378	Ephes 2: 4 – 10
378	John 12: 36
378	John 15: 1 – 4
378	Philip 4: 13
378	Matt 10: 38
378	Rev 12: 5
378	Psalm 2: 6 – 8
379	Gen 3: 24
379	Jer 33: 3
379	Matt 6: 8
379	Jer 31: 33
379	Rev 12: 7 – 9
379	Job 1: 6, 7
379	Rev 12: 10
379	Col 2: 14, 15
379	Rom 8: 28
379	Luke 11: 22
379	Ephes 1: 7
379	Heb 9: 12 - 15
379	Heb 13: 20, 21
379	Luke 1: 26 – 35
380	1 John 1: 9

Page No.	Bible Ref bk / chap / vs
Chapter Twenty One	
380	Gen 1: 1 – Rev 22:21
380	James 1: 2, 3
381	Psalm 91: 11
381	Prov 3: 5
381	Rom 8: 28
381	Rev 14: 6, 7
382	John 3: 16
382	Rom 3: 10 - 18
382	Rom 3: 23
382	Rom 6: 23
382	John 5: 28, 29
382	1 John 4: 18
382	2 Corin 1: 3
382	Ephes 3: 8 – 12
382	Rom 3: 24 – 26
383	Acts 4: 10 – 12
383	Ephes 2: 4 – 10
383	Gal 2: 20
383	John 3: 3 – 8
383	1 Peter 1: 23
383	Rom 16: 25 – 27
383	2 Corin 5: 21
383	Isa 53: 4 – 6
383	1 Peter 2: 24
383	Matt 27: 22 - 25
383	John 1: 1 – 5
383	Luke 1: 26 – 34
383	John 1: 14
383	John 1: 29
383	John 3: 16
383	1 Peter 1: 18 – 21
383	Matt 16: 21
383	Luke 24: 34
383	Acts 2: 22 – 24
384	Rom 6: 23
384	Heb 9: 27, 28
384	John 8: 58
384	Rev 1: 8
384	John 19: 30
384	Mark 10: 45
384	1 Peter 1: 17 – 23
384	Dan 12: 2, 3
384	John 14: 6
384	John 11: 25
385	Ephes 2: 3 – 6
385	Rom 8: 2
385	Romans 6: 4
385	1 John 4: 8
385	John 17: 1 – 5
385	1 Peter 1: 23
385	John 3: 3 – 8
385	John 19: 30
385	Heb 9: 27
386	Isa 5: 13, 14
386	Ephes 2: 8
386	Rom 3: 23 – 26
386	Acts 2: 21
386	Joel 2: 28 – 32
386	1 Tim 2: 5
386	Dan 7: 13, 14
386	Rom 10: 12, 13
386	Rom 5: 18, 19
386	Luke 4: 18
386	Joel 2: 10, 11
386	Ephes 1: 4
387	1 Peter 5: 8
387	1 Tim 2: 7
387	1 Corin 1: 17, 18

Page No.	Bible Ref bk / chap / vs	Page No.	Bible Ref bk / chap / vs
390	Gen 28: 14	393	Phil 4: 19
390	Gal 3: 29	393	1 Kings 19: 12
390	Rom 9: 7	393	2 Tim 1: 7
390	Psalm 24: 7 – 10	393	Rom 8: 28
390	Isa 9: 6	393	John 15: 1 – 11
391	Exod 34: 29 – 32	393	Ephes 2: 8 – 10
391	Acts 4: 13	393	1 John 4: 4
392	Psalm 91: 9 – 12	393	2 Tim 4: 18
393	Phil 4: 13	393	Jude 24, 25